Bridget went to the larg

where she had stolen a sa
not wanting to shatter any
may have left behind.

"Gone," she said, staring at the empty shelves. "All of it." She wrapped her fingers between the metal rows of one of the shelves, felt the dissipating coolness of it. "He could go anywhere and start all over again."

She jerked the metal shelves out and hurled them to the concrete floor.

From over her shoulder Don peered into the empty cavern. "He wouldn't really infect Raleigh's drinking water with the virus, would he?"

"If he thought murdering thousands of innocent people would force the managed care companies to meet his demands, then yeah, he'd do it." Bridget glanced around. "I know I saw a phone down here the other day...there!"

At the counter she snatched up the handset. "Maybe the police can set up road blocks or something. Come on, damn thing! Where's the dial tone?" She mashed the button again and again.

"Think he closed his account with the phone company?" Don asked.

"Why would he bother?"

"True. What about the cell phone I gave you?"

"Sorry, it took a dive out of the tree."

"Then let's drive to the nearest house in that subdivision and call from there."

"Good idea...you go. I'm going to video this stuff while you're gone. Is your camera still in the car?"

"We don't need evidence that he's the creator of the virus anymore, Bridget," Don said. "He'll get the death sentence for what he did to Madeline."

"That's what they said about O.J." She paused, sniffed the air. "Do you smell that?"

"Smell what?" Don inhaled. "Wait a minute. That's—"

"*Gasoline,*" Bridget finished...

HIPPOCRATES SHATTERED

by

JOHN KARR

FOR BETTINA & TOM,

A LITTLE SUMMER READING FOR
YOU GUYS. YOU MAY RECOGNIZE SOME
OF THE SIGHTS. HOPE YOU LIKE IT...

John

An

Tsylett Press
Publication

www.TsylettPress.com

Ysylett Press, Inc.

Edited by: Valerie J. Patterson
Senior Editor: Sandra Dugas
Acquisitions Editor: Fredrick Hunt
Cover Art by: Imaginusional Graphics and Web Design
(www.imaginusional.com)

All rights reserved.

HIPPOCRATES SHATTERED
Copyright © 2010 by John Karr
ISBN 1-934337-40-4

Names, characters and incidents depicted in this novel are the inventions—and derived from the imagination—of the author. Any resemblance to persons (living or dead), organizations, locales, or events is coincidental. Any actual historical figures, locations, events, organizations or products that may be mentioned are done so in a fictitious manner, without intended harm or malice.

No part of this book may be reproduced or copied, electronically, mechanically, or manually, to include photocopying, scanning, recording, or transcribing; nor may it be transmitted by any electronic or mechanical means; nor may it be stored in any manner on any electronic or mechanical device without the express written permission of the publisher.

If you received this book from any source other than the publisher, or a publisher-approved vendor, please be aware that it is a pirated copy, and neither the publisher nor the author received any payment for its sale.

Ysylett Press, Inc.
www.YsylettPress.com

Published in the United States Of America
January 2010

Ysylett Press, Inc.
3616 Devils Three Jump Road
Little Plymouth, VA 23091

DEDICATION

For Robert Karr, Sr. and Lucille Karr
~ parents who prefer Thrillers to Horror Novels ~

ACKNOWLEDGMENT

Many thanks to Sandra Dugas
~ without whom this novel would not have made it ~

PROLOGUE

RAYNORR LAID THE hamhock beside the dog and watched as rheumy eyes gradually focused on the offering. Nostrils flared, cracked the dried mucus around them. Raynorr didn't need the stethoscope in his lab coat pocket to hear the rasp of the animal's lungs as they struggled to inflate with the aroma of fresh meat and bone.

A pale tongue emerged from within a frothy muzzle. Slowly it licked its chops. Doubtless, it still harbored vague memories of a time when it had been a healthy carnivore; a time when it would have ripped the meat from the bone, devoured it with ravenous vigor, and with strong jaws laden with sharp white teeth, set to work cracking the bone open for the succulent marrow within.

But now the dog's ears laid flat and its eyes bulged with desperation from their sockets. The animal could barely summon the strength to raise its head from the concrete floor. Panting despite the relative coolness of the shade, the dog turned from the hamhock and stared through the pen's chain-link fence to the surrounding field.

Raynorr jotted observations down in his notebook. *Managed a few bites last night, but even that is too much now.*

A familiar chill encircled his wrist. He stopped writing and gazed into the darkest corner of the pen.

With his thoughts, he greeted Death—pointed out the irony of their alliance.

As always, Death remained silent.

Raynorr kneeled.

He'd found the dog in a rusty pen at the county animal control shelter scheduled to be put down that very day. He did not deny the guilt he felt at saving the grateful beast only to end up destroying it himself, but he had needed one more trial, one more successful experiment, to prove that all his labor—all his pain—had finally paid off.

And as with any war, sacrifices had to be made.

Raynorr stroked the dog's head, little more than patchy fur stretched over a canine skull. The dog leaned into him and moaned.

He produced a hypodermic needle from his lab coat pocket. Expertly, his fingers found a suitable vein in the dog's foreleg. He inserted the needle and pulled back on the stopper. When the tube held five cc's of liquid red, he withdrew the needle. This time the dog didn't growl or snap at him. This time it merely whimpered. Quickly, he produced another needle and injected its contents through the loose skin on the back of the dog's neck.

"This will shield you from the pain," he said, stroking the dog's head after withdrawing the needle. "It'll be over soon, boy. You're the last. I'll be going for the real thing, now."

He could hear Cain and Abel, the German Shepherds he'd raised from ten-week old pups, barking in the woods beyond the field, probably in hot pursuit of a rabbit or squirrel. He almost smiled.

Unlike people, dogs will not abandon you. Unlike people, dogs do not know how to be cruel.

The muscles in his back went rock-hard. His lip curled into a sneer.

Unlike.. people!

Raynorr tried to suppress the rage but was too late. His bones ignited with it. It burned his skin like flash paper and boiled the blood in his veins.

The dog moaned. Soon the moan became a pitiful wail, as if the animal somehow knew Raynorr's agony.

Crack!

The dog fell silent.

Shaking and gasping for breath, Raynorr looked down. His hand was buried like a claw in the fur on the back of the dog's neck. A pale, flaccid tongue protruded between the dog's parted jaws. Its eyes stared blankly into the nether realm.

He pried his fingers from the dog's neck.

"They've done it again," he whispered.

His hands shook as he closed the dog's eyelids. He stared down at the animal for several minutes and then carried it to the house to examine in his lab. The hours slipped away.

That night he drove into north Raleigh.

Even with the powerful spotlights pointed up at it, the massive water tower still looked like a huge baton cut in half. The stem was stuck in the ground and rose eight stories until encountering the massive vessel that held the water and was decidedly turnip-shaped.

He turned from Six Forks Road onto the gravel pathway. A bunch of clumpy rhododendrons provided an excellent screen to park behind. Razor wire gleamed with menace atop the eight-foot fence that surrounded the base of the water tower. No matter. With the rush of passing traffic in his ears, Raynorr picked the lock on the gate. Unhurried, he walked up the caged, metal-mesh stairs that wound around the stem of the tower like a vine, until the traffic noise faded and he reached the top.

There was no enclosed walkway here, only a solitary handrail that led up the slope to the middle of the containment vessel, where the trap door was located. He supposed city workers periodically opened the trap door to take samples of the water from the very highest point in the tower. It took thirty seconds to pick the lock.

Hinges squeaked as he pulled the door open.

Raynorr stretched out. The surface of the water tower was hard and smooth, with enough residual heat from the day to feel through his tee-shirt and shorts.

He inhaled the steel mustiness of the small pocket of air inside and aimed his flashlight at the water. The beam blurred at the edges and went on and on before disappearing far within. He reached in and caressed the water's silky surface, then splashed his sweating face and gasped at the refreshing shock of it.

After some time he closed and re-locked the trap door.

One hand on the rail, he stood and stared up at the blazing stars that seemed to hover just beyond his outstretched arm. Fiery suns pulsed in a heavenly Morse code. Celestial power rained down. Absorbed through his porous skin, it energized every molecule of his being. The stars beckoned but he rejected them. Borne upon the winds of war came a rolling thunder. Days of reckoning were *finally* at hand.

Raynorr's lips stretched. After some time he realized he was grinning.

At last, he was ready.

ONE

"COME ON IN."

Bridget Devereaux entered the room to find her next patient upright at the edge of the bed, primping her wig while gazing into a hand-held mirror. The lime-green patient gown with ties at the upper and lower back was a snug but not overly tight fit on her. She glanced over the top of the mirror as Bridget approached. "You're too late, honey."

"Oh?"

"'Fraid so. They already put clean sheets on the bed. They're always right on time with the sheets."

Bridget smiled. "I'll let housekeeping know you approve of their work, Mrs. Wilson."

"You're not here for the sheets?"

"No, ma'am."

Mrs. Wilson lowered the mirror and squinted at Bridget's breast pocket. "Your nametag's all fuzzy and my darned bifocals're in the bathroom with the latest issue of *People*, but something tells me you're not a nurse."

"You're getting warmer." Bridget held out her hand. "I'm Bridget Devereaux. I'll be your—"

"You're the new doc?" Mrs. Wilson said, shaking Bridget's hand.

"Close. I have the medical degree but now I'm getting the real-life experience. I'm what the staff doctors call a PGY-One—Post-Graduate Year One—an intern. Ward Seven is my third rotation here at Chambers Hospital

"But you're so young! Or am I just getting old?"

"You're not old at sixty-one, Mrs. Wilson." Bridget nudged her wire-rimmed glasses up with the index finger of her left hand. The same hand held a clipboard with Mrs. Wilson's patient file clamped to it. Bridget silently noted that Mrs. Wilson's hand felt almost hot despite the relative cool temperature of the air-conditioned room. "Old is like a hundred and twenty. You're only halfway there—still a spring chicken."

4

"And how was kindergarten today, honey?"

Bridget laughed. She'd overheard the nurses say that Becky Wilson was a hoot.

Mrs. Wilson raised her mirror and resumed the adjustments to her wig. "Well, almost-Doctor Bridget Devereaux, you look like you could be on the cover of *Cosmo*! My goodness, smart and pretty and you've got curves, too! But I have to tell you, those white lab coats don't exactly flatter you girl docs—they just *don't* reveal enough, if you know what I mean. Then again, with your dark, sassy hair and nice figure you'd probably look good wrapped in duct tape."

"I doubt that, but it's very kind of you to say."

"One suggestion, hon—lose the glasses. You have such pretty eyes, you shouldn't hide 'em. Contacts are the way to go."

"Contacts would be nice, but glasses are more practical at the moment. Now, Mrs. Wilson, tell me how it's going with your—"

"My son is single again, you know. Perhaps you'd fancy a divorced man…?" Mrs. Wilson looked over the mirror at Bridget and raised her eyebrows. The contraction of her forehead muscles caused her wig to tilt slightly backward, revealing the smooth scalp beneath.

Bridget felt her cheeks redden. "Uh, I don't think so."

"Oh, come on! A pretty girl like you ought to have a man. Of course, Jerry prefers a longer-haired, and, well, less on-the-ball kind of woman, if you know what I mean. But after his first two wives, a smart one would be a refreshing change—at least for me. Want me to introduce you?"

"I don't think my boyfriend would approve."

"Boyfriend? The last doc told a nurse right here in front of me that he didn't have the time or energy for any relationships. Just between us girls, I think he only wanted the hit and run stuff. It's a wonder you have time for a beau."

Bridget nodded. "We manage to find a little time here and there. Travis has been grumbling a lot lately, but I think it'll all work out once I get a handle on my new rounds."

"Want to see a picture of my Jerry? He's almost handsome—and I'm not just saying that because I shot him out my birth canal."

Bridget laughed. "No thanks, really."

The wig eased down as Mrs. Wilson's eyebrows relaxed. "Oh, well. Never hurts to try." She pulled out a small brush and started applying facial powder. "My husband's coming to visit in an hour. Want to look my best, you know."

"How are you feeling?"

"Oh, good and bad, I guess. Had to throw up this morning and last night after the chemo. Felt pretty hot for a while there, too. Slept at some point. Didn't get enough, but it was better than nothing. Can't seem to stop drinking water, though."

"Chemotherapy dehydrates most people. Your mouth gets dry?"

"Sahara's got nothing on me, honey."

"Keep with some water, but don't drink so much you feel bloated. Ice chips work pretty well—just let them melt in your mouth. The chemo has adversely affected your saliva glands. They'll get better as you recover."

Mrs. Wilson nodded and continued with her touch ups, softly humming.

"You certainly seem to be in good spirits despite the rough treatment here," Bridget noted.

"My husband's coming to see me, dear."

"Okay if I take your B.P. and pulse and listen to your lungs?"

"You go right ahead and do your doctor thing, honey. I'm just going to do my eyes while you're at it, okay?"

"Deal."

Bridget set her clipboard down on a small table near the bed and pressed her middle finger to the underside of Mrs. Wilson's wrist as the older woman held up her mirror. Careful to note each throb of her patient's pulse, she studied her wristwatch for fifteen seconds. Twenty beats. Multiplied by four and she had eighty beats per minute while the patient was in a state of rest. Eighty was high but not alarming. No doubt the chemo was accountable, plus excitement over her husband.

She took Mrs. Wilson's temperature via digital ear thermometer. After five seconds there was a ding and the readout showed one hundred point five, verifying what Bridget had suspected: Mrs. Wilson had developed a low-grade fever since the last time the on-duty nurse had taken her vital signs.

Wrapping a thick Velcro band around Mrs. Wilson's upper arm, Bridget pumped the air ball. The needle in the gauge twitched with each beat of her patient's heart. B.P. was one-seventy over eighty-four. Elevated. As with her temp and pulse rate, it wasn't high enough to send up red flags, but it was elevated nonetheless.

Bridget noted the small beads of perspiration forming on her patient's brow. A few damp strands of her real hair, thin and sparse, had strayed from beneath the wig.

The stethoscope was next. Bridget placed the small drum in the palm of her hand for a few seconds, then moved it inside the rear slit of Mrs. Wilson's gown. She gently placed it at various locations and listened to her breathe.

"Thanks for warming it first, honey," Mrs. Wilson said, turning her head slightly over her shoulder in Bridget's direction. "That last doc always put it on me cold. I think he got a kick out of seeing me jump."

Bridget smiled but said nothing. She moved the stethoscope to Mrs. Wilson's chest and listened to her heart. The beat was quick but clean, with no discernable echo. There didn't seem to be a murmur; no backfilling of blood in any of the chambers. And if there were, it probably would have been noted in the patient's chart by the nurses or the other intern. Still, redundancy during examinations was always a good idea for patients undergoing aggressive treatments. And they didn't get much more aggressive than chemo.

One of the first things Bridget had learned as an intern was that it could be just as important to note the non-clinical details when making the rounds. The fact that Mrs. Wilson was lucid, sitting upright, optimistic—these were good signs. On the other hand, the low-grade temperature, visible perspiration on Mrs. Wilson's brow, elevated B.P. and pulse—in addition to the vomiting and restlessness—meant the chemo was taking its toll.

Bridget straightened and hung the stethoscope around her neck. She picked up the clipboard and wrote her observations on the chart.

"I think you should rest a bit, Mrs. Wilson. Your body's working hard right now, still trying to cope with yesterday's chemotherapy." She laid a consoling hand on her patient's shoulder and again felt the heat that emanated forth. "You look fine. Why not lie back for a little while?"

Mrs. Wilson reclined against the bed, the back support of which was angled high. "I—I am gettin' a little bushed. My husband can still visit me, can't he?"

"Of course, he can. I just want you to take it easy for a little while, that's all."

Mrs. Wilson dabbed at her brows with a tissue. "The last doc said Hodgkin's disease was an easy cancer."

Bridget frowned. "Nothing about cancer is easy."

"You know, he never did shake my hand or anything the way you did. Matter of fact, I don't think he ever really touched me the whole time he was here. He always let the nurses do all that. Never came in here without a nurse, for that matter. Talked more to the nurses than to me, like I was just some kind of experiment or something. I don't know."

"My mother had doctors like that. God, they used to make me and my sister so angry."

"What did you do?"

"Mama died too quickly for us to do much of anything."

"Cancer?"

"Ovarian."

"I'm so sorry, honey."

"Thanks. It happened a long time ago, when I was still a girl.

Listen, why don't you take off your wig? It's trapping a lot of your body heat."

"But I want to look…" Mrs. Wilson trailed off, frowning.

"Tell you what," Bridget said, tapping the pen lightly against her chin. "I'll have the nurses notify you through the intercom, here, when your husband arrives. You slip the wig on then. Sound good?"

Becky Wilson nodded.

Bridget helped take it off.

"Whew, that's better! Like takin' the lid off a boiling pot. Thanks, honey."

"The head nurse told me you like to walk in the courtyard with your husband. I suggest you don't do that until the latter part of his visit, after you've had a little more time to rest and—"

The intercom speaker overhead suddenly came to life. "Code Blue. Team One, Code Blue. Room three-oh-three. Repeat. Team One, Code Blue. Room three-oh-three."

Bridget tensed. The voice was controlled and monotone, but to Bridget, the impact was the same as putting her ear to a piercing smoke alarm.

Code Blue. Cardiopulmonary distress. A heart had stopped beating. Lungs no longer inflated. Death had swung to harvest yet another soul. The latest skirmish in an unwinnable war. Their job was to postpone the inevitable as long as possible.

Mrs. Wilson said something, but Bridget didn't have time for it at the moment. She tossed her clipboard on the small table next to Mrs. Wilson's bed and hurried from the room.

Bridget wasn't on the Primary Code Team known as Team One, but as an intern she was expected to help if the code went down in her area.

Room 303 was just at the end of this hallway.

Bridget had seen Margaret Morrison in 303 for the first time just an hour ago. The middle-aged woman had been conscious but unable to speak. Via small electrodes taped to her skin, she was connected to an EKG that constantly monitored her erratic heart rate. She had clear plastic tubes in her nostrils; tendrils from the oxygen machine that pumped enough O2 into her lungs to make a linebacker for the Charlotte Panthers perform Barishnokovian pirouettes. Mrs. Morrison also had a catheter in her arm. A Levodromoran drip had been set up.

Levo was not medicine. Levo was a powerful opiate that shielded patients from pain as they died.

As Bridget sprinted past visitors, nurses, orderlies, and the stray patient well enough to walk the cancer ward, she couldn't help thinking about something she'd read in Mrs. Morrison's patient file: four weeks ago she'd been given a clean bill of health by her personal physician.

At that time Margaret Morrison had shown no signs of the rampant leukemia that now ravaged her body. She'd been in good shape. Didn't have any health-eroding habits except a workaholic's tendency to work sixty hours a week. Her personal physician had ordered blood work, poked and prodded in all the usual places, even performed a Mammogram on her. Nothing out of the ordinary had shown up.

Four weeks ago she had been perfectly healthy.

Now she was on Levo and had gone Code Blue.

✳ ✳ ✳

Room 303 was close to Mrs. Wilson's room. Bridget was one of the first to arrive.

They made a gallant effort to revive Margaret Morrison. CPR. Epinephrine shots. Bridget herself had worked the defibrillator, shocking the dying woman with 700, 1000, and finally 1,700 volts.

To no avail.

Death had won.

The tension in the room eased away, replaced by quiet resignation.

The senior attending wrenched his gloves off and threw them into the hazardous waste bin.

The other doctors stood for a moment, then slowly disbursed.

"Time?" the senior asked softly. His hands were on his hips, head bowed.

A nurse called out the time.

The senior, in a kind of post adrenalin daze, walked slowly from the room. The others followed.

"Devereaux...toe tag her," the chief resident said, scribbling notes on a clipboard he held in the flat of his forearm. "Since you jumped in on the team, you get to fill out the death certificate."

Blake Hensely's scornful tone would have been evident to a child. Bridget looked at his handsome, arrogant face and then away. What should she have done, stepped back and waited for the others to arrive while Margaret Morrison died right in front of her?

Tell him off, she chastised herself. *Don't just keep it in.*

Not now. This woman just died.

Come on! He's still pissed that you turned down his offer for an oh-so-romantic screw in the supply room four weeks ago. He's been on your case ever since, and he's going to stay on your case until you—

Not...now!

Bridget walked on pillars of lead out of the room. At the

nearest nurse's station she pawed through one stack of forms and then another, unable to find the death certificates. A nurse handed her a clipboard with the necessary paperwork on it, along with the toe tags.

"Thanks," Bridget murmured.

Nurses weren't always so helpful with the necessary paperwork, especially to interns, whom they often deemed inferior. But for one fleeting moment, everyone, except perhaps the chief resident in charge of this year's interns, had been reminded of his or her own mortality.

✳ ✳ ✳

Later that day, in the Ward Seven break room, Bridget stood before a broad window and cracked open a can of apple juice.

Doesn't make sense, she thought, taking a gulp of the cold juice. *Leukemia provides warning signs. It doesn't just explode in the body like a bomb. But that's exactly what it did to Margaret Morrison. And now... God, she's not the only one who's had this...this accelerated leuk.*

After filling out the death certificate, Bridget had checked the hospital computer for similar cases. She'd run a search on all leukemia patients admitted within the past three months. There were twelve. But of that dozen, ten were either in remission or still undergoing treatments here at the hospital. These followed the normal pattern for the disease. But the other two...

As with Margaret Morrison, the onset of the disease for the other two patients had been sudden and debilitating. And also like Margaret Morrison, both had died within days of being admitted to Chambers.

Bridget stared out the window at the hundreds of parked cars baking in the punishing North Carolina sunshine. *Healthy one day. Dying the next. No time to even say goodbye to loved ones.*

Two nurses entered the break room, chatting with one another. Bridget watched in the window's reflection as one of them opened the refrigerator door and peered inside.

"...breaks my heart just to walk in there," one said, reaching for a brown bag in the refrigerator.

"She's just a child," the other said.

"My god, eleven years old. My daughter's age."

"They say she was running around just the other day. Competed in a swim meet, for God's sake. Now she's bedridden with leukemia? It doesn't make sense."

Bridget turned and stared at the nurses dressed in blue scrubs all the way down to their rubber-soled shoes. The nurses froze as they noticed Bridget for the first time.

"*What* did you say?" Bridget asked, Margaret Morrison's

pained, emaciated face suddenly haunting her.

"There's a new admittance with leukemia, Doctor."

"Room?"

"Three-twelve."

Bridget flung her can of juice; with a crash, the recycle bin rocked backward. Before it settled back in place she was out of the break room and rushing toward Room 312.

TWO

N OT YET SUMMER but already hot.
Sunlight streamed through the pitted windshield as Raynorr navigated around a fallen oak that had lain in the meadow so long. even the termites had forsaken it. He squinted against the glare and felt the lines around his eyes deepen. Raising a hand to shield his eyes, he turned the long Oldsmobile toward the gnarled hickory standing like a colossus to the east. Once the tree's distant form was centered on the hood, he flipped the driver's side visor down and glanced at the burlap bag on the passenger seat next to him.

He could almost make out the shriveled form inside.

He drove slowly, his foot off the accelerator, partly due to the solemn nature of his undertaking, partly because a boulder or ditch might be lying in wait beneath the chest-high weeds and grasses yielding to the spot-rusted front bumper. It wouldn't take much for the Olds to puncture a tire or get stuck despite the relatively dry ground.

Of course, a four-wheel drive would be infinitely more appropriate for this sort of undertaking, but that meant either a pick-up or sport utility vehicle. A full sized pick-up, even with an extended cab, didn't have enough protected interior for his lab equipment should he need to move in a hurry, a valid concern now that he was about to start the war.

As for a sport utility vehicle…

He doubted Helen still had the old Jeep from their early days of marriage.

Weeds and tall grass continued to disappear beneath the hood as Raynorr drove and reflected.

The gynecologist Helen had latched onto drove a shiny Mercedes. Must be difficult to fit the Raynorr girls and the new man's offspring into that perfect piece of shit car. But then, the girls probably don't even live with Helen anymore—Jan was the youngest and she'll turn…twenty-two this year.

He frowned as his stomach coiled and knotted. Last time he'd seen her, Jan had been twelve.

The Olds suddenly rocked from side to side as it crossed a dry, shallow gully. The shocks squealed in protest.

Fact: Helen hadn't recognized him at the restaurant in Raleigh the other night. Even gave him a flirty look. If she didn't recognize him, no one would.

Gently Raynorr patted the stiff form beneath the burlap bag, as if the dog were alive and merely resting on the seat next to him.

The car continued to push through his meadow.

The shocks squeaked almost constantly now as he traversed more uneven terrain. He watched, almost mesmerized, as hundreds of grasshoppers the size of his middle finger leapt into the air at the automobile's massive intrusion, their wings beating frantically in an effort to escape harm's way. Many thwacked off the windshield. Some hit the hood on their backs or sides and became seared to the black surface. Their long legs jerked and twitched as they went into their death throes.

Raynorr blanched. The acrid whiff of the bugs wasn't nearly as powerful as it had been *back then*, but it was enough. Enough to take him back to the battlefields and the mass funeral pyres. A reek so horrid it was rendered unforgettable. All it had needed this time was the burning exoskeletons of these hoppers to resurrect it.

He drove toward the massive hickory in the distance, unconcerned about possible infection from the virus that had served as the catalyst in the dog's death.

On one of the many counters he'd built in his basement laboratory, beneath a heat lamp, was a solitary petri dish with moist mouse tissue inside. This dish contained and restrained the generation of Raynorr Virus that had unlocked death in the dog.

Tomorrow he would use more of the same—on a two-legged beast.

Right now he would tend to the dog.

The dog was a soldier in a war it could not have begun to understand. It deserved an honorable burial.

A sheen of sweat now covered the lean muscles of his forearms. Sweat also dampened the back of his simple white t-shirt where it met the leather seat.

Inching into the shade of the massive hickory, Raynorr turned the car until it faced in the direction of his house, now almost a mile away. He shifted into park and turned off the ignition.

No sooner had the engine noise died when the chattering of hundreds of cicada began. The vibrating wings of the large, ugly bugs created a pulsating rhythm that rose and fell around him, from the meadow he'd just traversed to the nearby woods to the hundreds of hickory branches above him.

A light breeze drifted over him like a warm caress, in perfect synchronization with the cicadaec symphony. In the distance stood the tiny form of his small house, snugly sheltered from the blazing sun by a cluster of huge oaks that had been there since the Civil War.

From behind the steering wheel he stared at the tire tracks the Olds had laid down through the tall weeds and grasses of the meadow. Many of the stems were bending back up. One rose slowly here, another there. Four in a row to the right, three to the left. As he watched, more of them rose and swayed gently in the hot breeze. His eyelids grew heavy.

Raynorr's head eased back against the seat. The musical cicada carried him away.

At some point he became aware of a loud buzz in his ears.

His eyes snapped open.

He turned to find a writhing black swarm beside him. Thick-bodied flies crept over his arms and legs and face. He could see the stiff hairs protruding from their abdomens.

With a cry he lashed out, swatting and striking. He crushed them on his face, his arms, his legs, the seat. Some flew off the bag as he struck it, only to descend upon it again in a growing black army. A few deaths wouldn't deter them. They knew there was a worthy prize within the bag.

With a curse, he kicked the door open and leaped outside.

The buzzing wings, coupled with the oppressive heat that had grown even hotter while he had dozed, took him to a place where the sun blazed even hotter. A place where the humidity was even more stifling. A place where, instead of a dead dog, the winged hordes found the decomposing bodies of men, women, and children.

A wrecked man could find such a place beautiful, even as it drove him insane.

Sucking in air and fighting the urge to vomit, Raynorr stumbled from the car. He crushed a dried stick and caught the flashes of white tails in the distance as deer bounded off into the woods.

After a few moments he flung open the passenger side door, shooed some of the flies away and hauled the bag out of the car, setting it down some feet away. Returning, he noted the sun was well past its zenith and had begun its descent throughout the western skies.

Workman-like now, he retrieved the shovel and pickaxe from the trunk. At a well-shaded spot beneath the hickory tree he dropped the shovel. The steel head of the pick bit into the ground with a puff of red dust. Thirty minutes later he lowered the dog into the grave.

The repulsive, winged demons dove into the grave, formed

a writhing black mass on the burlap bag. Raynorr spat and let the flies work themselves into a frenzy. Their buzzing reached feverish heights. It drilled into his ears, tunneled through his brain, bored into his soul.

Flies.

He snuffed the greedy little bastards with red Carolina clay.

✳ ✳ ✳

Classical music stirred Raynorr's mind from its slumber. The radio signal came from a listener-supported, public radio station only eight miles away in Wake Forest. Each year he anonymously gave a generous contribution to help keep the station operational.

He reached in the dark. With a single click the lamp beside his bed banished the inky blackness. In the pale yellow ambiance he stared up at the cracked paint on the ceiling and let the music flow throughout every part of his body. When the radio shut itself off ten minutes later, he was completely awake.

And ready to kill.

THREE

W HITE FLUORESCENT GLARE flooded the hallway. The swollen
veins in Bridget's eyes responded by throbbing in merciless
repetition, forcing her to squint as she power-walked toward
Room 312.

Human traffic clogged the middle of the upcoming intersection.
Bridget cut a path close to the corner—too close. Her shoulder
thudded into the corner of the wall. The impact spun her upper
body sideways. She grunted but did not break stride.

Nice, Devereaux, she thought, squaring her shoulders. *Either
that wall moved or I'm dragging major butt.*

She passed the nurse's station and Mrs. Wilson's room and it
was then that someone in hard heels fell into step behind her. As
she wove between staff and patients, her follower did the same, a
pilot fish cruising in the wake of a shark. Bridget started to turn
and see who it was when a formal nurse's skirt, outdated but
bleached and pressed to perfection, flashed in the corner of her
eye.

Not you, Bridget thought. *Not now.*

A patient file was suddenly in Bridget's face. Now she felt less
like the shark and more like the pilot fish.

"I found a patient of yours flipping through this," the woman
said, easily keeping up with Bridget's pace.

Bridget glanced at the name at the top of the file. "Mrs.
Wilson's...oh, shoot. I left it on her table when the code went out."

"It should *not* be left anywhere but the nurse's station."

Bridget nodded but did not turn and did not slow. "You're
right. I made a mistake. Thank you, Nurse Watkins."

Three-twelve was down the next hallway, second room on
the right, just around the corner. Bridget craned her neck but the
room was not yet visible, and became even less so when Nurse
Watkins suddenly blocked her path.

Bridget tried to step around the stern, fifty-something with the
buxom figure of a forty-year-old, but the woman deftly fronted

Bridget once again. With her fists on her hips and her elbows jutting out, she seemed larger than she really was. The severe lines between the woman's thin eyebrows became cavernous as she frowned, and her eyes could pass for twin pieces of flint. She gripped Mrs. Wilson's file tightly against the underside of her forearm, almost like a weapon held at the ready.

"You can't make mistakes like this. It could be trouble."

"Look, I'm tired and now a new patient has been admitted with the same rapid leukemia that has killed three—"

"Tired? We all get tired. You can't jeopardize a patient's life just because you're tired. You've got to get with it, Doctor."

Bridget stared at her. She could easily picture Nurse Watkins as a crusty sea captain in the age of tall-masted ships, berating one of the hands for not swabbing the deck properly—even as they braced themselves to receive a full broadside from the enemy.

"Aren't you over-reacting, Nurse? No, I shouldn't have left the file on the table, but where's the catastrophe? So Mrs. Wilson read about her diagnosis and daily treatment, so what? She isn't going to up her chemo treatments, believe me. And aren't these files the patient's property anyway?"

But even as she said it, she realized she had made a sizeable error in leaving the file behind. The hospital lawyer had told her and her fellow incoming interns on Day One to be very careful with patient files. Patient files were not for "public consumption" as he had put it, nor were they for casual "patient consumption." The only way a patient or family member could see a file was if they submitted a formal—

"Request, Doctor. The files are to be accessed by patient and family only upon *written request*."

Pinned, Bridget thought. *I broke a rule, but Captain Ahab-arina here will just have to wait until after I see the patient in 312.* "You're absolutely right. I made a mistake. It won't happen again."

Judging by the flush that hit Nurse Watkins' face, it was obvious the woman considered the incident more than just a minor faux pas and a little fessin' up wasn't going to diffuse the situation. Bridget could almost feel the woman's body temperature rise in conjunction with her anger. Bridget felt herself shrink away from this glowering woman who had so many years of healthcare experience over her. Nurse Watkins was not a fledgling intern trying to sprout into the role of physician. She was the head nurse for Ward Seven, the cancer ward at Chambers Hospital, and had been for over twenty-five years.

So…? part of Bridget cried. *Stand up to her anyway. You've got to be assertive, girlfriend—there's no room in the world for a timid doctor. Stand up to her, even if you are wrong.*

Nurse Watkins' eyes narrowed and grew more intense. "Let

me ask you something, Doctor Devereaux. Suppose a patient discovers a patient file with her name on it—mistakenly left behind by a very busy and very *tired* doctor. And suppose this patient, who wants a bit more pain relief, takes a pen and bumps up her dosage of morphine?"

"Something tells me this isn't hypothetical."

"My most senior nurse responded to three Code Blues that day and two of them died. If that wasn't enough, a patient vomited on her as she took his blood pressure. She got further behind schedule after cleaning and consoling another patient who'd been lying in a pool of diarrhea. The next patient's file was on the table beside him. A negligent doctor left it there. My nurse mentally slipped. Didn't think to verify things. Tired and stressed, the increased dosage of morphine the patient had scrawled in just didn't register with her."

"It wasn't caught it in time, was it?"

"No."

Bridget swallowed. "What happened?"

"The patient coded and died. Admin found out why. The doctor was reprimanded. My nurse—whom I had worked with for ten years and relied upon virtually every day—was fired. I fought for her. I told the higher-ups what had happened, how it had all been a terrible accident. Do you think they listened to me?"

Bridget slowly shook her head.

"Damn right they didn't." A thin misty veil descended over Nurse Watkins' eyes. "They knew they had a lawsuit on their hands. In the end, they settled with the spouse of the deceased for one point three million. Now I don't give a damn about the money, this place makes that in about a week, but that day we lost a patient and a great nurse—all because a young doctor forgot to properly handle a patient file."

"The nurse…?"

"Blacklisted. Couldn't get a job changing bedpans in a retirement home. The doctor, meanwhile, has a thriving practice in the suburbs of Winston-Salem. So now my ex-nurse waits tables at the House of Pancakes on Hillsborough Street, trying to make ends meet for herself and her kids."

Bridget and Nurse Watkins faced each other in the hallway. Hospital workers and visitors passed and gave them the once-over.

"It won't happen again," Bridget said.

Nurse Watkins stared at her for a moment and then nodded. To Bridget's surprise, the woman's expression softened. "You've got to watch for these things. They can bite you. I know they work the hell out of you interns, out of all of us, but you've got to keep the little things—and the big things—in mind or the shit can hit the fan in fat, gooey globs."

Nurse Watkins moved to the side to let Bridget by. As she did, she raised her arm and glanced at the slender watch face on the underside of her wrist. "Isn't your shift over, Doctor?"

"Yes," Bridget said, resuming her trek. To her surprise the woman again fell in beside her. "You're the head nurse of this ward. What can you tell me about the patient in three-twelve?"

"Josephine Woods. Her parents admitted her. Eleven years old, only about ninety-five pounds. Pretty girl. Early stages of leukemia. Doctor Prescott was the admitting staff physician and your counterpart, Doctor Simpson, was with him when she came in. After Simpson did the usual blood tests, Prescott diagnosed her and then had Simpson take a sample from the bone marrow in her hip. The leuk hadn't spread there as yet, thank God."

"Why does she have leukemia?" Bridget asked. The question was rhetorical, posed to herself more than the nurse.

"Children get cancer," Nurse Watkins said, taking the question literally. Her eyes softened. "Sometimes they recover, sometimes they don't. It just seems so much worse when it happens to them, poor things. Strange the girl showed no symptoms until a couple days ago, and now she's here."

"Doesn't sound like standard leukemia. By the way, isn't it against the rules to discuss patients in a quasi-public setting?" Bridget flashed her a grin.

Nurse Watkins halted and scowled, but it was ruined by the hint of a smile. Bridget kept walking.

Bridget walked up to 312. She paused to let an exiting nurse pass, grimly noting Margaret Morrison's vacant room across the hall.

The door was open but a short curtain was drawn across the entrance. Bridget knocked on the doorframe. Unlike most other doctors, she waited before entering.

"Come in," said a strong male voice.

Bridget parted the curtain and stepped inside.

The parents sat leaning forward on the edge of their chairs, next to the bed that dominated the room. Their faces were drawn, their eyes glassy. The girl propped up on the bed appeared in much better shape than her parents. She smiled as Bridget entered.

"Hey! I'm Josephine."

"Hello there." Bridget said, surprised at the girl's upbeat demeanor. Her extended hand was eagerly grasped but weakly shaken. "You have such a pretty name, Josephine. I'm Doctor Devereaux, but you call me Bridget, okay?"

"Okay, Bridget. As long as you call me Jo."

"Can you squeeze my hand a little tighter than that, Jo?"

The girl's lips pressed together and the pressure on Bridget's hand increased a fraction. Bridget smiled, patting Jo's hand before releasing it. "Good, good. I had a feeling you were strong."

Jo nodded emphatically. "Daddy says I'm strong, too. But I'm usually tons stronger than this."

Her French-braids draped over her shoulders in crimson streams. Unlike a typical red head, she was tan and had few freckles. Her blue eyes appeared dry and lidded, despite her cheerful presentation. Her lips pinched together when her smile faded, as if reflecting the battle being waged within.

Bridget turned and held her hand out. "Hello, you must be Mom."

"Ellen Woods." After the initial grasp her hand slid away, as if she had forgotten about the handshake halfway through.

"And you're Dad?" Again Bridget held her hand out.

"Joe." He grasped her hand tightly, gave a single downward tug and then released, affording a glimpse of a tattoo, a bulldog with a spiked collar, Marine-style on the topside of his muscular forearm. His eyes, also bloodshot, appeared worried and angry at the same time.

"Do you have a family physician or pediatrician for Josephine?"

"Not really," Joe Woods said. "We see a different doc every time we step foot in the local clinic covered by my insurance. It's like they've got a damned revolving door or something—you see 'em for two minutes and they're gone. How's anyone supposed to get good treatment when they won't spend any time with you?"

"I see." Bridget turned to Josephine. "I'd like to ask my attending if I can be your doctor, if it's okay with your parents, of course."

"I don't get it," Joe Woods said. "Why do you have to ask anybody?"

"I am an intern. A doctor, but still under close supervision. Once approved, Jo will be under my care and treatment plan, though I'll consult with the chief resident and chief oncologist every step of the way."

Joe Woods was on his feet. "You're not a full doctor? The hell is this…? I want a real doctor in here."

"Daddy, I like her."

"I assure you that I can perform—" Bridget began.

"My daughter doesn't get amateurs!"

"Daddy, no!"

"Goddamn it, I want a—"

"Enough, Joe!" Ellen Woods said. "She's already shown more interest than the other one. He ordered samples, hooked her to that drip bag and then left without hardly a word."

Jaw muscles flexed. "Didn't appreciate that one damn bit."

"Sit! And let's hear what Doctor Devereaux has to say."

Joe Woods slowly sat, shaking his head. He looked up at Bridget. "Sorry, I just want what's best for my girl."

"I completely understand."

"Can you cut it?"

"Yes."

He eased back on the chair. "All right."

Bridget turned to Jo. "I missed you on my earlier rounds. This has got to be weird for you, huh? Can you tell me how you're feeling? No detail is too small."

"Oh, I'm kinda tired. The doctor who set up these tubes said that was normal with my type of sickness. He had the nurse take blood samples, said he needed to run a bunch of tests. Then he told us I'd probably need some kind of powerful medicine. Keemo somethin' or another. I didn't like the sound of it."

"Chemotherapy," Joe Woods said, almost choking. He looked away, gripped the arms of the chair tightly, raising the tendons on the back of his strong hands.

Ellen Woods' knee pistoned up and down.

Bridget cleared her throat. "I need to wait on the results of the tests before I recommend a treatment plan for you, but in all likelihood it will include the chemotherapy Dr. Simpson mentioned earlier. When did you first start feeling badly?"

"I was kind of weak after my swim meet. When was that, Momma? Yesterday?"

"It was Saturday, baby. Just two days ago."

"I swam fast at first but then my body just wouldn't go. I thought I was just tired. Now I'm starting to ache a lot. Kind of ache all over. But I'll get better, right? I want to do more swimming. I'll be able to do more swimming soon. Right, Doctor Bridget?"

Ellen Woods let out a moan that made Bridget inwardly cringe.

"You keep thinking about swimming and staying strong and I'll do everything I can on my end, Jo," Bridget said, her jaw tightening. "We'll kick this thing together."

But even as she said it, she could almost hear Blake Hensely's nasal voice in her mind. As chief resident, he had addressed all the new interns on their first day here at Chambers: "...and don't promise the patient *anything*. Try to be consoling, even slightly optimistic if you feel you have to, but don't give them false hope or make promises you can't keep. You are not God. The fact is you're going to lose more lives than you're going to save, so you might as well start with that understanding."

But Bridget didn't feel she was giving Josephine false hope—she really *would* do everything she could for her.

But how much could she hope to do? This leukemia strain had already killed at record speed.

Bridget bit the inside of her lip. *I don't want this girl coding on us. I don't want to put the defib paddles on her.*

She suppressed a shudder. "I'd like to get a blood sample from you, Jo."

"Well, I gave one already, but okay."

"Thanks, honey."

Mr. and Mrs. Woods appeared a trifle relieved at the part about the cancer being destroyed. Bridget knew that was overstepping the bounds, but she was willing to do whatever she could to keep the girl's high spirits from falling.

She made a show of looking around the room. "Of course, I didn't bring *any* of the stuff I need with me. Now how do you like that?"

Jo smiled.

Bridget leaned close, arched a brow. "Tell me, do I look like a ditzy blonde to you?"

"No!" Josephine laughed. "You've got *dark* hair!"

"Oh, you mean I'm a ditzy brunette, huh? Well, thanks a lot! Maybe I should color my hair blond, is that what you mean? You think I should buy some hair color the next time I'm at the store, don't you? Come on, we're pals now. You can tell me straight."

"No, don't do that!"

Bridget winked. "Okay, I'll hold off for now. Don't you go anywhere. I'll be right back."

She went to the nurse's station to get the syringe and gauze, her smile fading.

The night shift attending stood watching her. "Most interns do reasonable things like sleep or drink after their shift is over, Devereaux."

"Can I have Josephine Woods?"

"What makes you think you can do better than one of my crew?"

"I'm here, aren't I?"

The attending shrugged. "All right. She's yours."

✳ ✳ ✳

Bridget pushed open the stairwell door and walked wearily down the dim basement corridor. The warm air clung to her face, neck and hands. It was something she would have expected in the Amazon jungle, not in the basement of a hospital. The place reeked of rust and long-standing water. Goose bumps broke out down the middle of her back and she shuddered.

Wish they'd move the hematology lab upstairs somewhere, she thought. *At least spend a few bucks and get more lights down here.*

A network of sweating pipes hung overhead, that made her

think of the root systems beneath a forest floor.

Stray towel bins, wheelchairs, gurneys and patient beds in various stages of disrepair lined the walls. She heard muffled voices and distant crashes of towel bins being shoved through the swinging doors of the laundry room at the end of the tunnel, or rather, hallway. Seemed a lot like a tunnel to her, and not a very nice one.

Carrying Jo's packaged blood close to her breast, Bridget gratefully pushed open the hematology lab door. Inside the square room she found rows of counter tops, stools, microscopes and computers...but no people.

Cutbacks, she thought, recalling the memo handed out a few months ago stating that all but the first shift of lab workers had been phased out, opting instead for an on-call rotation. *Well, this can't wait for tomorrow. At least the air's easier to breathe in here.*

She broke the tape over the lid of the thin plastic container and opened it. Thumbing the plunger of a pipette, she extracted some of Josephine's blood and squirted it into a glass test tube. The narrow spout clicked against the inside of the tube. Bridget capped the tube and placed it into the containment bay of the centrifuge and clicked the machine on. The tube blurred in a high-speed spin that would separate the white and blood cells based on relative weight.

Bridget let the centrifuge do its thing for sixty seconds, then clicked it off and went to one of the stations. She dotted several slides with Josephine's blood, then squirted seven cc's into a separate test tube and took it to the box-like machine in the corner. She fed a narrow metal lead through a small hole in the rubber stopper, then pressed the start button to the Ciba Corning 800 Series Blood Analysis Unit.

She sealed the original plastic container, labeled it and set it in refrigerated storage. At the lab station, she positioned the first slide beneath the scanning electron microscope and looked at the monitor.

Ugh, too bright, she thought, squinting through her glasses at the ghostly images on the screen.

Her left bra cup decided to ride up on her as she stretched to adjust the monitor. Alone in the lab, she tugged at the lower band of the errant cup. Just as she pulled it down, a lab technician backed through the doorway. Quickly Bridget redirected her hand and reached for the test tube of Josephine's blood as if that had been her intention all along.

Great timing, Mister! Bridget thought, her cheeks flushing red.

"Evenin'," the tech said, his blue jeans swishing softly as he walked in. He carried a can of soda in his left hand.

He appeared to be in his early fifties, judging by the

combination of his bald pate, gray moustache and the distinct lines on his tanned face. Handsome, he was lean and muscular and stood over six feet tall, much taller than her own five foot six. With his white lab coat fully unbuttoned, he made no effort to hide an electric blue t-shirt emblazoned with a green dolphin sporting dark sunglasses and a toothy grin.

"Hello," Bridget said.

"I can take care of that if you'd like."

She decided he meant Jo's blood sample.

"No, thanks," Bridget said, setting the test tube into a small rack. She focused on the monitor and centered the slide she had made. "I'd like to see this one through myself. I appreciate it, though."

"Your time, young lady," he said, moving to another lab station where he began to shuffle some papers stacked next to his microscope.

Suddenly Bridget looked up. "What time *is* it?"

He checked his watch. "Seven oh three."

"At night?" But she realized she already knew the answer. He'd greeted her with "evening." *Administration must've realized they need a second shift lab worker after all.*

The lab tech smiled with rows of straight white teeth like the dolphin on his t-shirt. "Getting their money's worth from you interns, aren't they? Standard procedure, but I think it leads to mistakes. Anyhow...yes, it's seven oh three *at night*, though the sun won't set for another hour or so now that we are fully immersed in summer."

"Is there a phone in here?"

He quickly scanned the room. "Right there," he said, pointing to a section of wall near the door.

The way he said it made her think he hadn't been sure of the phone's location any more than she had been. She hurried to the phone. "I didn't think anyone worked here after five o'clock. Didn't they do away with the second and third shifts?"

"Yes, but I'm a contractor. I told them when I first started that I needed to work nonstandard hours. They were happy to get me so cheaply, I think. I'm semi-retired and I don't mind working alone."

"How did you know I was an intern? I don't recall meeting you."

For a moment the middle-aged lab tech seemed absorbed by his papers. He scrawled something down and then raised his eyebrows. The furrowed rows of his forehead were long, deep, and even. "They always put us on alert when new interns come in."

"They do?"

"Sure. That way we can charge for blood work that's otherwise free."

"So we're just part of the food chain, huh?"

"Hey, we've got to pay for our Porsches somehow."

"I see."

"Of course, mine bears a striking resemblance to a Ford Focus." He winked.

Bridget smiled and punched up her apartment phone number. As she did so she noticed the watch on her wrist. She'd been wearing it continuously for the past few days and had forgotten it was there. She no longer felt its weight. The phone rang once. When Travis picked up the other end, his words seemed sluggish.

"Chez Devereaux."

"Travis…hey, it's me. Look, I'm not going to be able to make it for dinner tonight. I'm sorry. I've got a new patient—"

"What else is new?" he said. "You know, I could have stayed at my own apartment and had tuna or something, but I thought we were going to eat together. Guess what? Wrong again. Now what am I supposed to do for food?"

"Well, there's leftover chicken in the fridge. You can heat that up. Peas in the freezer can go with it. It's what we were going to have anyway. All you have to do is nuke it."

"And you?" he asked, but it sounded to Bridget like he asked only because she might expect him to do so.

"I'll grab a pack of peanut-butter crackers and a soda here," she said.

"Yummy. So when are you going to get here? You've pulled your twenty-four-hour shift. Isn't that enough, already? Damn…"

"I'll probably be home in a couple of hours. A patient of mine coded and now a girl has just been admitted with the same symptoms."

"Think my day was all dandelion wine? Isn't easy working on a thesis while instructing Dr. Vransic's motivational psych lab class. Man, it's all I can do not to feel like one of those little white rats getting sparked on the electric grid."

She was about to tell him she'd be okay but stopped short. He had barely acknowledged her situation. People were dying here and all he could think of was the stresses involved in his pursuit of his doctorate in psychology? In may not be fun, but at least he'd live to pass or fail.

"Bridge?"

His pet name for her.

Her parents had died without saying, but Bridget was confident they had harbored no intentions of shortening her name.

"Bridge?"

She'd corrected Travis plenty about it. Now she sighed and let it go. Again.

"Bridge, you there?"

"Yeah, I'm here. Look, I'll see you in a while. Why don't you do some studying until I get there? That way you'll have it out of the way and we can have some time together."

"Can't study now…I'm brain-dead. Maybe I'll have a beer or two instead. Hey, your fridge is a little bare. Do you have some green in the drawer?"

Bridget frowned. "I was saving it for the movie tomorrow night. I thought we'd celebrate since I won't be on-call for two whole days. Doesn't that sound nice?"

"Yeah, but how 'bout I buy some beer and we'll save up for a movie some other time? Don't you think you'll want a beer when you get here?"

She looked at the wall.

"You're not saying anything," Travis observed. "Bridge?"

"Yes, Travis."

"Suddenly we're not communicating."

"I know."

"Why do you think that is?"

Already acting the part of clinical psychologist, she thought, her throat tightening. "I don't know. I just don't know about anything anymore. See you later."

Instead of waiting for his goodbye, she hung up and stared at the cracked paint on cinderblock wall. She wondered how she had let herself get involved with a handsome but self-absorbed guy six years her senior who rarely shared any of his own money.

Keep going, girl, Bridget told herself. *Keep going.*

She rubbed her burning eyes. *Probably shouldn't have hung up on him like that,* she thought. *Just didn't want to get into it right now.*

But you never confront him, a little voice whispered from the shadowy recesses of her mind. *You keep it all in instead of coming out with it.*

I don't have time for you now, she told the voice. *So beat it.*

It faded but did not leave entirely.

She went back to the microscope and watched the images on the monitor. Jo's normal white blood cells were in abundance along with the red blood cells. In fact, there was a respectable percentage of normal white cells. This was good. These leukocytes were soldiers in the battle against viruses and diseases.

But then other, much more ominous forms drifted across the monitor.

Bridget stiffened. A hand closed over her heart and started to squeeze.

There in the slide was direct evidence of the battle raging inside Jo's young body. Misshapen white blood cells—mutants. Normal leukocytes were uniform in size and shape and had smooth outer walls. These cells were puckered, squashed-looking, and even flattened.

The trademark of leukemia, these mutant clones of normal leukocytes were useless to the body. As the disease progressed, so too did the percentage of these abnormal white blood cells in the bloodstream and vital organs. Complications arose in the host body from the lack of normal white blood cells. Viral and bacterial infections often occurred.

And should the chemotherapy or other treatments fail, it was certain that Jo's leukemia would spread to her bone marrow. Should that happen, the production process would shift into high gear, swelling the number of useless white blood cells circulating throughout the bloodstream, hampering and eventually shutting down Josephine's breathing and circulation and organ function.

Bridget examined slide after slide and noted the same ratios of abnormal white blood cells in each. With a sinking feeling in her stomach, she slumped back in the chair.

Jo was healthy just a couple of days ago, Bridget thought. *Poor girl.*

Josephine is not lost, Devereaux! Many patients recover from leuk. I'll throw everything I've got at this fucking disease. I'll do a shaman's dance and fast for weeks if it'll help—

"Done with this?" the technician asked, looking at the Ciba 800, which had beeped loudly three times and now was doing so once every ten seconds.

"Yes," she said. "Since you're there, would you print the results?"

"Want me to run a comparison?"

"Thank you, yes. Young female. Eleven years old."

He hit a few buttons on the computer keyboard. "Done."

She snatched at the printout from the printer. The results came out in percentages, given along with what was standard in a child eleven years old. Everything verified what Bridget had seen on the microscope monitor. Normal red and white blood cell production was down—abnormal leukocyte production was up.

But so far it's not rampant, Bridget thought. *I may have a chance to help her beat it, with the help of…of…What's this?*

There was something else in the printed results the tech had given her. A protein in Jo's blood that the 800 Series had mysteriously labeled "Protein Matrix X."

X.

Unknown.

Bridget rubbed her burning eyes, blinked to clear the blurriness. Unknown protein—who…?

Think, Devereaux, think!

The human body absorbs and produces an array of proteins. What was unusual was that the computer hadn't identified this particular one. There wasn't much there, whatever it was, only .05 percent.

Maybe this "Protein Matrix X" is attributable to Jo's diet. It could be a natural occurrence in a certain percentage of the population, or maybe it's fairly common now and was unknown to the researchers who programmed the blood analyzer. Hell, I don't know. I'm not a research scientist.

And now that she was thinking about it, what did she really know? Four years of undergraduate study and four years of medical school. What made her think she knew anything about how to practice real medicine?

To hell with the doubts. Just keep looking.

For hours she scoured internet research sites, but found nothing to compare with the rapidity of this strain of leukemia.

She stared at the cracked paint on the wall of the lab. It was strange how that one big crack resembled lightning, a long jagged bolt in the dull gray surface of the paint. The tendrils of the bolt narrowed, traveled sideways and then up along the wall, forked, widened, forked and forked again. You could get lost following the tendrils around the room.

Her pulse throbbed at her temples.

Blinking was akin to eyelids scraping over sandpaper.

She went to the phone and dialed Jo's room.

"Hello?" Mrs. Woods said sleepily.

"It's Doctor Devereaux, Mrs. Woods. Sorry to wake you."

"That's all right. Did you find anything?"

"I'm afraid the original diagnosis was correct—Jo has acute myeloid leukemia. I will consult with the chief oncologist first thing in the morning. I'll go over the plan for the chemotherapy with you and your family immediately afterward. I'm very sorry."

Mrs. Woods coughed back a sob. "I understand."

Bridget sat for a long time, hearing that sob over and over again while staring at the lightning pattern in the wall.

Finally she stirred.

Time to turn in. Not doing any good as a zombie. Don't think I can drive without falling asleep behind the wheel. Need to call Travis…don't have the energy.

She said goodnight to the lab tech, who waved and watched her leave with a sympathetic look on his face. Too tired for the stairs this time, she trudged the gloomy hallway to the elevator, slumped against the wall and was hoisted to the third floor. Another endless hall. The joints of her ankles, knees and hips seemed to grate in their sockets, as if depleted of synovial fluid to lubricate them.

Bridget made it to the doctor's lounge. A row of empty cots and stacked blankets beckoned her. She flipped a worn pillow to the end of the first gurney, grasped a blanket that smelled like bleach and climbed on. She sat upright for a moment, felt her head begin to levitate. She eased down and pulled herself into the fetal position.

It's happening too fast, she thought. *Way too fast for normal leukemia. What's causing it?*

Bridget waited, but the answer never came.

And despite her weariness, sleep proved almost as elusive.

FOUR

O NE WEEK AFTER burying the dog in the field. The first human had succumbed to the Raynorr Virus, and its creator was on the hunt again.

He used the steering wheel to propel himself from the cab of the delivery truck. He slammed the door behind him and inhaled the soupy air that is a mainstay in the heart of North Carolina from June to early October. Beads of perspiration leaped onto his forearms and the smooth skin of his face and top of his head. He took a step and halted.

The blacktop gave a little beneath him, as if he stood on one of those floating islands of peat and vegetation that form in the swamps of the deep South. Silently absorbing a barrage of summer sun, the asphalt of the four service spaces bled tar onto the concrete curbs. Black bubbles bulged, grew thin in the walls and ruptured with a splatter and hiss.

He almost wished he could have cooled down longer in the air-conditioned cab. But what did it matter if his blue uniform had patches of sweat on it? He was supposed to be a working man, and working men sweat from their manual labor. At least the shirt and shorts were a reasonable part of the uniform. The heavy boots, on the other hand, were overkill. Sneakers would be more appropriate and they wouldn't bake his feet by the time his shift was over.

He pulled a cap from his back pocket and unfolded it. In the side-view mirror, Raynorr made sure the patch on the front—the two-dimensional crystal shaped like a garish diamond—was properly lined up with his angular nose, just as the manager-girl back at the Crystal Clear home office had decreed. He pulled the brim down lower than what she had recommended.

Just another delivery guy.

At the rear of the truck, he yanked the dolly from its hanger and set it upright on its metal lip and the two large wheels at the base of its spine. Quickly, he unfolded and locked into place the secondary wheels high up near the telescoping handle, then pulled the skeletal wagon to the side of the truck.

After unhitching the iron restraining arm, he shoved the cargo door upward. Hard plastic wheels shrieked in steel runners as the door rumbled and shook and folded slat by slat into the top of the truck. At the top it slammed into the catch, rocked back and forth twice and remained still.

He stared at the honeycomb of pentagonal bays. Most of the bays held empty water bottles. The bottles were cylindrical and made of dark blue plastic, easy to spot against drab corporate interiors. When filled, the bottles held five gallons of expensive Crystal Clear *spring* water that was really treated tap water from some Yankee state up North.

He didn't care if it was chemically treated filth skimmed off Boston Harbor. It suited his purposes to deliver the stuff and that was all that mattered.

Employing considerable strength for a man of any age, Raynorr pulled out and stacked the water jugs onto the horizontal dolly. When filled with water, each canister weighed forty pounds. He handled them without conscious effort, taking the opportunity to mentally replay the strategy for his mission inside the Foundation One building, the modern-day Tower of Babylon that now loomed over his back.

When he had two rows of seven on the dolly he took a red handkerchief from his back pocket and wiped the sweat from his face and arms. He looked at the pentagonal bays rising to the roof of the truck.

His personal bomb depot.

Those who worked full-time for Crystal would go back for another load, but not Raynorr. Four hours a day was all he needed as a water delivery man. He had his other *job* to go—one he had started, like this one, soon after perfecting the Raynorr Virus.

He recalled how he had insisted upon this particular delivery route when he first joined Crystal. "Lou Walters already handles the Crabtree Lake circuit", they told him. "You need to take another route, Gramps."

He took another route—but not for long. Four days after Raynorr was hired, Lou's truck became intimately acquainted with a telephone pole. The police found a bloody mass of human bone and tissue in a briar thicket thirty feet from the ruined truck. It seems Lou forgot to wear his seatbelt that day. They said he'd been drunk, but Raynorr knew the half-empty vodka bottle found in Lou's mangled truck had simply been a prop. Powdered barbiturates dissolved in a coffee thermos can mimic alcohol in so many ways. Lou was pronounced DOA at Chambers Hospital and his mortal remains were now decomposing at Memorial Gardens Cemetery off Route 70.

Raynorr now delivered to all the health insurance companies that had sprung up around Lake Crabtree in the years since he'd lost his practice. It was as if the building behind him now — Foundation Health Net — had ejected spores into the wind and they all landed around this small recreational lake near Research Triangle Park. In the span of a decade, no fewer than eight corporate castles appeared on the once-forested grounds around the lake — all paid for by the blood of the patients trapped in their networks.

Of course, the employees of these companies sprinted through the daily rat race and paid little attention to him. To them he wasn't Doctor Andrew Raynorr. To them he was just a blue-collar man, lower by several rungs than the slick corporate class they belonged to.

Raynorr pulled the bay door down but didn't lock it. He wheeled the dolly to the service entrance. A sheet of paper was taped to the service elevator doors. On it was scrawled: *Out of Order*.

He hesitated.

More people would notice him if he used the main elevators. Greater chance of recognition.

But by the time the virus was connected to a water delivery guy — *if* it ever was — he'd be long gone.

He didn't have to worry about delivering to anyone but the executives at these companies, since they only deemed themselves worthy of bottled water. From what the manager-girl at Crystal had told him, the underlings had to settle for the tap.

"Execs get the perks," she had said, aiming the remote and switching channels to another brainless talk show.

Raynorr had a few perks for the execs himself.

As he wheeled the dolly through the lobby, he was struck by the cool, almost chilly air. He shivered slightly, then forgot about temperature as his senses were overpowered by the perceived stench his surroundings. He nearly choked on the festering reek of power run amuck.

These are the ones that ruined him. No longer human, they are corporate maggots writhing about…oozing, vomiting, defecating slime throughout their nest.

The foulness had been here so long he doubted anyone else could detect it.

The carpeted lobby was thick with two-legged traffic. Men in conservative suits and women in skirt/suit combinations. They traveled alone or in pairs or small groups. All of them moved stiffly, as if they didn't want to wrinkle their clothes.

At the elevators, he pressed the *up* button and stared at the glowing, upward-pointing arrow. He had only a few seconds to wait before the button went dark, an electronic ding sounded, and the elevator doors parted.

A squadron of suits issued forth. The male suits wore controlled expressions. To a man they were clean-shaven, and their hairlines didn't dare approach their starched collars. The female suits had carefully painted eyes and lips and hair that would blend easily into a crowd.

All of the suits, male and female alike, spoke in low tones, as if they didn't want to risk someone overhearing them.

Raynorr looked down before anyone could look into his eyes.

When the elevator was empty, he started to push the dolly toward it. Five dark figures zipped by him to fill the void. One of the suits smirked at him.

"We're in a hurry."

He jerked the dolly up short and glared at the one who had spoken. He was a young man, probably in his late twenties, with slick blond hair and a lean, haughty face. He had an air of superiority about him, and Raynorr knew instantly the young man was some sort of manager or junior executive. Around him his underlings snickered.

He felt his legs tense, ready to spring. He fought the impulse to slap the yuppie leader to the floor. With supreme effort he succeeded in smoothing his face into proper neutrality. "I'll take the next one."

"Good idea," the leader said, not bothering to contain a nasally laugh. He leaned forward and made of show of looking him up and down. "Uh, kind of old for a water boy, aren't ya, Pops?"

"Bills don't pay attention to age," Raynorr returned, not quite succeeding in keeping the ice out of his tone.

"And I'll bet hospital bills stack up in a hurry when you're staring old age right in the kisser."

Raynorr showed his teeth. "Sometimes they stack up in a hurry for young people who seem healthy one day and suddenly take ill the next."

The underlings didn't laugh this time. Instead, they eyed Raynorr and one another and waited for their leader to respond.

The leader's sneer vanished. He slapped his hand to one of the doors to keep the elevator from closing. "Know what, Water Boy? I'm going to call Corporate Affairs and have them put one of those water rigs on my floor. Then I'll see to it that you deliver the water to me personally, Pops. Uh, I mean —" he made a show of leaning forward to read the name tag on Raynorr's uniform, "— Mike. How does that sound, *Mike?* Want to deliver water to a man half your age? A man who has thirty-four employees reporting to him?"

Raynorr didn't take his eyes off the younger man. "I think it would prove…enlightening."

A brief flicker of uncertainty in the leader's eyes. Then the uncertainty disappeared and the sneer returned. "You're damn right it will."

The leader took his hand from the door.

Laughter broke out as the elevator doors hesitated before starting to close.

"Fucking water boy tried to steal our lift and then gets uppity? Obviously doesn't know Hugh Croston is the next vice-president of operations."

The laughter faded as the elevator ascended.

Raynorr's hand shook despite his resolve to remain calm. He mashed the "up" button and waited for the next elevator a few feet away. This time he stood closer to the door with the dolly, assertively proclaiming his intention to anyone who may arrive behind him.

The underlings had spoken a name: *Hugh Croston.*

He'd remember that name.

The elevator dinged. Two women deep in conversation exited. Raynorr quickly pushed the dolly with its cargo inside, taking up nearly all the open space.

"Room for one more?" he heard, as he reached for the button to the eleventh and highest floor.

"Certainly," Raynorr said, pushing the button without looking at the speaker. There was room for another in the elevator, even with the full dolly. He felt the woman enter to stand diagonally from him.

He was surprised to see she was not a young business clone but was instead closer to his own age. Her eyes were dark and coolly calculating. Her make-up was noticeable but she had not overdone it. She had not attempted to blot out the fine lines of her face, only lessen them. She was perhaps ten to fifteen pounds overweight, but in her gray suit/skirt combo she appeared very poised.

He looked away but his gaze snapped right back to her.

Those eyes.

Raynorr considered bludgeoning her to death as soon as the elevator doors closed. He had groveled before her in this very same building, eleven years ago. You don't forget eyes you've begged to.

"Floor…?" Raynorr asked, almost choking. He shuffled a little closer to the side wall so she could have more room. He cleared his throat.

"You already pressed it. I'm going all the way up," she said, smiling at the doors as they closed before them. "I've got twenty minutes before my business lunch. Got off the elevator and realized I forgot my damn speech. My assistant might get flustered looking for it so back up I go. Besides, two sets of eyes are better than one." She laughed one of those laughs designed to help ease the tension between people who don't know each other.

"You must be very busy," Raynorr said.

"I'm the CEO of this company," she said. "I've got three hundred and eighty-seven employees beneath me. You could say I'm busy, all right." Again the polite, forced laugh.

Raynorr choked down the bitter acid that pooled in his mouth.

CEO?

Raynorr looked away. A trickle of sweat traced down the middle of his back and he shuddered. His temples pounded. His blood screamed for him to jerk her backward and splinter her spine over his knee.

She'd only been a director when he had surrendered his pride to her nine years ago. Was she too high up to be targeted? Strategically, he couldn't eliminate every CEO. The confusion would cripple the companies instead of galvanizing them into meeting his future demands. No, he couldn't target every CEO, but he could take one or two as examples. *Would she recognize him if he took off the hat?*

Doubtful. A memory so painful, so devastating to him probably had not been more than a passing thought to her.

What was this woman's name?

And why didn't he remember it? Had he blotted it out? Was he losing his mind?

As they traveled upward, she mentioned how hot it was outside and how glad she was that he had ventured into such heat to deliver the water that would slake her thirst.

He'd see to it she would never be thirsty again. Of course, she'd have to experience a significant amount of agony before arriving at that end.

On the eleventh floor the elevator dutifully halted. The doors parted with a subtle swishing sound. As she stepped out their eyes met. A name suddenly blazed before him.

Margaret Morrison.

Somehow he managed to restrain himself. As much as he wanted to, it would be the worst of follies to get physical. He'd get the death penalty for a brief moment of bliss as his knuckles ruined her face and his hands crushed her windpipe. He had no intention of sabotaging his carefully laid plans for a fleeting moment of ecstasy.

Instead, he gave her a warm smile from beneath the brim of the cap. She stepped from the elevator and started down the hallway to the right. He followed, wheeling the dolly after her.

"Bring that delicious water right on in!" she told him, opening the glass door to her executive suite and stepping through. She didn't bother holding the door for him.

As Raynorr negotiated the doorway, she marched past a young man in a dark suit and tie seated at a desk found before her private office. The young man's eyes widened as she bore down on him.

"Speech, Don! Where did I leave the damned thing?"

"You left the speech?"

"That's what I said. Now help me find it."

"It's got to be on your desk," he said, leaping from his chair. "I finished writing it last night. I printed it and laid it on your desk for you this morning. You said you looked it over…"

"I skimmed it—didn't have time to read every word. You did a good job. I picked up the wrong folder after my ten-thirty with that accounting dweeb."

Beside the CEO's office was a wooden-paneled wall with two sets of opened doors leading into a conference room. Inside the room was a vast mahogany table, polished to a mirror-like surface that reflected the sunlight streaming in from the windows.

Just outside the conference room, to the right of the opened doors, was one of two Crystal Clear water machines, along with a rack of empty blue bottles. The other water machine was in Margaret Morrison's office.

As Raynorr wheeled the dolly toward the water machine outside the conference room, he watched them rifle through the stacks of documents on her desk. Raynorr went to the rack of blue jugs, pulling his dolly like a wagon behind him though the manager-girl had said to always push the thing. Pulling had often resulted in damaged heels, even snapped Achilles' tendons, she had said, and that meant workers' compensation, something the company didn't like. Raynorr was careful as he pulled the dolly, but not for the company's sake.

Raynorr replaced the empty jugs on the rack with full ones, then stacked the empties on the recumbent dolly. He had three full jugs left on the dolly. They were for Margaret Morrison.

To make the hit he needed them out of the office.

"Goddamn it, where did I put that thing? I'm going to be late for this fucking luncheon! I know it's here somewhere."

"Found it, Margaret. It was on the sill."

"Thank God! What would I do without you, Don Mayhew?"

"I hate to think about it. Want me to come with you?"

"To make sure I don't lose it on the way? Not a bad idea but no, I need you here until Sherry can relieve you at twelve for your lunch. You know how jerks like the governor always want to call at lunchtime."

"By the way, he mentioned yesterday that his wife had come

down with one of those bad summertime colds."

Raynorr watched from the corners of his eyes as he worked. As their voices approached, he pretended to be absorbed in rearranging the empties on the dolly. Margaret Morrison rushed to the elevator with her assistant in tow.

"Send a card and flowers to the governor's home," she said. "Never hurts to keep him well greased." Raynorr felt her looking at him over her shoulder. "Don't forget the one in my office, Mr. Waterman. I get thirsty too, you know. The other guy forgot to get my personal bottles every other time he came out here."

He smiled...tried to keep the predatory feeling inside him from reflecting in his eyes. "I'll take care of you."

She didn't hear his reply. She was rattling off orders to the young man she had called Don Mayhew, who was nodding his head and saying he'd handle something or another. They disappeared down the hall.

Raynorr was sure he'd already been dismissed from her attention.

He wheeled the dolly to a point just outside her office. He picked up one of his full water bottles and stepped inside, his gaze immediately centering on the water dispenser identical to the one outside the conference room. The jug perched upside-down in it was empty. He scanned her desk as he made his way to the water dispenser and set this first bottle down. In the rack next it were two other empties.

He could hear the faint voices of the CEO and her assistant as they waited at the elevator. His heart began a rapid thrumming as he reached into his pocket for the slight bulge there. With the CEO's personal water supply in front of him, he took the sniper's bullet from his pocket. Needle-less, the syringe was stunted, which made it perfect. He could easily conceal it in the palm of his hand.

A coffee cup caught his eye on the paper-strewn desktop.

Three seconds and the bullet was on its way.

His hand didn't even shake as he did it.

"What are you doing?"

The administrative assistant's voice sliced through the pregnant silence that he hadn't realized had closed in around him.

Panic slammed into Raynorr's stomach like a punch. He slipped the syringe back into his pocket, his body blocking the movement from the assistant.

"Just admiring the CEO's desk," Raynorr said quickly. "I've never seen one before."

"Look, I'm not trying to be a jerk, but I don't think she'd want you scanning her stuff. There could be sensitive papers there."

"You're right, of course. My mistake."

The assistant nodded, apparently satisfied.

"She must be very important." He replaced the other two bottles and picked up the handle of the dolly to leave.

"She can set new policies and procedures for all the health insurance networks Foundation has created. Thousands of people are affected by the patient care changes she finalizes."

Raynorr pulled the dolly through the doorway. The assistant watched him closely, then followed him out.

"You look familiar somehow. Do I know you?" the assistant asked from behind him.

For the second time Raynorr took a shot in the stomach. He kept walking toward the elevator. Looking straight ahead he said, "I have one of those faces, it seems. I moved here from South Carolina just last month."

"Oh, I see. Sorry."

"No problem."

The assistant followed him to the elevator, watching while he thumbed the down arrow. To his relief the bell dinged almost immediately.

"Have a good day," Raynorr said as he pulled the dolly inside the elevator, his eyes hidden by the brim of the hat.

"You, too."

The elevator doors came together and Raynorr let out a gust of air, relief mixed with triumph.

Though time would show the definitive results, he'd just fired the most important shot in the war thus far. After years of preparation and experimentation, he had finally engaged the enemy at one of the highest levels!

Outside, he forced himself not to run for the water truck. He breathed deeply of the thick, sweet air. The heat banished the clinging chill he'd gotten while inside the corporate building. Doused by sunlight, the water of Crabtree Lake had turned to a pool of gold. He basked in the sight of it, made even richer by his accomplishment.

He looked up at the mirrored building and grinned. The chances were excellent that Margaret Morrison would ingest the Raynorr Virus at some point today. When she did, the fuse would be lit and she would meet her end in only days.

Of course, the addition of Morrison to his death count would not be enough to gain any real leverage against the insurance powers. They'd ignore his demands until he proved himself with more kills.

Didn't matter. He'd take them down stone by stone, or broaden his attack by the thousands. He'd fill Crabtree Lake with cadavers if he had to.

FIVE

SOMETHING PULLED BRIDGET from slumber's murky depths. Awareness clung to her as she rose through the fathoms toward the light. Eventually she surfaced, but did not exit, the warm waters of her unconsciousness. Fearing the moment would elude her, she did not stir upon the makeshift bed in the doctor's break room, for it was while in this state, in the nebulous zone between awareness and sleep, that *she* most often came.

Bridget kept her eyes shut and waited.

I feel you, she thought, her stomach fluttering with anticipation. *You're with me again.*

Within the darkness, pinpoints of colored light suddenly glowed and drifted toward one another. An outline formed, and then thousands of the tiny lights filled the inner darkened areas to create a woman's ghostly visage.

The face was nearly as familiar as Bridget's own, filled with warmth despite the ethereal presentation. She hovered close at the moment, but in reality Christine was an entire world removed from Bridget's yearning touch.

Don't think of that, Bridget told herself, *just let her come.*

Gazing upon her now reaffirmed what Bridget had always known: Christine had been beautiful. She had a model's visage— eyes of arresting blue, high cheekbones, full lips, a softly contoured jaw line framed by the jet-black hair of perpetual youth. She was so pleasing to gaze upon, so reassuring. Bridget's friends looked at pictures of Christine and remarked at how similar mother and daughter appeared—a compliment Bridget demurely denied but was secretly pleased to hear.

Bridget had never been to France, but one look at Christine's face and she was in her mother's homeland. Through Christine she could feel the vibrancy of Paris, the wonder of the Eiffel Tower and L'Arc d'Triumph and Notre Dame and the Louvre, the quiet force of the Seine as it flowed through Paris and into the picturesque countryside Van Gogh had depicted so brilliantly in so many of his works.

When Christine spoke in Bridget's mind, it was in a gentle whisper. Her French accent was distinct but not overwhelming, just as Bridget remembered it. "The little girl won't die, will she?"

"I don't know. This form of leukemia has killed adults in only *days*. It's in its earliest stage with Jo, but she's already in pain."

"She will live?"

"I hope so, *mon Mere*."

"You have to get more involved, *cher*. Fight the disease with everything you have, to the point where the girl feels you are beside her in her battle. Find a way to banish it from her body."

"What if I can't?"

"You are a doctor now, Bridget."

"Your doctors couldn't save you."

"You are different from them. Perhaps you can find something they have not considered."

"I'm just an intern. Researchers have been trying to cure cancer for decades. They, they—"

"*Qu'est que c'est*, daughter? What…?"

"They are beyond me. I'm just starting out."

"Never mind them, *cher*. Concentrate on what you must do to save Josephine and those like her. You can do it, I know you can."

"I can't move a mountain!"

"Perhaps not, but Josephine needs you to try." The beauty of Christine's smile caused Bridget's eyes to well. "Concentrate on what you must do. I love you, *cher*."

"Do you have to go so soon?"

"You can do it, my sweet."

"But when will I see you again? Please don't go…"

The edges of Christine's form began to fade into the surrounding darkness. Slowly at first, then faster and faster. Bridget reached out and tried to touch her mother, tried to keep her from receding into the darkness.

Please!

But Christine Devereaux's image was gone.

Bridget gasped and bolted upright. She opened her eyes to find the barren break room surrounding her. She blinked and wiped away the hot tears that traced down her cheeks.

Her heart thudded away. It boomed as if her chest was a hollow log, before gradually slowed to its normal pace. She took a deep breath and let it out with a sigh, waited as the familiar pain of lost years spread throughout every nerve of her body. She slumped forward for a moment, then forced herself to straighten on the cot.

She raised her arm and squinted at the blurry face of her watch.

Three-fifty in the morning.

She tried to remember when she had lain down. She'd gotten

perhaps four hours of sleep. It wasn't nearly enough, but it was better than nothing.

And seeing Christine, while bittersweet, had been anything but restful.

Jo.

Bridget swung her legs over the side. Standing unsteadily, she kneaded her trapezius muscle with one hand and tried to relieve the spasm that had set in there. As she worked the spasm, she shuffled to the lounge bathroom and splashed her face with cold water over and over again. Massaging her closed eyes with wet fingers, she moaned softly as the water seeped beneath her lids to put out the twin fires there. She cranked an arm's length of brown paper towel from the dispenser, tore it off and dabbed her face dry with it. A quick look in the mirror confirmed the fact that she looked as beat as she felt. She tossed the paper towel into the trash and hurried toward Jo's room.

The door was partially open. Bridget knocked softly and slowly walked in when invited to enter. Inside, it was dim but not dark, hushed but not silent. Mrs. Woods was asleep on the chair next to the window. The blinds were open and an orange glow from the sodium lights in the parking lot drifted in. Her feet were propped up on a stool and a blanket was pulled up over her body.

Jo was awake on the bed, reclining but not fully supine. She was the one who told Bridget to come in. Her eyes were large and pain-filled. To Bridget's surprise, Nurse Watkins was also there, pumping a rubber ball that sent air into the constricting armband to check Josephine's blood pressure.

Jo smiled weakly. "Hi Doctor Bridget."

Bridget returned the smile as best she could.

"Well, hello," Bridget said softly, not wanting to disturb the sleeping Mrs. Woods.

Nurse Watkins arched an eyebrow in greeting as Bridget went to the other side of the bed and sat on it facing Jo.

"Pressure's dropped a bit, Doctor," Nurse Watkins said.

She nodded but said nothing about it being a bad sign.

"How's it going, Jo?" Bridget asked.

"Not so good. I'm sorry."

"Hey, no sorries allowed in here. Is the pain bad?"

"It comes and goes. Right now it's not too bad."

"I'm working on getting you better. Nobody gets to stay longer than a few days on my watch, you know. I like you an' all but I want you back to your old self and out of here."

Jo nodded and smiled but suddenly her smile was erased by a grimace of pain that seemed unnatural on one so young. Her neck tensed into thin cords while her breath hissed between her teeth. Her fingers dug into Bridget's hand.

"Hang on, Jo. You hang on, now. You're going to make it."

Nurse Watkins held the girl's other hand as pain racked the young girl's body. Bridget glanced up to see the veteran nurse wipe quickly at her eyes. Finally Jo's body relaxed. Sweat beaded on her forehead, ran down her cheeks like tears. Bridget let go of her hand and retrieved a nearby hand towel from the bathroom. She held it in the sink and ran cool water over it, then returned to the bed and wiped gently at Jo's face and forehead. The girl sighed.

"How often are they coming?" Bridget asked softly.

"I'm not sure. It's not all the time. Just when I think they might go away, they come back. I'm scared of them, Doctor Bridget. Really getting scared of them."

"I'm going to increase the dosage of your pain-reliever right now." She jabbed at the dial pad of the computerized I.V. with her index finger. "There. That'll take care of them."

"Okay," Jo said, nodding her head.

Bridget looked at Nurse Watkins. "Please record the new dosage, Nurse Watkins. Also, I'm requesting every test under the sun done for her. Blood, urine, bone marrow. I want her vital signs entered into the computer every half hour for my analysis."

"Yes, Doctor. But you realize her insurance will not agree to all of the tests so soon after the initial tests."

"Who's the carrier?"

"Foundation Health Net of Raleigh, but does it matter?"

"Try them anyway. I'll pay out of my own pocket if I have to. What's a little more tacked onto my loan balance?"

Nurse Watkins nodded.

Jo's fingers gently curled around Bridget's forearm. The girl glanced at her sleeping mother and then back at Bridget. "Am I going to be all right, Doctor Bridget?" she asked.

Cold talons sank into Bridget's stomach. "You'll beat this thing, Jo. You may not know it but you're a fighter. You're going to have to fight really, really hard on this one, okay?"

She pulled at a strand of damp hair that clung to the side of her face. Her mouth was set. "I will."

"Good! And I will, too. I'm in your corner, honey. Together we'll knock this thing out. It doesn't stand a chance."

"Thanks, Doctor Bridget."

Bridget smiled. "Thank me when you walk out of here. I need to go study some more of your blood, okay?"

"Will you be back soon?"

"If you need me, push the orange button on the bed rail there for the nurse. They'll page me and I'll come running, okay?"

"Okay." Her eyelids drooped and she appeared half-asleep already.

As Bridget turned and walked out, Nurse Watkins said goodbye to the girl and followed. Together they walked down the hallway.

"I was surprised to see you, doctor. Your regular shift is over and you pulled on-call duty just yesterday."

Bridget looked at her, not sure if she was being sarcastic or not.

"I'm not the only one who's here on her own time."

Nurse Watkins tilted her head to the side and back in a kind of half-shrug. "She's so young. Just started to get a taste of life. Do you think the chemo will work?"

"If it doesn't, I'll try something else."

"I'm not doubting your intent or ability, Doctor, but just to make sure you're aware of the realities of today's medicine I'll say it again—some of the tests you're asking for aren't going to be considered normal and customary under her father's health coverage plan since many were already done when Jo first arrived. I'm not sure any additional testing will be covered at all."

"I need those tests. I'm getting more than a bad feeling that this is not standard leukemia we're talking about here. Jo's case seems to be like Margaret Morrison's, and neither is the norm for this type of leukemia, from what I've read."

"That's not what the insurance analysts care about."

"You seem worried about Jo, too. Would you help me with the higher-ups so we can order them anyway?"

"Yes, I do feel for her. I just want you to be aware of the attention all this will draw. Attention that may not be so good for a young intern."

"We need to know why her leukemia is advancing so goddamn quickly. I want to know every step the disease takes, whether it's forward or back. Damn the insurance companies and what they think is *usual and customary*—this isn't a case that falls into any known category."

They walked on. After a moment Bridget said, "Have you noticed the influx of leukemia patients here?"

"Yes, but I can distinctly remember two other heavy periods very similar to this."

"But were the patients healthy only days before they turned terminal?"

"I doubt it. It's rare that someone is perfectly healthy one day and a terminal leukemia patient the next."

Bridget stared down the length of the hall. "But in at least four of our newest leukemia patients we're seeing these accelerated reactions, including Jo and Mister Jeffers in three ten."

Nurse Watkins grasped Bridget's arm. "I don't think you've heard...Norman Jeffers died two hours ago. That's part of the reason I'm still here, I was on the code team."

Bridget pulled up. "That's less than four days. Leukemia doesn't appear from nowhere and kill this fast! Did he have an infection or some other determining factor?"

"No, they think the anemia from the disease was the ultimate cause of death. His body couldn't get the oxygen and sustenance it needed and it just failed."

Bridget felt as if she'd been mule kicked in the stomach. Her face went slack. She'd seen Mr. Jeffers only a handful of times since starting her rotation on Ward Seven. He wasn't her patient. Only in his late thirties, Mr. Jeffers had reportedly been vibrant and healthy until just a few days before he was admitted. He had been a businessman—an executive—for a local company in Raleigh. Divorced, his children were only in grade school.

"This is not right," Bridget said.

"It never is," Nurse Watkins said, angling for the nearby nurse's station that was little more than a counter behind which three nurses sat on stools doing paperwork. Nurse Watkins picked up a worn leather briefcase and started digging through it.

Bridget watched her begin some paperwork.

"None of this is right," Bridget said, only this time there was no one to hear. She followed her feet through the long hallways of the hospital. She passed fellow interns without acknowledging them, as well as the technicians and nurses working the graveyard shift.

She took the stairs to the basement and walked silently into the blood lab.

The same technician who had been there earlier (could it only have been last night?) was still here, staring into the monitor linked to his microscope. He had an intense look on his face. His gray eyebrows were furrowed, creating a deep valley between them. His upper lip was pulled slightly upward into half-smile, half-grimace. He appeared almost frightening.

Maybe his eyes are bad and he's straining to see something on the monitor, Bridget thought. *Either that or he's trying to make sense of something on the monitor itself.*

He noticed her only when he reached for a different slide on the counter top. Instantly the intense look vanished and was replaced with a half-smile. His angular face became friendly, with bold laugh lines standing out in his cheeks and the corners of his eyes.

"Couldn't stay away, huh?"

"I'm really into the dungeon-like atmosphere of this place," Bridget said.

"And I thought it was just me. Gargoyles, demons, vipers, skeletal remains—they all thrive in the bowels of a vast medical center where so many stricken people seek the cures for their afflictions."

"You must read Poe," she said, walking further into the nearly deserted lab.

He arched an eyebrow. "You're very perceptive, young lady. I have indeed been reading Mr. Poe's works. Preferred Hemingway in my youth and throughout most of my adult years, but as I age, I see more of Poe's tortured world and less of Hemingway's straight-laced and adventurous one."

Bridget pulled a stool out in front of one of the electron microscopes and produced a hand-sized notebook from her lab coat pocket, along with a pen. She crossed her legs, set the pad on her thigh and started writing down the name of the patients on Ward Seven who had been diagnosed with leukemia.

"And which are you?" she asked him, scrawling Jo's name down, followed by Margaret Morrison's and Norman Jeffers'.

"Me?" he said.

"Are you one of the aforementioned—gargoyle, demon, viper, or—what was that last one?"

"Skeletal remains."

"You're not that, so which are you?"

He turned and panned deliberately around the room. Finally his gaze came to rest upon her once more. He smiled. "I don't think I can be classified as one of the aforementioned."

"No?"

He shook his head. "No."

"Then how do you fit in?" she asked, the beginnings of a smile starting on her face.

"I am the curator of them all."

She laughed.

"Care for some coffee?" he asked.

The weariness in her bones weighted her to the chair. "Can I offer you my right arm?"

"I can get one any time from the morgue." His eyes glittered as he rose from the chair. He walked with easy, long strides to the far corner of the room where a dark coffee pot sat like a fat cat. "I can't guarantee how it will taste since I've never had proper training in coffee production, but I do guarantee a swift kick in the gluteus maximus."

"That's what I need."

Her eyes followed him, drawn to the only motion in the deserted room. He reached into the cabinet above the coffee machine and removed two black and white paper coffee cups from the stacks there. He poured the steaming black liquid into the cups and soon she smelled its wonderful, energizing aroma.

"Cream or sugar?" he asked, pulling out a drawer beneath the counter and reaching in.

"Please...one of each."

He grasped a sugar packet between his thumb and forefinger and shook it. It flapped back and forth against his fingers. He ripped the corner and let the sugar crystals slide into one of the cups. After repeating the process for the other cup he reached into one of the refrigerators used to hold blood samples and took out a pint of Half and Half. He opened it and poured a little in both cups. "My wife used to always take it black. I never could stand it enough to do that. I always have to tone the bitterness down."

"How does she take her coffee now?"

"She doesn't."

"She gave up coffee?"

"In a manner of speaking. She's dead."

"Oh, I'm so sorry."

"Thank you, but that's not necessary."

He put plastic stir sticks in the cups, then turned and walked toward Bridget with the steaming cups in hand and handed her one. She gratefully thanked him as she took it from him. He smiled at her and this time the smile appeared tinged with sadness.

"Gretchen's been dead three years this October," he said. "She had a severe stroke while raking leaves and never recovered. She went quickly, thank God. We had quite a wonderful life together."

Bridget raised the paper cup and felt the heat of the coffee on her lips. She took a careful sip, felt it trace a hot trail down her esophagus to pool in her stomach. "How long were you married?"

"Thirty-two years. I still think of myself as married to her. I'm not trying to be morbid, but she's still with me in many ways. We first met when I was in the army, stationed in Germany during the Cold War. She was a German country girl with blond hair who knew how to have a good time." With one long leg bent and the other propped on the floor, he sat on a stool opposite her and stirred his coffee. "Gretchen always knew how to have a good time." He took a sip. "So, how is your life going so far, Doctor Devereaux?"

She felt it odd for this dignified but older man to address her so formally. She glanced at his identification badge. "Please, Mr. McGuire, call me Bridget."

"As long as you call me Ian."

"But —"

"I dislike being called Mr. McGuire. I have to battle the impulse to turn and look over my shoulder for my father."

She smiled. "All right, Ian."

"Good. You know, you remind me of one of my daughters. Not that you look like Susan, but you carry yourselves in much the same way."

"Really? Is that a good way or a bad way?"

"Oh, quite good. Like you, she's also a very independent girl."

Independent? Bridget thought, picturing her boyfriend Travis and recalling her reluctance at confronting him, as well as some of the cliquish male doctors who had made offhand comments about her being the "best-looking doctor wanna-be in the place." Why hadn't she put them in their places? Too afraid to cause tension, even at the expense of her own well-being?

"I think you must be confusing independence with something else," she told him.

He studied her closely for a moment then shook his head. "No, that's it."

"I don't think so. Otherwise, I'd be more in charge of my life."

"You're not in charge of your life?"

"It sure doesn't feel like it." She sipped her coffee and looked away. "It feels like I'm being pulled here and there instead of actually plotting my course."

"Fate acts upon us all. We can point the bow of the ship in a certain direction but circumstance may carry us far from our plotted course."

"I'll say."

They sipped at the hot coffee in their cups.

"You surprised me when you walked in," Ian said. "Usually I have the lab all to myself. What brings you down to the dungeon again?"

"Blood."

"Well, you've come to the right place. Just blood in general or are you looking for a specific brand?"

She showed him the list of names on her pad. "A specific brand. Namely, I'd like to study samples from each of my patients with leukemia and those that were admitted before my rotation."

"We should have all the samples you need. I'm here for a few more hours. I'd be glad to give you a hand."

"But you've been here for a long time. Isn't your shift over?"

"Not yet. I work four ten-hour days. Eight p.m. until six a.m. Sometimes I get here a little early to get a jump on things. This way I get a long weekend. An extra day to fish and garden and clean up the house."

"And probably see your daughters."

His expression hardened. "I don't see my daughters much any more."

Oh, God, she thought, *I've opened a wound in the man.* "I'm so sorry. Are they…"

"Dead?" he smiled grimly. "No, they're quite alive. Just…out of touch. They're grown and have their own lives and careers and husbands. Since their mother died, they don't want much to do with me."

"That's terrible! You're their father."

"I drank heavily after Gretchen's death. I was probably unpleasant on a regular basis. I tried not to hurt them. I never laid a hand on them but maybe I hurt them anyway, I don't know. Pain comes in a lot of forms."

"Still, that's no reason they should abandon their father—especially a father who's alone now."

"Oh, I'm not completely alone. I have two dogs to keep me company. You'd be surprised how it raises your spirits to have dogs around. But, I cannot deny that I miss my daughters." He cocked his head to the side and back in a kind of shrugging motion. "Who knows, maybe they'll come around."

"I hope so. I never knew my father. He died when I was a baby. My mother died when I was ten. I can't tell you how many times I wished one or the other was still alive."

"It must have been very difficult for you."

She sipped at her coffee and shrugged. "My older sister and I were sent to state orphanages—sometimes together, sometimes not. She's six years older. As soon as she was eighteen she left the orphanage, found a job as a waitress in Raleigh and soon made enough money to file as my legal guardian. I stayed with Francine in her apartment, did chores around the house and went to school while she worked for the both of us. I did well in school and got a scholarship to help with college and then medical school. I worked any jobs I could on the side and Francine covered the rest. If it wasn't for Francine, I don't know where I'd be."

"She sounds like a terrific sister. Are you still in contact with her?"

Bridget nodded. "She lives over in Chapel Hill. She married a great guy, an instructor she met while going part-time to Wake Technical Community College. Now he's a professor at the University of North Carolina at Chapel Hill. She's got two kids and is getting her Master's Degree in criminal psychology at UNC."

"She's busy."

"Yeah, and she gets a big discount on tuition because Evan is now tenured. They have a beautiful family—something she and I didn't have after Mama died. They ask me over to their house every time we talk, but I've been swamped with my own work. I eat lunch or dinner with them at least one Sunday a month. It's kind of a sanctuary for me over there."

"Perhaps you'll have your own family before long?"

"If I could be so lucky."

They sat in silence and drank their coffee.

"Let's get to work on those blood samples of yours," Ian said, breaking the silence.

"Good idea."

✳ ✳ ✳

"Just what are we looking for in these samples?" Ian asked, interrupting her train of thought.

Bridget hit the print button and swiveled the stool to look at Ian. He was withdrawing a small amount of blood from one of the vials and dabbing it onto a slide. "The blood analyzer couldn't identify a particular protein matrix in Josephine Woods' blood — it labeled it *Protein Matrix X*. Tonight I've actually seen the matrix under the scope, and I've seen it in other early samples from our recently admitted leukemia patients. The strange thing is that it is not there in the latter samples taken from the same patients."

Ian frowned. "An unidentified protein matrix that disappears as time progresses?"

"Sounds crazy, huh?"

"Perhaps there's an error somewhere."

Bridget pointed to the monitor hooked to the powerful microscope. Several clumps of matter drifted amid the red blood cells on the screen. "But there it is, see?"

He looked in amazement at the monitor and then to her. "Very strange."

She nodded. "Let's keep looking. Maybe we can identify it."

The hours slipped away and her eyes began to throb. She squinted into the scope, adjusted the magnification in an effort to clear the fuzzy image, but was unsuccessful. She tried this three more times to no avail. Even the monitor's image was blurred. She raised her head and blinked repeatedly. Everything in the lab room remained fuzzy at the edges. Bridget yawned, wiped an ensuing tear from the corner of her eye, squinted at the clock. Six in the morning. Ian still peered into the blood samples they had set up together.

"Hey," she said to him. "Isn't your ten-hour shift over?"

"Yes, but I thought we were making progress in trying to identify this Protein X."

"We are, but you need to go home and go to sleep."

"I'm not the only one."

They worked for twenty more minutes.

She was getting nowhere. She couldn't think straight any more and her eyes had had it. She sat limply against the back support of the stool and rubbed her burning eyes. When she was done she looked over at Ian, who was yawning as he looked at his monitor. His glasses were perched on top of his balding head.

"I think we should shut it down for today," Bridget said to

him.

He looked up and blinked a few times, then glanced up at the clock. "I think you're right. I'm staring so hard I'm not being productive. Sorry."

"Don't be. We put a pretty good dent in the samples. I couldn't have examined nearly so many on my own. Thank you, Ian."

He nodded, slumped back in his stool. "You're welcome. Maybe we can get the rest tonight or tomorrow. Are you working tonight?"

"My shift starts at four in the afternoon. You?"

"I'll be here around midnight, sooner if I can make it. I think you may be on to something here, Doctor Devereaux. I've never seen an unidentified protein in such high percentages in humans. And right now we've only seen it in the recent leukemia patients."

"I don't know what it means, though," Bridget said. "Maybe after going over the rest of the samples I'll know something more. Right now the only thing I know is that this Protein Matrix X drops off to nothing as the leuk progresses. It just disappears."

She rubbed her eyes, tried to think but it was slow going. "I'm starving. Care for some breakfast in the cafeteria? It's on me—kind of a thank you for all your help."

Ian eyed the clock. "I'll take you up on that some other time. Right now I've got to be going." He walked to the door. When he looked back at her, he had a strange, almost forlorn look on his face. "I enjoyed working with you. It felt like bygone days had somehow returned."

Bridget rose. "We make a good team, Ian. Hey, if you can't do a full breakfast then how about some coffee for the road? I don't want you to fall asleep on the drive home."

"No, I must be going. We'll have more coffee tonight. Same place."

"Okay. See you then. And thanks again."

Ian nodded. "Get some rest, Doctor Devereaux. You look terrible."

She smiled wearily. She had the sudden thought that her father might have said much the same thing to her, had he lived long enough.

Bridget walked slowly down the dark hallway, her feet leading the way. She took the elevator up to the ground floor, then down two more long, white hallways. She passed doctors, nurses and a few patients who were with family members. It was seven in the morning and the hospital was starting to bustle with life.

The chief resident and some of the senior doctors were standing just outside the entrance to the cafeteria, conversing with one another. They were a group of white lab coats and dress slacks holding foam cups of steaming coffee in their hands.

Without pausing for thought, Bridget walked up to the chief resident. "Dr. Hensley, I don't mean to interrupt, but there's something happening here with some of our recent leuk patients. We're getting abnormal acceleration of the disease in a drastically short period of time. There's also a strange protein matrix present in the early stages—"

Blake Hensley looked down his long nose at her. "Devereaux, patients come here because of the extraordinary care we provide. We see all types of leukemia."

"But we've had four patients die in only days, and those four were perfectly healthy only a few weeks before their illness!"

"I'm sure those patients had symptoms before they were admitted. Many people don't come into the hospital until the last possible moment."

"Not like this...it can't be! I've been examining the blood samples down in the lab. I think we're seeing...I think there's a trend —"

"This is not an epidemic, Devereaux," Hensley said. "Are you saying this is an epidemic?"

For the first time the senior physicians around them looked on with more than bemused interest. Their condescending smiles faded and their sidelong glances snapped from her chest, or her rear end, up to her face.

Blake leaned closer, until he was almost looking straight down at her. "Is that what you're thinking, Dr. Devereaux? That this is some kind of *epidemic?*"

Feeling her cheeks redden, she looked away. Her body tensed into a steel rod.

"I hope to God you haven't been saying there's an epidemic going on here, Devereaux," Blake warned.

She blinked. "No, but something *is* happening here. Something we don't fully understand. There's some kind of unknown trait with our recent leukemia patients!"

"Of course, silly girl—they've all got cancer," the chief resident said.

The throng of doctors laughed. Bridget felt as if she'd been kicked in the stomach and paddled like a child at the same time. They watched her while they laughed, their eyes glinting. She knew what they were thinking: she's a foolish doctor-wanna-be with a lame-brained idea about the realities of cancer. Here is the girl who dared tell them—male physicians with a century's worth of experience collectively—something new about cancer in the modern age.

Bridget felt her face flush. "But these were healthy people just days before being admitted—and now they're *dead*. The onset is too sudden for normal leukemia. I think there may be some kind of common catalyst here."

Doctor Wellington, a senior orthopedic surgeon, pointed a finger at her. "I tell you what, *Doctor* Devereaux. If you can prove there is a *common catalyst* with your leukemia patients, then you can have my Jaguar." He winked at her.

"Uh, oh," one of the others said. "The Jag's on the line."

"Watch it now, George!" another said.

"Hey, why don't you let me have the Jag, George?"

"You've got a Jag already, Henry!"

"Ancient proverb say, 'One can never have too many Jags.'"

They all laughed.

Bridget's throat felt constricted, as if they were strangling her.

They turned and walked down the hallway, a gang of white smocks and God mentalities, laughing with one another, occasionally glancing over their shoulders and smirking at her.

Bridget's eyes narrowed into slits, her hands clenched and then shook.

Other doctors, hospital workers, nurses and patients walked by her as if she were a rock in the middle of a fast-moving stream. She thought she glimpsed Ian McGuire in her peripheral vision, but she wasn't sure. She was too busy burning holes in the backs of the doctor's heads as they walked away from her.

Dismissed! Zero possibility that what I'm saying is true! she thought.

They vanished around a far corner. She blinked at their disappearance, then drifted to the concrete wall and leaned against it as if it were the only thing that saved her from slumping to the white-tiled floor.

She felt an odd prickling sensation at the back of her head. Someone was watching her with more than passing interest. She turned. To her surprise Nurse Watkins stood behind her, her arms crossed over her sizable bosom, one narrow eyebrow cocked up high on her forehead. Her gaze was steady and cool.

"Something on your mind?" Bridget asked.

"Yes, actually. I was wondering if you're going to stand there like an angry little girl or are you going to get busy?"

"I've been busy since the moment I walked into this place!"

Nurse Watkins stepped closer. "*They* don't think you're right about the leuk," she said, nodding in the direction the doctors had taken.

"They're wrong. There is a common factor with our recent leuk patients, I know there is!"

Nurse Watkins nodded. As she did so, her right eyebrow arched upward. "I've often wondered what it would be like to own a Jaguar, haven't you?"

She turned and walked toward the elevators.

Now Bridget tried to burn holes in the back of Nurse Watkins' gray-haired head. But then the older woman's meaning sank in, forcing her anger and wounded pride to smolder in the background.

You're right, Nurse, Bridget thought, picturing the leering faces of Blake Hensley and the veteran doctors in her mind. *You're one hundred percent correct. They won't listen until I prove it to them.*

Bridget took a deep breath.

So that's exactly what I'm going to do.

SIX

Raynorr stepped from the elevator and inhaled the strife-torn air of Foundation Health Net like a wine connoisseur savoring the bouquet of a rare vintage. The dolly's well-oiled wheels were silent as he pulled it, wagon-like, through the fifth floor lobby and into the main work area where sixty employees were normally held captive inside a maze of pale blue cubicles. The workers were almost entirely gone now, but they were still vulnerable should he deem them worthy targets.

The gray carpet left no sign of his passage. Speckled blue and white wallpaper covered the perimeter walls, while dominating the area inside those walls was the maze of anemic blue cubicles. Each five-by-five, fabric-covered enclosure was a carbon copy of the one next to it.

Fluorescent white light showered down from above.

The ceiling lights had been placed in uniform rows stretching from one side of the building to the other. The white ceiling tiles between the rows of lights had thousands of tiny holes in them.

Thousands of tiny holes, Raynorr thought, *for thousands of tiny lives*.

No bold colors were visible here on the fifth floor, nor on any floor of the entire Foundation One building. The theme was reassuring sameness, reassuring blandness. Reject the self and work together as mindlessly as a colony of ants.

Raynorr was not duped by the corporate subliminal message. He knew what was occurring inside the placid walls of this place. Roiling beneath the pastels were the crimsons and greens that seethed in the minds of the people who schemed to get ahead in this unnatural environment. Sameness and cooperation might be the corporate image, but political infighting, professional jealousy, and office intrigue were the corporate reality.

A major corporate reality of Foundation Health Net was that Margaret Morrison was no longer its Chief Executive Officer.

The queen was dead.

With her sudden death came opportunity, the chance of a

lifetime for the underlings. Vast power and riches lie in store for the one who could defeat his or her rivals and bring his or her faction to the fore. Raynorr could easily imagine the eel-like slithers of factions trading sides depending upon concessions granted or taken away by various departmental vice-presidents vying for the CEO position. Low-ranking employees were merely pawns to be manipulated, but even pawns have ambition. Pawns want to be rooks, knights want to be bishops, and bishops—if they are ruthless enough—want to be king or queen.

Hugh Croston was an up-and-coming knight.

He was currently Director of Operations (knight), but the rumor was he would become the next Vice President of Operations (bishop) should the current vice president he had allied himself with get appointed as the next CEO (king).

Hugh Croston.

The name burned in Raynorr's mind in fiery letters.

This arrogant scum was going to be in charge of operations for the entire company? This morally-deprived corporate product was going to set policies for people who need medical attention?

Not if Raynorr could help it. And oh yes, he *could* help it.

Four floors below what used to be Margaret Morrison's penthouse office, Raynorr towed the dolly with the blue water jugs toward the water dispensers Croston had ordered the day of their confrontation at the elevator.

The war is going well, he thought, pulling the heavy dolly with the taut strength of his arms and legs. *As long as Bridget Devereaux remains ignorant of the realities of her leukemia patients, I will be victorious.*

Suddenly he halted, cocked his head as if straining to hear a faint sound.

What is this…? Raynorr thought. *Does an intern really pose a viable threat to me? Probably not, but she is an unknown variable…and unknown variables can ruin good work.*

Below the brim of his Crystal Clear Water hat he felt the ridge between his brows deepen. This inexperienced intern felt a lot like a problem. He resumed his journey toward the water dispensers and tried to keep from thinking about the unknown variable that was Bridget Devereaux.

He was striking fast, now. He had hit six of the nine insurance companies in the area. He'd been rewarded with eight kills, even getting a two-for-one from an insurance company called Willheim Everlasting.

The executives at Willheim must have been close associates, Raynorr thought. *Very close associates.*

He had verified five of the six kills, himself. The sixth one had been taken to a different hospital than the one he frequented. As far as he could determine, no one had discovered a pattern to the deaths. Not the police, not the media, not the employees of the companies themselves. Certainly there was no cross-competitor sharing of information. Rival companies seldom communicate with one another.

But there was one person who suspected a pattern.

And here he was again...back to Bridget Devereaux.

The idiots scoffed at her when she told them about the explosive leukemia in her patients, he thought. *She had been ill at ease before them, but she did not let her uneasiness stop her. Instead she pushed through and made her case. She has courage and drive and smarts — a potentially dangerous mix for me.*

The sound of approaching voices interrupted his musings. He would have to ponder Devereaux at a later time. This was, after all, a hit.

And the Croston *punk* was the object of the hit.

A sparse stream of workers in the latest business fashions of dark blue and black suits approached, on their way to the elevator lobby from which Raynorr had just come. The suits didn't speak a word to him as they passed, nor did he speak to them. They were intent upon temporary escape — the weekend — and he didn't want to risk becoming memorable by speaking to them.

He raised his wrist and checked his watch as he pulled the dolly. He frowned at the timepiece as if he were running late. The workers glided by as if he wasn't even there.

It was after six o'clock on a Friday. His last run for the day.

The best for last, he thought.

A hush floated over the cubicle maze that normally housed the worker ants. Most of the cubes were already empty, just as they had been last Friday after six o'clock and the previous Friday before that.

Raynorr brought the dolly to a halt before the water dispensers that stood just outside three adjacent offices that looked like a prison cell block. He glanced inside the offices as he passed by. The blinds in all three were pulled up to allow full appreciation of the green water of Crabtree Lake and the other mammoth insurance buildings surrounding it.

These were the only true offices on the entire floor, and all three were vacant.

He stood before the office of the Director of Operations. Like the others, Hugh Croston's office was lit solely by the thick golden rays of late afternoon sunshine. The overhead lights had been turned off.

I've prepared a double for you, Croston, Raynorr thought.

He turned and scanned the area for signs of activity over the sea of cubicles. He heard a far-away laugh and someone turned out the lights. Now the sunlight streaming into the three offices became the dominant light source for the entire floor. It was a poor source of lighting—the golden rays could penetrate no further than the outermost cubicle walls—but it was just right for the work Raynorr would perform.

There came the sounds of two female voices, then combined laughter, and then the ding of the elevator bell. The voices died and the place fell into a hushed silence—except for the faint sounds of fingers working a keyboard and, from the same location, the occasional click of a computer mouse.

There's one other person here, Raynorr thought, *but I'm fine as long as the keyboard remains active.*

Raynorr's legs cast long shadows on the carpet as he stole inside Croston's office.

A phone pulsed loudly somewhere over the first wall of cubes. He froze. The clacking keyboard fell silent. He was about to spin around and hurry back to the dolly when the clacking started up again.

The ringing went unanswered. After the fourth ring it ceased, the call probably going to voicemail. All Raynorr could hear was his own quick breathing and the faint clacking of the keyboard about four rows deep in the cubicle honeycomb.

Once at Croston's desk, his hand slipped into his hip pocket and closed around the syringe. The sound of the keyboard had faded. He saw no heads above the cubicle walls. Quickly, he scanned Croston's desk.

His heart now pumping rapid-fire, Raynorr located the object of his search, a simple coffee mug. He performed a quick discharge onto the walls of the mug, then swiped completely around the lip with the tip. He put the syringe in a plastic Ziploc bag, sealed it, put it in his pocket and hurried back to the water machines and the dolly. Rinsing the cup wouldn't eliminate all of Raynorr's virus, nor would adding hot coffee.

It didn't take much in order to kill, this virus of his.

No sooner had he bent to grasp one of the full water jugs when a voice slammed into the collective quiet.

"Mind if I fill up?"

Raynorr's back turned to steel. He stared at the carpet for a split second as though caught up in its blandness. Then he straightened and looked up at the thirty-something in a white shirt and black tie and gray slacks standing at his shoulder with a tall drinking cup in his hand. His sleeves were rolled up to the elbow.

"Ah—you startled me!" Raynorr exclaimed, telling the truth. His hand strayed to his front right pocket, making sure the syringe was well hidden. Had this man seen anything?

"Sorry about that."

"That's all right. I should have heard you coming. My hearing's not what it used to be."

The man nodded knowingly. "I don't hear a lot of stuff when I'm concentrating on my work, either. You're really going at it, stacking those water bottles. I didn't know you were even here until I stood up to stretch."

He was the one at the keyboard, Raynorr suddenly realized. *Did he see me inside Croston's office? I can't remember if the keyboard stopped clacking before or after I delivered the virus. He saw me here when he looked over the cube walls—but did he see me earlier than that?*

Raynorr swallowed the bitter taste of fear that had pooled in his mouth.

Surely he would have said something or called security. Maybe security is on the way and he's stalling me. No, they would have been here by now.

Searching the young man's face and listening to him, Raynorr got the feeling there was a kind of frankness to him, something the corporate life hadn't bled out of him—yet. There was, however, a weariness in his eyes where there shouldn't have been for a man in his early thirties. The weariness wasn't overpowering. It didn't hide the honesty in his eyes, but it did veil the inner light that should have shown through to the outside world. "You're working late for a Friday."

The man looked out the window. "Cutbacks are rumored to be coming down pretty soon, part of a re-org. I want my work to be all caught up in case the axe falls on me."

"Cutbacks? That's too bad. Think you'll be part of it?"

"I don't know." He thought about it for a second more and shrugged, though the worried look on his face thwarted his effort to appear nonchalant. "Yeah, now that I think about it, I'm sure I'll be shown to the street. I work pretty hard, but I don't see eye-to-eye with my manager on a lot of things. He'll use the re-org to get me out of here."

"Who's your manager?"

"Hugh Croston. Do you know him?"

Raynorr blinked. "No."

The man paused for a moment, as if wrestling with some sudden compulsion. He glanced over the cubicle walls, leaned to the side as if peering around the far corner. He took a step closer, his tone low as if he was trying to keep his words safe from prying ears.

"It's good you don't know Croston. I was assigned to him after my first manager resigned. Now that I work for Croston he confirms the fact that he's an asshole on a daily basis. All I hear out of him is cut, cut, cut. Cut treatments, cut procedures, cut examinations. I don't know what he expects me to do. I'm a financial analyst—not a goddamn alchemist who can turn iron into gold! He doesn't want to know the real picture. All he wants to know is how we can get more for less. He and his bosses want me to make the bottom line dance and sing when it has two broken legs. It's pretty ugly, man."

Raynorr's mouth nearly dropped open. Someone was employed here who knew first-hand the deviousness of his own company and was appalled by it? Was this possible? "Why don't you leave before they get you? Don't give them the satisfaction."

The worker grimaced as if wrestling with the thought. "I don't know…it's tough out there. I'm pretty competent, but I've never been outgoing—I just don't give a great interview."

"Perhaps a little practice…?"

"I do great with my wife asking the questions. I think my problem might be that I don't really fit well into a big organization. I'm different from most of the others around here. I don't know what it is, but I'm definitely different."

I can tell you what it is, Raynorr thought. *You don't play the corporate power game. What corporations like this call a team player is someone skilled at dumping their work off on someone else. They want masters at backstabbing and rumor-mongering, and, above all, they want someone proficient at keeping a moist lip lock on the boss's ass. If you don't play, you don't get anywhere. That's what is happening to you, my friend.*

"There's got to be a company looking for good honest workers out there somewhere," Raynorr said.

"Where?"

Raynorr shook his head. "I don't know. I just deliver the water."

"Maybe I should do that," the man said, with a bitter laugh.

"It doesn't pay all that much." Raynorr glanced at the man's wedding band. "Is your wife employed?"

"Yeah. We don't live extravagantly, but it takes both of us working full time to make ends meet."

"In my day only one member of the household really had to work. That was usually enough to pay the bills and still get ahead."

The man nodded. "It's not that way any more. Ever since I graduated from college it's been like this. If you don't want to pay rent all your life you've got to have someone else help with the mortgage payment."

They fell silent and watched as the smoldering orange globe outside began its descent through the haze-filled skies over Crabtree Lake. It was an odd silence, but Raynorr didn't mind it. This was a worker, not an executive, beside him.

"I'm Ted Samuels."

Raynorr looked at the offered hand for a split second then shook with the younger man. "Mike Davis," Raynorr said. "You'll do fine, Ted. Good workers like yourself should do just fine. Don't worry about the layoffs."

"You mean the *reassignment without destination* as they like to call it around here?" Ted said, with a sly smile. "I think I do need to worry."

"It's up to this Hugh Croston?"

"Totally. So now you can see how low my chances of survival here are."

"You never know—you may come out okay."

Ted bent at the water cooler, pressed the blue button over the spigot to let the water flow into his cup. "Thanks, Mike. I hope things do work out. Not a whole lot I can do about it if they don't, though. I'm not going to change just for them."

"There you go."

Raynorr stacked the last empty water bottle on his dolly as Ted Samuels filled his water cup at the machine. The sound of water spilling onto water was loud in the otherwise silent workplace. He picked up the dolly handle and began pulling it in the direction of the elevators. "Best of luck, Ted."

Holding his cup at chest level, the younger man nodded. "Thanks. Hey, maybe I'll see you around. My cube's four rows in, fifth from the right-side wall. Stop by next time you do your rounds—you can see if I survived or not."

"Something tells me you'll come out just fine."

"I don't think so, but thanks anyway. Have a good weekend."

The young man turned and walked away. His head was visible for a few moments above the cubicle walls, as if it were detached and floating down the aisles by itself, then it disappeared altogether as Ted Samuels sat in his cubicle.

Raynorr glanced in the darkened office of Hugh Croston as he passed by with the dolly. A shame Croston wasn't like Samuels. But then, none of this would be necessary if these health insurance companies were run by people like Ted Samuels.

He hit the *down* button on the wall panel. He heard the clacking of Ted's keyboard once more, and then it faded away as a ding sounded and the elevator doors parted. He stepped inside and pulled the dolly in behind him. As the doors closed his hand strayed to the bulge in his hip pocket.

Croston would be dead by the end of next week.

SEVEN

THE ELEVATOR DOORS parted and Hugh Croston stepped smoothly onto *his* floor of Foundation One. He carried himself with the confident ease of a lion cruising through the tall savannah grass. True, he was not yet king, but he was destined for greatness, of that there was no question. The only question was how to expedite his royal destiny.

At his side he carried a leather Gucci briefcase with the initials HJC engraved in gold-leaf on the front panel between the brass combination locks. He gripped the handle in a palm made uncomfortably moist from the sweat he had broken while trekking in from the parking lot.

Goddamn it, he thought. *Where's my reserved parking space? Screw the direct reports only policy—I'll be kickin' back in the CEO meetings soon enough. Hiking in from the back of the lot in a camel-haired suit on an eighty-degree morning—with air so thick it settles in your lungs like hot sludge—just ain't cuttin' the fuckin' mustard.*

He scowled.

Ain't cuttin the fuckin' mustard, he thought. *The old man used to say that all the time, especially when he was talking about the way I did my bullshit chores on the farm. Of course, the old man doesn't say that now that six feet of dirt separates his bones from the living world. No loss there. Even when he was sober he wasn't worth a damn. Never gave a shit about us kids, but he was a party animal who knew how to keep his girlfriends happy.*

The sad truth was that the old man did better by Hugh in death than he ever had in life. Hugh had inherited a third of the dairy farm, which he promptly sold to his older brother and sister for a good chunk of change. Hugh had then used the money to put himself through college and then graduate school where he received his Master's of Business Administration.

MBA city, bubba.

That simple piece of paper was direct evidence of what he had always known to be a personal truism: he was a cut above the rest of the pack—especially the pack in his crappy little hometown.

I'm worlds away from hosing cow shit out of the stalls, bubba, Croston thought, *and that's just how I'm going to keep it.*

And now that he thought about it, he hadn't been back to the farm or had more than cursory relations with his brother and sister since they buried the old man next to Mom, who'd been down there for a long, long time.

With a crooked finger he swiped at the tiny beads of sweat on his nose and turned in the direction of his office. No sooner had he turned the corner when he was greeted by the sight of Rachel Dillard sauntering in his direction.

He tried to keep his face neutral but probably didn't fully succeed.

She took long strides, her fine legs well showcased in the barely business-acceptable miniskirt. Dark hose drew his eyes to those perfect legs, and dark hose were his favorite on her—on any woman, for that matter.

As she came closer, he glanced up and noted how her breasts pushed at the fabric of her white blouse, revealing the flowery pattern of the white lace brassiere beneath the semi-sheer material of the blouse. Her boobs were silicon enhanced, of course. They didn't have that natural bounce that would have otherwise accompanied such long strides, but that was okay.

She swore to him she hadn't screwed Jerry Oberlin, the current senior Vice President of Sales and Marketing, in order to get the job as his personal assistant, and Croston more or less believed her. Jerry wouldn't have done anything that risky—at least, not right away. He didn't have the balls. Of course, the fool ogled her so much during the initial interview that only a complete idiot wouldn't have understood his intentions—never mind his wife and three kids and executive mansion in Raven Wood up by Falls Lake.

Hugh flashed his well-practiced smile at Rachel just as her lusciously full lips spread into a smile of her own. He tried to appear fresh despite the fact he'd been up late last night partying and playing hide the salami with the two sorority girls from North Carolina State University. Sunday nights he usually took a break from partying and screwing—not due to any moral or religious beliefs—but because he was usually exhausted, strung-out, and in dire need of rest. But the two babes from Saturday night had proven to be accomplished and uninhibited lovers, versed far beyond their mortal years, so he *had* to bring them back for an encore performance, despite the loss of his recuperation time.

"Good morning, Mr. Croston," Rachel Dillard said, loud enough for any passing ears to hear.

They slowed as they approached one another. With deliberate glances to the side, they tried to use misdirection to disguise the intimate knowledge they had of one another.

"Morning, Rachel. Jerry in today?"

"Not yet. But I'm sure he'll be in later." The sudden arch of her left eyebrow let him know the jerk was going to be in more than just the office later.

"Good, good. Would you mind telling him I'll be ready for our racquetball engagement at lunch today?"

"Certainly, Mr. Croston."

She glanced around with those daring green eyes. Seeing no one was close by, she whispered, "Why didn't you call me last night?"

"You said you'd be with Jerry at his cabin in the mountains all weekend," Croston whispered back.

"He brought me home before noon."

"I had to get some rest," he lied. "Thursday and Friday night wore me out."

She glanced slyly at him. "Ready for some more?"

"Oh, yeah. Hey, aren't you going to take minutes while Jerry meets with his direct reports at the usual Monday morning powwow?"

"Yeah, why?"

"I want to know what's going on, that's why."

"What's in it for me?"

Croston cocked his head, leaned closer. "You can fill me in while I give you a serious tongue lashing."

Her eyelids fluttered almost imperceptibly and her knees moved together a fraction of an inch. "Hugh, you're such a bad boy."

He grinned. "I know."

"When?"

"Later today. After close of business. Say, around six?"

"Uh, huh," she purred. She licked her ruby lips with a discrete but sensual stroke of her moist tongue that made them glisten. Despite last night's sexual escapades with the girls from N.C. State, Croston felt renewed stirrings.

He took a deep breath. "I need to sit down."

She smiled seductively. "Don't get too tired."

"Me? Never. Don't forget your notes from the meeting."

"I won't. And don't you forget that I'll be needing a big raise when you become V.P."

"Ten percent?"

"I was thinking more along the lines of fifteen to twenty."

"Hmmm. I'll have to see if your...performance...remains consistently above average."

"You haven't seen anything yet, stud."

"I like how that sounds," Croston said. "You *are* the best I've had in quite some time."

He winked. Slowly she groped him with her gaze, then she gave him a parting sidelong look that just about ignited his black silk boxers.

They went their separate ways. She to the elevators, he to his office. He liked how they both had expressed their goals and found a mutually beneficial advantage in maintaining cooperative relations with one another. It all fit in so well with the cooperative relations theme detailed in the weekly deluge of internal management leaflets and flyers and emails he received.

I love this place! Croston thought.

He flipped the light switch and strode into his office. This was his command center, his *domain, mother fucker.*

As he plopped his briefcase flat on the desk the overhead fluorescent lights flickered for a few seconds and then caught, blasting the room with brilliant white light. He needed a liberal shot of caffeine before starting his daily regimen of computer time and phone calls.

Cocaine would give a far better rush than the coffee, Croston thought. *But I'll have to wait for lunch on that. I've been doing more and more of it lately but that's because I can handle it. I'll slack off in a couple of days. Right now though, caffeine is the prudent drug of choice.*

He looked to the corner of the desk. There it was.

"Come to papa," he said, reaching for his coffee mug.

With his palm covering the top of the mug, hot-shot style, Croston walked out of his office toward the break room. Several lower-level employees said hello to him as he strutted by. Croston nearly blew them off, but then graced them with a nod at the last possible moment.

In the break room the heels of his shoes clacked on the slate-colored tile. The smell of coffee was pervasive and he breathed it in like a dying man breathes oxygen from a machine. He didn't bother rinsing out his mug.

It's just coffee upon coffee, he thought. *What germs are going to survive a steaming cup of fresh coffee?*

He made his way to the dual coffee machines on the counter top next to the refrigerator that he never used—he always purchased lunch instead of bringing it. He put his mug on the counter and poured the steaming black liquid into it, noting with annoyance that he had taken the last few ounces of coffee from the glass pot. He glanced up at the sheet of paper taped to the wall behind and above the coffee machines. In bold letters it read:

IF YOU ARE LEFT HOLDING AN EMPTY POT,
PLEASE BE CONSIDERATE AND MAKE ANOTHER,
...AND MAKE IT HOT!

Screw that, Croston thought. *I don't have time to do the housekeeping, bubba.*

He put the empty pot back on the burner and turned the burner off. He turned at the sound of footsteps approaching from behind.

Ted Samuels, he thought, laying predatory eyes on the other man. *How perfect.*

"Hi, Ted," Croston said warmly.

"Hugh," Ted returned, the edge of wariness evident in his tone. He reached into the refrigerator and put his brown bag inside.

"How are the revisions coming on my report?" Croston asked.

Samuels looked uncomfortable. "They're coming."

"Good. Say, if you don't mind, I'm kind of in a rush—would you make another pot of coffee?"

"I don't drink coffee."

Croston blinked. "I didn't ask if you drank the stuff, Ted. I asked you to make it."

Samuels looked at him with bold disdain.

Croston raised his chin and stared at Samuels. "We're not sure about your loyalty to the company, Ted. You're not as cooperative as we would expect, particularly when venturing outside your normal responsibilities. Don't you want to be cross-functionally cooperative?"

"The internal marketing memos I read about cross-functional cooperation didn't mention anything about making coffee, Hugh."

They stared at one another.

The moment stretched on.

Other heels clacked on the tile but neither man broke away to see who it was.

"Sure you don't want to make that coffee, Ted?"

"I gave you my answer. I don't drink the stuff. And even if I did, you poured out the last cup, so you should make the next batch."

Samuels' look of disdain turned into a glare that made Croston decidedly uncomfortable. He wanted to swallow the growing pool of saliva in his mouth but didn't want Samuels to see him gump like some pimple-faced kid trying to get the nerve up to ask a pretty girl for a date. So Croston stared into the eyes of Ted Samuels and hoped his gaze appeared icy enough.

"You know there're rumors of cutbacks, don't you Ted?"

Ted swallowed. "I've heard."

Croston nodded. "And you know I make the recommendations."

Ted looked at the coffee machine and then back at his boss. "I'm not doing it, Hugh." His hands clenched.

"I'll make it!" a new voice piped in. It was Parkins, shoving her frozen meal in the freezer. She slammed the freezer door and walked between the two men to the coffee machine. She reached for the pot handle and said, "I need a cup, anyway."

Samuels looked at her in surprise.

Croston took the opportunity to swallow before he drowned in his own spit. "Thank you, Julie," he said. "I knew I could count on you, at least."

She looked at him with thinly veiled disgust and went about making the new pot of coffee. Ted Samuels turned and walked away. Croston watched his white shirted back and pictured a red-ringed target there. He looked through his imaginary scope, put the crosshairs directly on the bull's eye, and pulled the trigger.

You're gone when layoffs are handed down, asshole, he thought. *Gone. I'll make you choke on your lay off papers, you straight-laced fuck! Of course, in case of a violent reaction I'll have a security guard stand just outside the office.*

Croston went inside and shut his office door a little too hard. As an afterthought he hoped no one took notice—he didn't want them to think someone had been able to piss him off. He gulped down the coffee and started returning phone calls. At nine o'clock he went back for more coffee.

And ingested even more of the Raynorr virus from the mug.

At ten forty-five he began to feel...off. By eleven-thirty he was very off. Even strange. By noon he knew he was coming down with something.

* * *

Fuck! Croston thought. *It's late summer, for Christ's sakes, not the fucking flu season!*

But it sure felt like the flu. His tee shirt clung wetly to his skin. The sweat soaked all the way through to his dress shirt. He wiped his forehead and looked at the glistening sweat left on the back of his red-splotched hand. He got up to check the thermostat. Seventy-five degrees. He thumbed the dial to eighty.

God, now he was shivering...

The phone chirped.

He picked it up, at the same time reading the name on the LCD window that stood like a tiny billboard above the numeric keypad of the phone.

"Hey, Rachel."

"That doesn't sound too energetic! Something wrong?"

"Not feeling too good."

"Too much rest over the weekend?"

"No, not that. Something else. Something...*medical.* Think I'm coming down with a bug. I know I am, in fact." He took a handkerchief from his back pocket and wiped his face.

"Oh, too bad, Hugh," she whispered. "I guess we'll have to postpone our little rendezvous. Or would you like me to come over there and play nurse?"

"How did the meeting go?"

"All sorts of interesting developments."

"Damn, I knew it! I need to hear this. Why don't you come over now?"

"Now? We can't do it now—people will know! They know I don't work for you. I just can't go over there, shut the door, and get down to it."

A wave of body aches slammed into him. He cringed and curled forward in his leather, studded chair as if he'd been kicked in the balls. "Just come over and give me a summary. It looks like the other stuff is out of the question right now."

"Gee, I hope it's nothing serious. You know, Jerry doesn't really know how to please a woman. I have to fake it all the time with him. I was hoping you could finish what he started."

"It's not serious. Haven't you ever had the fucking flu before?"

"Now, don't get testy, Hugh. Maybe we'll talk when you feel better. Over dinner. At a nice place. Say, Angus Barn or Margaux's or something."

"The summary…" he croaked, as another wave of body aches hit him. This time they were followed by shivers that ran up and down his spine. Drops of sweat dripped onto the polished surface of his desk and soaked into a corporate memo on self-empowerment, smearing the ink.

"I think Margaux's is better," Rachel continued, as if she hadn't heard him. "Of course, I don't usually go there unless someone takes me. My account just can't handle the sudden out flux of funds. But I always like to look at that huge aquarium they have in there. The service is excellent and the food is great and all the richies go there. Cool place. Don't you think so?"

Hugh didn't answer.

"…Hugh? Are you there?" she said.

She waited a moment. "What was that noise? Did you drop something?"

Another pause.

"Hugh!"

Hugh Croston slumped forward in his chair. His sweating forehead pressed hard on the polished desk while wave after wave of body aches attacked him from inside every one of his joints, throughout his chest and back, and from within his pelvic girdle. He gasped for air as new waves of pain rocked him even before the old ones fully receded. From far away he felt his bladder lose control. Hot urine pooled on his seat and flowed down his leg.

The edges of his vision took on a thick, black border. At first the border slowly closed in on him, inch by inch. But then it gained speed and rush in at him, closing off the outside world, shutting him out from all that was familiar to him. Shutting him out from the corporation.

He wanted to cry out but couldn't. The pain screwed his jaw shut. He wanted to do anything but feel this *agony*, but it wouldn't let up. It had him and it wasn't going to let him go.

He couldn't move, couldn't even scream. There was only the unrelenting assault of pain. More layers of blackness piled over him.

He couldn't see it, but deep inside he knew the phone was dangling by its cord over the arm of the chair, slowly spinning as Rachel Dillard's voice kept calling his name.

TUESDAY, JUNE 8

At some point Croston opened his eyes to see the hazy image of an IV bag hanging from a metal post above him. He blinked and then cringed, expecting that horrible pain to return. It didn't.

The clear solution in the bag ran through a clear tube until it merged with a thin plastic apparatus stuck into his arm. The name of this device stuck into his arm—the old man had needed one before he kicked in the hospital. It was a catheter.

He looked up to the white tiled ceiling, then down to the white curtain behind the IV stand.

Is this...? he thought.

"I see you're up," someone said, cutting the silence of the room. "That's good."

He turned his head in the direction of the voice until he looked at the other side of the bed and saw a black woman in a blue nurse's scrubs and a white coat standing over him. There was an identification badge pinned to her lapel. Part of a stethoscope dangled out of one of her coat pockets.

"So it's true," he said, his voice hoarse. He cleared his throat and swallowed. His tongue felt like a slab of meat.

She raised her eyebrows. "What's that, honey?"

"It's true."

"What's true?"

"...that I'm in a goddamned hospital."

She frowned, her delicately plucked eyebrows coming close together to form a ridge between. "This is a bad place to be takin' the Lord's name in vain, honey. Very bad place for that sort of behavior."

"Yeah? Why?"

"'Cause He's a frequent visitor here at Chambers Hospital." Her lips parted into a quick and easy smile. She flipped a thermometer in his mouth as he was about to reply, then she put the ends of the stethoscope in her ears. "Need to get some vitals, honey. Breathe for me."

After a moment she was finished.

"You're doing a lot better. A lot better. You were in rough shape when they brought you in here. I'll go get the doctor."

She left the room and he stared at the ceiling. He couldn't believe he was here. This was where *sick* people stayed. This is where *injured* people stayed. He didn't belong here. If there was one thing he was sure of, it was that hospitals were places to be avoided. Hell, he'd given a hundred presentations to his superiors demonstrating how expensive inpatient hospital treatments were. His job was to keep people out of places like this to keep costs to the network down. Now he was a lowly patient messing with the bottom line.

I'm only twenty-eight, for Christ's sake! he thought.

The nurse returned with a man with steel-gray hair, round plastic-framed glasses and a map of lines crisscrossing in a thousand directions on his cheek. To Croston he was the epitome of a living fossil. His hands shook as he examined some papers on a clipboard.

"I'm Doctor Phillips. I'm one of the attending physicians for the Foundation Health Network, of which you are a subscriber through your employer. You were unconscious when the Emergency Team brought you in. The on-duty physician in the emergency room examined you and then admitted you at one-ten Monday afternoon. In case you don't know, that was yesterday."

"Yesterday?"

He glanced up from the chart. "That's right. You've been pretty much unconscious for about a day and a half. Your body was close to dehydration so the admitting rightly started you on a glucose solution to get your fluids level back to where it should be."

"I was in so much pain before blacking out. What's wrong with me? Flu?"

He smiled. "I'd say exhaustion."

Croston blinked. Maybe he hadn't heard right. "You're kidding, aren't you?"

"No, I'm not. Your body was dangerously low on fluids, which probably led to your feeling...uncomfortable. Now, it's possible you had an infection of some sort since you had a fever, but since it was easily controlled within the first six hours and has now disappeared I really doubt it was an infection. Infections last longer than that. Your body temperature is now normal...a standard indication that the body has recuperated enough to stabilize bodily functions."

"No way was it simple exhaustion, doc. No way."

"Exhaustion and dehydration. Not your normal, everyday worry for someone who works indoors in an office. Your case was pretty serious in that you passed out and stayed out for a while despite our initial attempts to awaken you. But now that you've had rest and fluids, your fever has vanished. I think your body was so run down that it took on flu-like symptoms. Why, it's happened to me before after pushing my body beyond its limits. It's fairly common. What's not common is the blacking out. That's an indication that your exhaustion was pervasive, perhaps even extreme. Basically, the exhaustion and dehydration—coupled with the narcotics we found in your blood—took a big Godzilla bite out of your ass, son."

Croston felt his face go red.

The doctor looked pointedly at him. "How do you feel now?"

Croston took stock. "Well, pretty good, really," he said in dull amazement.

The doctor smiled. "We'd like to discharge you as soon as possible."

"Shouldn't we do more tests? I mean, this could be something serious."

"Why run all those expensive tests your health plan won't pay for? Your bank account got too much money in it?"

Hugh sank back into his pillow. He had a good title at work as Director of Operations but it didn't pay as much as he wished it did, of course. Partying was expensive. So was his car, his house, his designer clothes. So, did he have a lot of money?

"No," he told the doctor.

"Then I wouldn't recommend the tests. You were burning the candle at both ends and up the middle, young man. *That* was your problem. You need to rest. Go home and take a few days off work. Watch a bunch of fishing shows on television. Don't do anything more strenuously than a twenty minute walk."

"I hate walking. It's too slow. And are you serious...*fishing shows*?"

"You've got to learn to slow down. It could kill you someday. That's no joke. You young people think stress won't harm you, but it will. Make sure you leave the drugs and booze alone as well."

Croston frowned. "Next thing you'll be saying is to leave women alone."

"You married or engaged or anything?"

"Hell, no."

The doc pursed his lips as he scrawled something on a pad of paper. "Then the only woman you need to be seeing right now is your mother."

"Well, that's out," Croston said, blandly. "Look doc, this just doesn't seem right. I mean, I work out. It doesn't make sense that I'm in here because of exhaustion and dehydration. I really think you need to recommend more tests so the insurance will cover the cost."

"That's your opinion as a patient. My opinion — as that of a physician —is they're not necessary. Recommending expensive tests when they're not necessary is one of the things that drives up the cost of health insurance."

"But I'm healthy! Didn't you hear me, goddamn it? Something *else* has got to be wrong with me!"

The doctor's eyes went flat and dull behind the glasses. He turned and walked toward the door, paused there. "Yes, you are generally healthy, Mr. Croston. Healthy but exhausted. All you need to do is keep away from the drugs and booze and get some rest."

"But what if you missed something?"

"I've been practicing medicine for a long time, son—a long time. You can be confident of my expertise in the matter. All boiled down, you can bet I know what I'm doing."

"If it was funded by my insurance company would you do the tests?" Croston asked, though he already knew the answer. After all, he was part of the machine that influenced the policies of his own health network. He knew damn well the doctor would recommend the tests only if they were covered. The doctor was under considerable pressure from companies like Foundation to keep costs down.

Doctor Fossil opened the door and turned to observed him over his shoulder. "Good day, Mr. Croston. I'm glad to see your recovery has been so rapid. I'm discharging you under your own recognizance. The nurses will pass on a prescription to help your body regain its strength. They will also help check you out of the hospital. Take my advice: Drink plenty of fluids and get a lot of rest."

"But—"

"Good day, Mr. Croston."

"How about I stay here another day so you guys can keep an eye on me?"

But the doctor had disappeared and Croston knew the answer to that one, too. Policy dictated patients get in and out of the hospital as quickly as possible so as not to incur the staggering cost of an overnight stay.

The nurse came in, removed his I.V. and catheter, and then left.

The door slowly swung shut. For some reason, as it latched loudly in place, Croston had the sudden impression of someone locking him out of a building that harbored something he desperately needed.

He leaned over and grasped the phone off the little round table next to the bed. He dialed his number one crony and told him to come to the hospital and give him a ride home.

Simpson, always looking for any chance to remain in the boss' favor, immediately acquiesced.

Lightheaded, Croston moved slowly to the closet and retrieved his suit, which the orderlies or somebody had hung there. It smelled of piss and sweat. His boxers were stuffed in the inner breast pocket. He pressed the orange button with the stick figure of a nurse on it. When her voice came over the speaker in the other armrest he told her to bring him something clean to wear.

The loose-fitting pants and v-necked shirt were similar to the scrubs the doctors and nurses wore.

"These cost extra," she told him, laying the items on the bed.

"Put it on my fucking bill."

She left without another word.

He could have worn the slippers she brought along with the shirt and pants but decided not to. He looked ridiculous wearing his wingtips with the patient scrubs but damned if he'd wear those slippers. They reminded him of something a preschool child should be wearing. Future VP's don't wear that shit.

With his suit draped over his arm he ambled to the billing office and flashed them his Foundation Health Net card and told them to file his claim for him. Then he walked out the main entrance of the hospital with the circular driveway designed to facilitate the picking up/dropping off of patients. He sat on a bench and waited in the hot shade for his ride.

He wondered what he had missed in his two days away from the office.

Simpson arrived and Croston immediately pumped him for information. Naturally, Simpson didn't know anything of real use. The flunky was only a project leader, after all.

In his apartment parking lot he got out of Simpson's car and told him to keep an eye on things at work until tomorrow. Simpson heartily agreed to do just that, then told Croston to get lots of rest so he could get back to work soon. They really needed him, man. Really needed him *bad*.

Kiss ass.

Back at his apartment, Croston threw his suit on the lazy boy chair that faced the wide-screen television. He went to the kitchen to fix himself a large turkey and ham sandwich with four slices of Muenster cheese and lettuce and tomato and rich mayonnaise on an onion roll.

He grabbed a soda and some potato chips and took the

sandwich to the couch, flicked on the television to the Markets Channel and heard the latest Wall Street gossip and reports. After eating the sandwich he slumped back on the couch and slowly drifted off to sleep.

He had no idea how long he slept. He was awakened to the saliva suddenly pooling in his mouth. His eyes flashed open. Lurching upright, he projectile-vomited all over his coffee table, fully emptying the contents of his stomach.

Too much food after missing meals in the hospital? He thought, just before the noxious fumes overwhelmed him and he heaved some more. *Or is this something else? Wait a minute, Simpson said he had a stomach virus just two days ago. That bastard, I'll bet he's still contagious! But how could it hit me so soon…?*

In the light of the television he watched, dumbfounded, as his vomit leaked off the coffee table. Then it came again. His stomach heaved but this time nothing came out but more spit. Gasping for air, he tried to wait it out but the heaves kept coming. He was covered in sweat.

Finally the dry heaves passed and he gulped for air. He wiped his mouth with the back of his hand and slumped back in the couch. His head felt like it was floating, even flushed with blood as he knew it had to be from all the pressure generated by gut-heaving. He breathed deeply. His heart finally stopped banging against his rib cage. Thankfully he could no longer feel the machine-gun throb in the carotid arteries of his neck. He looked down at the table and then back up to the ceiling.

What a mess! he thought. *Now I've got to clean this shit up.*

Why are you doing this to me, God? he silently asked.

He grabbed the edge of the couch and slowly sat up. His head was a big bubble of gas adrift between his shoulders, held only by a thin line that was his spinal cord. His legs shook violently as he stood. In fact, his entire body shook like he was a heroin addict late for a fix.

He heard a crash and suddenly he was looking up at the ceiling with his back now in pain. Groaning, he turned his head to the side. His furniture stood around him like silent guards—except for the coffee table on which he had landed. The table legs had surrendered beneath the sudden onset of his weight and had broken from the table. Croston tried to get up. His hands slid on the slick, chunky surface of the table.

With his head turned to the side, Croston dry-heaved.

When the heaves subsided, he was left gasping for air once again. He tried to roll onto his stomach, failed, tried again, failed again, rested, then, after several minutes, threw his right leg over his left, and his arm over his body. This time he gained his side, yet teetered on the verge of rolling back. Straining to keep his face above his own puke, he made it onto his stomach. He stared down at parts of the partially digested sandwich, his revulsion giving away to a much more serious feeling, a feeling that told him this was all wrong, this shouldn't be happening to him, that he was a young lion and getting this sick and this goddamned *weak* was not natural, was not fair, was *not* in his plans!

This isn't happening, Croston thought.

But when his head fell into the puke because he couldn't hold it up, he knew he was in some serious shit.

Somehow he crawled to the phone on the end table. Somehow he punched the buttons for 911. He mumbled something they probably couldn't understand because he couldn't make sense of it himself. But at least they'd have a fix on him as soon as they answered the other end.

I don't get it! Croston tried to tell the voice on the other end. *I'm on my way to the top of the corporate ladder and I'm only twenty-eight years old, for Christ's sake! I don't get this!*

He started to cry.

Then he blacked out.

When he awoke he saw a beautiful woman observing him with weary eyes. She was wearing a white lab coat so he couldn't really get a good read on her body, though there were good swells at chest level.

"Mr. Croston, you're at Chamber's Medical Center," she told him. "I'm Doctor Devereaux. We've taken some blood and run some tests on you. I'm sorry to have to tell you that you have leukemia. Do you understand me, Mr. Croston? You have a blood cancer that needs treatment right away. I'm very sorry."

He blinked a few times to get the fuzziness out of the corners of his sight. He cleared his throat, which was sore and aching, doubtless a direct result from the puke-fest he'd had.

"Leukemia?" he rasped.

"I'm afraid so," she said. "Leukemia is a cancer of the blood. Signs of it include an unusually high count of abnormal white blood cells that infiltrate the bloodstream. The manufacture of normal red blood cells and platelet is adversely affected. These factors can lead to anemia, infection, and excessive bleeding. There're several ways —"

"I told Doctor Who-The-Fuck that something was wrong with me. He wouldn't run any more tests to make sure, that asshole. And now I've got leukemia? I'll sue him. I'll sue him blind!"

The Doctor Devereaux babe nodded. "I understand your frustration, Mr. Croston. Unfortunately, the external signs of leukemia occur after the disease has already set in. It could be that there were no signs of your malady until just last night when they brought you here and I admitted you."

"Hey, I work in the health industry, honey. I know damned well cancer just doesn't pop up out of nowhere."

"You're right, but its signs aren't always evident."

"There wasn't a…damn thing…wrong with me until Monday afternoon—I swear!"

The doc's eyes grew intense, almost magnetic. "Unfortunately we've had several leukemia cases recently with the same sudden onset as yours."

Croston swallowed and looked away. "How did it happen?"

"We're…not sure. It could have been triggered by an environmental catalyst, or chemical, or genes passed down from your parents."

"Wouldn't surprise me if I had a genetic disposition. Just like my old man to strike from the fucking grave."

"Some research suggests there could even be a correlation to certain lesser viruses."

"Leukemia has a high cure rate, doesn't it?" Croston asked quickly, trying to remember the statistics that had crossed his computer monitor on the monthly reports.

The lady doc nodded. "Yes, one form of leukemia does have a high cure rate. Unfortunately you have Acute Myeloid Leukemia, which has seen a rise in the survival rate over the last thirty years but is still very serious. I'm going to present four treatment paths for you. Chemotherapy, spleen removal and bone marrow transplant, experimental drugs, and, of course, there is always the option to do nothing…"

As she explained his treatment alternatives, Croston's attention drifted away. His eyes moved from her lips to her eyes to the ceiling to the wall and back again and all the while a single thought kept spinning in his head.

I don't want to die!

EIGHT

"I'M SORRY TO tell you that your leukemia is extremely accelerated, Mr. Croston," Bridget said, after explaining the treatment alternatives to her latest patient. "It...has already taken hold in the bone marrow of your hips and is rapidly spreading to—"

"But this doesn't make goddamned sense! I was fine three days ago—*fine!*"

"I know it's frightening, Mr. Croston. I'll do everything I can to help you through this."

"Oh, yeah? Well, no offense, but you're not exactly a veteran at this, are you? You don't look old enough to be long out of med school."

"I assure you, I can —"

"So, what are you, an intern?"

She opened her mouth to respond, but he cut her off.

"Save it. At least you take the time to talk to me. So tell me, *Doctor Intern*, just how many others have come down with a case of this fast-acting leukemia shit?"

Bridget took a deep breath and let it out. "Several."

"Wonderful."

Her gaze drifted over his head to the eggshell white wall behind him. "I'm at a loss to explain the sudden onset of the disease. It could be that the cancer was operating in the background, not creating enough of a disturbance to be noticed. Or maybe it was dormant and something triggered its sudden release."

"These several other patients—did they make it?"

"We have one undergoing treatment now."

"One? That's all? What about the others?"

"I'm very sorry, Mr. Croston," Bridget repeated.

"Give me an update, honey. Just how will *sorry* make me better?"

She looked down. "It won't. Not directly, anyway."

"And not indirectly, either. So save it."

Croston made a fist and gripped it tightly in the palm of his other hand. He worked his fingers over his knuckles, squeezing and releasing, again and again, while his lower lip quivered. "I—I just can't believe this is happening to me," he said, his voice barely audible.

Help him, for God's sake, Bridget thought. *Can't you see he needs you?*

"Generally chemotherapy has the highest rate of recovery in leukemia patients," she said. "Because your leukemia is so accelerated, we need to initiate treatment right away. Do you agree?"

"Hell yes, I agree!"

"Okay. I'll work up the treatment plan and inform the nurses. They'll give you a complete run-down on what to expect with the chemo. Is there anything else I can do for you in the meantime?"

Hugh Croston's eyes glistened. "Just leave."

He turned away on the pillow but before he did she saw tears streak down the sides of his face.

Bridget's heart felt as if it were being wrung by twisting, constricting hands.

This is so difficult, she thought, *but that's how it must be. Maybe after years of informing patients they have cancer, my voice might not waver and sound so meek, but I will never allow myself to become accustomed to this. I will never let myself become aloof and unmoved like the doctor who told Mama she had cancer, almost fifteen years ago now.*

She sensed she probably would not have liked Hugh Croston as a person if she had ever met him outside these bleak hospital walls, but that had no bearing here—the man's *life* was in her hands.

"Can we contact someone on your behalf, Mr. Croston?" Bridget asked. "You don't have to have their numbers memorized. If you give me names and general locales, I can have our volunteers track down phone numbers, if it all possible. I'll take it from there and contact your people personally."

Croston stared out the window for a long time before answering. New tears traveled familiar pathways down his cheeks. His Adam's apple moved as he swallowed and then spoke. "My brother and sister still live in Hickory Grove, North Carolina, the piss ant little town where I grew up. I don't have Hank's number on me—it's at home, but his last name is the same as mine. Information should be able to get you the number. You can call him and he can let my sister in on the good news. They probably won't give a shit, but tell Henry and he can pass it on to Susan. Maybe they'll stop squeezing cow tits long enough to pay me a visit."

"All right, I'll do that. Anyone else?"

"No."

Bridget nodded, though Hugh Croston had turned away from

her. "I'll be back soon."

He gave a half-wave of dismissal just as his shoulders began to hitch.

Bridget slipped through the opening in the curtain, passed through the doorway and into the hallway, where she paused and jotted down the names of his relatives in his patient file. As she did so she noticed in a distracted kind of way that her handwriting had gone from fair to bad to atrocious during these past months of her internship.

She chose not to pass the request to contact Mr. Croston's relatives onto the volunteers. The elderly and retirees and corporate wives who needed something productive to do, as well as the high school/college kids looking to bolster their barren resumes in order to get into medical or physical therapy schools where competition is fierce, were perfect volunteers for handling requests like family contact calls, but they might let it slip to management that a doctor wanted to make her own calls, and management here at Chambers would throw a fit at that bit of inefficiency. No, Bridget had told him she would make the call personally, and that's exactly what she'd do.

Not all of the leukemia patients admitted here at Chambers have the same locomotive onset and progression—just a subset of the total number, Bridget thought, frowning as she wrote. The thing is, all of them are recent admissions. Why does the leuk in this subset kill so quickly?

The pen moved to the margin of the paper and created aimless designs.

I'm losing every time, Bridget realized. *No one has survived this terrible leuk strain. Maybe I'm not cut out to be a doctor after all. Maybe it takes something I don't have. Maybe I should just quit before any more of my patients die.*

Will quitting prevent them from dying? another part of her mind countered.

No.

Do any other doctors have a better understanding of what is happening here?

They don't even want to know about it.

So how exactly do your patients benefit from this display of self-pity?

They don't.

Then get on with it, girl!

Bridget regained control of the pen. In Hugh Croston's file she scrawled down orders for his chemotherapy and a gambit of standard and nonstandard blood, urine, and bone marrow tests. She knew some of the tests weren't normal procedure for cancer patients—weren't *normal and customary* under Croston's insurance plan—but to hell with that. She needed to know everything that was going on in this man's body as far as the disease was concerned. If it continued to spread, she was going to know how quickly and how far it spread. If it was curtailed and went into remission from the chemo treatments, she was going to know the exact point at which it was curtailed and the speed at which it went into remission.

I'm going to track this bastard disease every step of the way, Bridget thought.

She gave the chart directly to one of the nurses on Croston's watch. The woman's eyebrows rose in surprise but otherwise she didn't question the slew of tests. Bridget watched her for a moment and then walked away.

I wonder why she didn't fight me? Bridget thought. *She didn't even give me a dirty look. It is extra work on them, all these tests. Did Nurse Watkins tell her staff to support me or something?*

It was early evening and Bridget's rounds were officially over. Again the stress of the day and the ever-present weariness had settled deep into her body and she ached for the luxury of sleep.

Hospital workers walked up and down the hallways around her, some talking and laughing among themselves. Bridget stepped into the human traffic and flowed along with it, her direction unclear until she found herself at the room of Mrs. Wilson, the patient whom Bridget had first introduced herself to on her first day of her rotation on this ward.

She knocked on the door, which was partially open.

"Come on in!"

Mrs. Wilson was sitting up in bed, doing touch-up while peering into a hand-held mirror. She glanced over the top of it and kept doing the touch-up. "Doctor Bridget Devereaux! How are you doing, honey? Did you forget something from this morning, or did you change your mind about dating that son of mine?"

Bridget smiled. At least *one* of her patients was doing better. "I know I said goodbye to you earlier, but I wanted to see what it looked like for a cancer patient of mine to actually be discharged with good news."

Mrs. Wilson set the mirror down and beamed. "Well, here I am—take a mental picture! It feels like the weight of the world is off my shoulders, believe me. Thanks again for all your work. It was rough going there for a while, wasn't it?"

"Yes, it was. But you certainly pulled through with style."

"I don't know that my throwing-up or going bald was done with anything like style."

"All that matters is that you made it, Mrs. Wilson."

"You sound like an old man sitting on a mountain. How old did you say you were?"

Bridget smiled. "Twenty-six."

"Too young for talk like that, dear. Way too young." After a moment Mrs. Wilson's smile faded. "I had no choice with it, of course. It was so scary...not knowing if I'd make it through the summer or not. People came to visit and that usually made me feel better but in the end it was my body that was the battleground and they couldn't really help me with that. You helped me though, Doctor."

"I was glad to. It's my job."

"Oh, you did more than just your job, and you know it! You really cared and that means a lot to me. Makes a difference, honey, it really does." She smiled sadly. "Bill would be lost without me. I've got to be around to take care of him. Yep, got to be around to take care of him."

An almost girlish look of excitement overcame Mrs. Wilson as she pointed a thin finger at the table near the window. Amidst the clutter of personal items, books, two wig stands, cards and varying arrangements of flowers stood a new vase of gorgeous red roses.

"See what he sent me this morning? He's on his way, you know. Quick! Toss me one from the table there."

"Blond or brunet?"

"Blond today, honey. Definitely blond today."

Bridget handed her the wig. Mrs. Wilson fitted it to her head with practiced precision, then plucked at some of the longer strands. "What do you think?"

"Marilyn Monroe?"

"Nah...Sharon Stone."

"Mrs. Wilson!" Bridget exclaimed in mock surprise.

"What? You don't think us older folks know how to have a good time?"

"Of course you do," Bridget said, grinning. "It's just that Sharon Stone's kind of, uh..."

Mrs. Wilson winked. "Oh, I know she's *wild*, honey! Bill gets all red in the face when I joke him about it but I know he likes her. He's seen her movies at least a hundred times. Well, I have a surprise for him tonight, let me tell you. Going to rent one of her videos and not see it all, if you know what I mean!"

Bridget laughed. "I got you."

Mrs. Wilson stopped primping and looked at Bridget with misty eyes. "I really couldn't have made it without you."

"Oh, I think you would have. Please promise to give me a call every once in a while to let me know how you're doing."

"Of course I will. You need to take care of yourself, too. You're a beautiful young woman, but you're looking a bit run-down lately. I think these folks are pushin' you too hard."

"Nothing I can't handle. I'll be fine. You go out and enjoy your new life."

"Give me another hug, honey."

Afterward Bridget looked her patient over. Mrs. Wilson had put on Passion perfume and done her make-up and wig just right. "You're beautiful, Mrs. Wilson."

"Thank you so much, Bridget Devereaux," Mrs. Wilson whispered. "You saved me."

"Oh, you probably helped me more than I helped you."

"Now that's nonsense. Don't let things get to you, honey. Life's too short to put up with much crap from people. Life's just way too short for that nonsense. You got to pick your path and go for it, and don't let anyone steer you away from what you know is right."

Bridget moved to the door and opened it. Mrs. Wilson's husband was walking down the hallway toward his wife's room. "Here he comes," Bridget said.

"Oh, I'm actually nervous…at my age!"

"Take care, Mrs. Wilson."

"Bye, honey."

Bridget left and smiled as she passed Bill Wilson, who had a bouquet of orchids raised high in one hand like he was carrying the Olympic torch. He said hello to Bridget, knocked twice on the door and then disappeared into the room where his wife had undergone the assault on her body known as chemotherapy.

In Becky Wilson's case it had worked.

But the warm, hopeful feeling Bridget had in Mrs. Wilson's presence soon departed—as Bridget had known it would. It had been perched so precariously upon her shoulder that there was no way to keep it from falling off. She let her mind idle and soon found herself at Jo's room, down the hall and around the corner from Mrs. Wilson's room. She had already been here twice during her shift.

Bridget knocked softly on the door but no one answered. She took a deep breath and quietly stepped inside.

Jo was in bed asleep. Her face twitched as she slept, as did her fingertips upon her blanket, and beneath closed lids her eyes went back and forth in Rapid Eye Movement, or REM sleep, the time when humans dream their deepest dreams.

The bed seemed vast. It looked as if it would consume Jo's frail body at any moment. She had lost much of her appetite due to the chemo. Athletically trim when they first admitted her over a week ago, now her smooth cheeks had sunken and her eye sockets had darkened. Her strawberry-blond hair had thinned but not abandoned her; instead it had taken on the delicate appearance of fine, silken strands.

The morphine dripping into her IV was highly addictive, but twelve hours ago this tough, brave girl had pleaded for relief. The pain pills Bridget had started her on had suddenly become woefully inadequate. After explaining the addictive nature of the morphine to the girl's parents and to Jo herself, Bridget started her on the potent opiate.

The shades in the room were drawn because sunlight now hurt Jo's eyes.

The room was lit only by a blue television screen. Bridget sat on the side of the bed and held one of the girl's hands. Jo's brow furrowed and her mouth tugged downward. She moaned softly but remained asleep. Seconds later a brief smile flashed on her mouth and her eyebrows raised fine lines in her forehead. Her lips moved as if she were talking to someone in her dreams. Then the frown came again. She moaned softly and then her face relaxed and she appeared almost serene. The cycle repeated itself twice as Bridget looked on.

The girl's parents entered the room. They nodded to Bridget who could only nod back, when what she wanted to do is tell them how awful it was that their daughter was undergoing such an ordeal.

Bridget removed a syringe and gently pulled Jo's arm closer and overturned it. She carefully inserted the needle into the catheter and withdrew five cc's of blood, more than enough to get an accurate reading of her white and red blood cell count, as well as a platelet count.

As she moved to the door, Joe Woods spoke. "Just a sec, Doctor."

"Yes, Mr. Woods?"

"I should probably go in to work now. I can clean my client's offices anytime before the start of the next business day, but tonight I've got to get there earlier. If you think Jo's in for a rough stretch I can call and have my head guy handle the job. I just, you know, I don't want to be gone if Jo's going to hit a rough stretch."

There were dark circles beneath his eyes, but no surrender in the eyes themselves. His eyes glistened from unshed tears while Ellen Woods' eyes were scarlet and puffy and now she wiped a tear from her cheek with the back of her trembling hand.

"Jo is resting as much as possible given her abnormal circumstances," Bridget told them. "I've prescribed enough painkiller to keep her sleeping comfortably until the morning. Her heart rate and breathing are monitored by the machines and relayed back to the nursing station, and I've got the nurses coming in every twenty minutes to check on her. Bottom line: she'll be well-cared for. If you stay, you'll only see her sleeping. I would suggest you go to your job, and then go home and get some rest.

You both need rest. It's probably better to be with her tomorrow when she receives the next injection of chemo."

The parents glanced at one another and then Mrs. Woods nodded. They went to Jo and kissed her on the cheek and held her hand.

"We'll see you in the morning, kid," Mr. Woods said.

"Goodnight, baby," Mrs. Woods said, the dark rings beneath her eyes looking terrible in the dim light from the television.

Jo stirred on the bed but did not waken as they departed.

"They'll be back soon," Bridget said softly. "They'll be back soon."

She stood for a moment with the red syringe held between her thumb and first two fingers of her right hand. She looked around and realized she hadn't brought a transporting case for the blood, nor had she set up a sterilized tray in which to rest the syringe while she hunted for a transporting case.

Oh, well, she thought. I'm not going to trash this sample and take more of the girl's precious blood because of my own stupidity.

There was no transporting case in the cabinet at the far end of the room, but she did find a thin test tube with a rubber stopper encased in a sterile plastic wrapping. She carefully set the syringe down on the counter and pulled the plastic wrapping from the test tube. She picked up the needle, squirted Jo's blood into the test tube, dropped the syringe into the metal holding can with the skull and crossbones sticker on it, and then secured the rubber stopper on top of the test tube.

She found a bottle of ammonia and a sponge on a lower cabinet and poured a large circle of the ammonia on the exact spot where she had placed the syringe, though the needle had not contacted the counter top. She used the sponge to wipe the germ-killing solution over the entire counter top, then put the ammonia back where she found it and placed the sponge into the bio-hazardous waste container in the bathroom. Such containers were present in every patient's room and usually contained items such as bandages, tampons, disposable wipes, etc. — anything that had blood or other potentially lethal bodily fluids on it.

She took up the test tube with Jo's red blood inside and held it inside her lab coat pocket. "I'll check in on you again before I go home, Jo."

Though she slept, a hint of a smile touched the corners of Jo's mouth.

"I'd like to think you heard me," Bridget said. "I'll be back in a while."

Bridget turned from the girl on the bed but didn't see the veteran nurse until she almost bumped into her just inside Jo's doorway. Her arms were crossed over her chest and her thin lips were pressed firmly together in a straight line.

"Nurse Watkins," Bridget said by way of acknowledgment. Her tone was reserved and guarded, uncertain of the woman's disposition. Whatever the case, Bridget was on her own time and didn't have much of that.

"A word with you, Doctor?" Nurse Watkins said.

"It'll have to be quick. I have to get down to the lab."

Nurse Watkins visibly stiffened. "All right." She glanced at Josephine and then gently closed the door to the room after Bridget exited.

They walked to an unpopulated section of the hallway. Bridget turned and looked at the older woman. "What's up?"

"I hope you don't transfer blood samples like that all the time, Doctor."

"I should have gotten a transport case, I know. It slipped my mind until after I drew the sample."

"A slip of mind can get you into trouble, Doctor."

"Is there a reason why you're pointing this out? I appreciate constructive criticism and even just plain criticism as long as it's warranted, but you seem to have a personal problem with me. Am I right?"

Nurse Watkins glanced up and down the hallway before responding. "I don't have a problem with you, Doctor. In fact, I think you have guts and you really care about your patients. I'm on your ass about the little things because *they* will take the little things when they can't get anything else."

Bridget frowned. "What are you talking about?"

"They're gunning for you. They're looking for ammunition to use against you."

"What? Who is?"

"The male power consortium that runs this hospital, that's who."

"I don't believe it."

"Believe it."

"But why would they?"

"Because they are men from the old school and you are an assertive female intern willing to try anything to get her patients better."

"I'm not surprised, but for some reason I thought they just didn't like the fact that I'm an intern, not fit to walk in their shadow."

"No doubt some of both."

"But you're a woman and you've got a lot of authority around here. I don't see how you've been discriminated against or harassed."

"Nursing has historically been a female dominated department.

There is no power-sharing in the nursing department, no threat to the male ego."

"But there have been thousands of female doctors over the past twenty-five years! It's not like I'm some kind of new phenomenon."

"Then you haven't seen any of it?"

"I don't know. Blake Hensley came on to me and I rejected him and he's kind of had it in for me ever since, but I thought that was just a personal grudge. Outside the cafeteria one of the doctors called me a silly girl in front of the others. You were there—they laughed at me. God, I was so mad and embarrassed! But I didn't think anyone was actively discriminating against me."

"They've learned to go underground with it. Except for slip-ups like that one outside the cafeteria, it's now mostly covert stuff. They know they can get into a lot of trouble with lawsuits and bad publicity if things are done out in the open."

"This is so incredible…"

"You've got to keep your eyes open for discreet symptoms."

"Are you sure about this?"

"That incident in the hallway when they laughed at you was just one little snippet. I don't usually eavesdrop on the doctors, but my nurses and I have overheard bits and pieces of conversation from the male doctors. They're out to get you, Bridget."

"But why? I haven't done anything wrong!"

"They don't like the fact that you've insinuated something strange is going on with some of the leukemia patients here. They don't like the fact that there's a chance you're right and they didn't discover it first. Basically, an upstart female intern who doesn't know her place is a threat to them."

"But it's the patients they should be thinking about," Bridget said. "What difference does any of that other crap make?"

"Power? Control? Tradition? Fear of publicity, maybe? I don't know—I'm just telling you what you're up against. Look for the little things, the subtle things, and you'll see. You're a gifted intern, and you'll make a great doctor, but you've got to watch for the minor things like handling needles and patient files because they're just waiting for you to slip up. I think you can guess how they feel about those extra, uninsured tests you've ordered for your leuk patients."

"But I *need* those tests! They could find something I've missed."

"Yes, they can. I'm just saying they'll use it against you since many of the tests are beyond what the insurance company considers *usual and customary*."

They stood in silence for a moment.

"The bottom line is they're looking to bounce me out of the

internship program, aren't they?" Bridget asked. She bit the inside of her lip to keep the tears at bay. Everything went fuzzy at the sides despite her efforts. She blinked rapidly.

Nurse Watkins looked down and nodded. "They want you meek and mild all right. And they definitely don't want you making waves that could hurt their business deal."

"Selling the hospital?"

Nurse Watkins nodded. "You know what a shit Handlaw is, and how it all rolls downhill. Would you put it past them to kick you out?"

"I'm only trying to help my patients, for God's sake."

"Look, Bridget. I'm not fanatical about women's rights, but my daughter damn well deserves the same opportunities as my sons. I'm an old battleaxe, three years from retirement. I could turn away from all of this and be safe, but that's not the way I live. You're fighting for your patients, and I respect that. I wanted to make sure you knew the consequences before you went any further."

"Forewarned is forearmed," Bridget said, and wished she could be as strong as the woman before her. "I don't suppose you have any suggestions...?"

Nurse Watkins turned slightly as if to go, then halted. "Watch yourself. Small mistakes give them ammo to keep you quiet or send you packing. The path has split before you and now you've got to choose. On one path, you're at the beginning of your career and you're not God—you can only do so much by yourself. No one could blame you for backing off."

"And the other path?"

"The other...if you don't fight for these patients, who will? I'm a damn good nurse, but I can only do so much. If I could do it over, I'd put my ass through medical school." Nurse Watkins frowned. "Listen, both paths are covered in shit. It's not nice and it's not fair and you're gonna step in it no matter what. You have to decide what to do, Doctor Devereaux, and then you're going to have to live with it."

Bridget felt a moan wriggle up into her throat. She didn't dare say anything for fear of letting it out.

"I'm sorry, Bridget. I'll help you if I can, but you've got to choose." Nurse Watkins walked down the hallway and disappeared among the staff workers at the far end.

Bridget stared after her.

NINE

K EEP GOING, GIRL, Bridget thought, as she walked tentatively through the dim basement hallway. *Who's going to research this accelerated leuk if you don't? No one, that's who.*

She passed the same barren beds and bent-armed I.V. stands and broken wheelchairs that had been shoved against the walls and forgotten.

This is one great big safety violation, she thought. *I'll bet OSHA doesn't even inspect this area, so the higher-ups just ignore it all. But from what Nurse Watkins just told me, if a certain intern carrying a glass test tube of patient blood in her pocket tripped and fell and had to fill out an incident report, they'd take instant notice—and not in a good way.*
A steady hum filled the air, punctuated by the sounds of distant crashes as aluminum carts, pushed by ghostly-looking orderlies at the far end of the dim hallway, collided with the swinging metal doors of the laundry room. When the doors swung open the hum of the huge washers and dryers suddenly swelled, only to fade once again as the doors swung shut.

Her gaze tracked to the only other motion in the hall. Three ghostly figures in white scrubs rammed their carts into the far laundry room door. The distance was such that the crashing sounds met her ears a full second after the orderlies themselves disappeared into the laundry room.

Now this is just a tad unnerving, Bridget thought. It took all of about twenty seconds for the real world to get replaced by the twilight zone.

As the last specter disappeared, she found herself alone in the hallway. Her skin suddenly crawled. Goose bumps started inward from between her shoulder blades and up the sides of her neck and over her entire head, prickling the thousands upon thousands of root-hairs there.

Bridget shuddered.

This is still part of the hospital, she told herself. *It's not the Catacombs or a cemetery. Then again, a fair amount of human ash does find its way into the nooks and crannies around the incinerators.*

Bridget shoved open the crimson door of the hematology lab and slipped inside. After several seconds she was able to relax enough to get her shoulders down from around her neck. All the overhead fluorescent lights were at full burn. As she squinted, she could feel the sharp ache in each constricting eye muscle, an ache that testified to her lack of sleep over the past weeks.

A couple of lab workers dressed in powder-blue lab coats were hovering around a microscope at the rear of the room. Bridget hadn't seen them before. One was a woman with short-cropped hair. The man beside her had a long ponytail that almost wagged like a dog's tail as he moved his head during their conversation.

They glanced at her and then continued with their conversation. Bridget placed the latest sample of Jo's blood next to the first microscope she came upon.

Ian McGuire was nowhere to be seen.

She felt a twinge of disappointment that the middle-aged gentleman was not here. She checked her watch and realized that it was only eight forty-five. Ian's shift didn't begin until midnight.

She flicked on the power switch to the microscope and the associated viewing monitor and then turned to the lab workers at the back of the room. "Excuse me."

They broke off their conversation and looked at her.

"Hey," the guy said.

The woman with the close-cropped hair raised her thin eyebrows.

"Do y'all know if Ian left any messages for me?" Bridget asked them.

Their faces went blank.

"Who?" the woman said.

"Ian. Ian McGuire."

"I don't know any Ian McGuire." She looked at her companion. "Andy?"

"Nope," Andy said, taking the opportunity to let his gaze drift over Bridget's body. "Does he work here at the hospital?"

"He works here in the lab, on the graveyard shift. Maybe he's only part-time."

"'Ian McGuire'...sounds like he belongs in a Saint Patrick's Day parade," the woman said, laughing. "I'd probably be looking for a pot of gold to appear at his feet or something."

Andy rocked his head back and forth and grinned. "I hear you. Hey, Doc," he said to Bridget. "I think we'd remember the dude. We work radiology together, Jackie and me, evening shift, but we're on-call, here, so we get down here most nights. When did you say he worked?

"I'm not sure, evening hours."

"Well, we've got this covered four to eleven-thirty, Monday

through Friday for the past year, right Jackster? You'd think we'd overlap with this guy once in a while if he worked here.

Bridget slowly nodded, suddenly unsure of her facts. "But he had a badge on and everything. This is only my second time down here before midnight. Maybe he—"

"Maybe Debbie got a temp or hired the dude in the past few weeks or something and just forgot to tell us. Wouldn't be the first time," Andy said.

"Yeah, that's probably it." Bridget eased onto the stool and turned slowly around to face her microscope.

The lab techs returned to their conversation while Bridget tore the wrap from a specimen tray and brought out enough sticky labels to identify the slides she would make. She carefully made six new slides from Jo's latest blood sample and placed them one at a time beneath the microscope.

The abnormal white blood cells drifted on the monitor like pollution in a stream.

She went to the back of the room and employed the 800 Series Blood Analysis System. Jo's latest sample did not contain the unknown protein matrix found earlier in her samples.

What does this mean? she wondered. Was Protein Matrix X a random event, or was it truly connected to this accelerated leukemia? If it was connected, why has it disappeared in Jo's current blood samples?

She put the samples from the other leuk patients through a battery of tests and had the computer run the analysis. At some point Andy and Jackie walked by and opened the door.

"Goodnight, Doctor," the female lab tech said.

"Yeah, take it easy, Doc," Andy said over his shoulder.

Bridget blinked, took her glasses off and rubbed her eyes. It was eleven-fifteen. "Good night."

She watched the mechanical arm connecting the door to the wall slowly fold inward on itself. Bridget was now alone in the room. She rose from the stool and stretched, flexing the muscles in her legs while reaching for the ceiling. She rubbed her numbed buttocks, then went to the climate controlled storage room to retrieve earlier samples of Jo's blood.

She closed the door and turned around to find a man standing before her. She jumped and nearly dropped the test tubes. "Ian— you scared me!"

He stared intently down at her, as if he was unsure of her in some way. His electric blue eyes almost burned with intensity.

Bridget swallowed. "Everything…all right?"

He blinked but still did not say anything.

"Ian?" She took a step back and almost turned to look for a heavy object to defend herself with. Finally, Ian spoke.

"We made a mistake."

She let out the breath she'd been unconsciously holding. "Oh?"

"The protein matrix is a dead end. It's simply a random occurrence in the early samples."

"Then you don't think it's a by-product of the leukemia itself?"

"No. I've been studying the samples. The protein matrix is a random occurrence. There's a possibility I'm wrong, but I don't think so." He placed a small red cooler on the counter.

"Damn." She frowned. "Damn, damn, *damn!*"

"I'm sorry."

"Well, let's recheck them. Let's get them all under the scopes and run them through the analyzer again. Maybe we'll see some other common element. There's got to be something else going on with this strain of leukemia. Got to be."

"You're the boss."

"You know, Ian, for a minute there I thought you weren't well or something. You seemed…" she paused and searched for a low-key way to put it, "…like you weren't sure of things."

"I didn't know how to break the news to you. Unable to find just the right words, I simply blurted it out."

So that was what he was wrestling with, she thought. *He was trying to figure out how to spare my feelings. That's sweet.*

He smiled and the intensity of his eyes faded but did not vanish. "Besides, I've been thinking a lot and that always fries a synapse or two in the old gray matter, especially now that I'm old."

She smiled wearily. "You're not old. Look, it hurts me to think, too. You didn't happen to bring any of that delicious coffee with you, did you? I know I said I'd bring the next batch, but I've fallen behind in my groceries and everything. I haven't even been home in almost three days. I've been taking showers here and living in these hospital-provided scrubs, snatching sleep here and there, but it's never enough, you know?"

Ian nodded. "I didn't think you'd have the time to get out, so you'll be pleased with this…" He reached into his lab coat pocket and produced a plastic bag stuffed with dark grounds. "I stopped at the gourmet coffee shop on Six Forks Road earlier today. Inhale." He pulled the plastic bag open and held it up.

The smooth, mellow aroma almost made her knees give out. "Irish Cream?"

"Indeed."

"Bliss!" She looked pointedly at him. "Caffeinated?"

"Is there another kind?"

"Let's get it into the pot!"

"You got it."

At the coffee maker, she tossed the old, stale brew down the sink while Ian found a filter and scooped out five heaping scoops from the bag with a tablespoon.

"So, what exactly makes you think we made a mistake in the blood samples?" she asked, returning with the clean pot of water and waiting as he pushed the loaded filter into the machine.

"The unidentified protein matrix should be present in all of the samples taken at the onset of the leukemia and it's not," he said. "This leads me to conclude that the presence of protein matrix X is a random occurrence in some of your patients and isn't a true by-product of the leukemia."

"Why, Ian, you sound like a doctor."

He smiled, but somehow the smile looked strained on his face. "I've just been doing a little research, that's all. Obviously I'm no doctor—I haven't had the training you've had in the field. Call it a mix of observation, years of work as a lab tech, and a somewhat educated hunch."

Ian popped the lid off the little red cooler and reached inside. He then held up five thin glass test tubes bound together with a rubber band, each with rubber stoppers capping them off. "I took samples from our samples and took them home with me to examine in my basement lab."

He inserted the tubes carefully in a plastic holder on the counter.

"You've got a lab in your basement?" Bridget said, looking from the vials to Ian in wonder.

The coffee was ready. The pot bulged with the dark, aromatic liquid. Ian poured Bridget a steaming cup and then one for himself. He reached for the powdered cream next to the machine and she for the sugar.

"After thirty years of lab work I finally had enough money to get an electron microscope and some basic materials," Ian said, stirring his cup with a plastic spoon. "My favorite aunt left me money when she died. She was quite a bit younger than my mother, and I think she felt some degree of personal responsibility in providing a maternal figure in my life after my mother died at a rather young age. Aunt Margaret knew I wanted a personal lab for research, and left me money when she died to help me attain it."

"I see."

"It would have been impossible without her. The lab is not great, but it is adequate. I do my own research there on occasion. It turns out the blood samples taken from patients Morrison and Jeffers and Peale when they were first admitted to the hospital don't show the presence of protein matrix X after all. It *is* in the Woods' sample and two others, but is not something consistently present throughout all the recent leuk patients."

Bridget tapped her stir stick on the edge of her foam cup. "I don't understand — the analyzer showed the protein matrix in all the early samples of *all* the accelerated leuk patients."

"I ran these samples through once more and this time they didn't show it. Perhaps we were just tired the first time, I don't know. But like you said, we'll check them again."

"Sure," but even as Bridget said it she felt the wind leave her sails. She had thought they had really been on to some kind of pattern with the peculiar protein matrix. It could have led them to a way to attack the leuk at its earliest stages.

"We'll check out those samples once more and see if you agree," Ian said, moving to the next microscope on the counter and sitting on the tall wooden stool there.

During the next four and a half hours she had Ian do most of the footwork while she did the analysis. She had him prepare the test tubes and the slides while she scrutinized sample after sample and entered them into the computer. Together they went through all the samples of the accelerated leukemia patients.

Immersed in work, the hours passed quickly. Occasional glances at the clock told her that time was slipping away from her, and away from her patients. The accelerated leukemia in Josephine Woods and Hugh Croston grew stronger with each passing hour despite her treatments.

Bridget rubbed her eyes, tried to relieve the burn. Was unsuccessful.

Finally Bridget slumped on a stool before one of the computers and kneaded her forehead. Bar graphs and pie charts in rainbow colors appeared in each quadrant of the monitor.

"I just don't get it," she said to Ian. "Protein Matrix X appears in some but not all of the early samples, just like you said. I could have sworn it was present in *all* the early ones. Now why would I have thought that? Where did I go wrong?"

Ian returned the last sample to the refrigerator for storage. He shook his head regrettably. "I don't know. You were tired, I was tired, and we both missed the big picture. I'm sorry, I thought you had something there, as well."

She sighed. "I was just hoping the protein matrix was some previously undiscovered factor. I thought it might lead to a real understanding of this accelerated strain of BEING, or — and I know this is dreaming, but what-the-hell — maybe even lead to a cure." She rubbed her temples and stared at the microscope. "Nothing like reaching for the moon, huh?"

"You really care for your patients."

"Isn't that what a doctor is supposed to do?"

"Yes, but many don't. Not even most of them. It's one thing to evaluate a patient and work up a diagnosis and treatment plan, and another to actually get involved on a personal level. I knew a doctor like you once, years ago, but not many since." He looked away. "No, not many since."

Silence fell between them. Bridget wanted to press him on the subject but held back.

"I have to go now," he said, after a moment. "Have an early appointment, so I'm working a short shift tonight. The tired old bones trapped beneath this skin bag are crying out for bed. You ought to go home and get some real sleep yourself, young lady."

Had he lived, my father might have said something like that to me, she thought. *I wish I could have heard him say it just once.* "I look pretty rough, huh?"

"On the contrary, you are quite beautiful. Simply tired, that's all."

"Oh, you're just being nice. I should crash on the cot in the third floor doctor's lounge, but I've done that the last few nights straight. I probably should go home for a little while. I *need* to go home for a little while."

"Home would be good for you," Ian said.

"I could see my boyfriend for a few minutes before he heads out to teach his classes at NC State. I've got tomorrow off from my rounds, you know, but I'll probably come in anyway. Is that tomorrow or today? I get confused. How about you? Will you be here for the graveyard shift tomorrow?"

"No, I've got other business I must attend to. I recommend you take your day off. You've got to be close to falling prey to exhaustion."

"But my patients need —"

"You've worked hard for them. They are progressing through the treatment plans you worked up, aren't they?"

"Yes, but they're far from—"

"You need to get away from here, even if it's sitting home and reading a book while sipping a glass of wine. You need to do anything but think about this place—at least for twenty-four hours. You will come back rejuvenated."

"Maybe you're right. I'll see if Travis wants to see a movie at the Rialto. You can get beer and wine there, you know."

Ian smiled. "Old style theater with a huge stage. They have English beer on tap there. Makes for a good time even if the movie is bad. Enjoy yourself."

"Thanks, Ian. See you the day after tomorrow."

He walked out of the lab and the smile on her face faded after him. There was something she had wanted to ask him—something she had forgotten. Now what was it?

Think, Bridget commanded herself. *Think. It must not have been important or you wouldn't have forgotten, you airhead!*

Suddenly Bridget stood and ran for the door. Yanking on the handle, she flung the door open and ran a few steps into the dim hallway, ready to call out to Ian, wanting him to hang on a minute.

Ian wasn't there.

Bridget looked up and down the corridor, but didn't see Ian, nor did she hear any footsteps or latching doors oranything.

Moves fast for an older guy, Bridget thought. *Should at least see him down by the elevators there or going toward the laundry, but it's like he's vanished.*

She had meant to kid him about needing to get around at the lab a little more; the two evening shift lab workers hadn't even known he worked here. Oh, well, it would have to wait until after her day off.

She frowned. *Should I really take the day off?* she thought. *If I wasn't such a walking zombie I'd stay. I'll just work a little longer...*

TEN

R AYNORR FOLLOWED CLOSELY behind an orderly pushing a rumbling waste bin. When the orderly veered toward the nurse's station of Ward Two Raynorr kept to his original course, his gaze fixed straight ahead. As expected, the back of his head suddenly tingled. Would the nurses behind the large desk challenge him this time?

He doubted it.

They hadn't done so before, they had no reason to now.

The tingling sensation faded as the nurses silently accepted his presence and focused their attention elsewhere.

His grip on the objects in his lab coat pocket was firm but not too tight. His breathing was only slightly accelerated. Pulse was steady. He was keenly alert, but at the same time his shoulders and trapezius muscles were relaxed. No fear preyed upon his mind. No butterflies fluttered in his stomach.

He was beyond the nurses station now. He moved down a sub-corridor and followed it to a little-used stairwell. It ran up the rear of the patient tower like a spinal column, connecting to other hallways that connected to other pods, other wards.

Raynorr climbed to the third floor and silently entered the hallway that led to Ward Seven.

He saw no nurses. And at four-o'clock in the morning, no visitors either. Tucking the official-looking clipboard beneath his left arm, Raynorr pushed open the door to Room 315. The syringes and test tubes in the small vinyl kit he carried clinked softly as he pivoted to allow the door to shut behind him.

Now Raynorr filled his lungs with the intoxicating blend of vengeance and grim expectation. He seemed to float toward the curtain that harbored the object of his mission. He parted the curtain and slipped inside.

With the exception of the unconscious moaning of its tenant, Hugh Croston's hospital room was quiet. The overhead lights were off and the blinds over the broad windows were shut, but the mercury-yellow lights from the parking lot glowed eerily in the gaps between each narrow blind. A simple pitcher of water and a stack of paper cups were the only items on the oval table next to the bed. A print of Monet's *Purple Lilacs in Vase* hung on the wall above the table, and above the head of the bed Van Gogh's savagely colorful brushstrokes were captured in a print of *The Wheat Field*.

Doubtless Croston had given the masterpieces little more than a cursory glance, but that was understandable. Croston had to have a lot on his mind now that he was dying.

In the rails of the bed were two sets of buttons. They positioned the bed, worked the television, radio, and some of the lights. There was also the large red button with a stick-figured nurse ingrained upon it. Push that button and you could speak to the nurse through a small microphone and she could respond via the four-inch speaker on the opposite bed rail. Push that button, remain silent, and the nurse came running.

The head of Croston's bed angled slightly from the middle, partially raised, while its occupant lay asleep, curled in the fetal position.

Intravenous fluid dripped steadily from a clear plastic bag and into a milky-white plastic conduit. Below the conduit the fluid entered a programmable blue box that had a dozen buttons and an LCD readout that glowed bright green with numbers. The computer in the box measured, tracked, recorded and dispensed the IV fluid into the final stretch of plastic tubing that connected to the catheter stuck into Croston's arm.

Raynorr was not overly familiar with the computerized IV box. It had not been something he had used much in his days as a practicing physician. He had simply prescribed the dosages for his patients and let the nurses work the box. The one thing he knew for certain about the box was that a piercing alarm went off when the IV bag was empty, or when the tubing became blocked and the fluid backed up and couldn't enter the patient's body.

Of course, Raynorr had no desire for the alarm to go off.

Thanks to his unauthorized access into the hospital's computers, Raynorr had entered the Patient-Tracking System and gained the details of Croston's stay thus far, as well as his schedule of events for the future.

The nurses wouldn't check on Croston for another half hour, when the IV fluid was close to empty. The fluid in the bag was a morphine solution to help poor Croston sleep through his pain.

He would be in considerable pain without the morphine, Raynorr thought, a slow smile spreading over his face. *Considerable* pain.

He placed the clipboard and blood kit on the table, his gloved hands looking opaque and dull in the half light of the room. He dumped the tissues from Croston's trashcan into the bathroom trash and placed the empty can beneath the IV tube. Then he reached into his lab coat pocket and withdrew a large safety pin.

He unfastened the pin, exposing the sharp point. Between his thumb and forefinger he pinched a section of the plastic IV tube, below the blue monitoring box. Holding the tube firmly, he lanced it with the pin. The sharp point went through the tube and protruded from the far side of the tube.

Already fluid oozed from around the pin.

Raynorr made circles with the pin. The hole widened. More fluid oozed from around the pin, reflecting the light in slow-forming droplets that soon fell into the trashcan. Fat droplets formed and fell. Raynorr withdrew the pin and let go of the tube. Now the drops really came. They dripped into the can and hit the bottom in soft splats, one after the other, too fast for him to count.

Raynorr carefully re-fastened the pin into its protective sheath. Hospitals by definition were breeding grounds for viruses and bacteria. Wouldn't want to get pricked in a germ-laden place like this, would he? He was just arriving at the most critical phase of the war—he couldn't get bogged down with illness now.

He dropped the pin into his pocket and sat in one of the guest chairs.

He crossed his legs, propped his chin with his thumb and forefinger, and waited.

The precious fluid leaked out in a steady stream and fell into the trashcan. Like a garden fountain, he found the sound of it soothing.

He glanced at his watch and observed Croston.

The tremors had already set in.

Hugh Croston's body shook as if he were undergoing some low-level electric shock. His moans grew louder. The muscles in his neck flexed and released, as did those of his skinny forearms. His eyelids fluttered.

Looks like someone's having a nightmare, Raynorr thought. *Wait until he wakes up.*

After one hundred and forty seconds, Hugh Croston opened his eyes.

His moans ended with the rise of his eyelids. Drool started from the corners of his mouth, and his lips were stretched thin from days of grimacing. Beads of sweat clung to his forehead and dampened what Raynorr had first seen as a carefully coiffed head of blond hair while at the Foundation One Building. Croston stared straight down at the foot of the bed, his pupils almost completely dilated. He blinked rapidly and raised his head from the pillow.

Raynorr sat motionless. "Hello, Hot Shot."

Croston sat up clumsily, the dope still coursing through his veins slowing his mind and body.

"Who—who's there?" he said, his voice little more than a croak. His eyes became huge as he looked around.

His gaze passed over Raynorr without pause and continued on in their desperate search. "Who is it...nurse? Doctor Devereaux?"

"I am afraid that like Elvis, Doctor Bridget Devereaux has left the building," Raynorr said.

Slowly Croston focused on the source of the words. The confusion evident on his face was nearly childlike in its over dramatization, but it contained not a shred of a child's innocence. "Who are you? What are you doing here? I don't know you!"

"Of course you don't—you dismiss people once they've served your purposes. How arrogant of you. Quite a price on arrogance these days, isn't there?"

Raynorr uncrossed his legs and leaned forward on the chair. He glared at Croston and the unbridled malevolence in that glare made Croston blanche. "Tell me, Hot Shot, I've been curious for such a long time, why exactly do you think you're qualified to form a valid opinion on medical practices?"

"I—I don't know what you're talking about! Get away from me! Get out of my room! Where's the goddamned nurse?" His gaze zeroed in on the nurse's button located on the bed rail.

"I wouldn't do that."

Croston, fully awake now and visibly alarmed, looked wide-eyed at Raynorr.

Raynorr pointed to the IV tube that dripped into the trash can. "I rerouted your IV. I need your strict attention for this, you understand."

Croston craned his neck to see his precious Morphine drip out of the tube. "What are you going to do?"

Raynorr shrugged. "Hard to say. There are so many options." He reached slowly into his lab coat pocket and raised a shiny scalpel up to one of the beams of light that squeezed through a slit in the blinds. Balancing the blade expertly between his thumb and forefinger, he angled it so the light glinted off its keen edge and into Croston's eyes. "All I had planned to do is talk to you, but that will certainly change if you press that button, you understand. I'm sure you're aware that the nursing department is grossly understaffed due to corporate cut backs...you can never be sure how long it will take before one shows up. Tell me, have you ever pressed that button before?"

"Yes, and a nurse came to the room!"

"And how long did it take for the nurse to arrive?"

Raynorr watched as the young man swallowed and then blinked. Raynorr gave him a sliver of credit when Croston lifted his chin resolutely and tried to lie.

"A few seconds."

Raynorr waited, his eyes on his enemy. He waited as the sweat beads bonded together and streaked down the young man's face, visibly dampening the sheets. When finally Raynorr did speak, his words came out slowly, deliberately.

"Given the right circumstances, seconds can feel like hours."

In a blur Raynorr was on his feet. The scalpel blade creased the tender skin of Croston's throat, not enough to summon blood, but enough to let Croston realize just how truly vulnerable he was. Croston gasped and froze. His eyes bugged out and he stared straight ahead.

Raynorr leaned down and whispered in Croston's ear. "How long do you think it would take me to ventilate your throat, stroll past the nurses station to the parking lot, then drive away? Think it would take very long to do that, Hugh, my man?"

Croston's chin trembled, his eyes filled with tears that spilled out and slid down the slick surface of his sweating face. "P-p-please no! You said…you said you just wanted to talk!"

"I know, but now I think I've changed my mind. You see, Hot Shot, you're dying. Salvation just is not in the cards for you. If they would have run more tests on you then maybe, just maybe, they would have figured out that there was a virus inside you causing your own body to unleash leukemia upon itself. But you know first-hand how insurance companies don't want to cover a lot of *unnecessary* tests, now don't you, Hot Shot?"

Croston moaned.

"Better watch those body shakes, Hugh," Raynorr warned. "They might just cause the blade to sink in, which…may not be a bad thing. This blade could save you a lot of discomfort. It could relieve the pain you're in now that the morphine isn't making it into your body. This could be a merciful way for you to check out, you understand. Care to go for it?"

"No! *Please, no!*"

"You don't think you're going to survive, do you?"

Croston's eyes squeezed shut. *"Please…"*

"Now I wonder when you last employed that word."

"God!"

"Or *that* one? Fool. God abandoned this world long ago. How else did our health care system fall into the hands of fools like you, Hot Shot? I mean, it just *has* to be the work of the devil!" Raynorr laughed.

Croston squeezed his eyes shut and moaned. The tremors grew, causing him to shake violently on the bed. Sweat and tears came fast now.

"Hard to concentrate with this thing on your throat, I know," Raynorr said. With a flick of his wrist he withdrew the blade. He returned to the chair, this time sitting on the edge of it. Resting the blade on the arm of the chair so Croston's wide eyes could see it, he produced a plastic bag with a length of IV tubing from inside his pocket. He opened the bag and removed the tube.

"Pain?"

Croston, his entire body shaking from what had to be an exquisite mix of fear and pain, nodded his head several times.

Raynorr considered the bulging arteries in Croston's neck. *It would be extremely gratifying to draw the blade over those snakes. Just let the bastard bleed out.*

Croston moaned.

His body tensed so hard he could have been carved from rock.

Raynorr shook his head. *The blade was not the way to do it,* he thought. *Croston wouldn't suffer near enough to make up for what his kind has done to me and countless others like me.*

Raynorr held up the punctured section of tube. "Well, let's see what we can do here."

Raynorr pulled the tube completely from the valve at the base of the computerized box. The clear liquid dripped directly into the trashcan and the alarm did not go off. Raynorr quickly slid the new tube he'd brought with him onto the valve, unhooked the old tube from the catheter in Croston's arm and let it drop. He stood and scrutinized the entire length of the new tube while the fluid dripped out.

"Hook it up! Please...the pain! I can't take it!"

"Wouldn't want to introduce any air bubbles into your veins, Hot Shot," Raynorr explained, as the fluid traveled through the tube like thick water through a hose. "Pass an air bubble or two into the heart and it'd be over just as quickly as if my scalpel had sliced your carotid artery. And to be honest, I'd rather not have the nurses see you flat-line any earlier than necessary."

He hooked the IV tube into Croston's catheter.

Croston immediately let out a sigh.

"Oh, come on. It doesn't work that quickly," Raynorr said, with a sardonic smile. "Amazing what the mind will do for relief, though. Just amazing."

"Who are you?" Croston mumbled.

"Just a drug-induced dream of yours. In another minute or two you'll be fast asleep, but before you go back to la-la land, I want you to tell me who's holding the cards in your organization."

"What?"

"Tell me who the other players are in Foundation Health Net. Who else has the authority to approve those idiotic policies you send up the chain of command with such gusto."

"Why—why do you want to know?"

"Let's just say I'd like to guess who else might come down with a case of sudden leukemia."

Croston stared blankly at him for a long time before speaking. "I don't understand."

The younger man sank back onto his pillow. *Funny how he was calmer now that the scalpel had been removed from his throat and the drugs had started to kick in,* Raynorr thought.

"Maybe they'll wake up now," Raynorr said patiently, sitting back in the chair and slowly stroking his chin. "Don't you think it's odd that business people—people like yourself—are setting healthcare guidelines and policies when they don't have a shred of medical training?"

"But we don't need medical training! We use statistics to develop new policies. We have reports and analysts and cost-benefit—"

"Feel good about that now, do you? Statistics? Using statistics is the difference between performing surgery and watching it on The Learning Channel. Your policies are far too rigid. They cannot begin to cover the individual differences that are prevalent in a diverse human population."

"But that's what's most, most..." Croston blinked his eyes slowly, swallowed, then paused for a moment. "...cost-effective."

Raynorr glared at him. "You're the standard deviation for men in their early thirties, Hot Shot. Oh what a feeling, huh babe?"

Croston sobbed and turned his head away.

Raynorr turned and slid the scalpel into his pocket.

Croston squeezed his eyes closed as if he wanted to shut out Raynorr, shut out his cancer, shut out the entire world. Tears still flowed from beneath his eyelids, soaking the neckline of the patient gown he wore. He moaned. *"God help me!"*

"Weren't you listening? It's too late for that. Now, the players?"

"I can only remember one."

Raynorr sighed. "Give it to me."

"Oberlin. Jerry Oberlin."

"Department?"

"Sales...and Marketing."

"Vice-president, senior manager, or what?"

"V.P."

This Jerry Oberlin wasn't on Mike the Water-Boy's delivery route. Raynorr would have to get to him some other way.

"Powerful?" Raynorr asked.

"He has...the final say in the policy and pricing structure. He's been the lead candidate for the CEO ever since Margaret Morrison died." He looked over at Raynorr in fearful realization. "Wait— did you...?" he asked. His horrified look finished the question.

"Your situation is remarkably similar to Margaret Morrison's, wouldn't you say?"

"You killed her, and now you're killing me..." He trailed off, too weak to infuse any power into his words.

"Now you've got a grip on things, Hot Shot! Before you pass out from the rush of drugs back into your system, tell me more about this Jerry Oberlin. Is he a stay-at-home man or an out-on-the-towner?"

"Likes to be seen."

"Wife? Kids?"

"Yes."

"Girlfriend, too?"

Tears flowed from Croston's eyes. "Yes."

"What establishments does he frequent?"

Croston's head dropped to his chest.

Raynorr leaped up and grabbed Croston's chin. "You're going to tell me, you corporate puke! Where does Oberlin hang out?"

Croston's eyes widened and immediately began to sink once more. He mumbled something that sounded like *Anderson's*. Anderson's was a swank jazz house in downtown Raleigh.

"Andersons?"

"He-he'll be there Thursday night. We were supposed to be celebrating…all the new promotions. I was supposed to be there," he barely whispered.

"Really? Well, I wouldn't make any plans, Junior." Raynorr winked. "And thanks. Maybe you've learned something here tonight…maybe not."

He let go of Croston's chin.

Croston fell back on the bed as if the life had already drained from his body. His head sank into the pillow. The tears continued to leak from his beneath his eyelids though he was now totally unconscious.

Raynorr reached over the side rail and pressed the button to lower the bed to a horizontal position. He dumped the fluid from the trashcan into the toilet and flushed. With some paper towels he cleaned the stray drops of fluid from the floor, then he picked up his clipboard and kit and walked out of the room, leaving Croston to meet his well-deserved fate.

ELEVEN

SUDDEN, IRRITATING BEEPS knifed their way into Bridget's ears. The sound of the pager going off filled the silent lab. She hit a button to quiet it and then unclamped it from her waistband. She pressed another button and the LCD readout lit up.

1005.

It wasn't the nurse's station, the source of ninety-nine percent of her pages. The nurses were the ones who alerted her about status changes in her patients when she wasn't actually out on the floor of Ward Seven. This was a number she was not acquainted with. It was the extension of a phone number from the first floor.

The administrative floor.

She glanced at the clock. Eight o'clock in the morning. God. She'd worked the entire night in the lab and now her bones felt as if they'd been filled with lead. She *had* to get home and get some real sleep after this page was taken care of.

She found a phone list tacked to a cork board on one of the walls. Didn't have to read further than the first line on the list. She read the name across from extension 1005 and suddenly had to swallow.

Handlaw. Gerard Handlaw.

The Chief Executive Officer was paging her to his office number first thing in the morning.

She picked up a phone and punched his number. He picked up on the first ring.

"This is Handlaw."

His voice was deep, his words measured and unhurried. He spoke like a man who wanted you to know he had power. His greeting almost demanded she state her business right then and there.

She cleared the second lump in her throat. "This is Bridget Devereaux. Did you...did you page me?"

"Yes, Miss Devereaux. I see by the extension on my phone readout that you are down in the hematology lab. I'd like for you to catch the elevator up and stop by this morning."

"Now?"

"That would be perfect."

"I'll be there in a few moments."

The line went dead.

She held the receiver for a moment and then slowly put it down.

He had called her *Miss* Devereaux—not *Doctor* Devereaux. She wasn't hung up on titles, but administration *was*, and normally they used them when they spoke to you.

Oh, shit.

The warnings from Nurse Watkins suddenly echoed in her ears while unwanted images swooped down upon her. She pictured Gerard Handlaw telling her to gather her things and leave the hospital. Gerard Handlaw telling her she had bucked the system and now she was going to pay for it. Get ready, little girl, 'cause your lifelong dream of becoming a doctor has just been slam-dunked into the toilet.

Her stomach twisted into a knot as she walked to the elevator. Surely they wouldn't do anything more than give her a warning.

She'd worked so hard to become a doctor. She *had* to become a doctor.

Had to.

Should be there by now.

The signs in the upper corners of the hallways probably held the information she needed, but was the Chief Executive Office located in Hospital Affairs, or Strategic Business, or Public Relations?

This is pathetic, Bridget thought. *Mr. Handlaw wants to see me in his office and I can't figure out where the damned place is!*

Hovering close to the wall as visitors and staff darted by like an endless school of fish in a stream, Bridget grasped the sleeve of a passing volunteer.

"I'm sorry sir—the CEO's office? I can't find the CEO's office. Can you help me?"

The elderly man peered at her as if she were an escapee from the psych ward. "Left back there at the junction, young lady. You can find Mr. Handlaw's office in the Strategic Business wing."

She was already moving. "Thank you!" she called to the volunteer over her shoulder.

Come on, come on, she thought. *What's the worst that can happen? Will the world end? No. Will your lifelong dream get flushed? Don't answer that. All I'm trying to do is treat my patients. If he's got a problem with my methods then I don't belong here anyway. Dream or no dream, I can't just do what's normal and customary while my patients suffer and die around me.*

Just as the volunteer had said, the Executive Office was located in the Strategic Business Wing. Corporate lingo. It certainly hadn't been intuitively obvious where the office was, especially after working straight through the last twenty-four hours.

The door opened into a thickly-carpeted waiting area that had a lot of mirrors and leather-studded chairs along the walls. To the left a woman was standing in front of a large desk as if she had been waiting all morning for Bridget to arrive.

Bridget briefly wondered why she hadn't seen the woman on the cover of *Cosmo*. Perfect blond hair, perfect figure, perfect makeup, and boobs big enough to distract the most stalwart of men. At one time Bridget would have walked over hot coals to have boobs that size.

Who am I kidding? she thought. *I'd walk over hot coals now for boobs that size if that's all it took to get a pair.*

Bridget walked toward the office manager, trying not to glance self-consciously down at her own scrubs and lab coat and sneakers as she did so. *Probably a lot of plastic involved*, she thought. *Wouldn't stay too long in the sun, lady.*

What's Handlaw going to do to me?

Bridget tried to smile but the muscles of her face and lips threatened to tremble. Not wanting to look like a frightened schoolgirl having to see the principal for misbehaving, Bridget skipped the smile.

"I'm Bridget Devereaux," she said. *I come in peace*, she nearly added, catching herself just as her tongue positioned itself to utter the first syllable. She almost giggled.

"Mr. Handlaw is expecting you," Ms. Perfect Plastic Goddess said, not bothering to introduce herself. "He said to show you in right away. Shall we?"

She smiled at Bridget in a practiced sort of way and gestured gracefully toward the double doors at the opposite end of the room. Gold bracelets jingled and the rings on her fingers glinted.

They walked toward an arched doorway. The closed double doors were of darkly stained wood that had been polished to such a high degree that they reflected light. On the doors were two large brass handles. Bridget kept her hands in her lab coat pockets. As they walked, Bridget in sneakers and Ms. Perfect Plastic Goddess in her high heels, Bridget glanced out of the corners of her eyes at the woman's sizeable bosom.

Sure enough, no noticeable bounce.

Bridget felt a shadow of a smile cross her lips. Ms. Perfect Plastic had indeed paid in money or favors for the right to the title. Ms. Perfect Plastic knocked once on the door and pushed it open. She stepped to the side and gestured for Bridget to enter.

There he was, sitting behind a massive desk stained so dark it appeared almost black. *Noire, as Mama would have said.*

"Doctor Devereaux is here, Mr. Handlaw."

As large as the desk was, it did not overwhelm the man in the pressed white shirt and red tie sitting behind it. Bridget gathered he was a tall man, six feet something or another. He looked to be in his early fifties, and was probably only slightly overweight—it was hard to tell with him sitting behind the desk. He was clean-shaven and wore gold-rimmed glasses and he had dark, fuller brush hair that revealed no hint of turning gray. Without looking up from the documents he was examining, Gerard Handlaw pointed a thick finger at one of the leather guest chairs that looked as if it might get crushed by the massive desk at any moment.

"Sit down, Miss Devereaux. That's all, Vivienne."

Bridget swallowed hard and did as directed. She crossed her legs and tried to relax enough to smooth the frown ridge between her eyes but didn't quite make it.

Now that she was closer to him, she could see on his shirtsleeve cuffs were brass cufflinks shaped into the letters GH. As far as Chambers Hospital was concerned, this was *The Man*. He called the shots, and right now Bridget had the anxious feeling he was about to call *her* shot. To distract herself, she took in her surroundings.

Mistake!

Hundreds of volumes of handsomely bound medical journals and classic novels and business books were displayed in heavy oak bookshelves that stretched from floor to the ceiling. The man was not only well versed in the subject matter of his profession, he also appeared to be a scholar of sorts, someone who could probably quote passages from *Plato's Republic* and Shakespeare's *Taming of the Shrew* in the same breath.

He's either a master at bullshitting, or he's an intellectual giant, or some dangerous composite of both, she thought. *Get tough, Devereaux. You've got as much right to the air on this planet as this man does. Get tough!*

When she looked back from the daunting bookshelves she found he had set his fountain pen down and was scrutinizing her from behind his glasses.

Bridget swallowed.

"I consider myself a frank person, Miss Devereaux. I don't like to mince words when there are issues to be resolved. The fact of the matter is that I have a meeting in twenty-six minutes—a very important meeting. Important for me, my administration, the board of trustees, and every employee of this hospital, as well as the patients who seek this hospital out."

She noted the order in which he listed everyone.

He paused to stare directly at her for a few seconds, a move that was as obvious in its power-play intent as it was effective. Bridget forced herself to remain still and not squirm in the chair.

"Okay," she said, raising her eyebrows expectantly. Her tone was not petulant or subservient, yielding or confrontational. It was a noncommittal, a wait-and-see tone. What might be an ever-so-slight smile touched a corner of his mouth. So, that smile said, she wasn't going to fall to pieces right away, but Handlaw held all the cards and they both knew it. The smile vanished.

"Several representatives from Allied Health Care will be in my next meeting. Have you ever heard of them?"

"The representatives?"

He blinked. "Allied Health."

"Yes, I've heard of them. They're very...large."

"They're also *very interested* in our hospital."

Bridget waited, not wanting to look too much like a dunce by asking him exactly it meant for Allied to be *very interested* in the hospital.

"Doubtless you are aware of this because it is of public record, but I'll say it anyway just to make sure we're on the same page together. I have been given the green light, shall we say, from the Board of Trustees to convert this establishment from a nonprofit status to one that is privately owned and operated. With no binding obligations to serve the community, we will soon be free to operate in a manner that fully maximizes revenue. In this way everyone will benefit."

Everyone, huh? What about the patients without adequate healthcare? The ones we are currently obligated to treat regardless if they can pay out of pocket or not? These people will be turned away even if they are bleeding to death in that water fountain outside your window, Mr. Handlaw.

He waited for her response. When she offered only silence, he continued in a cool, deliberate manner. "As a for-profit organization, we can charge for services at a level more consistent with the true market rate, not just what insurance A, B, or C or Medicaid dictates. We'll be able to afford better doctors, better equipment, perform higher levels of research, etcetera."

He leaned forward. "Allied Health has emerged as a formidable power in the health care industry of the entire nation, Miss Devereaux. They are very interested in our joining their network and will soon place a bid on our hospital. Provided the terms and conditions are acceptable to all parties, we will probably accept their bid. But as an astute woman you were aware of all this, weren't you?"

"I heard the rumors. I didn't want to believe them."

"The Board has already passed a measure to grow the hospital into a for-profit organization by a ratio of nine to three. The three votes of dissension were from idealistic individuals, people of narrow vision who could not be persuaded, despite my best lobbying efforts." The skin around Handlaw's eyes tightened as he said it.

He swiveled his chair a few degrees to his right so he could look through the large windows and observe the large stone fountain at the hospital's main entrance. Bridget followed his gaze. Between the crepe myrtle trees she could see nine spouts of water describe nine graceful arcs toward the center of the fountain. The nine spouts shot over the water's surface like liquid artillery and merged with a single jet of water that spouted six feet before succumbing to earth's gravity and falling upon itself.

"How do you like the internship program here at Chambers Hospital, Miss Devereaux?" Handlaw asked, still gazing out the window.

Bridget's mind flashed a warning. "I like it. It's tough and challenging, the way it should be."

"Doctor Hensley, your chief resident, has informed me of the considerable number of tests you've ordered for some of your patients—tests that he himself did not approve and tests that do not specifically fall under the guidelines of their insurance coverage. Is this true?"

Bridget felt her face flush hotly. *Thanks a lot, Blake, you asshole.* She stared at Handlaw's profile as he continued to observe the outside fountain. "Yes, I ordered a lot of tests for my leukemia patients, but I did it for very good reasons. They have an abnormal strain of leukemia, one that is accelerated in both its onset and its life cycle. It's so fast that it's scary. So far no one has lived through it. I thought it was a good idea to find out as much as possible about both my patients and the disease and the only way to do that was to—"

Handlaw suddenly turned and skewered her with a penetrating gaze. "—to order a slew of expensive tests that your own chief resident considers nonessential? Who do you think you *are*, Devereaux? Jonas Salk in search of penicillin?"

She shifted in the chair. "But I need to find out more about this disease. It's not like normal leukemia. It kills so—"

"We are not in the business of having interns perform our research for us! You are in your first year as an intern, Devereaux. You don't have the necessary training to perform research on your patients. It's not sound, it's not cost-effective, and it could put this hospital at great risk if it ever got out that one of our interns had the balls to do her own research at hospital expense and reached a bunch of false conclusions about an already established disease. You should be aware of your proper position as"—he paused and looked away for a split second as though he was about to say something insulting and just barely caught himself in time—"as a freshman intern," he finished.

Her hands gripped the arms of the chair until her knuckles glowed white through the skin. *You mean my proper position as a female freshman intern, don't you?* she wanted to demand. Instead, she said, "Yes, sir."

He stared at her and said nothing.

Bridget felt the blood pump across her temples.

"But Mr. Handlaw, my research and tests are *vital*. Doctors Jenkins and Rathspell, who are also interns, have ordered similar tests for their lung disease patients. I don't see where there's any—"

"Jenkins and Rathspell had their resident's approval on the matter *before* ordering the tests."

"My patients were dying! They're dying now!"

"Nevertheless, Jenkins and Rathspell followed proper procedures and gained approval whereas you did not, Miss Devereaux." Handlaw's eyes might have been two pieces of granite stuck in his skull.

She was on the edge of the chair before she realized it. "My patients are dying from an undocumented strain of leukemia. Standard leukemia takes weeks or months or years to kill and my patients are dying from it in *days*. If I thought it would help save them, or better understand the disease, then I'd have their kitchen sinks tested!"

Handlaw didn't move. Her outpouring of emotion had about as much effect on him as a gnat singing the blues atop an elephant's ass.

Slowly he raised his eyebrows, wrinkling his forehead. "Doctor Hensley also tells me that you think we may have some kind of epidemic on our hands."

"I don't know if we have an epidemic or not," Bridget said, "but I do know that this strain of AML comes out of nowhere and explodes inside our patients who were perfectly healthy only days earlier. It's like there's a virus or something out there that's —"

Bridget cut herself off and stared.

A virus…!

"Devereaux, there is absolutely no scientific evidence of leukemia being passed from individual to individual as a virus," Handlaw told her. "If there was such a thing it would have been identified by now."

But what if it was caused by a virus? she thought, her mind suddenly alive with new possibilities. The unidentified protein matrix might not be a by-product of the AML so much as it might be something left over by a *virus* that had triggered the AML.

"I read in a medical journal that oncogenes—genes that are important during early growth but then lie dormant after childhood—might unlock cancer in the body if acted upon by a stimulus," Bridget said, more to herself than Handlaw. "That stimulus could come from radiation or chemicals like nicotine or even a *virus*. For the first time we may actually be seeing a virus trigger—"

"Enough of this! Pay strict adherence to our established policies and procedures, Devereaux," Handlaw said. "We do *not* need bad press at this hospital while we're undergoing negotiations with Allied Health."

She shook her head. "Bad press...? Don't hospitals receive recognition for identifying new strains of—"

"Is it so difficult to understand? If we found ourselves battling something we couldn't identify and couldn't cure, you can imagine the image that would project of our medical competence. Which is why we don't want to draw attention to any seemingly aberrant cases at the moment, especially without thorough, dedicated, research to prove such a diagnosis—all of which requires staff and expensive equipment. Are you hearing me?"

She looked up, not certain she'd really heard what he'd just said. "Wh-what?"

"Not clear enough for you? Very well...I will not allow an intern at this hospital to create waves with the residents and staff, and possibly the outside community, that might adversely affect this buy out."

"But-but what about my patients—?"

"Do you understand the meaning of the word expulsion, *Miss* Devereaux?"

His words gathered menacingly around her.

Bridget nodded. "Yes, sir."

Handlaw sat back in his leather-studded chair and observed her coolly. The mention of getting expelled was enough to cower any intern and he damned well knew it.

The next minute, Bridget was on her feet. "Tell me, Mr. Handlaw, what do you gain from the Allied deal?"

He blinked. "That's not your concern."

"A hundred-thousand in bonus and profit sharing? Two hundred thousand? Three, four, five?"

"You're out of line, Devereaux!"

"A million? Will you be getting a million dollars, Mr. Handlaw? Hard to care about the welfare of anyone when there's a million dollars at stake, isn't it?"

His face darkened. He leaped to his feet and leaned over his massive desk toward her. He looked like he'd rip her to shreds if that desk wasn't blocking his way. An angry vein rose like a snake down the center of his red forehead.

"Now you listen to me, you little cunt. I don't know who you think you are but to me you're *nothing!* Do you have any idea how many interns I've seen come and go through this place? You're one of thousands! Out of those thousands there were maybe twenty who tried to cut against the grain. And do you know what? Those twenty were all *women*. They weren't up to our standards and I threw their asses out on the street. Now they're maids and whores and waitresses and real estate agents instead of doctors. Do you *really* think I'm going to let some female intern buck *my* system and give me a bunch of lip?"

Bridget backed toward the door. Handlaw may as well have swung his beefy hand and slapped her across the face. "That's— that's inappropriate and you know it!"

"Why should you be any different from the others, Devereaux? You have no money. Your family has no money. Hell, you don't even have a family. You're *nothing!* You've scraped through by the skin on your teeth but that's not nearly enough to get you through this program, honey."

"You *bastard*—"

"You watch that sweet ass of yours, Devereaux. I can make you gone in the blink of an eye. And I can make sure no other hospital in this country will touch you with a ten foot pole. Now you get the hell out of my office. I've got to schmooze these Allied Health morons in this meeting, and I don't want you around."

Bridget's trembling hand fumbled with the door latch. Finally she got it open. She flung the door wide so hard that it banged into the wall and she ran out into the waiting room, unable to choke back the tears.

Ms. Plastic rose from her desk. "Is something wrong?"

Bridget didn't bother answering. She burst into the outside hallway and ran for the nearest exit.

TWELVE

A SCARLET ORB SMOLDERED behind the tall pines at the fringes of the hospital parking lot. Bridget waited for the thin line of trees to ignite like giant matchsticks and spew purple-black columns into the thankless morning sky.

"Do it," she commanded the orb, "and take me while you're at it."

But the sun didn't ignite the trees. It was huge and eternal and answered only to itself. It had lorded over this small planet for *eons*; the genesis and extinction of countless species had taken place beneath its omniscient stare—why would it care to relieve the troubles of one insignificant intern?

It would provide yet another sweltering day in the heart of North Carolina...and nothing more.

Staring at the angry orb looming over her path, Bridget struggled to keep the emotional maelstrom inside her from wrecking her composure any more than it already had. She wandered up one row of parking spaces and down another, always keeping her face turned toward her fiery companion.

Red sky in morning, sailor take warning. I've been warned, all right.

Engines approached around her, idled and then shut off. Car doors slammed shut and more cars rolled into the vast lot. Shoes clopped on the blacktop. Here and there a voice sounded.

Bridget walked on.

I could lose everything I've worked so hard for.

Concentrate on the sun, she told herself.

It was so massive, so red. Surely its vast surface was covered in oceans of blood. The sight of it was anything but tranquil, but the explosions and swirling chaos that were its true nature appeared to be held in a state of precarious check.

I need to be like the sun. I need to remain calm on the outside.

But the pressure that had built inside her while in Gerard Handlaw's office now pressed at the walls of her being. It leaked out through tiny fissures in her body like water through the hairline cracks in an old clay pot.

Don't give up. Don't.Don't.Don't.Don't!

Bridget couldn't breathe. Her lungs seemed to spasm and hitch. A wheezing rasp escaped her constricted throat.

Damn this...! The edges of her sight rippled and glistened. The parked cars she passed became irritatingly vague. She could see clearly only when she looked straight ahead, and even then only for a few seconds at a time before more tears came. Swiping at her eyes, she urged her wooden legs on until she was almost marching across the asphalt.

Keep moving! Bridget ordered herself.

Slowly her breathing found a natural rhythm. The shimmering edges of her sight became clearer. The tear ducts had closed, or at least narrowed. At least she could wipe the damned tears away now. The tunnel vision she had experienced slowly opened like those holes in the old Hollywood movies that would widen until finally the entire screen was filled with an image. For the first time Bridget understood exactly where she was.

She was in the main hospital parking lot, the one mandated for visitor use only. It was acres of blacktop dotted at precise intervals with tall metal light posts and islands of trees and shrubs. Right now it was choked with hundreds of cars and vans and pickups.

She took a deep breath, and then another. The thick summer air clung to her brachial passages, but she gratefully inhaled it...anything to taste real air and not the stifling mix inside the hospital.

Funny, Bridget couldn't remember the last time she'd actually been outside for longer than it took to walk to her car. Surely it couldn't have been that long ago—

Blackballed. You've been blackballed. Handlaw's going to throw you out on your ass if you don't play by the rules.

But hadn't she taken time out from the hospital for a run in the heat only yesterday? Or had that been the day before? It was yesterday *and* the day before. Instead of lunch she'd gone for a run. The temperature had been in the nineties and the overhead sun had tried to punish her as she ran. She'd been grimly satisfied as sweat had flowed from every pore in her body, drenching her spandex shorts and half-top and making her skin glisten. The shower had felt so refreshing afterward.

Flushed. Your career'll get flushed before it even gets off the ground, honey.

Bridget needed to work out for at least a half hour on even the busiest days. The on-site health center was a treasure. She could do aerobics or lift weights there. But yesterday she had gone for a run outdoors and showered at the health center and had left her sweaty clothes inside her car.

Her car...!

That's why she was out here. Now, where had she parked?

Flushed.

On your ass.

Blackballed.

Bridget shivered.

She turned from the sun and hurried to the employee parking deck. She felt inside her hip pocket and pulled out her keys. Where was her purse?

Oh yeah, she had left it in the gym bag in the car. Normally she would have brought it into the hospital with her but she had figured her period was another week away and she didn't need the tampons just yet. Her wallet was in the purse, which wasn't the smartest thing to do. There had been a few break-ins despite the security cameras that were all over the place, but even if a thief did get her purse, he or she wouldn't come away with much of anything. A single credit card with a modest credit limit, and ten or fifteen dollars. Other than that, she carried in the purse nothing of any real monetary value. One look at her car and a thief would know that. Where had she parked the bucket of bolts, anyway?

Gerard Handlaw.

The car.

...sexist bastard!

Where's that stupid car?

Scream, part of her said. *Stop distracting yourself and scream.*

No.

Go on, you know you want to.

I won't!

Oh, come on. You want to scream until your lungs bleed—just open up and it'll come. It's already right there inside your throat. You'll feel better, I guarantee.

I won't give him that.

He's not here. He won't know.

I'll know.

And your point is...?

He might flush me down the toilet but I'm not going to give up. I don't care that he's the CEO of this hospital. He's an uncaring asshole if he doesn't want to acknowledge what's really going on with my patients. I won't allow a man like that to get to me.

Nice, but did you forget you've cried already?

That was before I recovered, a little.

You call this being recovered? You're a mess and you know it. The psyche ward would be calling for the straightjacket right now if you walked in on them, missy.

I said "a little", now SHUT UP!

To her surprise, the other voice retreated to some dark corner of her subconscious. From there it waited with peering eyes for another opportunity to pounce—and there would be another opportunity, she was certain of it.

With her mind a trifle less cluttered, she soon found the Corolla. All she had to do was look for a rusted body with a discernable downward slope toward the driver's side. A four-door sedan, the car was twelve years old and splotched so badly with rust that it looked like it had some kind of automotive infection. Where there was actually a stretch of real metal, the discerning eye might be able to tell the paint had once been red. Of course the red had been sun-baked away so badly that it now might be classified as a shade of pink heretofore unknown in the modern world.

It had taken four years of waiting tables as an undergrad to pay for it, but now it was Bridget's outright, complete with rust spots and tilted body, one hundred forty-eight thousand mile speedometer, bad shocks, and the blue exhaust cloud that shot out like a genie from the exhaust pipe when she first cranked it up.

Bridget got in and turned on the ignition. The car shuddered as the engine started. The pistons fired well enough to keep it going after the initial bout of obligatory sputtering.

Ready to back out of the space, Bridget looked over her shoulder, raised her left foot to engage the clutch and pressed down on the gas pedal with her right. The car had a tendency to stall out unless she gave it a good dose of gas when starting off, so she pressed the accelerator down a bit farther.

The car sprang forward. Bridget gasped and slammed her foot on the brake. The bumper lurched to a stop only inches from the cement wall of the parking deck. She could count the tiny pockmarks in it. The car sputtered and stalled out. It coughed a few times and remained still.

She grasped the wheel and fought the urge to break down.

Easy, girl, Bridget told herself. *You're rattled and tired right now. Just take it easy. Now push the clutch in and turn the key...*

This time she succeeded in backing out of the spot. The car lanced through the blue cloud behind her.

I'll call Travis first and then Francine, she thought. *Surely Travis'll put aside his own worries long enough to understand what this means to me. In fact, he might still be at my place from last night. It's before nine and his first class isn't until ten thirty.*

She sped along the gently winding roads of the hospital driveway. On the surrounding manicured grounds, jets of water shot out from pop-up sprinkler heads in diagonal patterns that crisscrossed one another and sparkled in the morning sun. Many of the male residents and staff doctors not-so-jokingly spoke of fashioning a putting green out here. Never mind that patients would be watching with envy from the windows of their rooms as they either recovered or slipped closer to death.

Bridget shoved the brake pedal to the floor. The car lurched to a halt. She stared at the road ahead.

What will happen to my patients if Handlaw throws me out? They'll get standard treatments, standard tests, standard attention. None of the other docs will understand or care like I do. My patients might die despite my best, but at least I know what they're going through, and I'll fight for them.

A car horn blared behind her. She jumped, straining the seatbelt. Turning to look over her shoulder, she saw a dark-blue BMW sedan at the stop sign to her left. The driver had his arm out the window and was giving her a hurry-the-hell-up rotating motion. It dawned on her that she was blocking the intersection. She shifted into first and squealed her tires as she bolted through to the other side.

I need to learn more about this accelerated leukemia, but if I don't get some rest I'm not going to be of any use to anyone. I'm scheduled off today. I need to take it. Hopefully Blake Hensely hasn't yet countered any of the treatments or tests I ordered in my patient's files. Hopefully.

Her rising panic retreated to a neutral corner and waited for another chance to come out swinging.

Travis will help me through this, she was sure of it.

She drove the twenty-minute ride to the North Carolina State University campus in a little under fourteen minutes. As the landscape sped by, she kept thinking about how wonderful it was going to be to feel Travis' arms around her, shielding her from the rest of the world while she melted into his chest.

She took the right off Hillsborough Street and onto Gormon, just blocks from the N.C. State University campus. She'd moved there from Chapel Hill after she'd graduated from UNC medical school to be closer to Travis. His own apartment was on campus, but he spent just as much, if not more, time at her place, using the key she had given him after nine months of exclusive dating. Her apartments were garden style, three-story buildings that held twelve apartments to each building. The buildings were a bit older than most in the area—bordering on thirty years old— which was why she could afford one. The style was a bit rustic, but she had no problem with that. A casual eye would never know they were that old just by looking at them, since the maintenance and upkeep were first-rate.

There were well-trimmed hedges near the apartment buildings. A cluster of sizeable Bradford Pear trees stood in front of each building. In springtime the trees fairly exploded with bleach-white blossoms for about two weeks, after which the petals fell like snow to the ground. Thick green grass covered the areas around the trees and buildings, bordered by concrete sidewalks. Lining the sidewalks were rows of yellow and purple winged pansies.

After bouncing over two speed bumps, Bridget arrived at her building.

Relief came when she spotted Travis' Mustang GT. Her tires chirped when she parked alongside. The engine was still sputtering as she dashed up the sidewalk toward the stairs. She wished Travis was looking out the window or on the balcony. He'd see the hurt on her face and come charging down the stairs toward her, his arms open wide and his face reflecting her pain without even knowing what had caused it.

She took the stairs two at a time. She pushed off like the runner she was, propelling her body up and using the rail for extra pull. The first floor landing came and went. She took the turn to the left, up the next flight, another turn to the left, another flight, and then she was on the second floor landing.

Come on, come on, she thought, breathing deeper now.

A neighbor slipped a key into her lock and turned her head at Bridget's sudden arrival. "Good morning."

"Hi," Bridget said, unable to think of the woman's name though they had often exchanged greetings with one another. She crossed the landing in three long strides and was gone up the stairs.

A turn to the left and she dashed up the next flight.

She was moments away from feeling Travis' arms around her. The third floor!

She didn't bother fishing her keys out of her pocket. Travis normally left the door unlocked in the mornings after getting the newspaper. He had insisted they split the cost of the subscription even though she knew she would rarely have the time to read the paper.

The 303 on her door was a beacon. It drew her in, ever closer, to the comfort that awaited inside her apartment in her boyfriend's arms.

The paper was still on the welcome mat. Normally Travis would be sipping his second cup of coffee and scrutinizing the editorials by now. Bridget left the paper where it was and reached for the doorknob.

It didn't turn.

Well, if he slept late and hadn't gotten the paper, then of course the door would be locked.

Her hand dove into her pocket and retrieved her keys. She stared at them as they quivered in her trembling hand. Which one was her apartment door key?

Funny how stress can make you forget everyday things. She finally remembered and thumbed to the correct key.

Bridget put the key in and turned the knob. She wanted to burst inside and blurt out what had happened to her in Handlaw's office but at the same time she didn't want to startle Travis.

She shouldered the door open and hurried inside.

It was dim. The shades were drawn in both the living room and kitchen. The rising sun lit the edges of the windows where the shades didn't quite meet up to the window frames, causing an eerie crimson glow to permeate the entire apartment.

The door to the bedroom was partially open, but not enough for her to see inside. She couldn't tell if Travis was still lying on the bed or if he was in the bathroom taking his morning shower.

She inhaled to call his name, then suddenly held her breath.

Something wasn't right.

Something was different.

Her heart started drumming away within her chest. She exhaled slowly, without calling his name.

There was the distinct residual smell of cigarette smoke in the apartment, which wasn't right because she insisted Travis go outside to fire up his Chesterfield's. Granted she'd been away for what amounted to the better part of three days and maybe he'd taken liberty with her hard-and-fast rule, but there was something else in the air, some underlying scent that hovered just below the sharp stench of the cigarette smoke.

She moved tentatively toward the bedroom door as she glanced about. Her gaze passed over the worn but useable couch, the scratched coffee table, the new television that had been a Christmas gift from Francine last year. It stuck out because it looked too new for the place but she wasn't about to complain. Nothing unusual there.

Bridget looked to the kitchen. The small white kitchen table was clean, but there were a few of his dishes in the sink. Surprisingly enough, Travis had cooked something, and the dishes were the remnants of the meals he hadn't bothered to clean up. No surprise there. She had told him often enough that she wasn't his mother but she usually ended up cleaning his mess after he bowed out with one excuse or another.

She veered into the kitchen, her eyes narrowing. The cigarette odor was stronger here, as was that underlying scent. She glanced to the counter top nook between the refrigerator and the entrance wall. There, hidden from the access way leading to the bedroom, was a ring of five brown beer bottles surrounding a thin, gold-colored ashtray of tin or aluminum with at least eight crushed cigarette butts in it.

Spent cigarettes and stale beer didn't cause that underlying odor, though, and she couldn't dismiss the uneasy feeling that began to knot her stomach.

She turned and was about to exit the kitchen when she suddenly froze.

Wait a minute.

She zeroed in on the ashtray.

Several of the filters were dark where Travis' lips had contacted the cigarette. Not burned, but dark—when they should have been white.

Bridget's heart thudded like a wild thing within her breast.

These dark smudges looked a lot like—

She flicked on the light, leaned over the counter and picked up one of the dark filters.

Lipstick.

Oh, God.

She stared at the stain.

…whose?

Does it matter?

Now wait. Travis has friends who smoke, and some of them happen to be women. It could be that he had a few friends over—

She suddenly realized that underlying odor was not stale beer, it was hair spray. Hair spray and perfume.

She charged the bedroom door. She shoved the door wide and flicked on the lights. The door banged loudly off the rubber stopper on the wall and came back to strike her shoulder and fly away once more. She barely felt it.

"What the hell…?" Bridget heard Travis utter.

Light flooded the bedroom. It left no shadows. There were clothes strewn about at the foot of the bed. Blue jeans. His jeans, and another pair. A brand for women. A brand Bridget didn't wear. Near the jeans were other clothes. A large tee shirt, white briefs, a bra and panties.

There were two forms beneath the sheets and now two heads shot up from two separate pillows.

Bridget's throat felt like it constricted to the size of a straw. Every muscle in her body tensed. She wanted to scream but her throat wouldn't let her.

The two of them bolted upright, exposing their naked torsos. The woman had a tangled rat's nest for hair. She blinked and squinted and raised a hand to shield her eyes from the penetrating glare of the overhead light. The bimbo didn't even bother to cover her boobs. "What's goin' on?"

"Bridge?" Travis said, leaning forward and blinking. "Shit, Bridge, hold on a minute. I—"

"Cheating *BASTARD!*"

"This doesn't mean anything, Bridge. It was just one of those things."

The bimbo shrugged her bare shoulders as if this was a normal, everyday occurrence. "Hey girl, you weren't around—"

"*SHUT YOUR FUCKING MOUTH!*" Bridget jabbed her index finger at the bimbo while her other hand balled into a fist.

119

The bimbo's eyes went wide. Her mouth opened as if to issue some face-saving retort but then she took another look at Bridget's livid face and her ready-to-spring stance and remained quiet.

"Get out! Both of you—get your clothes and get the hell out my apartment!" Bridget bent, grabbed the pile at the foot of the bed and flung it at them in a heap. *"OUT!"*

"But Bridge…hang on a sec. You're taking this all wrong. It wasn't anything I meant to do!"

"Get out, Travis!" She spat out his name as if it were poison. She noticed his keys on the dresser. She went over and yanked her apartment key from his chain. She flung the others at him. They hit him on the chest and bounced into his lap.

"Ow!"

"You're lucky I don't do worse than that. *Now move it!"*

They got out at the far side of the bed and started pulling their clothes on.

"Told you we should have gone to your place like last time," the bimbo said to Travis, as she knelt and grabbed her sandals.

Bridget's eyes grew wider. *"GET THE FUCK OUT!"*

"Let us get our goddamned clothes on," Travis mumbled.

Her iron was perched on the ironing board next to the far wall. Bridget leaped, grabbed it and held it high before their amazed faces. *"OUTSIDE!* You try to put those clothes on in here and I swear to *God* I'll smash your fucking heads with this iron—I SWEAR TO GOD I WILL!" She leaped onto the bed with the iron in her hand and jumped down on their side. With her free hand she shoved the naked duo toward the door.

"You're crazy!" the bimbo cried, as she and Travis the Betrayer, Travis the Cheater, Travis *the Fucking bastard. Fucking low life scum how could he do this to me?* moved quickly through the doorway.

"GET OUT!"

"But what about my things?" Travis asked, daring to look over his shoulder at Bridget.

"MOVE!" Bridget was a heartbeat away from swinging the iron.

Bimbo and Travis ran for the door. Without hesitation they stepped out onto the third floor landing. They tried to shield their privates with their clothes held tightly against their bodies. Bridget followed closely on their heels. At the stairwell they stopped.

"I'm not going out in public without my clothes on!" the bimbo said, dropping her clothes and picking up her panties.

"Keep going!"

"Goddamn it, Bridge, isn't this good enough?"

"Now that you're out of my life, I want you out of my building!"

Three of five doors to the other apartments were already open, and the other two doors opened at the new sounds of altercation. The tenants, all men and women in their twenties and thirties, most of them students, stood and stared and didn't say a word.

"Pick up your clothes and move!" Bridget told the bimbo.

Bridget forced them all the way down the stairwell. She halted on the final stair of the ground floor. They were now out in the parking lot, bending to get their underwear on and then their jeans. Every tenant in the building was out and watching. Some of them murmured, some gave verbal support to Bridget with *Go girl!* and *That's it, kick him out of here!*, some laughed outright.

The bimbo was now crying, evidently not enjoying the public humiliation. Though his face blazed red, Travis was completely silent. He shot a look at Bridget, who hadn't been able to keep the tears from her own flaming face.

"If I ever see you around here, you'll be wearing this iron in your skull," Bridget said between clenched teeth.

"Bridge—"

"My name is *Bridget!*"

He looked as if he'd been slapped. For the first time she saw a hint of remorse on his face, as if he'd only just now understood who she was and what they could have had together.

"I'm sorry," he said.

She turned and walked up the stairs, dragging the cord to the iron behind her. She ignored the searching looks from the other tenants. After reaching the third floor landing once more, she went into her apartment and softly closed the door behind her. She went to the bedroom and pulled open the glass door leading out to the balcony. Then she pulled out the single drawer she had allowed him to use for his clothes. She scooped the disorderly collection of his tee shirts and shorts and jeans into her arms, went out to the balcony, and threw them over the rail.

Travis and the bimbo, now fully dressed, just watched, the bimbo with her mouth wide open, as the clothes fell with a *whomp!* onto the hood of Travis' Mustang.

Laughter and exclamations followed from the other tenants. Bridget walked back inside and slid the glass door shut behind her.

Fresh tears started from Bridget's already raw, puffy eyes. She ripped the sheets from the bed, stripping it and the pillows bare. Disgusted, she returned to the balcony and, as with the clothes a moment earlier, hurled sheets and pillowcases over the side. This time she didn't watch as they fell to the earth. Instead she went back inside to the hall closet and took out another set of sheets. She succeeded in throwing the bottom sheet upon the bed before suddenly halting in mid-motion. She stood there for a long time listening to the silence of the apartment around her.

First Handlaw and now this, Bridget thought. *How wonderful things are going.*

Her shoulders hitched as she sobbed. From the depths of her soul a cry escaped her, a cry that was both pathetic and frightening at the same time.

She wrapped the sheet around her body and shuffled to the living room. There, she fell onto the couch and curled into the fetal position, then cried harder than she had ever cried before... except for the afternoon when she'd come home from school to find Christine, who seemed too young to call *Mother,* dead on the living room floor.

THIRTEEN

RAYNORR AWOKE WITHOUT truly waking. His head listed to the side and his eyes remained shut. The rocking chair in which he sat in the shade of his front porch was motionless. At some base level of cognition he registered the warm puffs of a hot breeze upon his bare legs, arms and face, as well as the hard press of the wooden rocker against his lower back and buttocks. He was aware of these things but he did not actively consider them, nor did he actively consider anything else.

For some time he remained thus, a point of sentience suspended inside the unmoving shell that was his body. Later he would reflect upon this odd state of being and surmise that perhaps death included such a state, a state where consciousness is present without the added elements of active thought. Or perhaps this state was more indicative of pre-life, or of existence within the womb itself.

Ever so gradually, white luminescent threads of thought wormed their way into the vast emptiness of his mind. Instinctively, he recognized the threads, and did not welcome their presence. They squirmed and twitched and crawled about, grotesquely intermingling in a thousand different directions at once. They were all that comprised the essence of human life. Experiences, emotion, raw intelligence, logic and illogic, needs, wants, and ultimately, self-awareness—all of it now converged in a wild orgy, carried upon the backs of these writhing threads and sewed into the black canvas that was his soul.

Years ago the threads had laced together gracefully, as if weaving a silken tapestry. Now they moved like a horde of maggots on a deer carcass.

They engulfed his sentience and formed what he now actively recognized as a composite of his life.

It was no longer a young life. The fringes were decayed. Spider veins ran through it. It was pale and shriveled.

Does this life have worth?

He wondered.

The answer hid from him inside the emptiness of his existence. He searched desperately for it, but the answer continued to elude him.

His terror mounted. He felt his soul cracking beneath the strain. In a final attempt he searched another darkened alcove of his mind, and there he found his answer. He seized it with all the fervor of a drowning man clutching at a lifeline.

The war is my life now! Faces flashed in his mind. His children, his wife, his many patients and colleagues with whom he had once been close. There was no warmth in their gazes. They stared at him as if he were some loathsome creature beneath their contempt. As one they turned their backs to him and faded away.

I remember, Raynorr thought.

He grimaced. A familiar ache lanced where his heart used to be.

He remembered Rwanda. And the country that had been Zaire when he'd first arrived and was now ridiculously called the *Democratic* Republic of Congo. He remembered crossing the Congo River so many times he lost count after his first two years there. He remembered Zambia and malaria-ravaged Tanzania. The squalid conditions, sweltering heat, and endless miles of sick and dying refugees. Mind-numbing slaughter of thousands. Pulling infants from the shriveled breasts of their dead mothers. Confusion and pain in the older children's huge eyes. Children— mere walking skeletons who regurgitated even the tiniest rations of mashed rice that he gave them.

He had worked around the clock treating refugees in crowded tent hospitals, dispensing food and medicine and trekking miles on foot to administer Red Cross immunizations to villagers.

The perpetual struggle for food. The murders that had taken place over bowls of rancid rice. He remembered thinking that surely someone or something would hold accountable those who were responsible for the cruelty he witnessed. For a long time he'd waited…and nothing had changed.

Man did not stop the cruelty.

Nor did man's governments.

Nor did man's gods.

I hold them all accountable, he'd thought back then, as he sewed the skin over the stump of a leg of a thirteen-year-old girl whose only crime had been living in a hut within a half-mile of a firefight.

He made the girl as comfortable as he could with his paltry supplies, then he retrieved from his pack the Tutsi blade given to him as a gift by a grateful soldier whose son he'd saved. He pressed his thumb to the blade and a thick drop of red appeared.*I cannot combat an army, but I can target the murderers and thieves who prey upon these refugees.*

And the Tutsi blade held the criminals *accountable.*

One by one their numbers dwindled. Some were found in the bush with their throats slashed. Some were never found at all.

Word spread about Raynorr—over time creating legends about Ray-Nor, the medicine man who could heal with one hand and kill with the other.

Eight murderers brandishing blades had once surrounded him in the middle of a refugee camp. He had cursed them and raised the Tutsi blade to defend himself despite their numbers. He had been prepared to fight and die when suddenly the murderers were set upon by scores of men and women and children who, in the span of minutes, turned the murderers into vulture pickings. He wept openly as they chanted and celebrated around him and his hospital huts until the moon was high in the night sky.

He used a field microscope to identify the ancestor of the Raynorr Virus in the blood samples taken from ill Hutu and Tutsi villagers.

I will use this virus to create a lethal strain.

And I will hold accountable those who have desecrated American healthcare.

Raynorr's eyes now gradually focused on the weather beaten floorboards of his front porch in Wake Forest, North Carolina.

I could return to Africa. I have many friends there and would be welcomed at any airport. Even the soldiers would welcome me, grateful that I helped someone in their families or villages. I wouldn't even need to purchase tickets—they would be delivered the day after my call. All I have to do is give the word and I can disappear from American soil for good.

He watched a dragonfly alight on the edge of the porch floor and slowly work its four white-dotted wings up and down.

But I cannot leave, yet. My work here is far from complete.

He raised his head. The upper support of the rocker creaked as he raised his arms overhead and thrust his legs out and stretched. His joints popped and snapped but that didn't bother him; there was no real pain associated with the sounds. As he stretched, he filled every brachial tube in his lungs with the hot summer air, held it for a ten count, and then exhaled it with an audible whoosh. The stretch completed, he rubbed his forehead in circular patterns.

Wednesday. Hump day. And his chosen day to rest and rejuvenate.

He squinted against the glare hovering just outside the shade afforded by the mighty oaks that surrounded his small house. Beyond the oaks, at the edge of the overgrown field that began on the west side of the house, rose a sea of oak and beech and pine trees in full summer flourish. They marked the beginning of a deep forest that ran for miles to the west and north. Many of the trees on the border with the overgrown field were covered in long kudzu vines, the wide green leaves of which masked the true shape of the trees and made them appear as misshapen monsters.

These vine-covered trees on the perimeter of the forest and the oaks around his small house harbored hundreds of cicadas, who now gave rise to their sporadic chi-chi-chi-chittering. In seconds others picked up on the sound and joined in. Their noise marked the heat of the day as well as any thermometer. Of course, they chittered at night, too, but it was a telltale sign that the day was hot when the cicada chittered.

He flicked a finger across his nose to swipe at the beads of sweat that had formed there. He looked at the worn floorboards of the porch, noting with disinterest how the blue paint had long since faded to gray and had given way to bare wood in many areas.

Cain and Abel lay panting softly beside him, their red tongues jabbing beyond their white fangs. By late spring the dogs had shed their heavy winter coats but the black and tan fur that remained was little comfort in the summer time, even in the shade of his front porch.

Raynorr began to rock in the chair, the steady creaks adding to the cicada's chitter and the whispery breeze.

What are the real threats to the war? That young corporate man with the unusual streak of integrity? Ted Samuels didn't let on, but he may have seen me enter Croston's office. Doctor Bridget Devereaux? She's sharp, but too trusting. She hasn't even considered the possibility that I sabotaged her patients' blood samples.

John McLaughlin of the McLaughlin Group political talk show materialized in the empty chair next to Raynorr, his eyes wide and owlish. He barked in his abrupt Yankee style, "Next issue! Will Doctor Andrew Raynorr's sniper missions come to a close this week? I ask you, Doctor Raynorr."

"Absolutely, John," he said, rocking back and forth on the porch. "After Jerry Oberlin is brought down, the sniper missions will no longer be necessary. Soon I will send my demands out to the insurance cartel. The insurance companies will recognize my ability to destabilize them with the Raynorr Virus and they will be compelled to make policy changes in both patient care and physician relations."

McLaughlin raised his chin. "That the sniper missions will come to a close is the *correct* answer!" He crossed his legs and leaned closer to Raynorr. "But Andrew, do you *really* think these insurance criminals will agree to your demands? Are they intelligent enough to heed your warnings? Will they even care?"

"They will when their own lives, and the lives of their families, are at stake, John," Raynorr said.

"But these are large conglomerations that have purposefully sucked themselves dry of all humanity, Doctor. They will not listen!"

"Perhaps not."

"Prediction, Doctor?"

"Should they be foolish enough to ignore me, I've got something far bigger in mind that will force them to comply."

"How much bigger?"

"An order of magnitude, John. An order of magnitude."

"Interesting, Doctor!" McLaughlin turned to the oak trees in the front yard. "Tune in next time to find out the results of Doctor Raynorr's war on the insurance companies. Bye-bye!"

Around Raynorr the cicada chorus rose to a full, pounding crescendo.

Pressure built inside him. It had to be let out. Cain and Abel looked up as he leaped from the old wooden rocker. He caught the center porch post in the crook of his arm, leaned out over the edge, threw back his head and laughed.

Raynorr's laughter gradually quieted to a throaty chuckle. He wiped the sweat from his forehead and stared at the browning weeds in the field beyond the trees.

Strange how you can get lost in the chaotic uniformity of it all.

Chaotic uniformity. Now that's interesting. Yes...interesting.

At some point—he couldn't tell exactly when—he turned and opened the screen door. It moaned in protest. Then he turned the knob of the old wooden door and shoved hard to disengage it from the frame. The dingy, yellowed curtains over the three upper glass panes in the door flew upward from the sudden push. He held both doors open and looked down at his German Shepherds.

"Come."

Both dogs immediately gained their feet. With a clatter of paw nails the dogs were through the door and into the much cooler environment inside the house. When it became apparent that the master was not heading for the kitchen where a snack might be had, both went to lay near the air ducts, through which cool air was flowing into the sparsely furnished living room.

Raynorr padded through the living room and down the small hallway toward the locked basement door. He shivered. It wasn't that it was chilly in the house—he kept the thermostat around eighty—it was just so much hotter outdoors where he'd napped for the better part of an hour.

At least ninety in the shade today. Maybe ninety-five. Good thing I had that central air put in, and that dehumidifier down in the basement lab.

From his front shorts pocket he fished out his keys and unlocked the deadbolt he'd installed on the basement door. He took the first step down and flicked on the light, closing the door behind him but not locking it, confident the dogs would warn him far in advance of any unexpected visitors.

His hand gliding down on the smooth rail, he walked down the twelve stairs, glancing at the drab gray cement wall on his left as he descended. The stairs squeaked beneath him, each a slightly different pitch from the other. To his right was the open air of the basement, cool and dry. As he descended, he inhaled the sharp, lingering odor of bleach, a given for a sterile environment.

He hadn't bothered to wall-in the stairwell. He didn't have guests. No one would be peeking down in the basement.

At the base of the stairs the concrete floor was cool beneath his bare feet. He flicked on two more switches and the entire room was bathed in white light. There was no visible dust or dirt or hair on the floor; he was meticulous about keeping his laboratory clean. He didn't want skewed results from bacteria or dust mites that a simple cleaning possibly could have prevented.

He saw no reason to finish the basement. The sparse interior suited his needs quite adequately. The gray concrete slabs of the house foundation were the only walls down here. Overhead, the vents and air tubes for the central air were exposed. Rows of fluorescent lights hung from chains nailed to the flooring joists. Two long wooden lab tables commanded the center of the room, stretching nearly from one wall to the other. Like the cabinets and shelves along the walls, he had made the tables with his own hands, using basic lumber and nails and polyurethane coating purchased from the local hardware store in Wake Forest. The furnishings were neither polished nor ornate, but they were sturdy and straight and met his needs quite adequately.

Atop the long tables, two labyrinthine structures silently greeted him. To Raynorr they were works of art. At first glance chaotic, they consisted of hundreds of feet of interwoven plastic tubing, connected here and there to beakers and heating elements and containment bays held aloft on flat metal stands.

He approached his creations reverently, letting his eyes travel along the familiar networks of tubing that he supposed the uninitiated would consider almost maddening.

The smaller of the two glass and plastic constructions, the one on the table nearest the stairwell, was his original configuration. In it he developed successive generations of the original, milder virus that had come directly from Africa.

He opened the large refrigerator at the far side of the basement. Industrial-sized, the refrigerator housed hundreds of closed petri dishes in small cardboard boxes. The petri dishes on the right-hand side held animal tissue and the self-replicating, non-lethal virus he'd brought from Africa.

The petri dishes on the left held the completely lethal but non-replicating strain he called the Raynorr Virus.

He raised an eyebrow in sudden contemplation.

Perhaps I should call my creation the Raynorr Catalyst. It would be more accurate since the lethal strain doesn't replicate itself—I have to spawn it from the non-lethal virus each time.

He frowned. Raynorr Catalyst would be more accurate, but at the moment altogether irrelevant.

He closed the refrigerator and went to his supply cabinet. He'd succumbed to the non-lethal strain himself while in Africa, and had been cot-laden for five days and weakened for twelve. The virus attacked the body through the respiratory system to induce fever, headache, body aches and fits of deep coughing. But that wasn't the worst of it. The virus caused the body to drastically shut down its production of red blood cells, a condition known as anemia. The body continued on this course even after the virus itself had been dispatched by common antibiotics from the body. It was the onset of anemia that had first attracted his serious attention to the unknown African virus. After studying it closely with crude field equipment, he saw the potential in it. Returning to America, it had taken three years of constant experimentation to spawn the Raynorr Virus.

The fact that the Raynorr Virus couldn't reproduce itself meant it was an evolutionary dead end. It was an interesting phenomenon, but he didn't have time to fully pursue it. In his spare time he worked to create a reproductive strain, but as yet had been unsuccessful. For now, it more than suited his purposes as a kind of viral bullet, infiltrating the host body at incredible speed, forcing into action the dormant oncogenes of healthy cells that immediately began producing wildly accelerated leukemia.

And the leukemia, once unleashed, *was* incredibly adept at replication. It attacked the ripe blood-producing cells of the body and reproduced itself in a mad rush within these cells. This was repeated millions of times each hour—a fantastic rate—bringing the host to Death's door in just days.

Raynorr reached in his supply cabinet and held up a large syringe.

The Raynorr Virus might not be able to replicate itself, he thought, *but it doesn't take much of it to kill. It is extremely resistant. Even chlorine, the Grim Reaper of most viruses, has little effect on it. It can survive in treated drinking water long enough to be drawn through the taps and consumed.*

He studied the syringe.

I could pack enough of the virus into one of these horse-sized tubes to kill hundreds, he thought. Quadruple the dose and as many as a thousand random sacrifices could be taken from the general population.

He lowered the large syringe and checked the date displayed on his watch. Thursday was only twenty-four hours away. From what Croston had said, Thursday night Jerry Oberlin would be attending the company event...a night out on the town.

Out on the town, and therefore vulnerable.

Raynorr put the large syringe back in the cabinet.

Soon, he thought.

He climbed the stairs and locked the door behind him.

Raynorr went into the bedroom and changed into loose-fitting shorts, white socks, and a red headband. He removed a colorful handkerchief from a neat stack that occupied the left corner of the sock drawer, then went to the closet for his running shoes. The bed squeaked as he sat on the edge and put the socks and shoes on. He stretched his hamstrings and calves, gave the dogs a couple of quick pats, and held the door open for them. He stepped out on the porch and penetrated the wall of summer heat.

The dogs followed at his heels as he jogged along the crude driveway—two dirt trails that led toward the road. The grass was high between the trails. Beyond the pocket of oaks around his house were four square miles of abandoned tobacco field, now overgrown with waist-high wild grasses, poke weed, and blooming goldenrod. Intermittently a handful of ancient beech trees loomed. He could imagine the tobacco pickers resting beneath those trees in an attempt to cool themselves in the shade.

Now, an increasing number of young pine, maple and oak trees rose above the grasses and weeds. In a few years the trees would grow and the old tobacco field would thicken into a forest.

As he jogged, the ever-present cicada sang around him while plump green and brown grasshoppers jumped and flew for short distances away from him.

After the quarter-mile of his dirt driveway, he reached the gravel and dirt road that was State Road 1202. Here he commanded the dogs to stay.

He didn't have to repeat himself. Their tongues were already hanging out and they were panting from the heat. Raynorr felt large beads of sweat form on the skin of his mostly bald head. Another couple of minutes and the sweat would run in rivulets down to the sweatband.

The dogs went to lie in the shade of an oak tree that stood fifty feet from the end of the driveway. They watched him as he jogged onto the glaring slash that was SR 1202.

He was only a few minutes into the run when a pickup sped down the road toward him, raising a cloud of dust behind it. It was one of those full-sized jobs, with an extended cab and a sharp blue metallic finish.

The driver was blond, perhaps in her early forties. She sported a black cowgirl hat and a sleeveless denim shirt. And a full figure.

She slowed and smiled as she passed. Before he realized what he was doing he raised his hand and gave a short wave, sweat flying in drops from his forearm.She waved back and sped away. The rising plume of dust following the pickup grew smaller and smaller as he turned and watched. Her license plate was one of those personalized ones that help fund the highway wildflower program and cost ten dollars more than a standard plate.

RU4REAL?

Raynorr had no idea what her name was, but he'd seen her at the Piggly Wiggly supermarket once with two teenage boys at her side. They had joked with her and called her *Momma* and she had given them playful slaps on their butts when they'd asked her to buy them some beer. She had made eye contact with Raynorr and he had said hello. She'd returned his greeting with a smile and that had been the extent of the exchange.

Now, seeing her again on this dusty road, he remembered how attracted he'd been to her. The quick intelligence in her flashing eyes brought forth a longing in him.

He wondered where this country woman with the blond hair and the bold manner lived. It had to be fairly close.

He sped up, his breath coming harder.

There's no time for flirting! I must remain focused on the war.

Still, he couldn't deny the longing he felt.

The last time he'd actually had more than just sex with a woman had been in Africa. She had been a traveling doctor like himself. She'd been killed when soldiers massacred a village in the Congo.

He was in gear, now. He was sweating profusely and liked it. He was a well-oiled machine. Without slowing, he wiped the sweat from his eyes with the handkerchief. His steady breathing and the crunch of his footfalls on the gravel and dirt road were the only sounds. He was a being in motion in an otherwise static environment.

The sun beat down on his head and shoulders, and though it was taxing him he enjoyed the feeling. It reminded him of running on the border of the Sahara Desert, which he had done on two separate occasions during his years in Africa. He had given the desert respect by only running a short mile out and then returning to the camp. He'd done it in the early hours of the morning, but even then the heat had been oppressive. He had done well, though, maintaining a steady pace and remaining poised throughout the runs. At first the tribe's people had looked upon him as if he'd been crazy. But if he wanted to run naked in the desert that was fine with them, as long as they could send one of their own along with him for safety.

Now he ran along State Route 1202 and passed long stretches of barbed wire fencing, the wire red-brown from years of rust. The fence posts were mostly dried and splintered, but now and again some were claimed by honeysuckle and jasmine vines, and appeared to have had put down roots and turned once more into trees. Cattle grazed in fields fenced in by the barbed wire. He passed old shacks of warped wood and tin roofs, long ago abandoned and now in various stages of decay. Some leaned at extreme angles, like carnival fun houses. These had the look of imminent danger, as if they would blow down in the next storm, though they had stood this way for the three years he'd lived here. In the back woods he spied a few trailers and houses, but he encountered no one.

The blonde in the pickup drove by again in the opposite direction. Another smile. Another wave.

Something about her…Maybe just the way she looked.

At the twenty-minute mark he planted his front foot, pivoted, and jogged back in the direction he'd come. His shorts were soaked with sweat and when he swung his arms several drops flew off him to land in the dusty road. Feeling good, he pushed it and made it back to his driveway trail in seventeen minutes. Cain and Abel rose from beneath the shade of the tree at his arrival.

On a whim he told them to stay and, instead of turning into his driveway, he continued to jog down SR1202 for another two minutes. He gazed at both sides of the road, passed a growing number of houses he had seen only a few times while scouting the area around him. After four minutes he was about to turn around when he noticed a small subdivision that sprang up from old farmland. It was odd to see paved roads stemming from the dirt and gravel of SR1202, but there they were.

He turned into Meadow View Acres and onto the sun-softened blacktop. He could feel the heat rise up through the rubber of his shoes. The houses were modest and new, spaced perhaps an acre apart, with long straight driveways leading into single car garages. The lots were sodded and young trees were secured by lines attached to stakes in the ground.

Construction continued on the houses at the far ends of the roads. At the finished homes a few people washed their cars and a few children dared the heat and rode bicycles down the long driveways. Some waved to him as if he were a resident here. He waved back and followed the semicircular main road to the far end, electing not to pursue the three other roads that met with this one. At the last house before SR1202 he glanced into the shaded garage and stared.

There it was—metallic blue pickup, license plate RU4REAL?

So this was where she lived. There was a small hatchback parked in the driveway slip. It had a number of rock band stickers on the bumper and clear ones on the window of the hatch. One of her boys probably drove it.

He felt a sharp tug on his stomach as he looked at the modest house. At the grocery store he had noticed no rings on her fingers although that didn't always mean a woman wasn't married. Surely a woman with her looks had a man already, but maybe not.

Maybe he should talk to her.

What? There's no time for this. You've had your peek, now go home, old man.

Near the entrance of his driveway Cain and Abel were waiting. They wagged their tails and circled him and whined as he slowed and then walked the quarter mile back to the house.

Sweat flooded from his every pore. Abel tried to lick the salty stuff from Raynorr's wrist but he put an end to it with a quick, "No, boy."

With his dogs at his side, he went to the coiled green hose attached to the outside faucet and picked up the end. The dogs bolted and watched him from a distance, visibly dreading the idea of possibly getting a bath, though they would hurl themselves into a scum-choked creek without hesitation. He cranked the faucet open and let the warm water stream out for a minute. He was after the cool stuff.

The water splashed onto a brown patch of weeds, the likes of which comprised his yard. When the water turned cool, he drank deeply. Then he held the hose up high and let the water flow down on his head and shoulders. He shivered. He completed the outdoor shower and drank some more, the water filling his stomach.

Raynorr needed to drink a lot of water, now, as he cooled down. He didn't want to be taking repeated bathroom breaks at the restaurant tonight while targeting Jerry Oberlin, the last of the individual assassinations before he sent out his demands.

FOURTEEN

$\int$ OMETHING TICKED AWAY in Bridget's mind. Something big.

I don't want to know about it, Bridget thought, cringing.

A safer alternative was to study the poster that hung on the living room wall. The image leaped out at her. It was only a cheap reprint of the real thing, but the manic color and bold brushstrokes of *Starry Night* held her gaze as if she were caught in the same desperate fervor Vincent van Gogh must have felt while creating the original, more than a century earlier.

Lying motionless on the couch, she stared at the print while the ticking in her head grew more insistent.

Bridget pondered van Gogh. The troubled painter had created over a thousand works of unsettling beauty. Toward the end of his life he'd battled increasingly violent bouts of insanity, and was institutionalized twice, once voluntarily and once involuntarily. A few months after his second release, he sought relief in the form of a loaded gun. On July 29, 1890, two and a half days after firing a bullet into his chest, at the height of the summer when his beloved sunflowers were in full blaze and his skills as a painter were at their most refined, van Gogh died. He was thirty-seven and had been painting only ten years. The quintessential struggling artist, van Gogh sold only one painting during his lifetime. Now his works were world-renown and sold for millions.

What terrible irony, Bridget thought, as the ticking in her head grew louder, and then louder still.

She winced.

Then, as if severed by a swinging scythe, the ticking stopped.

Bridget squirmed on the couch, convinced that both the poster and Vincent van Gogh were soon going to be rendered totally inconsequential.

Unfortunately, she was right.

Within her, reality silently detonated. The blast leveled her paltry avoidance defenses. Shrapnel tore through her brain, leaving only strips of gray matter behind. More of it blasted outward from her torso, shredding her insides and leaving them hanging in tatters.

Bridget groaned. She grasped her head with one arm and wrapped the other arm around her mid section and squeezed with all her strength.

*I don't want to know about this…*She pulled her legs up into the fetal position.

But here it is anyhow, sister. Travis cheated on you. Handlaw sexually harassed you and threatened to throw you out of the intern program. Nobody but you and your patients are taking this accelerated strain of leukemia seriously, and while you know what it's about, you don't know how to fight it. And Jo—the little girl who reminds you so much of you at her age—is slipping further and further away. Now isn't life just grand, honey? A glorious bowl of cherries, wouldn't you say?

Bridget squeezed her eyes shut and felt the double burn there. She'd cried so much. She bit her lip as two more searing drops oozed like lava between her eyelids.

She opened her eyes and blinked rapidly.

Do something!

She didn't move.

Come on, do something!

Do what? she thought.

Run. Don't think…just run!

With a wild swing she hurled the sheet from her body and was off the couch before it settled. She hurried to the bedroom. The pants she had slept in dropped to the carpeted floor, followed by her shirt and bra. Hunting in the dresser, she snatched a sports bra, half-shirt, shorts and socks and yanked them all on. She tugged on the strings of her running shoes, doubled knotted them so there was no chance she would have to break strides and retie them.

She grabbed the yellow sports radio from the kitchen counter, wrapped the Velcro band around her upper arm, and cursed like a sailor when the band didn't cling the first time. She got it nice and tight and snaked the earphone wire beneath her half-shirt to cut down on the swing. She thumbed the radio on and immediately her favorite rock station sent Nirvana's "Lithium" pounding into her ears.

Bridget glanced at the stove clock…2:30. She'd gotten home around nine-thirty or ten. She'd slept about four hours.

Seems to be my limit these days.

She slammed the door shut, locked it with the key that hung from her wristband, then raced down the three flights of stairs and hit the glaring white sidewalks at a pace just shy of all out.

Her legs felt weak at first, but soon they stretched into long strides, keeping in rhythm with her steady breathing. Hedges and parked cars baking in the sun blurred in her peripheral vision.

A few people heard her coming and moved out of her way. She passed them as if they were road signs.

Run, and keep running, she thought, lungs dealing easily with the steamy air.

Run!

The sun beat down on her head but that meant nothing. Sweat flew from her pumping arms. The music in her ears pounded with a driving beat, spurring her faster and faster, up steep hills without slowing and down the other sides so fast she could barely get one foot to land before the other hit. Long straightaways vanished before she knew it, as did steady inclines. Apartment buildings fell back and gave way to forest.

Farther and farther she ran, down Gorman Street until it passed over the 440 Beltline. Still she ran, barely noticing the cars and trucks on the highway below. Now there were wider patches of forest separated by housing subdivision entrances. The sidewalks disappeared and she leaped the curb and ran on the hot asphalt at the side of the road. The heat from the soft blacktop rose through the souls of her shoes and into her feet. On she went, not caring about anything but running for her life.

The miles swept by beneath her feet.

She had no idea how long she had been at it when her breathing changed from heavily labored to outright burning. Her shoulders slumped forward. Again and again she had to wipe at her eyes to keep the stinging sweat away from them. Fire licked into her brachial passages with each breath and her body slowed despite her frantic urging to keep going. By sheer force of will she kept going, but she realized the end was near. She was a runner, but not a marathon runner.

A hill rose to her right, breaking the steadily wooded landscape with a rising tide of tall golden grasses and flowering weeds. She turned from the road and ran up the hill, her breath coming in rapid gasps now. Her legs protested at having to travel up the sudden rise. Her quad muscles quivered and threatened to go out on her if she foolishly persisted in running. She slowed to a fast walk, still pumping her arms though her shoulders began to ache horribly.

Go, go, go! To the top—right to the top!

Grasses bent before her and here and there thorns of almost invisible briars sliced into her shins and calves, drawing thin, precise lines of red blood.

The pain was sharp and immediate but not, she thought, altogether unwelcome.

Gaining the top of the rise, she slowed and turned off her radio, pulling the tabs from her ears and the small receiver from her arm. She held them in the palm of her hand as she walked in a circle, letting her breath and heart rate slow.

There was a clearing here, along with four simple benches that she could not see from below. There was also a paved asphalt trail leading up one side of the hill and down the other; one leading through a green way that cut through the woods and the other leading down to a small lake. She had no idea this park had even existed.

From up here she could see for miles in every direction. The trees in the distance became fuzzy from the high humidity. As she gazed about, her breathing calmed. No longer were her lungs filled with fire. With her hands on her hips, sweat dripped from her onto the trail.

Birds sang and crickets chirped and the cicada made good with their rising and falling chittering. The big ugly bugs sounded like an engine revving up, slowly at first then progressively louder until falling into an abrupt silence, only to start with the slow revving all over again.

The sun seemed to burn her hair. She needed to find some shade.

She found herself heading down the trail to the lake, where a couple of wind surfers were making the most of a paltry breeze. In the shade at the edge of the lake she found a water fountain and a bench and after taking a long drink that saturated every one of her internal organs she sat on the bench and gazed at the lake, squinting against the glare reflected off its surface. The breeze, though barely more than a steady puff, soon cooled her, evaporating some of the sweat from her body. She sank back against the hard plastic ribs of the bench and watched the wind surfers meander across the lake while her legs continued to quiver from the run. After a while they, too, calmed down.

The tall oak and beech trees that provided her shade were in full summer green. More of them rose around the rim of the lake, except to the east, where a vast golden carpet of wild grasses met the water of the lake. The golden field struck a pleasing contrast with the emerald tree leaves and the aqua-tinted lake water.

Blue-spotted dragonflies raced and hovered and dove around the shallows just before her, some landing in a thick clump of cattails that jutted high above the lake. Now and then some large fish jumped out of the water, going after minnows or flying insects and splashing at the surface before diving below once more.

Bridget knew this place was beautiful—but right now its full beauty was lost on her. It was as if she were encased in a glass bubble that kept her from fully enjoying the serenity of her surroundings.

I still don't want to deal with it. I want to be one of the trees around this lake. I don't want to know anything except the soil and air and rain and the birds that perch on my branches.

A child's wish.

True, but I'll get through this somehow.

She wasn't sure if she should believe herself or not.

She rose from the bench, and without a farewell glance began the long journey back to her apartment. She knew she could only jog a mile or two more and then she'd be forced to walk, but that was okay. The main thing was to keep going. Just keep going.

I've got a little time to pull myself together, she thought, forcing her legs to jog a little faster. *Today's Wednesday and I'm not scheduled to work at the hospital until Friday night's graveyard shift.*

After the better part of an hour, she entered her apartment complex.

Her quivering thigh muscles had turned to Jell-O. She had just enough left in them to start up the stairs. Again she dripped sweat from what seemed like every pore. She used the handrail to haul herself up the stairs. On the second floor landing she looked up to see the same neighbor who had been there earlier today, just before the Travis travesty.

Travis travesty. Nothing like a little drama to make a gal feel better. Now what's this woman's name?

She was perhaps a few years older than Bridget—late twenties or early thirties. She had inquisitive eyes and short, dark hair. Her sleeveless sundress displayed long limbs and a dark tan. Compared to her, Bridget had all the color of Casper the ghost.

"Oh, hey there," the woman said, bending to pull a load of wash onto the landing. She straightened and let the door shut as she took a step closer to Bridget. "I'm so sorry for you, Bridget. I wasn't trying to overhear earlier but you know…"

Bridget stiffened at the sudden ache in her chest. "Hard not to hear when it's a public spectacle. Nothing like the whole apartment complex knowing your boyfriend has cheated on you in your own bed."

"It's so *awful*. He's a snake for doing that to you. I know this isn't going to make you feel any better but I've been in the same shitty situation."

"You've been through this?"

"About six months ago. Surprised you didn't notice when the asshole stopped parking out front in his blue Corvette."

"I remember the car."

"Best thing about him. He cheated on me with my best friend at the time. Friends don't get in the way of hormones, or so they say. In this case they were right."

Name? Bridget thought. *Name, name, name, goddamn it what's her name? "G"—it starts with a "G." Gretchen? No, that's not it. Gwen? Gilda? No! Oh, well, bite the bullet.* "I'm sorry," Bridget said. "My brain has gone numb. I'm not exactly sure of your name..."

The woman smiled. "That's all right. We've never really introduced ourselves. I had the misfortune to be named Gretel."

"Gretel?"

"Yeah. Go ahead and laugh." She appeared expectant.

"I wouldn't do that."

"Then you're one of the few. No biggie—hey, I laugh at it myself. Mom and Dad wanted to either keep the German folklore thing alive or were downing too many Peppermint Schnapps when they named me. All my life I've had this nagging feeling I should be shacking up in a gingerbread house with an Alpine stud named Hansel."

Bridget smiled. "Gretel. It's pretty. Unusual and pretty at the same time."

"Well, thanks. I like yours, too. But unlike Bridget, Gretel has its obvious problems. After I tell them my name, most people look at my short black hair and six foot body and get real quiet. I know what they're thinking—'where's the little girl with rosy cheeks and long golden braids?' And I *know* they're dying to ask me if I've ever stuffed a witch's ass into a burning stove."

Bridget smiled.

"Hey, over the years the name thing can get on your nerves. Now I go by Greta instead of Gretel. Of course, like everything else in my life, being called Greta isn't a perfect solution, either. Greta Garbo was a blonde but *hey!* at least she was a real woman and not some damned fairy tale." Greta suddenly rolled her eyes. "God, I am *such* a jerk. Here I am bitching about nothing when you've just been through hell with your boyfriend. I hope you know that this thing is his fault and not yours."

Bridget leaned against the wall. It felt cool to her bare shoulder. "I can't help thinking that if I wasn't at work so much, or if I was prettier or had bigger boobs—"

Greta cut the air with a slicing motion of her hand and shook her head at the same time, causing her hair to dance back and forth. "No, no, no! You can *not* go there! This was his little penis head thinking for him and nothing else. I don't know a whole lot about you, but I can tell you're beautiful and smart and I'll bet a month's rent you like to go out and have fun when you can. This is *not* your fault! I know you're probably not going to believe me, but he wasn't worth your time if he's going to pull shit like this on you."

"Thanks. So, how did you get over it?"

"All of it? Only with time. Seems the old cliché is true, after all. You get on with your life and after a while it fades away. I won't lie to you, it takes a while. In the meantime I suggest you party."

"I don't feel much like partying."

"You will when you have a couple of margaritas with me after I do these clothes and you get a shower."

Bridget had to smile again. "Thanks, but I really don't think—"

"You have to work?"

"No, not tonight."

"Early in the morning?"

"Friday night."

Greta raised her chin. "Then I won't take *no* for an answer. If you don't come down here in an hour I'll camp outside your door with a blender and one of those ugly orange extension cords."

Bridget thought for a moment. "Well, having a drink does sound better than sitting around taking turns crying then beating my mattress."

"Hey, you bet it does. We'll have a drink or two here and then we'll hit a couple bars. You like dancing?"

"Used to. I think I've forgotten how. Travis never wanted to take me. Always said it was a waste of time unless you were there to pick someone up."

"Travis? That's the snake's name?"

"You got it."

"Sounds like he should be swigging beers and farting around some campfire."

Bridget smiled and leaned a little more weight on her thighs. Immediately they began to quiver. "You know, I kind of over did it on my run—like by about ten miles. I'm not sure these legs'll be able to do any dancing."

"Honey, those legs of yours look like they could take ten more miles at a full sprint. Besides, you'd be amazed at the healing powers of tequila once it hits the bloodstream. I'm surprised they didn't teach you that in medical school."

"No, they left that one out for some reason."

Greta cocked a slim dark eyebrow. "Documented fact. It's temporary, of course, but tequila can get the motor running when all else fails, believe me."

"Well in that case I'd better go get cleaned up. Thanks, Greta. Really." Bridget started up the stairs.

Greta picked up her load of laundry and headed down the stairwell in the opposite direction. The laundry room was on the first floor. "Hey Bridget, if you're not down in an hour I'm sending the cops up after you."

"I'll be ready."

"I'll leave the door unlocked so just come on in. I've got a great view of the traffic on Gorman Street from my balcony. Keep that in mind and I'll bet you'll barely be able to stand still long enough to get your eyeliner on."

"A view of Gorman Street...I'm getting goose bumps!" Bridget said, again using the rail to help pull herself up the stairs.

Greta's throaty laugh followed Bridget up the stairwell.

＊ ＊ ＊

Cuervo Gold pumped through Bridget's veins. Hyper dance music thundered in rapid fire beats down on her and the other dancers on the dance floor. Laser lights and strobe lights and wall lights and floor lights pulsed in time with the music, cutting the smoky air. Bridget could see patterns of light on the back of her eyelids when she blinked. She and the others bumped and grinded, shimmied and spun, did bunny hops forward and back, waved their hands high in the air and, rockin' to the beat, shook their derrieres.

Derriere, Bridget thought, *that's French!*

She laughed at the absurdity of it.

She didn't recognize a lot of the tracks the disc jockey was playing, but they were *phresh, baby!* and she let music and tequila take over her mind and body.

Now lasers of red and green cut through the smoky air in precise, flickering lines, drawing weird, spinning shapes in the air and on various body parts of the dancers.

And drawing other, unwelcome images: Misshapen white blood cells. Margaret Morrison. Handlaw. Travis. Even Jo. Especially Jo.

Despite the booze and dancing, she couldn't beat it all back. The will to party drained from her. She hung out ten more minutes but it was no use. "Greta! Sorry, but I think I'm going to head home."

"You sure, girl? There's a lot of night left…"

"Thought I might be able to short it out with alcohol but it all keeps circling back."

"Even with that cute guy over there checking you out? He doesn't look sleazy either."

Bridget made eye contact with him and looked away. "Cute, but no, sorry."

"Yeah, you got rocked with that scum boyfriend," Greta said. "Another guy might take your mind off…?"

"I don't think I want anyone around me for a while. Thanks for bringing me out, Greta, but I'm going to head back home. I'll call a cab. Are you coming back or are you going to stick around for a while?"

"Well, that guy at the end of the bar with the tight jeans and white shirt and delightfully hairy chest wants to show me his shell collection, but I'm going to pass. You seen one shell collection and you've seen 'em all. Cab's a good idea, though. We don't have to call—there's usually half a dozen waiting outside this place by now."

Greta was right. Outside they had no trouble getting a cab. As they arrived at the apartments Bridget wanted to pay for the entire ten-dollar ride but Greta quickly gave the cabbie thirteen before Bridget could think to protest.

Bridget halted in front of the stairs. Her entire body ached to the bone. Greta stepped on the first stair, her high heels clacking once and then no more as she turned and waited for Bridget.

"What's wrong?" Greta asked.

Bridget leaned heavily on the handrail. All she could think about was her nice, comfortable bed and the joy it would soon offer her. "I feel like I just did a whole day of aerobics. My legs are shaking so badly I don't know if they're going to be much help up these stairs. Oh, why didn't I pick the first floor when I was moving in?"

Greta laughed, took her arm and helped her up the stairs. "Wouldn't have that great view of the pool if you did that, would you? Come on."

Together they made it up to the third floor and Bridget's apartment. Greta patted her on the back. "You can manage the key, right?"

"As long as it doesn't jump away." Bridget smiled wearily at Greta. "Thanks for helping me out. It's been great not wallowing in my own self-pity."

Greta smiled, and for the first time a weary light entered her eyes. "Hey, it's no fun going through that crap alone and I know it. I had a blast tonight. Until today I haven't met any girl who could keep up with me on the tequila. You come on down anytime and let me know how it's going. I'll drop in on you from time to time. 'Night, honey." She leaned against the wall and slipped her shoes off, first the right and then the left. With a nonchalant wave she walked across the landing and disappeared down the stairs.

Bridget stepped inside her apartment to find it silent and void of any life. Normally *he'd* be here, and if he was asleep in the bedroom there'd be signs he was here: book bag, books on the dining room table, an empty glass or beer bottle on the kitchen counter. Now there were no signs of his presence at all.

The yellow glow from the parking lot eased through the blinds. She locked the deadbolt behind her and flipped her shoes somewhere into the living room. Closing the blinds in her bedroom, she peeled off the miniskirt and flimsy bra and walked around in her panties.

She flicked on the bathroom light and threw his toothbrush in the trash with an exclamation of disgust. Her hand shook as she tried to get the paste onto her own toothbrush. A few rapid strokes and her teeth were done. Letting the water run, she removed her makeup with cold cream and a few splashes of cool water. She dabbed at her face with a towel and swiped at the light switch as she walked out of the bathroom. She missed the switch, didn't bother with another try. Instead she flopped on the bed and pulled the sheets up to her chin.

While the bed spun, she waited for sleep to claim her. It didn't take long.

THURSDAY, JUNE 10

The next morning Bridget awoke to sudden and complete awareness. Her head hurt but not so badly that she couldn't move. She turned and looked at the clock. Six in the morning. She had thought to sleep until at least noon but hadn't counted on the anxiety she had repressed with last night's alcohol to come creeping to the fore while she slept.

The leukemia. There's something wrong with it, and it isn't just the incredible speed at which it attacks. Something's also wrong with the samples Ian McGuire and I analyzed. Something I overlooked...but what?

The faces of Travis and Gerard Handlaw appeared in her mind.

They laughed at her.

Bridget went to the kitchen and ate a slice of cracked wheat bread, washing it down with a few gulps of milk. Then she went into the bathroom and downed three aspirin.

Her stomach groaned but she wasn't in serious danger of throwing up, which surprised her since she wasn't a heavy drinker. She guessed that the dancing had sweated a lot of it out of her system.

Bridget held her hands up and watched as her fingers twitched and jittered.

Should go back to sleep. Thank goodness I don't have to work tonight. I'm so tired.

She crawled back into bed and pulled the sheets up to her chin. In moments she was asleep.

FIFTEEN

RAYNORR RAISED HIS chin and straightened his tie in the full-length mirror. After pinching the base of the double Windsor, his movements slowed.

The mirror.

The smoked, oval-shaped glass was large enough to dive through, and was encased in a hand-carved, black mahogany frame. It was one of the few items he had shipped to the United States before departing Africa. It had been a gift from N'Buta Shantu, now Chief Medical Field Officer of Tanzania. Raynorr had worked side by side in the bush with N'Buta for nearly two years, tending to the sick and the injured and the dying.

Miniature heads with hollow eye sockets stared back at Raynorr from the frame. They watched him in noncommittal silence. The heads were fashioned one atop the other and comprised every inch of the twin supports and oval frame.

"They are likenesses of real people," N'Buta had told him, pointing at the disconcerting faces with a scarred finger. "They were members of a nameless village that was terrorized and then wiped out completely by rebels with automatic rifles and grenades. Even the artist who fashioned the mirror was murdered. Strangely, his creation was spared the onslaught of the bullets that took his life.

"Look upon them and remember us, Andrew. Remember us while you fight your enemies in America," N'Buta had said. "Remember and know you are always welcome here."

"I will never forget. Goodbye, N'Buta."

"I will not say goodbye because we will meet again. That day will be a great day and we will celebrate. I will step down from this posh job you talked them into giving me and together we will heal the sick as we did when we were real men." He nodded his head for emphasis, and to Raynorr that simple movement had conveyed the dignity and honesty that filled the soul of N'Buta Shantu.

They did not shake hands. They were too close for that.

"Until then," Raynorr had said, and he had climbed into the hold of the cargo plane.

Now the silent faces of the mirror frame did indeed cause him to remember those he had known during his stay in Africa. Some of his friends yet lived, as was the case of N'Buta, whom he emailed through the Internet on a regular basis, but the majority of them were dead. Some had died quickly, slaughtered by soldiers of one political faction or another, but many had died slowly, from malnutrition and disease.

He stared at the faces in the frame until his body ached for him to move. He forced his attention from them to his own image, trapped as it was in the smoked glass. Perhaps his own likeness would someday be carved into the mirror.

The coat and slacks he wore were of finely brushed virgin wool, charcoal gray with thin, powder-blue pinstripes that added a subtle but significant degree of class to the suit. Beneath the suit coat he wore a stark white shirt with a high, stiff collar that buttoned to the body of the shirt with two tiny buttons. Brass cufflinks were affixed to the shirtsleeves where they met his wrists. The tie was a silken affair, with a mottled pattern of black and brown and white. Distinct, but not ostentatious. A single bold crease ran down the length of each pant leg, drawing his line of sight down to the polished wingtips on his feet.

Sharp and expensive. Should fit right in at Anderson's tonight.

Smoothly he turned to the side, unbuttoned the coat and pulled the right half over his hip while easing his hand into the hip pocket of his trousers. He grunted in disdain at the sudden impression that came to him; he looked like one of those middle-aged models given a token page or two in the Dillard's catalog.

He slipped his hand in and out of the pocket, coming out empty twice.

The third time a slim needle-less syringe appeared in his hand, almost invisible between his third and index fingers, the tiny cap already flicked into the pocket by his thumb.

Quickly he raised the hand and made a fist. A thin stream of tap water shot out from the syringe and into the brimming highball glass on the dresser. His hand was back at his side in the next instant. The entire motion was executed so quickly that he barely could observe the transfer, and he was actively looking for it.

It was a movement he'd practiced at least a hundred and fifty times now and he had to admit he was quite good at it. Quite good. In fact, expert. He slipped his hand into the pocket and withdrew it once more. The syringe was gone.

Yes, he favored these pleated trousers. Of course, they were the entire reason he'd bought the overly-expensive suit to begin with.

With only half-interest, he checked his look again in the mirror. He'd gone to the barber shop—hair salon, he corrected himself with distaste, it seemed true barbers were an extinct species these days—on Main Street in Wake Forest and directed the young woman with the rat's nest of hair to give him a very close cut on the small amount of hair he still had around the sides of his head. *She did a good job,* he thought, angling his head this way and that, searching for flaws. He found none.

Nor did he find any in his general appearance.

His head and face were bronzed by the sun. The gray of his side hair and finely etched lines of his face gave him a kind of wizened, outdoorsy look. He filled the suit well, with no sign of a belly thanks to his strict exercise regimen. And though the years had been exacting, he was unbowed.

Tonight I will feast at Anderson's.

The phone rang, interrupting his train of thought. Calmly he walked to the other side of the bed and picked it up.

"Yes?"

"This is Suzanne."

"Hello, Suzanne. I take it you're from the escort agency."

"That's right. Are you..." she paused as if reading from a note, "...Henry James?"

"Indeed, I am. Do you read much, Suzanne?"

"Oh, yes. I'm always flipping through the latest issue of Cosmopolitan or Vogue."

"Any novels?"

"Well, just those true crime ones and ones about movie stars and singers."

"I see," he said, arching an eyebrow at her definition of a novel. "Well, we have something in common. Did you read the one from the maid who worked in the Cruise house for six months?"

"Oh, yes. Can you believe all that stuff between Tom and Katie?"

"It *is* amazing, isn't it? Why don't we discuss it over dinner?"

"That would be so perfect. See, we're getting along already. So, are you ready to go out on the town?"

"Indeed, I was just smoothing out the ruffles in my suit. We'll meet in the lobby of Anderson's at six o'clock sharp. Is that satisfactory?"

"Anderson's? You must have some money burning a hole in your pocket."

He pulled out his billfold from his inner coat pocket and peered at the four freshly-minted Ben Franklins.

"Indeed, I do. Suzanne, I must apologize to you. I would gladly pick you up at your place of residence but the agency said it wasn't recommended due to safety reasons...which I most wholeheartedly agree with."

"Well, it's safer this way," she said. "There's a lot of strange people out there who aren't nearly as sociable as you, Henry."

"It seems as if they're all coming out of the woodwork, doesn't it?"

"Oh, you wouldn't believe it! I mean, I only do this part-time, but I see a weirdo at least every other week."

You're due then. "Tell me all about it at Anderson's."

"Sure will," she promised. "I just can't wait to meet you! Oh—but there's one more thing before we hang up, Henry, just so there's no, uh, awkward moments. Did the agency explain the code of conduct to you?"

"They were quite clear. I have you as a dinner guest for the evening and perhaps a drink or two afterward. Anything more is not part of the deal and entirely optional for you, as it rightly should be."

"Any questions?"

"None. It was as if I'd written the policy myself." He could sense the relief at the other end of the line.

"Well, that's perfect then," she said. "I'm really excited about meeting you, Henry. Now, they told me you're a distinguished gentleman around fifty-five, clean-shaven, and you'll be wearing a suit."

"That's right. And you're in your late teens."

She laughed. "You're a kidder! I like that."

"Seriously, Suzanne. I need the company of a mature woman, someone who has seen a bit of the world. Early forties would be perfect."

"I'm not quite in my forties but I think you'll find me very mature."

"I'm sure I will. What will you be wearing? Just in case you don't spot me right away."

"Cream-colored dress with pearls, dark stockings and heels. I've got long auburn hair."

"Very good. Meet me in the outer lobby at six o'clock."

"Not the bar lobby?"

"I would prefer the outer lobby where they sell the expensive ties with the name of the place on them and the cigars. I want to be sure I don't mistake you for someone else. It would prove quite embarrassing. The outer lobby, if you please."

"Outer lobby. Got it."

"I'll see you there."

"Goodbye, Henry."

"Until we meet, Suzanne."

He hung up and went downstairs to load the syringe with the Raynorr Virus suspended in a saline solution.

He still had an hour left after loading the syringe. Plenty of time in which to gain a status check.

He removed the suit coat and carefully hung it up, then sat in a straight-backed chair before a small desk in the bedroom. From his briefcase he took out his laptop computer.

It had been child's play to persuade the computer operator to provide him with an access number, user-id and password. All Raynorr had said was that he needed to dial up from home to input blood-analysis data or his manager would make his ass grass. That, and a case of tequila had sealed the deal. The operator had given him the account number and password of a recently departed programmer.

Now he connected to the hospital's Local Area Network, or LAN. He clicked on *records* and typed in *Croston, Hugh*. In the blink of an eye the patient information screen showed him patient name, address, phone, insurance plan, and other data. But the only two fields he cared about were name, death-indicator, and expiration date.

All were filled.

"I'll toast your death tonight, Hot Shot."

Raynorr checked on two other victims he'd successfully infected earlier in the week. He noted how their vital signs were dropping with the passage of each day. It wouldn't be long before they followed Croston to the morgue. He clicked his way out of the network and signed off.

He picked up the phone and dialed the hospital's main number.

"Chambers Hospital, this is Miriam. Can I help you?"

"I hope so, Miriam," Raynorr said. "I've lost a friend at your hospital. He died of a terrible disease and now I'm wondering where to send the flowers. I—I don't want to disturb his family. They're going through enough, right now. I was wondering if they left any word about the funeral arrangements?"

"I'm so sorry. The name of your friend, sir?"

"Croston. Hugh Croston."

"One moment, please."

He waited in silence.

"Yes, here it is. A Mr. Jacob Croston, listed here as brother to the deceased, has left the following church address..."

Raynorr wrote it down.

"Services will be held the day after tomorrow," she added.

"Thank you so very much, Miriam."

"You're very welcome, sir."

He might just have to break with tradition and attend the funeral. There was no danger of discovery, so he might as well bask in the glory of Croston's death.

148

Raynorr pulled slowly into the parking lot of Anderson's Restaurant and looked for more than an empty space in which to park the rented Cadillac. Up and down the rows of the large lot he drove, feeling like Death himself in a black carriage, though instead of a scythe he carried a small syringe.

With the air-conditioning turned up high to compensate for the added heat of the suit, he cruised past the assorted Jaguars, BMWs and Mercedes that gleamed in the late afternoon sun. He paid particular attention to the Jags, and for the license plate Croston had told him Jerry Oberlin used: NSUREXEC.

Croston had said there was supposed to be a company party tonight. And a party animal like Oberlin wouldn't miss a good party, so surely he would be here—

A flash of chrome cut into Raynorr's eye. He turned.

A dark brown Jag pulled into the parking lot entrance and headed down the first row. It slowed to wait for a couple of patrons to get into their Mercedes and pull out of a space. Raynorr slowly eased the black Caddy behind the Jag and read the license plate.

Oberlin.

And he was alone. So he hadn't brought his wife. A true player.

Croston had said the man was a habitual cheater. Raynorr doubted he would eat dinner by himself, and with any luck he would order a drink in the lounge before going to a table.

His heart beat a tad quicker. Not much, but a little. This was, after all, his first hit in a public place. The chance of someone seeing him was greater.

And so was the thrill, he had to admit.

Oberlin pulled the Jag into the parking space and got out just as Raynorr eased the Caddy past him. Oberlin was probably in his early fifties, stood around five ten, and at the most weighed a hundred and forty pounds. He had narrow shoulders and a thin bone structure that made him appear almost delicate. He wore a light brown suit that was probably made of camelhair. Raynorr took a mental snapshot of his target's sunken cheeks, paste-white skin, and fuller-brush style hair dyed black. The contrast between the pale skin and jet-black hair was not a pleasant one.

This is a man who avoids the outdoors, Raynorr decided. He's a product of the corporate world. Long hours beneath fluorescent lights, little or no exercise, little or no grasp of what it means to have a real life. And yet this puny man holds the power to dictate health care policies that affect thousands of lives.

Raynorr had to suppress a sneer. *I promise you "a death not of a customary manner," as Edgar Allan Poe had put it.*

A car beeped impatiently behind him. He glared into the rear view mirror at the driver of a shiny Mercedes and didn't move his foot from the brake pedal. The man looked away.

Only then did Raynorr ease off the brake and guide the Caddy to the rear of the parking lot. He left a number of empty spaces between it and the nearest luxury car.

He got out of the car without bothering to lock it. Who would steal a Cadillac with all these far more luxurious vehicles at hand? Besides, the Caddy's a rental. So what if it gets stolen?

He glanced at his reflection in the driver's side window. The reddish orange light from the sinking sun struck him full in the face. The light was warm on his tanned skin.

He lingered for a moment next to the Caddy and let the heat and humidity surround him. If Anderson's was anything like it had been seven years ago, it was going to be frigid inside, even with all those live bodies cavorting with one another.

He buttoned the coat with his right hand only. His steady fingers performed the task so smoothly as to make it nearly indiscernible. One moment his hand was there and the next it was gone, the coat buttoned. He started to adjust the tie but then thought better of it. It was already perfectly straight.

He pivoted and strode toward the vast building that had once been a tobacco warehouse. The brick facade had been painted white. The jutting overhang at the main entrance was a recent addition and added a touch of 1940's nostalgia to the place. It also kept the rain off patrons who were dropped off. Running the length of the overhang were neon lights that glowed blue and spelled "Anderson's" in a classy free hand script.

Raynorr pushed through the double doors and strode inside the restaurant, the hard heels of his shoes clacking on the wooden floor of the outer lobby. Groups and couples who didn't drink or simply didn't want to deal with the crowd in the lounge sat on the leather benches here or struck poses near the walls while waiting for their names to be called over the loudspeaker.

Oberlin wouldn't be caught just staring at the woodwork with commoners. He's here for a rendezvous, one that most likely doesn't include his wife. He's either sitting in the restaurant already or he's in the lounge near the long bar with the solid brass hand and foot rails that run from one end to the other.

He couldn't see the bar for all the people clustered around it, but he knew from his earlier life that the bar itself had been hand-crafted from solid oak in High Point, North Carolina, and had been coated with a quarter inch of polyurethane that was so hard you couldn't drive a knife into it at full swing. He'd seen a bartender try it once on a dare when the floor manager was nowhere to be seen. But that had been a long time ago. A lifetime ago. A lifetime ago when he had belonged to the high-society crowd that now clustered inside this place.

Raynorr stood in the circle of light that enveloped a podium where an attractive hostess in a low-cut dress waited. She had long dark hair that shone in the spotlight. She smiled in a practiced manner and he knew then why she was the greeting hostess.

"Welcome to Anderson's, sir."

"Thank you, young lady. Pleasure being here."

She raised her pencil thin eyebrows. "Do you have a reservation or shall I put you on the waiting list? There's about an hour wait for a dinner table, thirty minutes for a seat at the raw bar."

Raynorr tilted his head. "I do indeed have a reservation. Henry James, party of two, though I have arrived a bit early and my dinner guest is not here, as yet."

The hostess skimmed down her list, using a shiny pen held just above the paper as a pointer. "Ah, here it is. James—party of two. I have you."

"Do you, now?"

"Yes. You're just a little early, like you said. Your table is still not yet available. Would you care to have a drink in the lounge or wait out here?"

"Do they serve beer in the lounge?"

"Oh, yes, sir."

"Then the lounge will be fine. Thank you, young lady."

"My pleasure, sir," she said, and she smiled again like she meant it. "The pager will light up when your table is available. Should be only a few minutes."

He leaned a bit closer to the podium and she looked up at him as he spoke. "Tell me, did the management here show impeccable taste by purposefully hiring such a beauty as yourself or was it simply random fortune?"

She blinked for a moment, uncertain. Then her dark eyes widened in surprise and her pupils dilated with pleasure. And for the first time, her true smile came through, touching her eyes where it hadn't before. "Oh, my! You *are* a charmer, Mr. James."

"Ever thought about running away with an old man?"

She leaned closer to him, so close he could easily see the swell of her breasts. She gazed mischievously up at him. "I haven't seen any old men tonight, but when I do, I'll definitely consider it."

Raynorr smiled. "Now who's charming who?" he asked, and with a wink he eased into the crowd at the bar and was absorbed into them, a virus into a living cell.

Jazz pulsed loudly through an impressive array of overhead speakers. People raised their voices to be heard, driving the noise level higher. Cigarette smoke enveloped Raynorr and sent its burning tendrils into his nose and lungs. He drifted around the tables of couples, singles, and small groups, and the people crowding between the tables. Many looked his way, registered him for a fleeting moment and then continued scanning the crowd.

The mode of dress ranged from black jeans to suits for the men, black jeans and dresses and miniskirts for the women. Apparently plunging necklines were "in" this year. *Nothing wrong with that,* Raynorr thought.

There were many smiles, some real, most social replicas of the real thing, and a lot of laughter. Several women of various ages openly checked him out, and he held their gazes with his own for a moment before resuming his search.

The crowd parted near the bar. Raynorr seized the opening and stepped through, searching.

There.

Oberlin sat at a high table just twenty feet away. A throng of people hovered between his table and the bar. Oberlin had his back to the bar, his side to Raynorr. At the table with him was an attractive woman in a sleeveless dress held up by two spaghetti straps that snugged the dress to her ample cleavage, crisscrossed, then disappeared somewhere behind her. As he moved closer, he noticed there was an empty martini glass in front of Oberlin and a wine glass before the woman. The first round was gone. Would Oberlin order another?

Surely a man who drank martinis would order more than one.

Oberlin wasn't fighting the crowd at the bar for the attention of the bartenders, so he must be using one of the three cocktail waitresses working the floor in long black dresses and bared shoulders.

Raynorr looked around as he shouldered his way smoothly through a gap that appeared between a woman in an orange sundress and heels and two younger men who checked her out with sidelong glances. They tried to appear casual as they ogled her, raising their bottles of beer to cover their lips as they spoke. As he worked his way toward Oberlin's table, Raynorr spotted a cocktail waitress carrying a full tray of drinks, mouthing "excuse me's" to get through the crowd. She was heading in Oberlin's direction from the opposite end of the bar.

Among the other drinks on the tray was a martini glass with a green olive in it.

Raynorr's opportunity was suddenly here. He had wanted some time to set up and get his bearings but if Oberlin was called to his dinner table then the hit would be entirely too risky and Raynorr would have to wait for another night. And he had no intention of setting this evening up all over again. A few more quick steps and a turn of his shoulders and he was in position.

The cocktail waitress smiled as a couple stepped to the side and suddenly she was only a few feet from Oberlin's table. Raynorr focused on the martini with the green olive skewered by one of those little plastic swords. Quickly, he slid his hand in his front pocket and flicked the cap off the syringe. He held the syringe between his index and middle fingers.

Camouflaged as part of the crowd, Raynorr was within striking distance. A woman in a daring crimson dress stood next to him. Her bare back was inches from his left arm. A pair of suits unwittingly shielded him from more peering eyes. He stood facing the bar at an angle. To the casual observer he appeared to be trying to catch the bartender's eye, though in reality his entire universe had narrowed to the three people at the table beside him.

The waitress stood between Oberlin and his date. She smiled at them, placed a fresh glass of wine on the table before the woman, took her empty glass, placed a fresh martini just to the right of Oberlin's empty, then took his empty and placed it on her tray.

Raynorr glanced at Oberlin's martini glass and then away.

Oberlin withdrew his wallet from his coat pocket and thumbed through it while the waitress hovered at the table, one of those small cash and change holders waiting in the center of her tray.

Raynorr eased his hand from his pocket and held it at his side.

Oberlin and the waitress were distracted by the money transaction. Two out of three. But the woman—

Raynorr glanced at Oberlin's date. She was looking directly at him. Not at his hand, but at his face. While Oberlin was busy, she was taking the opportunity to check out the field and her gaze had settled on him.

For the first time that evening Raynorr's heartbeat started to race.

He couldn't do it while she watched.

The moment was slipping away. Oberlin held out a ten-dollar bill and the waitress grasped it and placed it in her tray. She began to make change.

Raynorr had to act soon or the moment would be lost.

He had to distract Oberlin's date.

He shifted his gaze to a point over her shoulder. He nodded and smiled to the imaginary person there.

She took a sip of wine and casually turned to see who was usurping his attention.

Raynorr turned in the direction of the bar, hand moving smoothly up his side, syringe nestled in his palm. He raised his arm as if checking his watch. His forearm came up, out, and over. His hand hesitated over Oberlin's glass. A quick squeeze.

Transfer complete.

Raynorr stepped between the suits and let the crowd fill in around him. The syringe was already back in his pocket.

A few moments later he had a pint of beer in hand. He raised the glass to his lips and took a deep swallow of the frothy brew. He glanced over at Oberlin's table as he did so. The target and his date appeared to be chatting. She smiled at Oberlin as her jaw moved. Oberlin raised his martini, stirred it with the impaled olive, and then drained it just as his name was called over the loudspeaker.

Raynorr smiled, drank deeply, took a breath, then drained his pint completely. Turning sideways to fill in a gap between two other patrons, he placed the empty pint on the bar and watched for a moment as the foam slid down the inner walls of the glass.

"Do it again?" the bartender asked, leaning over the bar toward him. Her long hair gently skimmed the polyurethane surface.

He raised an eyebrow. She was at least twenty-five years younger than himself. "Why not?"

She nodded, was about to turn away but then paused. He smiled at her and she smiled back, her gaze directly meeting his. After a moment she went to get him another beer. She placed the pint of dark brew in front of him. "Three fifty," she said, giving him a smile that brought out the dimples in her cheeks.

He took her gently by the hand. She let out an exclamation of surprise and pleasure when he caressed her palm with a twenty-dollar bill. He closed her fingers around it. Patting her hand lightly, he let go.

"Thank you for the exquisite service."

She gazed down at the twenty and then looked up at him. "Well, thank you. If you need anything else, just ask for Tracy."

"I will be sure to do that, Tracy. Right now I'm going to dine. What do you recommend from the menu?"

She leaned closer to him from over the bar, providing a very nice view of her ample cleavage. "It's all good, but the oysters are *incredible*. A suave gentleman like yourself should always sample the oysters."

"Oysters! I really don't know if I should..." he leaned forward over the bar until his face was inches from hers. "To be honest with you, Tracy, darlin', oysters seem to get me incredibly horny. And since I live alone, it's not always conducive to the evening." He leaned back and watched as her cheeks darkened with a very fetching blush. "You understand, don't you?"

Her fingernails swept back and forth over the palm he had recently caressed. "A fine-looking man like yourself shouldn't be living alone."

"I agree. Why don't you and I get together sometime?"

"But I don't even know your name..."

"How thoughtless of me. I'm Henry James."

"Like the author?"

"Exactly."

She held out her hand for him to take once more. When he did, she smiled. "You *will* stop by later, won't you, Henry?"

"Of course. After dinner I will order Crown Royal on the rocks from you."

She cocked her head and looked into his eyes. "I'll bring it myself."

"That's a promise, you understand."

"Yes, it is."

He winked at her and started toward the podium where the hostess stood. He noticed a woman in her early forties wearing a cream-colored dress with pearls, dark stockings and heels. She was attractive and had long auburn hair. It had to be Suzanne, his paid escort for the evening. She checked her watch and Raynorr looked at his own. She was six minutes early.

Raynorr slid beside a large man in a double-breasted suit and turned to watch Suzanne. He raised his beer to his lips. His eyes remained fixed upon her as she craned her neck and searched the outer lobby area where they had agreed to meet.

Apparently satisfied he was not in the building, yet, she made her way to the bar. He could have rubbed elbows with her as she passed right next to him. Instead, he pretended to drink. She put her hand on various male arms and smiled prettily for them as she slid through the crowd to the bar. There she impatiently waved a ten-dollar bill, intent upon catching the eye of one of the bartenders.

Raynorr's eyes narrowed into slits. *What else would she do that she isn't supposed to?* he wondered. *Here she is sneaking to the bar for a drink when I expressly ordered her to remain in the outer lobby!*

His heartbeat pounded in his ears.

How dare she disobey!

Casting furtively around the bar area, Suzanne was apparently unaware that he was glaring at her from just two people away. The fingers of her free hand tapped impatiently on the bar. Tracy, the bartender he had spoken with earlier and the one he was going to have sex with later this evening, raised her chin and asked Suzanne a question that Raynorr couldn't hear but one he knew anyway.

Something to drink?

Suzanne told her and Tracy did her bidding, returning with a shot glass of what was probably vodka and a glass of wine. Suzanne tossed the ten onto the bar and downed the shot in a single gulp. Then she took a sip of wine. She tapped the shot glass impatiently on the bar. She wanted another.

Raynorr reached into his pocket and felt the second slim syringe there, the one he had brought as a back up for the first. Tracy took Suzanne's empty shot glass and walked down the bar to where the vodka bottles were. Raynorr flicked the cap off the syringe and eased around the two people between himself and Suzanne.

She tapped on the bar with her nails, watching intently as Tracy dipped the head of the vodka bottle and poured another shot. She was in the process of returning the bottle to the shelf when Raynorr made his move.

Suzanne's wine glass was positioned six inches to the right of her body—six inches in his favor. Suzanne leaned forward, her forearm on the bar and her fingernails tapping away.

The bass notes of the jazz music throbbed in his ears. A quick look around and he decided it was clear. With an almost imperceptible flick of his wrist Suzanne's wine glass now harbored the Raynorr Virus.

Raynorr disappeared into the crowd and placed his beer glass on one of the cocktail waitress's trays as she sponged off a table.

Raynorr walked past the hostess podium, through the outer lobby and went outside. He walked a short distance to a bench where he sat for exactly five minutes. He then rose, pushed open the door and re-entered the restaurant as if arriving for the first time that evening.

And there was Suzanne, sitting in the outer lobby just as he had directed. Her legs were crossed to reveal a slit in the dress that came up to her mid-thigh. She had nice legs. She watched him with naked interest as he approached. He bent at the waist and offered his hand while forcing a half-smile on his face.

"Suzanne?"

She smiled and took his hand. "Hello, Henry. Nice to meet you."

"The pleasure's all mine. I hope you haven't been waiting long?"

She rose and he started to let go of her hand but she pressed her hand firmly into his. "Oh, no. I just got here a minute ago. You're younger than I expected. There's no way you're in your early fifties."

"I have to confess you're right. I'm fifty-seven."

"Well, you're a very handsome and distinguished man." Her breath smelled of mint, though the underlying aroma of alcohol was still discernable. "It's not often that I get this lucky."

"Out of the two of us, I'm definitely the fortunate one." *Especially since you'll be dead in four days.* "Shall we check on our table?"

The hostess was the same pretty, young woman as his first time in, but she didn't let on that she had seen him before.

"Is the James table ready, my dear?" he asked.

"Ready and waiting, Mr. James." Her smile to Suzanne was perfunctory, part of her job performance. "Would you please follow me?"

She led them to a private booth and placed the menus on opposite sides of the table. "Enjoy your dinner, Mr. James." She ignored Suzanne.

"Thank you, I intend on doing just that." Raynorr watched as Suzanne sat and slid toward the middle of the seat.

They had calamari for an appetizer, which went well with the zinfandel wine. Both ordered broiled seafood platters for entrees, had more wine. They spoke of things great and small, most of the time small. He watched her closely, something she no doubt took as avid male interest in her notable womanly attributes, when in actuality he was imagining what kind of corpse she would make.

After dinner he checked his watch. "Suzanne, I must apologize to you. I must end our evening early as something unexpected has cropped up. He pulled her hand to him and pressed three of the hundred dollar bills in her palm. "I've had a very pleasant evening, but these matters will not wait, you understand."

Her eyes widened in surprise as she looked at the three hundred dollars in her hand. She didn't let her surprise keep her from stashing it almost immediately into her purse. "Henry, thank you. But is something wrong? I—I thought we were getting along so well."

"It's not that. These are things out of my control."

She slowly nodded, then leaned closer. "Let me be honest with you, Henry. I find you to be a very attractive man. I'd like to spend some more time with you."

"I am sorry. These matters will not wait."

"Would you like to drive me home? Perhaps you have time for a drink in my condo. It's not far."

"Perhaps another time. I'll call a cab for you."

"No, I can drive. I've only had the two glasses of wine."

He stared at her.

She looked away, obviously uncomfortable. "Well, I'll just be leaving, then. No need to walk me out. Thank you for the lovely evening, Henry." She couldn't keep the hurt out of her voice as she said it.

"Goodbye, Suzanne." He didn't stand when she slid out of the booth.

She looked quizzically at him for a moment and then strode away.

Perhaps this was the first time she had been rejected by a paying customer. Raynorr didn't care. He had given her explicit instructions and she had disobeyed them. Now she was going to pay with her life. In a war there is no tolerance for those who disobey direct orders. Had she recognized him at the bar she could have jeopardized his assignment.

He paid the bill and asked the waitress to hand a written message to Tracy the bartender. It read: *I'm ready for my Crown Royal on the rocks.*

Five minutes later Tracy left the bar and brought two glasses of Crown over ice to his table. She smiled as she stood before him. "I've got your order, Mr. James."

"Indeed, you do."

"It looks like there's room at your table for another."

"Indeed, it does." He stood and pulled out a chair. "Please."

Sitting side by side they sipped their drinks and talked. She was studying for her master's degree in psychology from NC State, putting herself through the program by bartending. He found her intelligence and wit quite refreshing.

Later he followed Tracy in the rented Cadillac to her apartment. She proved to be a fiery and uninhibited sex partner, and he rewarded her with an hour and a half of intermittent orgasms.

In the darkness of the early morning she stood in a white robe, blocking the apartment door as he cradled the suit coat in the crook of his arm.

"You didn't ask for my number, but I work five nights a week at Anderson's," she said. "I'd like to see you again, Henry."

Raynorr wrapped an arm around her waist, pulled her close and kissed her. She pressed into him and he knew it would be the last time he felt the warmth and fullness of her lips and exquisite body. He wouldn't call on her again. It had been a lark. An opportunity that had presented itself and he had taken it. He had far too much to do to get involved with anyone at this time, especially a woman his youngest daughter's age.

"Maybe I'll see you at Anderson's sometime," Raynorr said, and walked out of the apartment.

SIXTEEN

Bridget woke early feeling more refreshed than she had in a long time.

Just needed some solid sleep, I guess.

She languidly stretched, then pushed aside her covers and sat up. Her stomach immediately rumbled and she realized that she'd hadn't had anything substantial to eat since Wednesday afternoon. She'd virtually slept all of yesterday away, waking only twice to get a drink of water and go to the bathroom. Sleep had been the balm her body needed and her mind had been happy to comply with hours of dreamless slumber.

After fixing herself a light breakfast of toast and juice, she donned her running gear and went for a short two and a half miler. She didn't push it this time. She had to work tonight and didn't want to wear herself out early. A moderate pace was best. When she returned to the apartment, she took a long hot shower and dressed in comfortable shorts and a tee.

She went to the living room, sat on the couch and picked up the phone from the end table to punch in a number. It rang once and then came a stern greeting.

"Ward Seven, Nurse Watkins. How can I help you?"

Curse the woman for sounding fresh and alert, Bridget thought. *Didn't she just work the night shift?*

"Hello?" Nurse Watkins asked, her tone got across the message that the caller had seconds in which to reply or it was cut off time.

"Hey, it's Bridget Devereaux."

"Bridget—uh, Doctor Devereaux."

The nurse's voice was hushed and strained, as if she'd turned away from the direction she'd been facing and was trying not to be overheard. "Where have you *been*? I tried to reach you until midnight last night. Didn't you get the messages I left on your machine?"

"Messages?" Bridget stood and looked over at the kitchen counter where an angry "3" burned on the LCD readout of her answering machine. She tugged on a handful of damp hair. "God—I never thought to check. What's going on?"

"This damned leukemia has killed again."

Bridget swallowed. "Who?"

"Hugh Croston. He coded yesterday and we couldn't get him back. Blood tests showed almost no healthy cells in his bloodstream, white or red. I've never seen or heard of someone dying so quickly from leukemia in all my years."

"But I admitted Mr. Croston only a day and a half ago…"

"That's what I'm saying. He was young and healthy only last week. Yesterday, he told Nurse Williams he'd had a routine physical with full blood work two weeks ago and everything had been fine. I just don't understand it. Even acute leukemia doesn't kill like the goddamned bubonic plague."

"I'm beginning to think this strain has a lot in common with the black plague, Nurse Watkins. Was Abrams attending in my absence?"

"Yes. He kept Mr. Croston relatively pain-free, but Mr. Croston seemed to get very delusional toward the end. He kept saying he'd been assaulted by one of our hospital staff. Said it was a crazy man who had planted the disease inside his body, and just went on and on like that until he passed out. When he woke back up he started all over again."

"He said someone *planted* the disease?"

"That's right."

Bridget frowned. "I can see why he might have felt that way. One day you're strong and healthy, a corporate executive on the rise, and the next you're dying with a disease that's going to end your life in record time. Factor in a high dose of morphine and it could seem as if someone planted the disease inside his body."

There was a pause on both ends of the line before Bridget asked in a tentative voice, "How's Jo?"

"She's fighting, brave thing, but the leukemia is growing stronger inside her. Even without the lab results, you can tell just by looking at her that her red blood cell count is down. She's losing strength and her pain is worse. She had a bad nosebleed that lasted for twenty minutes before we could get it to stop. I'm not sure she's going to make it through the chemo."

"Not her, too," Bridget whispered.

"I know your feelings for the girl, Doctor. She's lasted the longest out of all the recent leuk patients, but…I think it may be time to prepare for the worst. She'd really like to see you. One of her parents is always with her but she's been asking for you. She knew it was your day off yesterday and she didn't want me to page you."

Bridget bit her lip. "I'll be there in forty minutes."

"Doctor, before you hang up…"

"Yes?"

"News travels fast around here. I understand you're taking heat for trying to raise a red flag about this leukemia thing."

"You might say that," Bridget said tersely, trying to ice the outrage she felt at Gerard Handlaw and not quite making it. "Handlaw threatened to throw me out of the internship program. Then he sexually harassed me in his office—used sexually abusive language."

"He did what?"

"That's right. The president of the hospital. Nice, huh?"

Nurse Watkins' voice dropped to a whisper. "That bastard. I've heard rumors of him doing this kind of thing before. Even so, you can't go to Human Resources on this."

"I'd be dismissed just as fast as they could draw up the letter."

"You can't afford to get thrown out of here. It'll end your career before it even starts."

"I know. Thanks for the warning, Nurse Watkins."

"Barbara."

"Barbara. The problem is that I don't have solid proof that this is a new type of leukemia. Without more evidence I can't back up the alarm I'm sending out and they know that."

"What about the rapid onset of death?"

"They'll claim it's just circumstantial."

"But we've lost *six* patients."

"They still won't call it an epidemic."

"They would if it was Legionnaire's."

"Yeah, but they can identify Legionnaire's Disease. I can't differentiate this leuk from regular AML except by its explosive reproduction. There was something with an unidentified protein matrix, but it didn't lead anywhere."

"Damn it. Why don't they listen?"

"Money."

"Always."

"They want to keep things quiet until after the hospital is sold. Handlaw told me that himself in his office."

"Handlaw. If you can get me evidence that he's putting profit ahead of patients, I know someone who may be able to help with him."

"Who?"

"I can't tell you right now. Just find something and get it to me—but try to do it quietly so they don't throw you out of here first."

Bridget tried to clear the lump that rose in her throat. "I'm still going to treat my patients the way I think is right. I'm going to run my tests and I'm not backing down on my position that we're in the middle of some kind of unknown epidemic, here."

Bridget paused.

"Problem is, I don't think they're going to tolerate me much longer."

✳ ✳ ✳

Bridget's car idled roughly at the side of the entrance road leading into the hospital campus. Arrow-straight rows of ornamental pear trees stood at attention on both sides of the road. It was into the shade afforded by these Bradford pears that Bridget had guided the little hatchback, and it was here that she now clicked off the air conditioner and slowly rolled down the window, her eyes locked, trance-like, on the massive structure at the bottom of the sloping road.

Chambers Hospital is really a castle. A modern-day castle about to be sacked by invaders wearing suits and ties.

Her arm wouldn't move. Dully she realized the window was down as far as it could go. With the glass barrier lowered, a rare morning breeze drifted into the car. Her shoulders tensed as warm, thick air breathed down her neck. She wanted to blame her trembling solely on the car's vibrations, but why fool herself? Certainly the car wasn't responsible for the dread that had turned her stomach into one great big knot.

No one wants to acknowledge that my patients are dying from a new strain of leukemia, Bridget thought. *Not the administration, not the staff doctors, not the residents. Not even my fellow interns. Only the nurses, the front-line defenders. But if my own hospital won't back me up, certainly the people at the Center for Disease Control in Atlanta won't believe me without further proof.*

Bridget tugged nervously at the cuffs of her lab coat and stared as people came and went through the hospital's main entrance.

Handlaw's going to throw me out. And then what will I do? Will I break down? Will I become a victim? Or will I have the courage to fight and keep going?

Her stomach knotted once more as her gaze wandered over the hospital grounds. The vast patient and visitor parking lots were filling with vehicles of every imaginable type, from rusty pick-up trucks with cracked windshields and spot-rusted bodies to freshly minted Jaguars, so shiny you had to squint to look at them.

Sickness and injury pay no attention to social standing.

Mothers were stricken with disease just as often as the most ruthless CEO. Chambers Hospital was a nonprofit organization, with a mandate to treat all patients regardless of their ability to pay—hence the spectrum of vehicles present in the parking lot. But that would all change with the buyout Gerard Handlaw was orchestrating. Allied Health was a corporation. Patient care would no longer be *the goal*. Profit, as in the if-you-ain't-got-the-money-you-ain't-gonna-get-treated kind of profit, would become *the goal*, despite the propaganda Allied would spew into the media after the buyout.

Allied's first act would be to create a new charter for the hospital. The old charter, set down a hundred and fifty years ago by humanitarian and wealthy businessman John Chambers, a man with a vision of reasonable healthcare for all, would be shredded.

And you won't see many rusted pickups in the patient parking lots then.

She took a deep breath, but it didn't help much.

A sudden gust bent the branches of the trees around her and scattered her hair. She lifted her gaze skyward just as a thick cluster of purple clouds smothered the morning sun. In seconds a huge shadow claimed the hospital, the vast parking lots and parking decks, the islands of green and everyone walking from their cars to the hospital.

She'd heard the warnings on the radio as she'd driven here. These angry-looking clouds were the first in a line of violent thunderstorms moving into the area, the result of an approaching cold front clashing with the hot, soupy air around Raleigh. There was a severe thunderstorm warning posted for the area for the next four hours. Lightning, heavy winds, hail and a deluge of rain had already engulfed the Triad area to the west and it was all working its way eastward toward the coast.

Cars passed. Her gaze fell once more on the massive building at the bottom of the hill. Beneath the shadow of the approaching storm the hospital appeared like Modred's Castle, cruel and sinister.

Can't stay here, woman. Can't just wait for things to happen. Got to get moving.

She shifted into first gear, glanced over her shoulder, and eased out into the entrance road. After a moment she turned onto a side road that led to the employee parking deck. She slowed at the wooden yellow arm that blocked her way. Taking her employee identification card from her purse, she leaned out the window and slid the card through the reader while easing the car forward in anticipation of the arm raising. But it didn't go up. Didn't even twitch. She nearly ran into it with the car, had to slam on the brakes to keep the bumper from hitting it. Her tires chirped their annoyance at the sudden halt. She frowned, pushed the card into the reader again. Nothing.

Again, with the card.

Again, nothing.

Someone beeped a horn angrily behind her. She ignored

whoever it was and tried the card one more time.

Still nothing. The yellow arm mocked her with its brilliant color. The red reflectors attached to it seemed to wink at her as if they had some kind of inside scoop she didn't know about.

Bridget bit her lip. *Is it happening, then? Is this the first indication I'm getting thrown out?*

The sky became a massive bruise. The shadowy veil that enveloped the world grew darker. Winds gusted and then fell completely still. The fine hairs on Bridget's arms and neck stood on end and she had to resist the urge to cower in her seat. She put the car in reverse and started to back up. Another beep sounded, and then an all-out blare. She slammed on the brakes. Her car lurched up and down like a johnboat in rough seas.

"Oh, great."

Horrified, Bridget gazed into the rearview mirror as the Mercedes behind her shot backward, tires screeching to avoid harm. She had a pretty good feeling the guy was not mouthing kind words of understanding at her.

Bridget backed the car away from the yellow arm, ignoring the doctor in the Mercedes though she could feel his eyes boring into her. She parked in the visitor's lot. The security guys would write her a parking ticket if they discovered her car with its green employee sticker out here, but what could matter less at this point?

Lightning flashed in a series of blue-white brilliancies. The resulting thunder rumbled deep inside her chest.

There's no way the security guys are going to brave this storm anytime soon, Bridget thought.

She rolled up her window and got out of the car just as the first big raindrops pelted the area in a haphazard blitz, smashing into the blacktop and car hoods and roofs, and stinging her face.

She slammed the door and raced for the main entrance along with several other people. Bridget outstripped them and reached the protective overhang extending from the main doors of the hospital first. She risked a glance over her shoulder just as a jagged streak of lightning cut downward through the purple sky to the ground. Something exploded like an artillery blast.

Bridget gasped. A few of the others cried out. All of them stampeded through the automatic doors. No one said more than a few words, but the sense of urgency in their quick steps and tight faces was unmistakable. As they formed a throng around the front desk, she broke off from them. She knew where she needed to go. Thunder continued to explode outside in rapid, cannon-like succession, warning away all who would dare venture forth beneath its awesome power.

As if galvanized by the storm, Bridget hurried through the

hallways and headed for Jo's room. To lessen the chance of Jo contracting infection while in her weakened state, Bridget grabbed a paper mask from the nurse's station and quickly strapped it over her nose and mouth. Then she picked up the patient records. On impulse, she also grabbed a syringe and slipped it into her coat pocket. If the nursing staff hadn't taken a blood sample recently, she would do it herself.

She rapped lightly on the door. When no one answered she gently pushed the door open and parted the privacy curtain. Jo was alone in the room, propped up by the angle of the bed. Her eyes were closed. Bridget gazed on the girl's sunken eyes and cheeks and had to clench her teeth to keep the cry in her throat from escaping.

She went to the girl's side, grasped her thin wrist and felt for Jo's pulse. For fifteen seconds she counted the reluctant beats.

Bridget closed her eyes and offered a silent prayer, something she hadn't done since the day her mother had died.

Blinking to keep the tears at bay, Bridget pulled the stethoscope from her lab coat pocket and listened to Jo's lungs. The girl's breathing was shallow, but there was no indication of blocked brachial passages. Her temperature was normal, a good sign there was no infection. The fever she had been running when she had been first admitted was gone. There was at least that.

Bridget then checked the flow of fluids from the computerized IV, her eyes continually straying to Jo's face as the girl slept a troubled sleep.

The flesh appeared tightly drawn over the bones of Jo's pale countenance. Her skin retained none of the summer tan it had held the day of her admittance. Now spider webs of thin blue veins were visible around her eyes and on her cheeks as her skin degraded into translucency. Crease lines appeared between the girl's furrowed brows, blatant signs of the pain she endured as she battled the disease inside her youthful body.

Where's Jo's mother? Bridget wondered. *It's not like Mrs. Woods to be away.*

There was a familiar-looking purse on one of the guest chairs. Judging by the way the strap had doubled over on itself and hung over the arm of the chair, it appeared to have been thrown there. Jo's mother was here; she must have just stepped out for a meal or a cigarette, or something.

She glanced through the chart and satisfied herself that blood had been drawn recently. Then she moved to the door. She would talk to the Woods family later. Right now the logical part of her mind was crying out for her to do something that might benefit Jo, like getting down to the lab to further analyze the blood samples.

Reluctant to leave, but knowing she had to in order to help

her patient, Bridget reached for the door handle. It was there an instant before it should have been, the metal handle in her palm and pushing toward her.

She stepped to the side as the disheveled form of Jo's mother pulled up short, a paper mask over her nose and mouth. Obviously, Mrs. Woods knew Jo's body was wide open to infection right now.

"Oh, I didn't see you, Doctor," Mrs. Woods said, walking slowly into the room. "I know you're doing what you can, but my little girl doesn't look well." Over the mask her eyes glistened.

"She's fighting, Mrs. Woods. Her pulse is low and her breathing is shallow, but I've seen patients who appeared much weaker pull through." During Bridget's brief experience as an intern she'd seen no such thing—she'd heard of it, though. "Quite frequently there's a dip in health before the chemotherapy fully wipes out the cancer-producing cells. The dip is due to the chemo taking out both the good and bad cells. Jo has avoided infection so far and that's a pretty good victory in itself. Now her body can focus on rebounding instead of fighting a virus."

Mrs. Wood's eyes appeared hopeful, but not convinced. The dark circles surrounding them were testimony to the battle she, too, was fighting.

"I could write you a prescription for some sleeping pills," Bridget offered. "Nothing powerful, just enough to let you rest."

Placing a can of soda next to the untouched food tray on the small table, Mrs. Woods went to her daughter's side and gently caressed her troubled brow. "No, thank you. I want to be alert if my Jo gets any worse."

Bridget bit the inside of her lip. "How is your husband?"

"Drinking a lot when he's not working. He comes in here and breaks down. It's almost better that he keeps working. There's plenty of backlog out there for him. He's hired a couple of extra workers. Offices need to be cleaned every night of the business week, you know?"

Bridget nodded. "Yes, they do." What could she say that would help? "I'll be back before I start my shift, Mrs. Woods."

"You're not on your rounds now?"

"Not officially."

"I see. Well, thank you. It was good of you to check in on Jo on your own time. I know doctors don't usually do that. Jo really likes it when you come by. She says she wants to be a doctor when she grows up—just like Doctor Bridget. When does your shift begin?"

Bridget swallowed. *Doctor Bridget might never make it to being a real doctor.* "My shift begins at four. How about if I come back around three-thirty or so?"

"I'll try and make sure she's awake. She won't want to miss you."

"I'll see both of you then."

Bridget offered the best smile she could summon and realized Mrs. Woods couldn't see it because of the mask. Bridget turned and left the room, closing the door softly behind her. She took off the mask and hurried down the hallway. She passed the nurses station where two nurses were on their feet, reaching for supplies and checking paperwork. They froze as she approached.

"Y'all look busy," Bridget said, pulling the patient list clipboard from the hook and examining it.

"Busier than a one-legged woman at an ass-kicking contest."

The other rolled her eyes. "God, that's old. Hello, Doctor."

"Is Nurse Watkins in?" Bridget asked.

"She's on break right now. How are you doing?"

Bridget's eyebrows rose. The nurses had never asked how she was doing before. They had never been truly hostile, but they hadn't been friendly, either, despite her frequent attempts at levity with them. They were watching her closely for some reason. And that reason had to be Barbara Watkins. "I'm doing a lot better than my patients. Have you been checking on Josephine?"

"Every twenty. Poor girl. She'll make it, though. I have faith."

"We lost Hugh Croston on Wednesday," the other nurse pointed out.

"I know," Bridget said with a sigh. "I'm sorry I wasn't here to help him." She looked down at the list of patients and then up at the nurses.

"There was no saving him, Doctor. He went so fast—it was unreal. He shouldn't have gone that fast."

There was an awkward pause. The two nurses, who were five or six years older than Bridget, glanced at each other and then turned to Bridget.

"Look, we know what you're going through. Nurse Watkins told us after we heard some rumors floating around that they're trying to pressure you to keep this leukemia thing under wraps. We'd just like to say that we're with you. If there's anything we can do to help…"

"Anything," said the other.

"Thanks, I appreciate that." Bridget flipped through the names on the patient list. There were three new ones. One of the new ones had been diagnosed by Doctor Blake Hensley *with a sudden onset of leukemia*.

"What's the story with this new admission, this Mr. Oberlin?"

"They brought him in only an hour ago. He passed out at home. Preliminary tests show he's got the leuk."

"Treatment?"

"Doctor Williams is talking to Mrs. Oberlin about the options right now."

"Blood work?"

"Preliminary. Enough for the diagnosis."

"What about in-depth?"

One of the nurses pointed to a tray that held three slim vials of blood. "Pending. I was just about to take these samples down to Hemo for further analysis. But they're so understaffed down there, it may be a while before they get to it."

Bridget returned the patient list clipboard to the hook and grasped the tray. "I'll take it myself. I'm going down there anyway to do some analysis of my own. I'll enter the results into the computer for y'all to pull up. Give me half an hour. Who knows— maybe there's something in Mr. Oberlin's blood that I missed with the others."

"Good luck, Doctor."

"Let us know if we can help."

"Thanks," Bridget said, hurrying to the elevators with the three slim vials in hand. One of the four elevator doors parted just as she arrived. As she stood before it, three residents stepped out, laughing with one another. The men noticed Bridget and fell silent. Their gazes hardened and their facial expressions changed from jovial to masks of forced neutrality. They stepped out of the elevator and started to walk by her as if she wasn't there.

"Is this elevator going down?" she asked, glancing up at the arrows above the door just as she was about to enter.

"Oh, yeah," the tallest of the three said. "It's going down, all right."

"Definitely going down," said the other.

"How 'bout you, Devereaux?" said the third.

"Excuse me?"

"Oh, nothing."

"Never mind."

They turned their backs to her and walked away, but not before she caught them elbowing one another and snickering.

Bridget's eyes narrowed as the elevator doors shut. *Assholes. But were their remarks sexual innuendo or were they referring to my prospects as a physician? Both, probably.*

The doors parted to reveal the dilapidated basement once again. She stepped out and immediately noticed several more of the overhead lights were out. The same scattered tables and wheelchairs were still strewn throughout the long hallway, only now they resided beneath an even thicker veil of darkness. She thought she glimpsed a scurrying form dart from one shadow to another and then disappear beneath a long aluminum table used to transport cadavers to and from the morgue.

Mouse? Or rat?

Bridget shuddered. Did it matter? She'd handled both types of rodents in a laboratory setting, but caged in a lab was one thing and seeing them scamper about in the bowels of a hospital was another. These vermin could easily be infested with virus-laden parasites. She blanched. Disgusting. She'd definitely let maintenance know about this, just as soon as she got the chance.

As her skin crawled in a sweeping pattern from the base of her neck out to her shoulders, she pushed the door of the Hematology Lab open. In contrast to the dim hallway, the overhead lights here burned so brightly they made her squint. It was only after she arrived at a lab station, with its electron microscope and symbiotic computer, test tubes and clean slides, that she noticed the other two people in the room.

They were the same lab technicians who had been here the last time. She thought of Travis and what he'd done to her, and Handlaw and what he'd threatened her with, and boy it seemed a lot longer than two days ago.

The male lab tech watched her as she set her tray down. She said hello and he gave a small wave back. The girl had her eyes glued to the microscope at first, but after a moment she looked up and said "Hi", then scribbled something down on a pad.

"Are you two the only ones working today?" Bridget asked, using a slim dropper to dip into the test tubes containing Jerry Oberlin's blood. She carefully placed two small drops on each of the glass slides she had laid out in a row before her. When a pregnant pause followed, she glanced at the others.

They looked at one another, and for the first time Bridget noticed their faces appeared almost grim.

"Feels like we're the last two blood techs period," the guy said.

"They've cut us back so much, it almost seems that way," the girl said. "Two others are out on vacation, but even so there's just the four of us on this shift right now. They had us on-call for the night shift. Now they've taken us off that…"

Bridget blinked. "That's terrible."

"Tell us about it."

"Let me guess—they did this for the sale?"

"Sure," said the guy. "To make the bottom line look more attractive. After the hospital gets bought, they'll probably hire some temps or even more staff to help with the load. It's all bullshit smoke and mirrors, man."

"Meanwhile we're drowning in work," the other said. "Take those tests you're running—if they're standard it could be hours before we could get to it."

"That's way too long."

"It sucks," the guy said. "But even if you told us you needed it stat, we still couldn't drop what we're doing and get to your stuff."

"The other samples we have are all needed stat, as well. So there's a queue," the woman said.

"But my patients are dying."

The guy's long hair bounced as he nodded. "I hate to say it, but so are others. Ultimately the patients are going to suffer by the sale of this place." He wiped his brow with the back of his gloved hand. "I think it's safe to say the level of care in this place has just dropped a few hundred notches."

"Some'll be paying with their lives, all right," the woman said.

"It just gets better and better," Bridget said, turning back to her vials and slides.

She ran the blood tests on the Oberlin samples and entered the results into the computer. Then she called the nurse's station to let them know the results had been entered in Mr. Oberlin's patient records.

To her surprise, the blood analyzer identified, once again, Protein Matrix X—the unknown element she had originally thought might play a role in the explosive leukemia.

But Ian McGuire had said he'd proven the matrix was only a random event.

Bridget studied Mr. Oberlin's blood on the computer monitor hooked to the powerful microscope. Cancerous leukemia cells and healthy red and white blood cells were present, as were abnormally-shaped red and white blood cells that were products of the leukemia.

And with the help of the computer software, she was able to locate and identify several occurrences of Protein Matrix X.

Small victory, that, she thought, gazing at the monitor.

A small spiral-shaped organism drifted into view. It bypassed the cancerous cells and hovered near a healthy red blood cell as if sizing it up. As Bridget watched, the organism suddenly speared the healthy cell with its pointed end. The end penetrated deeply, and now the two entities drifted and bumped into other cells like drunken dance partners on a crowded ballroom floor.

Bridget stared, almost forgetting to breathe.

The spiral-shaped organism began drilling itself into the live cell.

She'd never seen this spiral-shaped organism before. The computer software couldn't identify it. However, it did classify it as a virus.

The virus drilled itself completely into the healthy cell. For a moment nothing happened. The cell drifted aimlessly with the virus inside it. Then the virus ruptured into pieces inside the cell.

Bridget jerked back but did not take her eyes from the

monitor.

Now viral fragments were swept to one side of the cell, as if the cell was cleaning house. The fragments were unrecognizable as the original virus. In the next instant the cell ejected the fragments outside its walls.

Bridget's face went slack.

That's the unknown protein matrix! Protein Matrix X is a waste product created by the reaction of this virus inside a healthy cell!

The cell that had been penetrated by the virus now writhed like a dying animal. It changed to a sickly reddish-orange color and the cell walls, once smooth, became chaotic and spiked. It drifted about in the slide, very alive and suddenly menacing. It attacked three other healthy cells as she watched. Seconds later there were four independent cancer cells looking for victims in Mr. Oberlin's blood. Then there were sixteen cancer cells.

With enough cell supply, there would soon be one hundred and fifty-six cancer cells, then twenty-four thousand, three hundred thirty-six, then...

"Oh my God," Bridget whispered, her pulse thudding in her ears.

Until now this had only been theory. She'd read about it in medical journals and on the Internet, but to her knowledge no one had actually witnessed a viral reaction that caused a healthy cell to become cancerous. In Jerry Oberlin's blood, and, she now suspected, in the blood of all her leukemia patients, the leukemic process had been both created and grossly accelerated by this unknown virus. After the virus did its dirty work and died off, there was a leukemia explosion within the body and then, with frightening speed, death to the host.

With trembling hands she examined Oberlin's other samples. Twice more she witnessed the same incredible process.

This is it!

Bridget turned to the computer and clacked away at the keyboard. In her doctor's notes she documented her findings. When she was finished, she returned to further examine the samples.

The spiral-shaped viral bodies were getting harder to locate, but the number of leukemia cells were still growing at an incredible rate.

Then, from all three samples, the virus simply *disappeared.* There was no evidence it had ever been there at all, except for the scattered occurrences of Protein Matrix X.

Bridget slumped back on the stool and stared.

There went her evidence of the whole process. How could she convince anyone of her findings without showing them the entire process?

Frantically, Bridget pulled up records of her early patients—Margaret Morrison and the others—on the computer.

As a by-product of the viral/cell reaction, she thought, *the protein matrix should have been present in all of the early blood samples. And yet, Ian McGuire proved it was simply a random occurrence.*

She clicked the mouse a few times.

I don't understand…

Bridget studied the numbers and percentages and breakdowns of the early samples taken from the accelerated leuk patients. All of it seemed correct. What was she missing?

She took off her glasses and rubbed the contact points on her nose. After a moment she put the glasses back on and leaned forward to peer at the columns of data on the monitor.

The sizes of the early samples are inconsistent. Five cubic centimeters. It's standard practice to use a sample twice. I know the samples I took were all ten cc's. Why have only five been entered into the computer? Did Ian make a mistake?

She clicked on another screen and examined the later samples from the leuk patients. All of these were ten cc's, as they should be.

Why would they have used only five cc's in the early samples?

Bridget glanced up as the two lab workers entered through the door and returned to their stools. She'd barely registered when they'd left fifteen minutes earlier for their break, but she noticed them now. "Hey, did you guys ever meet Ian McGuire yet?"

The guy arched an eyebrow and shook his head. "Nope, but I'm looking forward to it. He's a mystery man. I checked with our manager. She said she didn't hire any temps named McGuire. If he was a staff guy, we'd know him."

"Are you sure he isn't a doctor doing some of his own analysis, like you?" the woman asked.

"No," Bridget said. "He was a lab tech. I tried to pull his name up in the employee database but it doesn't come back with anything even close. It's weird because I worked with him a couple of nights in a row—he was very helpful and he had an identification badge and everything."

"That's weird, all right," the woman said.

"Yeah, man," the guy said. "I keep expecting Rod Serling to jump out from behind the cabinets."

Bridget nodded and turned back to her computer. So, who was Ian? *No one even knows him but me.*

And then that thought she didn't want to entertain…*Did Ian sabotage the blood samples? But why would he? What reason could he possibly have?*

Her leg pistoned up and down on the stool.

Maybe Ian was hired by Gerard Handlaw to throw me off the epidemic trail. A dirty thing to do, but it would fit right in with what I know of Handlaw. But Ian was here before I started making waves about the leuk. He couldn't have been hired by Handlaw, or any of the staff doctors.

Her leg stopped.

Ian was acting…on…his…own. But he'd been outwardly nice and personable, almost fatherly—why would he sabotage the samples? He had to have a reason. I need to find out where and when my patients first caught the virus. Are others exposed to it? Where does it come from?

She glanced up at the clock. Three twenty-five. Whoops! Time had gotten away from her. She'd told Mrs. Woods she'd stop by to see Jo before her shift started, around three-thirty. Time to get moving.

Bridget packed up the samples as fast as she could and put them back into cold storage.

"Leaving us?" the male lab worker asked.

"Running late."

"See you next time, Doc," the woman said.

Bridget barely heard her. She was out the door and scrambling for the staircase that led out of the dungeon that was the hospital basement. She'd make her destination faster under her own steam, not having to wait for the elevator to make its inevitable stops.

She burst out onto the third floor and almost ran to the nurse's station of Ward Seven. The same two nurses from before were standing there, peering down the other hallways. When they saw her, their eyes grew wide.

A man in a business suit stood nearby, conversing with a physician in a white lab coat. The physician was a staff doctor and the man in the suit was from Administration, a direct reporter to Gerard Handlaw. Bridget didn't know their names. They hadn't seen her, yet.

The nurses started to shuffle things around on the counter, but they stared at Bridget as they did so.

Bridget slowed.

One of the nurses held up her hand and Bridget stopped. The other nurse picked up a phone and Nurse Watkins suddenly appeared outside a room between Bridget and the nursing station. The look on her face made Bridget's heart sink.

Nurse Watkins glanced over her shoulder at the two men waiting at the nurse's station and then took Bridget by the arm. She turned her around and led her to a recessed alcove.

"It's happening, isn't it?" Bridget asked.

"I'm so sorry. I didn't hear about it until just now, damn it all! Now you listen to me—you're one of the best young doctors I've ever worked with. Don't you pay attention to these fools. They don't know a goddamn thing about healthcare! Don't listen to them, hear me?"

Bridget swallowed. "It's really happening."

"I have a friend on the Board of Trustees. I'll get in touch with him about this. Maybe he can do something."

"Thanks, but with the hospital up for sale, I don't think that'll do much good. Isn't the Board backing Handlaw?"

"Not my friend. He's been against that sexist son of a bitch from the get-go."

Suddenly Bridget grasped the older woman's arm. "Listen—I found the secret to this leukemia epidemic."

Nurse Watkin's mouth dropped open. *"What?"*

"Just now in the lab. I saw it in Mr. Oberlin's blood. The problem is that the evidence gets absorbed by the cells in one hell of a hurry. If you want to help, here's what you can do—get Mr. Oberlin on antibiotics along with his chemo."

"But antibiotics won't stop leukemia, nor any cancer."

"Our accelerated leuk is caused by a virus that stays active in the body for only a day or so, two at max. The virus acts as a catalyst to transform healthy cells into super leuk cells that can replicate themselves at a devastating rate. Right now Mr. Oberlin's blood contains both the virus and the leuk cells. Attack both and we may save him. Otherwise he's dead—just like the others."

"Oh, God…But what about Jo? Why has the leuk taken so long with her?"

"Jo must not have been fully exposed to the virus or she'd be dead by now. Instead of a power punch, she must have received only a glancing blow. Her blood doesn't show any of the protein matrix by-product, so my guess is she's beyond the viral-reactionary stage—the virus has already done its dirty work. The leuk is active in her, though not as strong as in the others. The best thing for her is to stay on the chemo and hope for the best.

"Right now I need to pay Jo a visit." Bridget stepped out of the alcove. Nurse Watkins stepped out with her. Bridget glanced over at the men who had just noticed them, and turned and walked toward her like executioners. "It's been great working with you, Barbara. I've learned a lot."

"What are you going to do?"

"I need to find the source of this virus, and to do that I need to know more about my patients. I'll—I'll just have do it without having to worry about my career as a doctor." She tried to force a smile but the tears were already building behind her eyes.

Are you going to fight, or be a victim?

"You call me," Nurse Watkins said, pushing something into Bridget's hand. "My home number is on that card. You call anytime, day or night."

"I may need more of your help, especially with information about our patients. Some of it may go against the rules."

"Screw the rules."

The men finally reached her and now stood expectantly behind Nurse Watkins. Bridget gently pushed her to the side.

Nurse Watkins glared at the men with open contempt.

"I think Linda needs you at the nurse's station, Nurse Watkins," Bridget said.

Nurse Watkins looked at Bridget, then marched right between the men, who had to step quickly to the side to get out of her way.

The administrator, Handlaw's flunky, had a serious expression on his round face. His eyes seemed to bulge from behind his round-rimmed glasses. "Bridget Devereaux, I'm George Waxton and this is Doctor Phillips. If you'll follow us, we need to converse with you in my office."

Bridget stared at them.

Decide. Victim or fighter?

"Let's go, then," Bridget said, following Nurse Watkins' lead and stepping deliberately between the two.

They had to hurry to catch up to her.

SEVENTEEN

Bridget's steps fell silent and quick, contrasting sharply with the clatter of the two men who struggled to keep up with her. Nurses and doctors and orderlies stepped aside to stare in sudden quiet as the three marched by.

Bridget didn't need to see the faces of George Waxton—rather George Waxton the Third, as she'd often seen his name on hospital letterhead—or Doctor Phillips to know they were shooting angry glares at her back while still trying to appear dignified to the rest of the hospital population. She could feel the heat from those looks. Evidently, the men didn't appreciate having to march through the hospital hallways like storm troopers of the Third Reich.

No doubt they wanted her to go demurely to her fate. No doubt they wanted to tell her to slow down but didn't want to appear weak.

*Too bad.*After almost stumbling down three flights of stairs to the first floor, her companions finally did mumble something about slowing, but she ignored them. The greedy fools had scoffed at her warnings about the leukemia epidemic and now they were going to throw her out of the internship program. To hell with slowing and to hell with *them*.

She could hear them wheezing slightly, sucking air into then squeezing it out of their lungs. She bumped up the pace another notch. She was charging fast now, and her dubious escorts had to pump their arms to keep up.

Closing in on the fancy wooden doors that led to Gerard Handlaw's executive suite, she put on a sudden burst of speed. When her hand closed on one of the handles she was several paces in front of them.

"Now wait a damn minute, Devereaux!" George Waxton said. "That's *not* where we're going. We're going to do this in my office."

She turned and glared at him, seconds away from shredding the fat from his pudgy red cheeks with her fingernails.

"That's quite enough of this foolishness, Doctor Devereaux." Doctor Phillips began unabashedly jogging toward her, now.

"Save it," Bridget said, throwing open the door to Handlaw's suite. She threw it so hard it banged against the rubber stopper on the wall and rebounded. She slipped inside an instant before it caught her. The faces of Handlaw's flunkies were replaced by dark wood grain.

The receptionist—big fake boobs, teased hair, non-prescription glasses and all— saw Bridget and let out a strange cry. She leapt to her feet and tried to intercept Bridget, catching up to her at the door to Handlaw's office.

"You can't go in there!"

The secretary grabbed Bridget's arm, her fake nails breaking as she dug her fingers in. Bridget jerked her arm away and the secretary's grip was broken as easily as a child's. Now Bridget held the secretary fast by *her* arm. Bridget's other hand let go the door handle and balled into a fist. In a sudden flashing image Bridget could see her fist crashing into Ms. Perfect's face, fake glasses and pert nose and all. She could see it with all the distinct violence of the thunderstorm raging outside.

Not the way. Not the way, Devereaux.

She held her fist in check. Barely.

The office door flew open and Waxton and Phillips charged through. "Get away from Mr. Handlaw's—"

"You can't go in there!"

Bridget pushed Handlaw's secretary aside and shoved the door to Handlaw's personal office open. She stepped inside and slammed the door behind her. Handlaw wasn't at his desk, nor were his visitors from Allied Health sitting in the guest chairs around his desk.

Her eyes darted to the expansive meeting area across the room. There she saw three balding men in their late forties or early fifties in suits. At the head of the meeting table sat Handlaw himself, sporting a snazzy double-breasted. The others looked at her in surprise, but Handlaw's face was set in stone, the consummate business politician. Only a flicker of annoyance glinted in his narrow eyes as she approached.

Waxton and Phillips entered the room behind her. She glanced at them over her shoulder and then looked down at Handlaw. "Certainly the chief executive officer of this hospital can perform this task without requiring additional assistance from his lieutenants."

All gazes were fixed on Handlaw. He motioned the subordinates away with a single flick of his fingers. Waxton and Phillips glared at Bridget, then retreated to Handlaw's desk. They crouched in the guest chairs around Handlaw's desk, ready to spring at a moment's notice.

"Gentlemen, I believe that will have to suffice for now," Handlaw said. "I must call an end to this meeting so that I may attend to a rather distasteful matter."

There was a murmur of surprise from the men and they started to rise from their seats.

Bridget's face flushed so hot it must be on fire. Of course, he wouldn't want witnessed to this conversation. He'd dismiss these men and can her, and that would be that.

No!

She approached the table with her hands held up. "Gentlemen—wait! Don't rush off! Doctor Handlaw wants to dismiss me from the intern program and I'd like you to hear why."

The reps, caught in a half-crouch, glanced at each other uncertainly.

"We'll discuss this in *private*, Miss Devereaux!" Handlaw said.

She ignored him and addressed the others. "Isn't an entire career worth five minutes of your time?"

The men eased down into their seats.

"It boils down to this, gentlemen," she said. "In the past eight weeks we've lost seven patients to leukemia, a blood cancer of which I'm sure you're familiar. These seven patients died within *days* of their initial diagnosis. In each case there was a sudden, debilitating onset of the disease, rapid decline, followed by death in less than seventy-two hours. Normally leukemia doesn't kill anywhere near this quickly. At first I didn't understand why, but now I do: the accelerated leukemia is triggered by a *virus*, a virus I discovered just moments ago."

She gauged their reaction. There might as well have been four mannequins sitting around the table.

"Really, Devereaux," Handlaw said. "You're not a researcher. What makes you think you're qualified—"

"My tests were valid. With the microscope, I saw the virus turn healthy cells into leukemia cells. And these newly-created cancer cells are *voracious*. They preyed on other cells at a frightening pace, spreading leukemia like wildfire within the host."

Handlaw raised his eyebrows in a show of mock amazement. Then he smiled at the Allied reps in a see-she's-so-fucking-far-out-there kind of way. "Gentlemen, our specialists found no such virus in blood samples taken from the same patients."

Bridget leaned forward. "That's because the virus is temporary. It doesn't replicate itself. It gets dismantled in the healthy cells as part of the reaction. Twelve to twenty-four hours after initial contact with the host, the virus is gone. It gets the ball rolling and the accelerated leukemia takes over from there. As far as I can tell with our computers, this virus is unknown. In the last two months we've lost all but one of our leukemia patients to it. Therefore, I must conclude that we're in the early stages of an epidemic."

The reps turned to one another, murmuring comments of

surprise and doubt.

Bridget continued, looking each representative squarely in the eyes in turn. "The administration won't listen to me because they don't want to blow the sale of this place to you people. They don't want any bad publicity because we failed to identify a possible epidemic and notify the public. They are sacrificing lives for money!"

The reps looked at Handlaw.

He made a show of checking his Rolex. "Devereaux, your shift was due to begin at four today, how could you possibly have had time to examine blood samples?"

"I've been practically camping out here in order to do my own research."

"Oh? From what your chief resident told me, you weren't here yesterday, or the day before," Handlaw pointed out, arching an eyebrow.

"No…I…I was…exhausted."

One of the reps spoke for the first time. "You said death resulted in all but one of your cases, young lady?"

"That's right."

"What about that case?"

Bridget swallowed. "She's a young girl. She's hanging on, but only barely. Chemotherapy may or may not save her."

"But surely an epidemic would take the life of a young girl." Handlaw seized the opening.

"I don't believe she was exposed to a concentrated level of the virus."

"You don't *believe*?" Handlaw said, a smile of mockery on his wide, heavy face. "This hospital is a place of medical knowledge, built upon what is known and what is proven. Personal beliefs are inconsequential unless backed up by fact. Surely even you are aware of this, *Miss* Devereaux."

There it was again, *Miss Devereaux* instead of *Doctor Devereaux*. "The virus breaks down quickly after cell infiltration. It explodes, really, and the waste is ejected from the cell as a useless protein. I haven't seen the virus in Jo, but early on I did see the protein waste-product. She's lived this long because she didn't get infected with enough of the virus to cause a quick death."

"You know that for a fact?"

"Well…no…but I believe—"

"There's that word again, *Miss* Devereaux." Handlaw propped his elbows on the arms of his chair and bridged his fingers before him, the tips of one hand lightly touching the tips of the other. "Your *beliefs* are no more than whimsical fancy without hard evidence. I'm afraid we cannot have our patients exposed to a steady diet of such stuff, wouldn't you agree, gentlemen?"

To a man they nodded and watched her as if she were some sort of odd curiosity.

And just like that, Handlaw walled her in.

Bridget slammed her open hand on the table. *"You don't have the balls to admit I'm right!"*

All the men except for Handlaw jerked away from the table. Handlaw just stared at her with his glinting eyes and that slight upward tugging at the corners of his mouth. He might as well be grinning from ear to ear. He had won. There never really had been much of a chance of persuading them. And now, she realized with a sinking feeling in her stomach, striking the table had thrown her completely out of contention.

Way to go, Bridget-old-gal.

Handlaw bolted to his feet, an expression of almost genuine alarm plastered on his face. "You're out of line, Devereaux."

"You know I'm right," she said between clenched teeth. "And when I prove this epidemic is not fantasy, you're going to look like the greedy, stone-hearted bastard you really are. In fact," she eyed each man at the table, "all of you are going to look pretty bad. It'll take years of corporate bullshit propaganda to get your careers back on track after this."

"My word!" one of the reps said.

"What is the meaning…" started another.

"Gentlemen, I'm very sorry," Handlaw said. "As you can see, she's very much out of control." He reached for the phone. "Security will escort her out."

Bridget straightened. "Don't bother. I'm leaving."

She stormed out of his office and through the outer office, flunkies Waxton and Phillips right behind her. Handlaw's secretary looked up at her.

"Ding dong the witch is dead, right?" Bridget said.

His secretary stiffened. "We can't have incompetent doctors here. You're a danger to the patients—"

Bridget stopped short, forcing Waxton and Phillips to halt behind her.

"That's the official lie? Look, they want to throw me out because I've stumbled across a cancer epidemic and they don't want to know about it. Seven people have died already but they don't want it getting out. They don't want any 'hysterical' warnings from a lowly intern to jeopardize the sale of this hospital."

The secretary blinked. "But Gerard said—"

"Did he also tell you you'd have a job after the hospital changed hands?"

"A promotion. In the public relations department."

"Don't you think Allied Health is going to bring in their own people to run the place *their* way? Handlaw'll get a cushy job until the transition is complete, then they'll have him resign quietly and he'll fade away, taking his millions with him. But don't be surprised when the new management brings in their own secretaries. Your days are numbered, too, honey."

Shock was the last expression Bridget saw cross the secretary's face before she marched out of the office.

She stormed through the main lobby and out of the hospital. Heavy winds immediately buffeted her. As she stepped from beneath the protective overhang, a sheet of rain slammed into her. In three seconds she was completely soaked.

Lightning exposed the bruised world around her in momentary still life. It flashed again and again, slicing the air, cutting with abandon. On its heels came thunder that shook her very bones. She walked away from the hospital without hurrying. She kept her head up, letting the rain sting her face and wash away the tears that now flowed despite her anger.

Another flash of lightning and she suddenly knew the world had changed in a thousand ways at once.

Handlaw is not the real enemy, she thought. *He's a complete asshole, but he's not the real enemy. The real enemy is the virus, and I'm the only one who can do anything about it.*

Shivering and dripping wet, she found her car. She climbed in, put the key in the ignition and started it. It chugged at first and she revved the engine. Normally loud and sputtering, the engine noise was barely audible over the crashing thunder. The car vibrated roughly as it idled. She was about to put it in first gear when she suddenly froze.

Jo.

The girl in Room 305 had been expecting Bridget to check in on her.

"She really enjoys your visits," Mrs. Woods had said. "She wants to be a doctor like you when she grows up."

Except I'm no longer a doctor. Right or wrong, they've thrown me out of the program. Still, I told her I'd come see her.

She turned off the car. She had to shove the door open because the wind wanted to keep it closed. She stepped out and in seconds was soaked all over again. The wind pushed her toward the hospital and she let it take her, riding it toward the main entrance.

She walked through the hallways, her hair and clothes soaked to the skin and dripping water onto the floors. People can always be counted on to stare at anything strange, and this time was no exception. Family and friends of patients, patients themselves, doctors, nurses, and orderlies seemed to find the sight of her instantly compelling.

Her shoes squeaked as she walked.

The cool air of the hospital made her shiver. If she unclenched her jaw, her teeth would chatter.

"I'm so sorry, Doctor," one of the nurses told her as she reached the Ward Seven nursing station. "It's not right what they've done to you."

She grasped a facemask and nodded, not daring to speak right now. A second nurse placed a towel in her hands and draped another over her shoulders.

"Thank you," Bridget managed to say.

Blake Hensley came around the corner. He saw her and pounced, an intense expression on his chief resident's face. "I warned you but you wouldn't listen. Couldn't play by the rules, could you? A *prima donna*. You're not Chambers material. Get out. You're not welcome here."

"Are visitors no longer welcome here either, *Doctor*?" Bridget didn't know why her voice didn't crack.

A quizzical expression came over his face. "Of course, visitors are welcome."

Bridget pulled on the mask that would keep her germs from infecting Jo. "I'm visiting a friend."

Blake Hensley had nothing to say as Bridget walked toward Jo's room.

EIGHTEEN

H ICKORY GROVE WAS everything Raynorr had expected it to be, just a small Southern town of limited means and isolated nothingness. Driving down Main Street, he realized it was a tiny spec compared to Raleigh, which was only a modest city when compared to sprawling behemoths such as Atlanta.

People live in a place like this because they're born to it. That, or they've got something to hide. Like me.

It had taken over an hour to get here from his home in Wake Forest and he had pushed it, keeping the long black Oldsmobile ten miles an hour over the posted speed limit as he raced down country roads that were monotonously straight and bleached almost chalk-white from years of punishment beneath the harsh Carolina sun. The roads had taken him through field after massive field of farm crops. The first had been tobacco. The waist-high plants were almost ready for harvest; the leaves were broad and green and turning to gold, and a cluster of tiny white flowers protruded at the tops of the plants from the center stem, making the plants appear almost snow-capped. Soon field hands would lop off the flower heads, take the golden leaves from the lowest portion of the plants, then return in a few days to take the next layer closest to the ground. They'd repeat the process until the plant was completely bare.

Seven miles outside of Hickory Grove were long stretches of green crops that may have been soy or alfalfa, he wasn't sure which, having never been a farmer. On the outskirts of the town were vast fields of corn; stalk and silk-plumed armies that stood in tight formation over hundreds of acres, with each soldier standing five feet tall or better.

Then the cornfields had suddenly ended and he had slowed to the posted speed of thirty-five miles per hour as he entered the township of Hickory Grove.

Now he eased the Olds down Main Street, staring with a modicum of interest at the rows of neatly-kept homes, reminiscent of the Old South. The majority of the houses had to be at least fifty years old, some probably closer to a hundred. Most had wide front porches and gently sloping roofs. Protruding like giants from the green lawns were massive trunks of pecan and oak and pine. Closer to the road were smaller crepe myrtles, whose tough little green leaves were offset by bumblebee-infested flowers of pink, red, and white.

Raynorr encountered a total of three traffic lights while crossing through the heart of town. Halting at the third while it glared angrily at him, he noticed a few old men and women rocking on their porches while kids on summer break rode bikes and skateboarded down the side roads. He also counted three women, their shirts soaked with sweat, cutting grass, despite the dewdrops that sparkled like diamonds in the morning sun.

The red light went black. Below it stared an orb of cool green. He took his foot from the brake and pressed down on the accelerator. The car instantly shot forward.

At the center of town was the town hall, a hardware/feed store, an aging movie theater that was showing two movies that had been released almost six months earlier in Raleigh, a single fast food restaurant, two greasy spoons, two gas stations with various rusting cars in the side yards, and three separate churches—two Baptist and a Methodist.

The churches stood within a mile of one another. All three were neat and tidy; the bricks and siding and shingles were fresh-looking and the stained glass of each was intact. All three had white spires that rose high into the azure sky, far above the highest of the surrounding trees. The spires were so white Raynorr had to squint to look at them. The bronze crosses at the apexes of these spires glinted in the morning sun.

Easy to see who has the money in this town.

The Baptist parking lots were empty. The asphalt of these was deep black, so dark that they had to have been poured recently, perhaps as early as the first days of summer. Grids of almost neon white pulsed against the blacktops to mark the parking spaces.

The Methodist parking lot, while faded, was far more interesting, for it actually had vehicles in it.

Not so common for a Monday morning. Raynorr arched an eyebrow. *Either someone's getting married at a very peculiar time, or a funeral is underway.*

He smiled. *And I didn't drive all the way out here to see two people get hitched.*

A black hearse had backed into a solitary parking spot near the side entrance. A small overhang kept it shaded. Raynorr parked at the side of the road near the church and got out, quickly checking his reflection in the glass of the driver's side window.

As at Anderson's restaurant, he was dressed again in a suit, although this time his tie and the suit were black. He had wanted to wear a cheery red tie with mocking white power dots and a white suit, but had decided against it. He didn't particularly want to stand out any more than he already would as a stranger at a small funeral. Not that it would matter. He'd never see any of these people again.

He donned dark sunglasses and walked to the brick and mortar church, pulling the handle of one of the large white doors and entering through the main entrance. Inside it was cool and dim. Seemed the church had invested a lot in stained glass and air-conditioning but not so much in artificial lighting.

A hush settled around him as he strolled through the vestibule. Everywhere on the white walls were handmade posters done in bright blues and reds and greens and yellows. No doubt the posters were the work of young Bible School students, their artistic talents conveying what a wonderful world God had made and how great He was for making it.

He frowned and halted before the open chapel doors.

The children who made those innocent posters would someday find that the world is not so full of joy and bright color and everlasting love. Small hands would grow into adult hands that would be used to grip the sides of their heads in disbelief when they came to realize there was no real God, no higher power that took an active interest in their lives. Then they would realize the world was not as the clergy painted it, nor was it as Disney painted it. The world was a cold, uncaring place. These children would someday have to scrape and claw for daily survival. Happiness and good fortune, if attained, would at best be fleeting, the result of random chance.

And even then, if they're fortunate enough to gain some measure of happiness, it will get ripped away from them just as surely as mine was ripped away from me. That's reality. It's stark. Cold. Meaningless and maddening, but it is reality.

Somber organ music droned in his ears.

He entered the chapel.

Row after row of empty wooden pews led to the backs of a handful of men and women. The pews were angled so as to focus attention on the altar, where a scant few vases of flowers were propped around an open casket containing the worthless shell of Hugh Croston.

With a deliberate tread, he walked down the center aisle toward the casket. He could see the milky white, sunken cheeks and thin strands of hair on the corpse that only a week earlier had housed an arrogant young man in the prime of his life, a man rising through the corporate world on a fast track, a man who had made bottom-line driven recommendations on health care policies that had adversely affected the lives of thousands of people—including, in the end, his own.

It's possible you might have lived if your health insurance had covered the cost of those expensive diagnostic tests, Hugh-boy. Possible, but unlikely.

Suppressing the smile that tugged at the corners of his mouth, Raynorr passed the loose group of men and women sitting in silence or trading whispered conversation. Some looked his way but he kept his eyes on the body of Hugh Croston. He arrived at the altar and stood looking down into the casket.

The corpse looked thin and withdrawn and decidedly unnatural, almost plastic. There was an inadequate layer of beige makeup on its face and blatant rouge on its cheeks. Even through the ridiculous red lipstick, Raynorr's trained eye could make out the stitch pattern they'd used to secure Croston's lips.

Wouldn't want your mouth to fall open and have you making a big wide "O" at the gathered kinfolk.

Raynorr's cheek twitched.

With his back to the mourners, he bent and whispered in Croston's ear. "Not doing too good, now are you, Hot Shot? For some reason you don't look so proud anymore. In fact, you don't look very proud at all. I don't think folks liked you too much, Hot Shot. You didn't exactly draw a crowd, now did you?"

Raynorr's shoulders began to shake. *No, no. Can't do that now.*

"Where are your cronies from the corporation? Too busy to make your burial? Must have had a staff meeting today. Maybe they should have hired some professional wailers."

Despite his resolve, a snicker escaped his lips.

The sound of it in this place of reverential quiet tickled his ears. Another snicker followed the first. And then one after that. He tightened his upper body and had to clench his teeth to keep more from escaping.

But as Raynorr looked down at Croston's clownish makeup, he couldn't help but remember how the arrogant shit had cut him off at the elevator. He couldn't help but find this, the end result, *hysterical.*

Raynorr's breath hissed through his clenched teeth. It sounded like air escaping from a hose. More and more hissed out and then the mirth gained strength inside him, causing his shoulders to buck as if he were breaking in a bronco.

Can't hold back any longer.

He threw his head back and howled with laughter. The sound of it rebounded off the high ceiling and the walls and was carried to every corner of the acoustically sound chapel.

Murmurs and cries of disbelief from the mourners behind him made him turn and laugh louder, right in their astounded faces. Several men suddenly stood and shuffled past protruding knees to reach the aisle.

"He was a heartless bastard!" Raynorr cried, laughing and pointing at Croston's shell of a body. "Why mourn a heartless bastard like Hugh Croston?"

This time the cries were those of anger.

He laughed harder. "Don't you get it? He was *fucking* you people!"

"Ian?" A woman's voice, tension-filled, cut through the others. "Ian, what...what are you doing?"

Doctor Bridget Devereaux suddenly stood in the middle of the third pew. She wore a sleeveless black dress, a look of unbridled confusion and horror on her face.

Raynorr froze, his laughter collapsing beneath surprise.

Why is she here? Did she actually care for this human trash?

Raynorr bolted for the side exit as several men gained the center aisle. Addressing the congregation, he shouted: "Hugh Croston would have mourned none of you! Not one! Why mourn him?"

An instant before he shoved the door open he glimpsed Doctor Devereaux running down the length of the pew, heading for the side aisle.

Sure-footed, he noted, in the one part of his brain that wasn't tickled by the absurdity of mourning for such a heartless bastard as Hugh Croston. *Sure-footed and quick, but not nearly fast enough.*

Raynorr burst out into the glaring sunshine. He collided with the black hearse, throwing his hands out at the last moment. The black finish burned into the flesh of his palms. The pain started him laughing again, even harder than before. The hearse was as hot as an oven. Surely it would cook Croston on his way to his final resting place—

Baked Croston, anyone?...only three days old. It's a delicacy in these here parts. Ya don't git it but once't every thirty years!

He careened off the hearse and dashed for the Oldsmobile.

What an odd sensation to laugh while running, he thought as he sprinted with an athlete's ease.The laughs gushed out in a geyser of guffaws. He didn't attempt to contain them, doubted he could, even if he had the inclination...which he didn't.

Behind him he heard the side exit door slam against the brick wall. Voices and the sounds of heavy footfalls spilled out.

At the driver's door he fished the keys from his pocket, missed the keyhole the first time because his hand was shaking from his laughter. Finally, the keys slid into the lock. He was inside and revving the engine a second later. The tires squealed as he slammed the accelerator to the floorboard. The back-end of the long Olds fishtailed and he laughed even harder, hot tears flowing down his cheeks.

The handful of male mourners, probably Croston's limited

family members, jumped like startled grasshoppers to get out of his way as he barreled through their midst.

In the rearview he saw rising clouds of blue-black smoke appear behind him. In a sudden flash of inspiration he whipped the car to the right and put his left foot on the brake, even as the right remained on the accelerator. The tires screamed in tortured protest as he forced the Oldsmobile into a three hundred and sixty-degree turn, a stunt they used to call *doing a donut* in his high school days.

The sharp reek of burning rubber clung to the insides of his nostrils. His laughter blended with the screeching of the tires and for a few seconds he couldn't distinguish between the two.

Suddenly, Raynorr jerked the wheel to the left to straighten the car and tear down the street. As he passed the church he turned his head and there was Bridget Devereaux, standing on a green patch of grass and staring at him with a perplexed expression. Her exquisite mouth hung open and her blue eyes were wide and...hurt, he suddenly realized.

His daughters had looked at him like that whenever he had fought with his wife.

His laughter again died and this time didn't revive.

He raced out of the tiny town of Hickory Grove, his mind alive with the certainty that Doctor Bridget Devereaux knew *something* more than the fact that Ian McGuire wasn't just a lab worker at Chambers Hospital. She knew something else about him. He had hurt her—the look on her face had said as much. Did she know he had deliberately misled her by tampering with the patient blood samples?

Perhaps she even knew about the Raynorr Virus itself.

That was acceptable, should it be the case, for he needed the virus to gain some publicity, now. The insurance fools needed to know what they were dealing with.

But had Doctor Bridget Devereaux linked the Raynorr Virus directly to its creator?

If so, it made her a very real danger to his operation.

A danger he could not tolerate, despite his fondness for the gutsy young doctor.

∗ ∗ ∗

By the time he pulled into his driveway the euphoria of seeing Croston in his casket had long since worn off. His concerns over Bridget Devereaux, and the look on her face when she saw him at the funeral, nagged at him.

No, haunted him.

Cain and Abel greeted him with panting tongues and wagging

tails. Distractedly, he petted them, murmuring to them without knowing what he was saying.

He climbed the three steps leading up to the shaded porch. He pulled the screen door open and then unlocked and opened the front door. With the clatter of paw nails the dogs bee-lined to the air-conditioned coolness inside. He followed them in and went to the bedroom after checking the basement door to make sure it was locked, a habit of his. It was. The lab was safe. He changed out of the suit and tie and donned his headband, shorts, socks and sneakers. He ordered the dogs to stay inside and they were only too happy to oblige.

He closed the front door behind him without locking it, as always. The big shepherds were more than enough of a deterrent in the off chance someone came to the door.

At first he only walked down the driveway. He welcomed the fiery touch of the sun on his bald pate and shoulders and upper back. The gravel scrunched beneath his tread as he began the run, turning west on SR 1202 after his driveway ended.

Forty minutes later he returned, sweat flowing from every pore in his body. His shorts, underwear, even his socks and shoes, were soaked with sweat.

He sat on the single rocking chair on the porch, breathing hard. It hadn't been one of his better runs, or even a good one, for that matter. The distraction of Bridget Devereaux had kept cropping up in his mind, taking energy from him, depriving him of the necessary willpower he needed to really push himself.

But at least now he knew what he needed to do.

First, he needed more firepower. The Raynorr Virus was deadly and potent, but it lacked the ability to reproduce itself. He needed the threat of a true virus, a true epidemic. If his demands weren't met, or if his position was somehow compromised, he needed to be able to take out an entire city. Then the fools would bend to his will. Using a large dose of the current semi-virus may or may not work. But infect the drinking water of a city with a self-replicating version of the Raynorr Virus and *boom*! he had the equivalent of an atomic bomb.

And atomic bombs bring capitulation.

After taking a quick shower, he ate two peanut butter and apple butter sandwiches, heavy on both spreads, washed down with a large glass of skim milk. He carefully washed his hands and donned his lab coat and a thin pair of pants. He put on a breathing filter, a clear plastic visor, and thin latex gloves. Then he went to work in the basement lab, where he proceeded to develop altered generation after altered generation of the Raynorr Virus.

He added a control mechanism here, took one away there, introduced the virus to a wide array of tissue, temperature, and chemicals—all within his labyrinth of glass and tubes. Each experiment was carefully monitored and documented in his computer for additional analysis.

Possessed, he didn't tire. His entire universe shrank to the basement laboratory.

After two consecutive days and nights of painstaking work, he knew he was close. He drank pots of black coffee to remain awake and alert. Twenty hours after he started he finally succeeded. There, beneath the lens of his microscope, was Andrew Raynorr's equivalent of Oppenheimer's Atom Bomb.

I have my self-replicating virus! I did it!

He shut the lab down and went upstairs to take a shower. He then laid in his bed and stared at the ceiling. He couldn't sleep, despite his near exhaustion.

Might as well have a little celebration.

TUESDAY, JUNE 16 ... NIGHT

IT WAS DARK when he emerged from the house. He flicked open a hand-carved silver lighter that he'd picked up in a trade market in the "city" of Mbandaka, in Zaire—*now the Democratic Republic of Congo,* he reminded himself—and lit the five citronella tiki torches lining the porch. The torches were supposed to keep the mosquitoes to a minimum, though he had his doubts on their effectiveness. He went back inside the house and re-emerged with a thick cigar clamped between his middle and index fingers and a highball glass of whiskey, a double, in the palm of his hand. The dogs followed him out and he sat on the porch in the rocker, lit the cigar and sipped the drink while the tiki torches burned steadily in the windless night.

The chittering cicada broadcasted from the surrounding trees and the dark forest at the edge of the meadow. The fireflies glimmered in a wild array of mysterious lights. He stared at them as he alternated between the cigar and whiskey glass.

As he rocked in the chair a few vehicles passed by, their headlights lighting the trees on the far side of the road long before the whoosh! of tires and accelerated metal met his ears. He caught a glimpse of them as they blurred beneath the pale area light on the post at the end of the driveway.

One vehicle passed his house and then slowed before fading away. He heard the crunching of the gravel as the vehicle turned around and came back a few moments later. Again the headlights lit the trees and road, though this time at a much slower pace as the vehicle approached then turned into the two dirt tire lanes of his driveway.

Shaking off his comfortable buzz, he warily rose from the rocker. The dogs rushed off the porch to bark at the newcomer. No one had ever visited him here…perhaps they were lost.

Then he recognized the pickup truck.

It was the one driven by the blonde woman who lived in the subdivision farther down the road.

In the golden glow of the tiki torches she smiled at him through her windshield, then looked down at the barking dogs. He called them off and immediately they ran back to him. He ordered them to sit and stay and then, with his short-sleeved shirt completely unbuttoned, he walked out to greet his unexpected guest.

She rolled down the window and smiled at him. "I noticed your bug-torches from the road. Saw you in the rocker and wanted to know how a man could have such a contented look on his face without a woman nearby."

His eyebrows raised before he could stop them. Bold woman. Not afraid to break the ice. He liked that. The cigar smoke curled upward from his hand and over the cab of the pickup. He smiled. "Now that you mention it, the only thing that could make this evening any better would be the company of a beautiful woman. Would you happen to be available for a drink, per chance?"

"Only if you promise your dogs won't think of me as tonight's alternative to Alpo."

He laughed and it felt good. He wasn't at all tired. "They've been fed already tonight."

"Then I accept your offer for a drink. My house is all too quiet with my boys away an' all."

"I know what you mean," Raynorr said, nodding.

Setting the highball glass on the roof of her pickup, he opened the door and offered his hand. She slipped hers into his and he liked how it fit inside his palm—slender, with long, artistic fingers despite the fact she drove a pick-up truck. She wore a sleeveless shirt and one of those skorts, half skirt, half shorts. The first two buttons of her shirt were unfastened and he had to fight to keep his gaze from her ample cleavage. Her long legs led the way out of the pick-up.

She brushed a few errant strands of blond hair from her face. Perhaps it was a trick of the torchlight, but her eyes seemed to smolder as she gazed up at him. "I'm Madeline Harper."

"Anthony Burgess," Raynorr said, leading her into the inviting glow of the tiki torches. "I'm so glad you came for a visit, Madeline. This is truly one of life's unexpected delights. What will you have?"

"What you've got looks just fine to me."

NINETEEN

WEDNESDAY, JUNE 15 ... MORNING

THE SLEEVELESS SHIRT clung uncomfortably to the small of Bridget's back as she stepped onto the third floor landing of her apartment building.

Driving around with no AC in summertime'll do that. She rolled her shoulders in an effort to free her skin from the damp cloth.

Nice try, but that short climb up the stairs isn't what's making you perspire, sister.

Yeah, well...She eyed her apartment door.

Her hand trembled, causing the key to *tap-tap-tap-tap* against the doorknob.

Haven't been here for four days. Will I find Travis in bed with another woman? Or maybe Handlaw with a gun looking to finalize things?

Or Ian, laughing like a madman...

*She still couldn't fathom why he'd been at Hugh Croston's funeral. And every time she thought about his bizarre behavior...*She shuddered.

She took a deep breath and let it out with a hiss. Grasping her wrist firmly with her other hand, she succeeded in sliding the key into the lock. She pushed at the door and it swung slowly inward.

Inside, it was cool and dark.

Like a grave.

Now if I hadn't just been to a funeral...

Bridget stepped inside but left the door open behind her. She went first to the living room windows, where she hauled down on the drawstrings of the shades. The shades shrieked upward and bright mid-morning light streamed inside the apartment. Tossing her purse on the counter, she jerked on the shade cord at the kitchen window with the same result as before. On her way out of the kitchen she noticed a red "6" glowing on the tiny display window of her answering machine.

Not right now. Have to check things out first.

She went to the bedroom and peered in. The bed was made, the spread free of major wrinkles and only slightly askew.

No Travis in bed with a bimbo. No Travis at all. No Handlaw with a shotgun, either. And no Ian...thank God.

Acid sprang from the glands inside her mouth. She ran to the bathroom. Spitting into the sink, she was certain she was going to vomit the toast Francine had made her eat this morning. She groaned but it never happened. After a few moments she rinsed her mouth out and drank straight from the tap, then cupped the water and splashed her face. Gasping for air, she looked into the mirror. Water ran in rivulets down her face and dripped from her chin. The hair at the sides of her face was wet and clung to her skin.

Obviously the weekend away had not led to a full recovery.
There's no time for this.

She coughed, the origin of it deep in her lungs. She sniffled, pulled out the worn handkerchief she had borrowed from her brother-in-law and blew her nose.

"Nothing like having a summer cold to top off the problems list," she told her tired-looking reflection.

Wiping at her nose with the handkerchief, she returned to the living room to close the front door before heading back to the bedroom. She kicked her shoes in the general direction of the closet, peeled off her damp socks and threw them toward the simple plastic hamper she'd picked up at K-Mart for seven bucks. Feeling much cooler now, she didn't bother to change out of the shirt and shorts. Instead she went to the computer that was tucked into the corner of the room. The monitor and box were perched precariously on foldout tray tables. As the computer booted, Bridget picked up the phone and dialed a number she had long ago learned by heart.

Four rings and Francine's answering machine clicked on. The recorded voice of Erin, her sister's eldest daughter, high-pitched and beautiful, announced that the caller had reached the Gordon residence and the Gordons were busy right now. So could the caller please leave a name, number, and message after the beep? Thanks and have an extremely nice day!

"Hey everybody, it's me," Bridget said. "I'm back at my own place now. Thanks for letting me crash for the last few days, and thanks for the loan on the dress, Sis, for the funeral. I'll get it back to you after I get it dry-cleaned. I...I don't know what I would have done without you guys being there for me. I'm better now, except for this stupid cold. Got a lot to do. I'll tell ya about it all later. Love you guys. Bye for now."

Bridget hung up and focused on the computer monitor. She clicked on the lightning bolt icon to bring up the communications software. There was a stream of clicks and beeps, followed by the unmistakable shriek of a modem seeking connectivity. As the modem went through its paces, she had time to reflect.

She'd gone to Hugh Croston's funeral on a whim. She'd felt she owed him that small gesture. Not because she had known him; she really hadn't—not as a healthy person, anyhow. What she did know was that he'd been a demanding patient who had not treated anyone, including himself, very nicely. But the man had been dying. You can't expect people to be gracious when they're fighting death and losing.

Like her other leuk patients, Hugh Croston had spent his final days in a hospital room with tubes coming out of his arms and painkiller coursing through his veins.

Maybe I could have saved him if I had discovered this leukemia-producing virus sooner. If I'd spent more time in the lab…maybe, maybe not. Mr. Oberlin has already died from it, despite my feeble attempt to attack the virus directly. Only Jo—God save her—is still hanging on.

The modem screeched once more as if caught in the throes of a final agony, and then fell silent. The only sound in the apartment was that of Bridget's breathing as she stared blankly at the eggshell wall above the monitor.

I still don't understand Ian. He acted like a madman at the funeral. He has to know something about the virus or else he wouldn't have tampered with the blood samples. He derailed my analysis and made a mockery of the funeral of a man who died from the virus. And judging by his behavior today, it looked like he settled some kind of score with Croston, and did it by using the virus as a weapon.

Bridget's stomach slowly constricted.

I spent hours alone with him in the lab. He could have exposed me to the virus at any time, but he didn't. Why? I doubt he's a carrier. This virus is too much of a killer for that. He must be linked some other way.

She reached for the phonebook and opened it to the "M's". Naturally Ian McGuire wasn't listed. Most likely he'd used an alias and fashioned his own false hospital identification card, and had been confident enough to use it. He wanted to keep himself unknown, and had gone to great lengths to do it.

He's a man with a lot to hide. A man who, quite possibly, has murder on his agenda. And yet, he seemed so nice.

Devereaux, you are so naive. You just fall off the turnip truck, or what? Of course he seemed nice. He conned you into thinking he was something he wasn't.

Well, maybe I can find a lead, or a pattern or something in the hospital's patient files. If they haven't shut me out of the computer system…

She clicked the mouse, entered her logon ID and password at the hospital network sign-on screen, and crossed her fingers. After a moment the menu of functional hospital departments appeared on her monitor.

Yes!

Handlaw hadn't been thorough enough to revoke her access privileges.

The first file Bridget brought up was that of Josephine Woods. The girl's prognosis had worsened. Jo had begun to slide into a steady decline. She was at nadir, a condition that meant there were almost no healthy cells left in her bloodstream. The chemo and leuk had taken their toll. She had very few platelets, few red blood cells, and her white blood count was one-point-nine—normal was in the range of eight to twelve. The series of chemotherapy treatments were over and now it was wait-and-see time.

As per Bridget's last orders, Jo was receiving transfusions of red cells and platelets every twelve hours. White blood cells could not be transferred from one person to another without being attacked and rejected as foreign bodies by the host. White blood cells must be produced by the host. With her white blood cell count so dangerously low, Jo was at extreme risk of infection.

Now that she'd developed this cold, even wearing a mask, Bridget couldn't risk seeing Jo face-to-face. The common cold virus could prove fatal to the young girl.

"You keep fighting and I'll keep fighting for you, all right, Jo?" Bridget said to the monitor as she rocked back and forth in the chair, blinking back the tears.

She performed a search on all the leukemia patients who had died at Chambers Hospital in the last three years. Of those, only eight leuk patients—all of whom had been admitted in the past two months—showed an abnormal rate of decline and consequential death. Margaret Morrison had been among the first to succumb to the virus and consequential leukemia. She had coded and died on Bridget's first day in Ward Seven.

Did Margaret Morrison infect the others with the virus? No. Not by herself. The Ian Factor doesn't play into that. The real question was this: what did Margaret Morrison have in common with the other fatalities and Josephine Woods?

Bridget downloaded patient records to her own machine, an act that broke the hospital's policy of patient confidentiality.

Oh, well.

Bridget printed the patient profile data of each patient on her bubble jet. Then she went to the kitchen table, shoved the place mats and napkin holders off to one side and spread out the eleven sheets of paper. She examined each in detail. The accelerated leuk patients varied in age and weight and height, gender and fitness level. None of those details seemed to matter.

But they're all local to the Triangle area.

Bridget got on the phone and called other hospitals in North Carolina, those in Charlotte and Wilmington and Winston-Salem and Greensboro. They were responsive to her inquiries; Bridget didn't deem it necessary to inform them that she had recently been thrown out of the Chambers' internship program. Bottom line: These other hospitals all had leukemia patients, but it was standard leuk, not the accelerated variety.

Bridget hung up and poured over the sheets of paper once more. All but two—Jo Woods and a recent female admission listed as an "entertainer"—were employed by local health insurance companies.

Health insurance companies?

And all but the same two were influential employees of these companies.

Strange. All but two. What's different about Jo and this new arrival? Wait! Didn't Mrs. Woods say that just before Jo got sick, Mr. Woods had taken her to one of the offices he cleaned regularly?

Bridget's fingers raced through the yellow pages. She punched up a number.

"Woods Cleaners. This is Mary, how can I help you?"

"This is Doctor Devereaux. I'm Josephine's physician. Is Mr. Woods in?"

"No, he's on location right now, Doctor."

"Where?"

"I'm not sure."

"Doesn't he have a pager or a cell phone or something?"

"Yes, but he usually wants me to pass any information along."

"This is an emergency."

Mary complied. Bridget scrawled the number down on the side border of Jo's printout. She dialed the cell phone first, hoping that maybe he had it on. She heard it ring and her pulse sped up rapid-fire.

"Joe Woods."

"Mr. Woods, this is Bridget—uh, Doctor Devereaux."

There was a pause. Then, "Oh, God. Jo didn't—"

"No, not that! She's still fighting. She's a tough girl, she's going to pull through. I'm calling because I need some information from you. I need to know if you clean the offices of any health insurance corporations."

"Why?"

"Please!"

"Well, yeah, Foundation Health Net is one of our accounts. I landed the executive suite over there myself. Had to clean it when one of my girls quit on me to become a waitress. Why?"

"Foundation Health Net—Mr. Woods, thank you! I'll explain later."

Bridget hung up with the man's voice still sputtering questions.

She stared down at Margaret Morrison's printout.

Occupation: *CEO, Foundation Health Net.*

Bridget scrambled to get her shoes on. She snatched her keys and purse and ran out of the apartment. She heard the door slam shut when she was already five stairs down the stairwell.

She needed to get to Foundation Health and she needed to get there *now*.

TWENTY

THE SHOULDER BELT locked Bridget against the seat as she jammed on the brakes. The shocks squealed as the car rocked, boat-like, in the visitor's space. Filling the cracked windshield was the glass mountain of a building known as Foundation One. It glittered in the sun and, even through her sunglasses, Bridget had to squint to look at it. She cut the engine and was out in the soupy air before the last of the car's tremors subsided. She wanted to run inside the massive building, grab the first person she saw, and blurt out everything she knew about the virus and the danger everyone was in.

But who knows how these corporate types will take the news? I still don't have any concrete proof. If these folks are anything like Handlaw, they'll call security and slap a restraining order on me. No, before I say anything I need to find the right person to say it to.

She settled on an aggressive walk to the chrome-framed glass doors. Once inside, she stopped and stared, her mouth dropping open.

Beyond a raised, marble greeting desk was a vast cavern of a lobby. The ceiling was high and darkened, giving the impression there was nothing above it. Lights hung like stars from long golden wires. The perimeter walls were done in slabs of what had to be false marble. Veins of silver ran like lightning bolts diagonally through each slab. Several grand columns of the same material rose into the dim reaches of the ceiling. The floor was also done in faux blue marble, with each tile six feet long and six feet across. Large potted plants of lush green stood in marble vases so large and numerous they could have housed all of Ali Babba's forty thieves and then some.

At the far end of the lobby a gently flowing waterfall splashed into a large pond. Four stone koi belched streams of water to the center point of the pond. Around the water garden was a sea of green ivy and purple and violet-flowering hibiscus plants. Four large banana trees spread long green leaves like helicopter blades. Leather chairs and couches ringed the garden, and several men and women in natty business attire conversed with one another while sitting in them.

"The Romans would go gaga over this place," she murmured, walking toward the front desk. "Wonder where the purge troughs are."

No one else seemed to notice their surroundings.

Two receptionists were busy attending to several visiting suits. Bridget noticed a company directory standing by itself, like the directories in a shopping mall. Margaret Morrison was still listed on the directory; her office was on the fourteenth floor—the executive suite. One of the receptionists glanced toward Bridget with irritation but was caught up with the suits. Bridget smiled at her and headed for the elevator.

On the fourteenth floor she had the option of going right or left. The words FOUNDATION HEALTH dominated the marble wall before her.

She stood beneath the letters and looked first down one hall and then the other. The wall curved and she could garner no clues about how to get to the executive suite. Apparently, if you had reason to come up to the executive floor then you knew where you were going. She turned left and took two hesitant steps when she heard someone approach from the opposite hall.

"Are you lost?"

She spun around and looked at the forty-something man in the bleach-white shirt, coal-colored slacks and red paisley-patterned tie. "That obvious, huh?"

He didn't smile. Instead he checked her out from head to toe in a quick, practiced manner. A glint entered his coal black eyes. "Are you employed here at Foundation?"

"Uh, no." This guy didn't come across as the helpful type. Tell him the purpose of her visit and *poof!* two burly security guys would help make sure she found her way out. "No, I don't work here."

"Then, the lobby's downstairs."

"Okay." She cleared her throat. "Uh, look, I'm Bridget Devereaux. I'm here to, well, to find—"

Just then the elevator chime dinged and a younger man, perhaps in his late twenties, stepped out. Bridget stalled by watching him. Like the man pressing her for her intentions, this guy also wore a white shirt, slacks, and tie. His colors were a bit more relaxed, however, and his shirtsleeves were rolled up to his elbows.

She noticed the spark of interest in his eyes when he made eye contact with her—only his interest appeared warm whereas the other man's was coldly calculating. The younger man half-smiled in a cordial manner and was about to walk down the hallway to the right when she smiled broadly at him. He hesitated, perhaps wondering if he should know her.

"Just what *is* your business here?" the older man pressed, his tone increasingly agitated.

"He is," Bridget said, pointing to the younger man.

A flicker of confusion passed over the new man's face, but was quickly replaced with a crooked grin that looked damned close to genuine. He deftly changed direction and walked up to her just as the older man focused his attention on him.

The guy from the elevator beamed at Bridget and then frowned in an exaggerated manner while making a show of checking his watch. "*Here* you are! I was waiting down in the lobby, wondering if I'd be eating alone today, and you're up here chatting with the vice president of marketing."

"You know this person, Don?" the VP asked, his eyes narrowing.

"Indeed, I do. And do you know what?" He tilted his head as if letting the veep in on a little secret. "She's beautiful, but she's never on time. I'm sure you know the type, eh, Mr. Franchello?"

Franchello nodded, a tiny crack of a smile forming at the edges of his tightly pressed lips. "Yes, I certainly do." He looked down his long nose at Bridget. "Why didn't you say you were a friend of Don's, Ms. Devereaux?"

Bridget scrambled for an answer. Of course, she'd never seen "Don" before in her life...or had she? She shrugged and tried to appear embarrassed. "Just kind of forgot to mention it, that's all. He goes on about the office so much I thought I knew my way around. But as it turns out, I obviously don't. Sorry for the mix-up, Mr. Franchello."

"Well, come on, Dev," Don said. "We're going to be late. Oh, shoot! I forgot my keys in the office. Come on."

"Okay," Bridget said. As they walked away from the marketing exec, she glanced at Don and arched an eyebrow. "Dev?"

He grinned. She noticed how it was different from his polite smile. It made him seem boyish and more than a bit mischievous. "Well, I had to come up with something. Unfortunately, I've never seen you before. Wait a minute. Yes, I have. At the club..."

"Oh, yeah. You're the guy I saw on my way out. Sorry, I was in a bad place."

He held the glass door open for her and they stepped into a large office lobby that led to a busy-looking desk and another interior office. Bridget looked at the paneled walls and formal office furniture. To her right was a fish bowl meeting room that had glass walls and a glass door leading in. She heard the entrance door click shut behind her. She turned at the sound of his voice.

"I'm Don Mayhew." He was holding his hand out. "All of this isn't mine, I'm just the administrative assistant—no jokes, please! I took the job so I could earn money for night school. Answered an employment ad in the paper. It pays pretty well and I'm sure I'll be replaced when they decide on a new CEO, which should come down any day now."

"Bridget Devereaux." She shook his hand. His grip was firm but not tight, nor did he try to rotate her knuckles upward and grasp her fingers lightly, an overblown move that said, *"I'm such a regal snoot bag of a gentleman who knows how to hold a woman's hand properly."* His grip was warm and firm and vertical, and to her that meant he thought of her as an equal.

"Bridget Devereaux. Hmmm. *Francais, n'est pa?"*

His accent wasn't bad. Americanized, of course. But not bad. *"Tres bien, Monsieur Mayhew. Parlez vous…?"*

"Un peu—a little. High school stuff. I'd like to learn more, but hey, there's just not that many French-speaking people running around Raleigh, you know? Anyhow, a nice name—Bridget. A lot better than Dev, don't you think?"

She had to smile. "I think so. But Dev wasn't bad."

"At least I didn't call you Bridge."

A sharp jab of pain hit her in the stomach. She looked pointedly at him. Of course, he couldn't know the pain that name unleashed.

"Everything cool?" he asked, his face suddenly serious.

"Yes, I'm fine. Just a quirky body ache."

"Sorry to hear it. Well, what can I help you with, Ms. Bridget Devereaux?"

"Actually, I'm a physician."

"Oh, *Doctor* Devereaux."

Should she tell him she'd been thrown out of the hospital because she discovered a killer virus that the administration didn't want to know about? She turned her head to the side and sneezed. Just in time she succeeded in grabbing her handkerchief from her purse. She blew her nose and sneezed again.

"Bless you," Don said.

"Thanks." Her eyes watered and she wiped at them. When she turned back to him he was holding out a neatly folded, white handkerchief.

"I'd say the doctor has a cold," he said with a smile. He nodded in the direction of the handkerchief. "Please take it. If you don't mind me saying so, yours looks like it needs to hit the showers."

The tears at the inner corners of her eyes made the light around him shimmer, giving him a strange ethereal quality. She took the offered handkerchief. It was a simple cotton job like the ones her brother-in-law had. Very soft. She dabbed at the corners of her eyes with it and was able to clear her vision.

He appeared bemused. "So what brings a physician up to the executive suite of Foundation Corp?"

She hesitated. How do you say there's some kind of epidemic going around, possibly being perpetuated or even controlled by a middle-aged man whom she had worked with briefly in the blood lab? Well, if she was going to tell anyone, it may as well be this Don Mayhew.

She cleared her throat. "Well, of course you know Margaret Morrison died of leukemia less than two weeks ago..." She told him everything she knew about the virus, her patients, Ian McGuire, the administration's deaf ears, losing her internship, and her inability to go to the authorities concerning the virus without hard proof. She told him all of it.

✳ ✳ ✳

Raynorr jerked the dolly and recoiled at the shriek of metal scraping metal. When the dolly was withdrawn on a level plane the tiny wheels ran smoothly and quietly along the metal tracks, but in his haste he had pulled at an angle and had scraped the edge of the truck. Grimacing, he flattened the angle of his pull.

Haven't made that mistake since my first day. I'm not concentrating — why? Is it Bridget Devereaux?

Am I losing control?

Pushing the dolly, he went to the side of the truck and shoved the slatted metal doors upward. The doors folded section by section into the sleeve at the top of the truck, until the protruding handle halted it with a crash of metal on metal.

Devereaux is an X factor. Why did she attend Croston's funeral? What does she know about the Raynorr Virus, or Andrew Raynorr? Should she be removed from the equation?

Exposed inside the truck was the honeycomb of hexagonal bottle compartments, most of them occupied by water bottles that were full. At the end of his shift the majority of bays would hold empty bottles. But even at an increased pace, it was unlikely that he'd be able to make all his deliveries today. He'd just have to call his supervisor and tell her he'd be out tomorrow to finish the rest. She wouldn't like it, but that was too bad. She had no idea of how truly inconsequential she was. Of course, the only reason he kept this job was that being a water deliveryman gave him access to his targets and some inside news. The sum he was paid each week by the company was negligible.

With the sunlight reflecting off the glass exterior of Foundation Corporation behind him, Raynorr moved quickly. He loaded the dolly in under three minutes, completely unaware that two people inside the sandwich shop were watching him with much more than passing interest.

He wheeled the dolly inside the building. He'd started to sweat while loading the water bottles, and dark patches were visible on the blue uniform he wore. Inside the building he shivered.

This time the service elevator was operable. He made his first stop on the eighth floor, where Hugh Croston used to run the show but was now comfortably resting in a state of infinite oblivion six feet under.

He pulled the dolly toward the water bottle and rack that Hot Shot Croston had been so eager to have installed. Raynorr slowed as he approached Croston's old office, the office of Director of Operations. Glancing inside, he noticed someone behind the desk, staring into a computer monitor. The corporation hadn't taken long in finding a replacement for Hot Shot.

Raynorr looked at the nameplate on the wall next to the door: Ted Samuels.

Samuels. He was the man who had surprised Raynorr immediately after he'd planted the viral bullet in Croston's coffee mug.

At first Raynorr had thought Samuels suspected something, but as they'd engaged in conversation that hadn't seemed to be the case. Samuels had asked Raynorr nothing about being in Croston's office. Samuels was a hard working, levelheaded employee who had been trapped beneath Croston's oppressive regime, and who had been in danger of losing his job because he refused to skew the statistics the way Croston had wanted them skewed.

Raynorr felt a sense of satisfaction rise within him. If nothing else, he had gained a small victory in getting an honest man into a higher position where he could make fair, responsible judgments that were good for the patient, and not just the insurance provider.

He was about to pass the office when Ted Samuels suddenly looked over at him from behind the desk.

"Mike, do you have a minute?"

Samuels had remembered the name on Raynorr's uniform. Surprising. A trifle disconcerting, even. The man had a very good memory.

Raynorr stopped and glanced over his shoulder.

"Most of the employees are having lunch at the company picnic outside in the courtyard," Samuels said. "Nobody'll see you. Come on in and close the door."

He stepped warily inside the office, his satisfaction at seeing Samuels behind Croston's old desk suddenly replaced by increasing amounts of apprehension. What did Ted Samuels mean, *"nobody'll see you?"*

It meant he knew *something.*

Raynorr closed the door.

Samuels gestured to a leather-studded guest chair. "Have a

seat."

"You're the new Director?"

Samuels looked pained. "Yes."

"Excellent," Raynorr said. Despite his apprehension, a triumphant smile spread across his face as he sat across from Ted Samuels.

"No. It's not a good thing."

Raynorr's smile slipped a couple notches. "What do you mean?"

Samuels took off his glasses and rubbed the sides of his nose where they'd contacted his skin. He took his hand away and Raynorr noticed for the first time the black semicircles beneath the man's eyes. When he spoke, Samuels' tone was unsteady, as if his words were being squeezed out his windpipe. "What do I mean? I'll tell you. I mean that I had to sell my soul to get here, Mike, or whatever you're real name is."

Raynorr stiffened but before he could answer Samuels went on.

"Your name isn't Mike. You're nowhere close to being a simple Mike."

Raynorr started to reach for his wallet. "I have identification."

"Save it. I'm not interested in who you really are."

Raynorr blinked.

"It was a struggle to get this job," Samuels said. "I nearly lost it to my rivals." He paused and stared at Raynorr before continuing. "To make sure I won, I went against every shred of decency in my body. I skewered my rivals in meetings, stabbed them in the back with false rumors, painted them as subhuman. I kissed ass so much my lips are chapped and bleeding. Not exactly honorable, but in the end I got the position." He laughed bitterly.

Raynorr stared, dumbfounded. When he regained his wits he said, "But you're a good man who will listen to medical reason. Surely you'll do a better job than Hugh Croston."

"That's what I thought, at first, but it's just not that easy. Already I'm caught in their trap. The power pushes down from above. I'm just a conduit through which it flows to the peons beneath me. Profit is the one true God of this place, and the lives of the patients on our insurance plans are the unwitting sacrifices to that God. Instead of striking a balance between profit and sensible healthcare, I force my people to clip more wool from the sheep. I squeeze my people the same way Croston used to squeeze me. And if I don't squeeze, the higher-ups'll replace me with someone who will."

"Walk away," Raynorr said. "It's not worth it."

"I can't walk away. I've got a new car to pay for and we're thinking of moving into a bigger house. Now, I can't afford to lose this fucking job."

Raynorr sat silent.

Samuels continued. "And there are other things...like the women who suddenly think I'm the sexiest man alive and are willing to prove it to me right here in the office. Of course, Jenny doesn't know about them and I can't tell her—she wouldn't understand what a goddamned snake I've become. I'm still playing the role of loving husband, though she says I've been more withdrawn ever since I won this so-called 'promotion.' God, she thinks it's just me getting used to the new job!"

He took something out of his top desk drawer and held it in his lap. He looked down at it for a moment and then slowly up at Raynorr. "I saw you come out of Croston's office that night. You poisoned him, didn't you?"

Raynorr's tongue clove to the top of his mouth. His heart jackhammered against his ribs. He had to do something or his war would be over and he would be defeated.

"It started then, you know," Samuels said, his face tightening into a mask of self-loathing. "My corruption started when I saw you poison Croston. I could have called security on you and I didn't. I didn't understand it at the time, but I was hoping something would happen to that pompous bastard after you came out of there. And it did, didn't it?"

"I—I thought things would turn out for the better."

"You thought wrong."

"You can change things, Samuels. You're in the position to create change—"

"No. It will never change. It'll just get worse. They'll eat more and more of my soul until there's nothing left of the real Ted Samuels. I...I used to be a good man."

As he uttered this last statement, Ted Samuels, the new Director of Operations, raised his hand from his lap. The dull black metal of a .38 seemed to suck in all the light streaming in from the window behind him. He pointed the muzzle directly at Raynorr's chest.

Raynorr's legs stiffened and he slid up against the back of the chair. "No! You don't know what you're doing!"

Samuels' eyes lidded. "I know exactly what I'm doing."

Suddenly he brought his arm in and angled his wrist. Now the stubby gun muzzle was inside his mouth.

"No!" Raynorr cried.

A single report cracked the air. The back of Samuels' head exploded in a geyser of red and gray. The mix of blood and brains slammed into the blinds and the glass window behind him. The blinds crashed to the floor, revealing streaks of gore that slid slowly down the window. Samuels' eyes bulged out in his purpling face. He slumped forward in the chair and his arm fell into his lap. The gun remained in his grasp.

Raynorr was instantly on his feet, looking down at the dead man in horror. He spun, opened the door and dashed out, slamming it behind him. He grabbed the dolly and towed it to the service elevator at a run.

Incredibly, no one was rushing to Samuels' office in response to the shot. His heart machine-gunned, his breathing was ragged. The elevator dinged and he disappeared inside, jamming on the 'G' button.

✳ ✳ ✳

Don sank into one of the guest chairs, wearing a dazed expression. She sat in the one next to him and watched his face closely for signs of dismissal or disbelief.

"I know it's a lot to throw at you all at once but I don't have much time."

"You think this Ian guy is really linked to the virus?"

"I do—I just don't know how. He knows about the virus, I'm convinced of it. And at Hugh Croston's funeral…well, I told you about that."

"Yeah. Weird. Sounds like he's gone over the edge without a barrel. Listen, I'd like to help you. Margaret was demanding, at times, but she was always fair with me. If she was murdered by this Ian guy, or he knows something, then I feel I need to help any way I can."

"You can help by trying to remember anything unusual that might have happened right before Margaret Morrison fell ill."

"I'll try, but I'd like to help more than that. Let's face it, you could use someone on your side."

"Look, Don, you seem like a nice guy. I don't want to put you at risk."

"I don't just seem like a nice guy, I *am* a nice guy. But there's something else. You know that charming man you met in the hallway, Mr. Friendly Francello? He's likely to be voted the next CEO. You think he's going want me around? I ain't made right for that. So, really all I'm doing is sitting around waiting for the axe to fall. I feel useless and I want to help."

She studied him closely. There was no indication of insincerity. She nodded. "You're right, I could use the help. Now, can you remember anything unusual or even when she started feeling badly?"

He got up and went to the window. She followed, looking out with him at the incredible view of the bright blue sky and green lake, and so many trees that they stretched like a carpet into the horizon.

"It's not that it was long ago," he said softly. "It's just I don't recall anything unusual. She seemed fine the day before she went to the hospital. She held meetings, had me make some calls, schedule appointments, the usual routine. I came in the following day expecting the usual and they told me she had been taken to the hospital the night before. I went to see her twice and then she died before I could see her a third time."

"Do you know if she came in contact with a balding, middle-aged man?"

"You've just described almost every executive we have."

"Ian would probably be from outside the company, although I'm not sure of it."

"Margaret received visitors all the time who were of the balding, middle-aged man variety."

"Was she exposed to any sick people?"

"Not that I'm aware of."

"Did she eat or drink anything unusual?"

"Not here."

"What about the water supply?"

He turned and pointed at the large water bottle near the sitting area. "There's one in her office, too. I drink from both. I drank from both before and after she got sick. Nothing's happened to me."

She sighed. This wasn't getting them far. "Okay. Anything else? Even if you don't think it's important."

"She was on her way to a luncheon on the day she felt ill. Maybe something happened there."

"Where was that?"

"Jarrad's Restaurant down off Harrison Avenue."

"Okay, we'll need to check into it. Anything else?"

He looked intense as he tried to recall but finally he sighed and shook his head. "I tell you what—my stomach's grumbling so much I can't think. Did you have lunch yet?"

"No."

"Why don't we grab something at the deli downstairs and maybe something will come to me. I'm buying."

Her stomach growled at his mention of food. In spite of her cold, she was hungry, and a bit weak. She could use something to eat. "All right, but you don't have to buy. I've got some money."

"No, really, it's on me."

She didn't really want a man to buy her lunch, but he seemed nice and wanted to help and this was not a social occasion, so why not?

"Lead the way," she said.

The deli was tucked into a corner at the rear of the building. There were only five small tables in the place and they were all taken by the time she and Don turned from the cash register with their sandwiches and sodas in their hands. There was a tall counter next to the glass walls, and it was there that Don guided her. There were no stools, so they stood and ate and looked through the glass to the outside service loading bays. As they ate, Don asked her more about the virus, and more about the hospital administration.

"That Handlaw guy is an asshole for what he did to you. He needs to get pile-driven into the street. But the doctors—they should know better. They're all fools for not listening to you," Don said, leaning on the counter and taking another bite from his sandwich.

"They don't want to know anything while they're still negotiating the sale of the hospital. They're afraid an epidemic, especially if they can't get it under control, will rock the boat. Until people start dropping like flies they won't pay attention."

"What about the police?"

"I don't have enough hard evidence to prove there's an epidemic."

"But the viral reaction—triggering cancer in the cell—that should be enough proof."

She sniffed and used his handkerchief to wipe her nose. "I have no clear evidence, only what I witnessed with my own eyes and a theory. I need something more concrete." She turned her head and was able to bring the handkerchief up just in time.

He looked at her. "You don't have the virus, do you?"

"I'd be a lot worse off than this. A lot worse."

"Well, isn't there some governmental agency that investigates stuff like this? Some disease and virus agency?"

"CDC—Center for Disease Control. I tried them but they stonewalled me. I'm just an intern. They wanted to hear it from the senior doctors at Chambers, and you know how far I got with them."

"The CDC ought be checking things out no matter who reports it."

"Thing is, I don't know where this is all going. What's going to happen next with this virus? And what exactly does Ian have to do with it?"

He swallowed. "Pretty scary. And on top of it all, you've lost your internship because the fools wouldn't investigate your warnings. It's not right."

She looked outside so he wouldn't see that the tears making her eyes blur weren't due to her cold this time. "I wish—I wish no one was dying and you and I were just two people having lunch together."

"That would be nice," he said.

"But that isn't reality, is it? This lethal virus is out there. It has killed and will probably kill more, and a man who goes by Ian McGuire knows something about it, if not *all* about it."

Silence fell between them.

Bridget watched as a food truck pulled away from a service parking space, exposing a truck that had been parked on the far side of it. There was no one inside the Crystal Clear Water truck.

Suddenly a man pulling a stack of water bottles on a dolly appeared on the sidewalk. Sunshine illuminated him like a spotlight as he headed toward the Crystal Clear Water truck. The brim of his hat hid his features.

"That's got to be hot work," Bridget said, tilting her soda can in the direction of the deliveryman.

Don nodded. "Yeah...hey, I forgot about that guy. He delivers water to the executive suite. Other suites too, I imagine."

Bridget stiffened. "The executive suite...?"

"Yeah, that one, too. He was in Margaret's office the day before she was admitted to the hospital. Seemed pretty cool. Just another working guy."

Bridget pushed her glasses up with her index finger and squinted. The man's face was still hidden by the shadow cast by the brim of his hat.

"Hey," Don said. "You don't think...?"

Bridget studied the man. His head was angled downward, as if he didn't want anyone to see his face. He hurried with the dolly along the sidewalk that passing close to the deli. Suddenly, he looked up, as if gauging the distance back to his truck.

Sunlight hit him full in the face.

Bridget put down her soda.

Don looked at her. "Bridget, talk to me."

"That's Ian McGuire."

TWENTY-ONE

"Y OU'RE SURE HE won't see us?" Bridget asked, unable to tear her gaze from Ian.

"Didn't you notice how this building looks like a giant stack of mirrors?" Don said. "We can see out but he can't see in."

"It's just that if he sees me he'll know I've connected him to the virus."

"He won't see you," Don said.

They watched in anxious silence as Ian hauled his load toward the truck. The dolly was stacked waist-high with cobalt blue water bottles, all with unbroken seals over their mouths and a single fat air bubble inside that shook with the vibrations.

"Why didn't he swap out the bottles?" she asked.

"Good question," Don said, peering at the bottles. "I know the executive suite is running low on bottled water. All we've got are empties. He should have at least gotten those."

"It doesn't look like he replaced *any*."

They watched as Ian shoved the bottles back into the truck in rapid succession.

"He's working pretty darned fast," Bridget said. "Like he's trying to get away in a hurry."

"Do you really think he's using this virus to kill people? Maybe he's just an innocent carrier or something."

Bridget shook her head, keeping her eyes on the imposter outside. "He might be immune, but there's no way he's innocent."

"He just seems so—I don't know—regular."

Bridget jabbed the counter top with a forefinger. "That man out there sabotaged my patient's blood samples while in the guise of a lab technician. He delivers water here, where three victims of the virus worked. I bet if we follow him, we'll find he also delivers to the other health insurance companies in the area, the same companies that employed other victims of the disease. Throw in what he did at Hugh Croston's funeral and it all boils down to one thing: whoever this guy really is, he's using the virus to kill people."

"Too much for coincidence," Don said. "You think he does it by infecting that bottled water he delivers?"

"I think we'd see a lot more people dying if that was the case. People are dying, but not en mass. No, he's got some other method. He's being extremely selective about his targets."

"Wait a sec, wait a sec," Don said. "I remember now! When I walked in on him in Margaret's office, he had her coffee cup in his hand. He said he was admiring the logo and inscription but maybe he was —"

"—placing the virus inside the cup, knowing Margaret Morrison would probably be the only one to use it!" Bridget said.

Outside, Ian secured the dolly and yanked down the sliding doors to his truck.

"We've got to follow him," Don said, already abandoning his partially eaten sandwich on the counter, heading for the door.

"Hey, you might want to stay here." Bridget caught him by the shoulder. "I kind of dumped all of this in your lap. It doesn't really concern you directly. I can understand if—"

For the first time she saw a flicker of annoyance cross Don's handsome face. "This concerns me as much as it does you. Margaret's family deserves to know that she didn't just *take ill*, like they kept saying at her funeral. Besides, any decent person would try to stop this guy if they knew what he was up to."

"Okay, okay," Bridget said. "Don't get me wrong, I'm grateful for the company. I'll drive."

"Where's your car?"

"Up front in the visitor's lot."

"Closer than mine. Let's go!"

They bolted from the deli, down a long hallway and out through the front lobby, getting disapproving looks from others along the way.

* * *

Whispering to himself, Raynorr started the truck and pulled out into the parking lot, a little too fast.

Slow down, slow down.

He turned out onto the adjacent road.

Two police cars, their lights flashing blue and white, their sirens wailing at full blast, turned into the main Foundation One parking lot entrance.

Someone must have found Ted Samuels' lifeless body.

Raynorr watched the police cars disappear from his side mirror as he continued on his way.

* * *

Bridget's car sputtered on the first try of the ignition, then died. She goosed it harder the second time and it came chugging and sputtering to life.

"He's getting away," Don warned, pointing to the light blue water truck rolling out of the parking lot. "Truck's leaning bad around the curves…he's really moving out!"

"Keep your eye on him," Bridget said, looking over her shoulder as she backed the car out to the sound of screeching tires.

Don lurched forward and then back as she shifted and hit the gas. They raced toward the main exit out of the parking lot, narrowly avoiding a slow-moving sedan with a group of suits inside. One of the suits pointed at Don.

"Friends of yours?" Bridget's voice sounded tense to her own ears.

"Hardly. Those are execs. Everyone inside that car is a card-carrying member of Assholes 'R Us."

"I'm beginning to think being an asshole is a prerequisite for all management."

"There's a few who are decent people, but they're hard to find. Margaret was one of the rare ones."

Bridget did a California stop at the next intersection and then floored it. She had to close the distance to the water truck. A police siren suddenly wailed.

"Oh no!" Bridget said. "Are they after me?"

Bridget wanted to look but had to concentrate on the water truck, which had turned into the left-hand lane and was putting on some real speed. She lead-footed the accelerator and, after a two second hesitation, the car sprang forward. Don slung his elbow over the seat and turned around.

"They're heading toward the main building going into Foundation."

"Is this a common thing?"

"Not as far as I know," Don said. "Let me call Lisa at the front desk, she'll know something about it. She's the eyes and ears of the place."

Out of the corner of her eye Bridget saw Don dig in his inside coat pocket as she wove through traffic. They exited the business park with its nice lake and clumps of forest separating one vast building from another. The two lanes merged into one and the jerk in the right lane was speeding up to try and cut in front of her at the last second instead of taking the open slot behind her. Bridget pressed her machine forward, the engine whining, denying the jerk. Had she let him go in front of her, she'd be three cars behind the water truck instead of two. With a baleful glare and a flip of the bird, the other driver fell behind.

She heard beeps as Don punched numbers on his thin cellular phone. "Do all admin assistants carry those?"

"Margaret got me this thing so she could reach me any time

though she hardly ever called—

"Hi, Lisa? Don. What's up with the police? I just saw two of them turn into the parking lot."

There was a pause, then he said, "You're kidding." Pause. "You're not kidding. Jesus! What was his name again? Samuels? Poor guy." Another pause. "No, I never knew him. Took over for Hugh Croston? Yeah, I knew Croston—never thought much of him. Thanks, Lisa. I'll call you later." He lowered the cell phone.

"That didn't sound good," Bridget said.

"Ted Samuels shot himself. Somebody came back from lunch, walked into his office and found him slumped in his chair with a big mess on the window behind him. The gun was still in his hand."

"God, how awful!"

"Wonder if our water guy here had anything to do with it."

"He sure was in a hurry to leave."

"But why not just use the virus? From what you told me, it works fast enough."

"Maybe this Ted Samuels wasn't on Ian's list. Maybe this was something Ian hadn't seen coming."

They drove steadily, with two cars separating them from the water truck. They passed Raleigh-Durham Airport on Airport Boulevard and continued west on Route 70 toward Durham. After fifteen minutes they turned off 70 and headed east on Route 98 toward Wake Forest. They passed the landscaped entrances of various businesses and housing developments. Soon, these became fewer and fewer, and the stretches of forest and field became wider and wider. Now they passed standalone homes, clusters of doublewides, and tin-roofed shacks perched on cinder blocks. They traveled over three separate expanses of water that all had the same name: Falls Lake.

"I used to fish in this lake with my dad when I was growing up," Don said. "It's not all that wide but it runs for fifteen miles and has a quadrillion fingers. Used to be a river 'til the Army Corps of Engineers dammed it up, thirty years ago. Now it supplies the city of Raleigh's drinking water."

Bridget chewed the inside of her bottom lip. "Oh?"

"All the city water, anyway. A lot of the subdivisions outside city limits have well water." Don paused and then looked at her as she stared at the water truck. "Where do you think he's going?"

"Home, I hope."

"What if he's not?"

"We'll follow him until he does. We need to see if there's any hard evidence at his house that can implicate him in the murders of my patients."

"Have you ever tailed anyone before?"

She glanced at him. "No. You?"

He shook his head. "Never. But I guess like in the movies you can't get too close or he'll catch on."

Bridget nodded. "Hey, since you've got that cute little phone, give Crystal Clear Water Company a call and ask for the name of the guy who delivers to Foundation. Try and get an address for him."

"How do I do that?"

"I don't know—tell them you want to send him flowers or something."

"Flowers from another guy? They'll think I'm gay!"

"So?"

"So, I'm not gay!"

"Okay, but we need to try and get his address in case we lose him."

"All right, I'll try. But I don't think I'll sound genuine enough."

"Dial them up and then give me the phone."

Don called information and then had someone at Crystal Clear on the line. "Hold on, my co-worker wants to talk to with you." He put the phone to Bridget's ear.

She steered the car around a corner, glanced at Don, and took hold of the phone. "Uh, yes. I work with Don… Don…" She put the phone on her chest. "Sorry, what's your last name again?"

"Mayhew, and that's okay."

She held up the phone. "…Don Mayhew at Foundation Corporation. I just want to say that the man who delivers the water to us is really doing a great job. I think you guys ought to give him a raise, or at least a day off with pay. The bottles are always straight and he's been right on the money as far as timing. I'd like to send him a card in the mail but you know, I don't even know his name, much less his address. Could you help me with that? That's right, Foundation Corporation. The guy's in his mid-fifties, nice body—I guess you have to stay in shape for all that lifting and pulling and stuff, huh?"

She put the phone in the crook of her shoulder and held it there with her cheek, head tilted. She snapped her fingers at Don, made a writing motion with her free hand and pointed to the glove compartment. Digging in the glove compartment, he found a beat up looking pen and a napkin.

"Mike Blevans?" she said into the phone. "No, that's not right? Oh, *Evans*. Mike Evans. Forty-two twelve River Run Drive, Raleigh, two-seven-eight-oh-one. Thank you so much! Bye, now." She looked at Don. "Did you get that address?"

"It's a fake."

"Why do you say that?"

"For one thing, you've got to have six figures in the bank just to build a tin-roofed shack in River Run."

"Maybe he's got money. We don't know."

"It's not his address."

"How can you be so sure?"

"Because I've been there."

She looked at him. "I don't understand."

He looked away, but not before she saw the sadness that overcame his face. "That was Margaret's address. I went to the dinner party she held at her house last Christmas. Forty-two twelve, River Run Drive."

"I'm sorry." The sudden taste of acid flooded Bridget's mouth. "Ian must have targeted her from the beginning."

Bridget handed the phone to Don and slowed the car at a four-way stop. They were three cars behind the water truck. Ian or Mike or whatever his real name was had taken his cap off; Bridget could see his baldpate in one of the long side view mirrors. He looked right and left, checking out the cars already stopped there.

The water truck turned left. Two of the cars in front of Bridget went straight and the other went right. It was Bridget's turn to go.

Don said, "Wait for this other guy." With a repeated wave he motioned the driver of the dusty red pickup on the right to go ahead, even though he had arrived at the stop sign after Bridget. "We need him for a shield."

"But Ian's getting farther away!"

"This road's long and straight. We won't lose him. Go ahead."

Don was right.The road was long and straight. They used the pickup for cover, with Bridget edging out into the oncoming traffic lane periodically to make sure the blue water truck was still visible. Three miles farther down the bleached, cracked, asphalt the red truck turned off.

Don looked around. "Now we've got our asses hangin' out."

"I can't turn off now," Bridget said. "We might lose him if he turns down one of these side roads. I'll just hang back."

Five minutes later they were perhaps a half mile behind the blue water truck as it slowed and made a right off the road. Bridget slowed the car as they approached the dirt turn-off the truck had taken. She chewed at her lip. Leaning forward, she tried to peer into the entranceway the truck had taken but was thwarted by the high weed and wild grass-covered embankments. "I think he saw us."

"No way," Don said, also straining forward to look into the turn-off. "He's not expecting anyone to follow him."

"I think he's always on guard. Especially here. This is his road, his neighborhood—if you want to call all these fields and forests a neighborhood." The car crept closer to the entrance. "I think he's parked just inside that dirt entranceway and is waiting for us to pass."

After a moment, Don said, "You might be right."

Bridget unlatched her seatbelt and then Don's.

"Hey! What—" he started.

She grabbed his hand and put it on the wheel. "Drive!" she ordered, and then dove into the back seat to lie down below the window line, stiff as a board. "Get into the driver's seat. Hurry!"

The car lurched onto the thin strip of asphalt that was too thin to be called a shoulder. Don swore and the car warbled from his overcompensation and then warbled again as he overcompensated for the first overcompensation.

"Hurry!" Bridget said again, banging her head on the car body. "More gas! Here, put on my sunglasses." She threw them over the seat.

She felt him move into the driver's seat. He sped up an instant before reflected sunlight shone inside the car, just above Bridget's line of sight.

"Damn!" Don said, through what sounded like clenched teeth. "There he is. He's standin' at the back of the truck and staring right at me."

"Don't look at him. He doesn't really know you—maybe he won't suspect anything. Is there a number on the mailbox?"

"One eighty-six."

"Keep driving. Look casual."

"He's got dogs," Don said. His words were mumbled, as if he was trying to keep his lips from moving. "Big dogs."

Bridget swore she could feel Ian's gaze penetrating through the steel sides of the car, though she knew it wasn't true. If he spotted her, he'd know that she was on to him. He might leave and pick up in a different part of the state, or a different part of the country. And the killing would start all over again.

Her heart thudded dully in her ears and her chest felt as if it was on fire, but she didn't dare breathe.

"We're past him and going down the road," Don said.

She let her breath out in a whooshing gust. "Keep checking your rear view to see if he follows. Let me know when we're around some kind of curve."

After a few seconds she got anxious. "Well?"

"Not yet," Don said. "I told you this road was long and straight."

Finally she felt the car lean around a curve. "Clear?"

"Clear."

Bridget slumped into the back seat. "Oh, man that was close."

"There's a subdivision up there, see it? Want me to turn into it?"

"No, let's keep going."

"What's the plan?" Don asked.

"We can't do anything until he leaves. Then we've got to get in his house and see if there's some kind of evidence to take to the authorities. You did see a house or a trailer or something back where he was, didn't you?"

"More like a roof. I assume there was a house attached to it."

"And you said there were dogs?"

"Two big German Shepherds that looked like they could shred a crocodile. They were sitting like guards, one on each side of him. My guess is he's got 'em trained pretty well if they'll sit like that. But even if he does leave soon, how are we going to get past the dogs?"

Bridget thought for moment. "Don't we hit Wake Forest if we keep on this way?"

"That's what the sign said."

"They've got a grocery store and a pharmacy somewhere, right?"

"I guess so. You getting hungry since we didn't finish lunch back at the office deli?"

"Turn around and go back into that subdivision."

"I thought you wanted to go to Wake Forest."

"Drop me off first, then you go."

"I don't understand."

She stretched over the front seat and opened the glove compartment, took out a prescription pad and pen. "Give me your cell phone. I'll keep an eye on Ian's house so we'll know when he leaves. I need you to go into Wake Forest and buy a couple things, then call me from a pay phone. I'll call you when he leaves, and until then I'll check in with you every forty-five minutes or so. If you don't hear from me, call the police."

"Hey, I don't know about this," Don said. "It sounds pretty risky. I mean, he might be dangerous in more ways than one."

Bridget tried to swallow the lump in her throat and wasn't quite successful. "You're probably right."

"He might see you coming alongside the road."

"I'll go through the woods and stay on the far side of the road from his house."

Don handed her the slim phone. "What about the dogs?"

They pulled into the subdivision. Don let the car idle at the side of the entrance while Bridget scrawled something on the prescription pad. After a moment she tore the top sheet off and pressed it into Don's hand.

"This is a prescription for a strong sedative," she said. "Get this filled and buy two thick steaks and a sharp knife."

"Huh?"

"We'll give those dogs one hell of a food coma."

Don nodded. "I get it. Let the dogs eat the steaks with tranquilizers inside. Pretty smart. You learn that in medical school?"

"FBI trick I saw on television at my sister's house. You know the number of your cell phone, right?" She started digging in her purse. "I've got some money—"

"Look, Bridget. Why don't *you* go to the store and I'll keep on eye on that guy's place? You come back for me after you get the stuff."

"They'll check your ID for this stuff. Legally I can't write a prescription for myself, but I can for you. Here." She held out two twenties.

He pushed her hand gently back. "I've got it covered. Be careful, okay?"

"Right. Just don't stand me up."

His warm brown eyes and smiling face seemed to fill Bridget's world. "Only a fool would stand you up, Doc." His smile faded. "I mean it, watch yourself. That guy's a killer. I saw it in his eyes. Don't take any chances with him."

"I won't." She held up the cell phone. "Call me?"

"Wish it was for a date and not this."

"Yeah, me, too."

Bridget got out of the car and jogged toward the trees. A patch of thorny briars slashed at her legs despite her hasty efforts to avoid them. She winced at the thin streaks of blood.

Ouch, damn it.

No time for that...move!

TWENTY-TWO

A DOZEN MORE STRIDES and a sea of brown and green engulfed Bridget. To her right, progressively deeper shades of brown led to the inner forest, where direct light was thwarted from penetrating to the ground by a vast network of interwoven branches. Fifty feet to her left, towers of green basked in undiluted sunshine on the fringes of State Road 1202. She was grateful for the running shoes she wore.

Probably should be more careful, a part of Bridget warned. *The woods can be tricky. It's not like running on a jogging path, you know.*

I can do this, she countered.

Bridget zigzagged as the tree trunks came at her like a silent mob. She ducked the grasping arms and clutching fingers of low-level branches, leaped and stutter-stepped as rocks and sudden roots and ground vines came toward her like obstacles on a huge treadmill.

See? You just need to know how to—uh, oh!

Her leg didn't come when it was supposed to. The force of her hurtling body snapped the vine but it was too late. She flew three feet through the air and then slammed into the ground. Pain. She looked for the source. Her hands had found soft leaves and forgiving soil, but her right knee had struck a gnarled Holly root.

Her knee was a bloody patch of shredded skin, but she was able to flex and retract her leg with the help of some groaning. She pushed off the forest floor. Her knee hurt, but it wasn't broken or sprained and there was no time to baby it.

She could achieve only a gimpy half-jog at first, but after a few minutes her knee loosened up and she soon could manage a pace closer to a guarded run.

Impenetrable thickets of young pines forced her deeper into the woods. The air here was thick and unmoving and she had to open her mouth wide to get enough air to breathe. Within the shadows she ran, startling a number of rabbits and squirrels and birds. After navigating the thickets she angled back to her original course.

The road was intermittently visible through pockets in the green canvas to her left, a glaring streak of light that kept pace with her as she altered her course a hundred times, only to alter it back a hundred more.

It took her nineteen minutes to reach her destination. She could have made it to the woods directly across from Ian's house in half that time by running on the road, but the risk of him seeing her had been too great.

Gasping, she leaned an outstretched hand on the smooth trunk of a massive beech tree. After a moment she looked up. She couldn't see through the branches to the middle of the tree, and forget about the upper part. There were hundreds, perhaps thousands of branches that extended in every direction.

"Whoa, you're a...granddaddy," she breathed. "So this is what it looks like...when you're an ant."

She looked down to see her shirt was torn and wet with sweat. Blood trails snaked erratically down her leg from the red patch of mangled skin that was her knee. It stung as more sweat seeped into it. With the handkerchief Don had given her earlier, she dabbed at the dirt that clung to the wound.

Who was the jerk who thought running through the woods was easy? she thought, as her chest heaved.

She flexed the knee. It stung and smarted, but it wasn't bleeding badly. Besides, the real pain would come tomorrow and the day after.

The dirt path that served as Ian's driveway lay directly across the sun-baked road from where she stood. She was close to the road, now, having angled toward it with the last few paces of her dash. She could see where the mouth of his driveway had been created by a bulldozer pushing through the high embankment wall, that now acted as a privacy barrier for the house set back some distance from the road. Leaning this way and that, she could only see the shingles on the roof through a gap in the leaves.

Where's the water truck? Where's Ian, or those dogs? Damn it, I can't see diddly from down here!

She looked up at the big beech again. The lowest branch was within jumping range. But how high would she have to climb before gaining a better vantage point?

Only one way to find out.

Taking a few steps back, she drew a deep breath then rushed forward. She leaped, catching the branch and swinging out and back before pulling and scrambling up onto the branch and reaching for the next.

Let's forget about acrophobia. How 'bout the cicada out here? They're chatterin' up a storm.

As she climbed from one branch to another, putting more distance between herself and the ground, she remembered reading where the fear of heights was really the fear of falling.

Now there's a newsflash.

Okay, okay. Maybe if I think this through it won't be so bad. People with acrophobia invariably picture in their minds what it would be like to fall from the height at which they find themselves. They imagine themselves going over a railing, slipping off a high ledge, or losing their balance while on a roof, a tall ladder, or a tree, and suddenly they get the urge to feel what it must be like to fall. Self-preservation centers in the brain try to combat this "perverse urge," as Edgar Poe put it. The centers for survival clang the alarms, kicking in the terror response that overrides the urge to experience the falling sensation.

So?

So, I'm going to think about holding tight to this tree, and I'm going to think about what Ian is doing and I don't have room to think about anything else, got it?

Hmmm…

She climbed to the next branch and looked out toward Ian's house. She forced herself to not look down, but some part of her brain wasn't as easy to control as her eyes. It knew the forest floor was already a substantial distance below. A damaging, if not altogether deadly, distance below.

Still can't see. Have to get higher.

She tried to concentrate on the leaves as she climbed. They were oval-shaped, with ridged veins extending out to the serrated edges in uniform harmony. Oddly, the leaves reminded her of ruffled potato chips. Each leaf was a tiny work of art, and they had to number in the hundreds of thousands. But as fine as these leaves were, they could do absolutely nothing to help her should she lose her balance and fall.

Don't go there, dummy!

Well, there's an awful lot of air around me all of a sudden. I might slip, might get weak and lose my grip. Then I will FALL and probably get knocked around by the lower branches on the way down. Don or the police will find a twisted rag doll. And Ian or whatever-his-real-name-is will just keep killing and killing.

Another voice sliced through the others. *Just keep going, girl. This isn't about you; it's about him. Now, do what you have to do!*

Her fingers trembled in an awful way as she reached, but once she grasped the branches, she held on so tightly she was sure her fingers would dig into the fabric of the wood itself.

Finally, a break in the leaves.

With her feet braced on branches wider than the distance between her shoulders, she leaned back against the main trunk and let out a huge gust of air. Most of her body was sheltered behind branches that twisted and turned and angled toward Ian's dirt driveway. The opening in the potato chip leaves was like a three-dimensional movie screen; on it played Ian's entire house and the driveway and the water truck that was parked, but not hidden from her view, behind the house.

"Truck's still there!" she whispered. "Good, good. Now take it easy and don't look down, baby." In defiance, her gaze began to stray toward the ground below. "Eyes up. Come on, eyes up! Figure out where he is and look for those dogs."

Moments later Ian and both dogs emerged from the house. Bridget stiffened. Though Ian looked like a middle-aged everyman in his T-shirt, shorts, white socks and sneakers, she knew him for what he truly was: a murderer. And here she was up a tree, spying on him. If he caught her up here...

And what about his canine pals?

Even from here the dogs looked big. Muscles rolled and flexed beneath their black and tan hides. Thick necks led to large, angular heads and dark muzzles. Their pointed ears reached almost to Ian's chest.

The trio stepped down from the front porch. Ian walked directly toward a big black car parked next to the water truck. The dogs milled about around his legs, tails wagging.

Ian carried a briefcase. He placed it in the trunk of the car that was so big and blocky it had to be American-made. Bridget could only make out the chrome "O" on the back of the trunk. She assumed it stood for Oldsmobile. Ian went back inside the house, this time with only one dog on his heels as the other did his business in the tall grass to the right of the driveway.

Bridget's pocket suddenly went off like an electronic alarm clock. Startled, she jumped, at the same time realizing that the ringing was coming from Don's cell phone.

Grab it quick or the dog might hear!

Her hand dove for the pocket. No sooner had her thumb brushed a button on the side of the phone that silenced the ring, than the knee she had fallen on earlier buckled. High in the tree, Bridget lost her balance.

Choking a cry, she flailed at the branches. Suddenly she could see herself plunging headlong, with the leaf-strewn forest floor rushing up to greet her like a nightmare. Her fingernails scraped the outer skin from the tree. Gravity pulled at her and she fell farther backward. At the last instant she clutched a green waif of a branch protruding from the belly of one of the major branches. It had all of four leaves growing from it. It was really just a twig.

But it was enough.

She used it to right herself on the big branch at her feet. Then she grabbed the branch that was shoulder height. She held onto it with both hands, a drowning woman clutching at a life preserver.

Sweat dripped from her brow and stung her eyes. She gasped for air while her heart thudded away in her throat. Caught up in the anxiety of the moment, she looked down for the first time. She was at least forty feet up. If she had fallen, she would have been killed, or at least paralyzed.

All at once it felt as if her head had somehow filled with helium. It was a balloon, attached only by ligaments and skin.

Don't you dare faint! Look up, look up!

Suddenly the cell phone rang again. Bridget shot a look toward the house.

The dog that was doing its business turned its head toward her tree. Its wolfish muzzle rose high to sniff the breeze. Its ears pivoted in Bridget's direction. The dog growled but did not bark. It looked right and left but could not find the source of its suspicion. Finished with its business, it took a step, kicked some wild grass in the direction of its handiwork, and then padded toward the end of the driveway.

Directly across the road from Bridget's tree.

Bridget threw herself against the trunk. Her hand dove into her pocket and she pulled out the phone, mashing the first keypad button her fingers contacted.

"Don?" she whispered, trying to catch at her hitching breath while jamming the phone to her ear.

"Yeah, it's me. Are you all right? What's happening? I tried calling and it went to voicemail—"

"I'm forty feet up a tree and almost fell out when you called the first time. One of Ian's dogs is suspicious so I've got to be quiet. Did you get everything?"

"Everything. Look, be careful up there. If this Ian guy catches you spying on him, man…"

Her breathing steadied and she realized that for some reason Don's voice had a calming effect on her. "I know. I'm all right. Ian's getting ready to go somewhere, I think. He's got a briefcase in the trunk. What's the number to the pay phone?"

He gave it to her.

"Hold on." She squeezed the phone between her cheek and shoulder and pulled a pen from her other pocket. Then she leaned against the tree trunk with no hands on the branches and her heart all but popping out her throat. She wrote the phone number on the back of her hand, barely able to read the numbers even as she wrote them for all the trembling going on. Fighting the urge to look down and satisfy that self-destructive thrill, she jammed the pen into her pocket, grasped the life-preserver branch with her left hand and the phone with her right.

"Got it," she said. "You'll—you'll be there, right?"

After all, she didn't really know Don Mayhew. A storm of images overcame her all at once; Don dozing in the car, or driving off, or catching a beer at the local dive, or following some big-boobed woman inside a motel room or—

"I'll be here, Bridget," he said. His tone was serious and caring at the same time.

The images in Bridget's mind stopped just as surely as if a blade had cut a celluloid movie strip. "Good," she breathed. "Good…thanks."

"So just how should I go about this steak and pills thing?"

The dog started to scan the tree branches. Bridget shrank back farther.

"Cut deep slits in the steaks and put four painkiller capsules in each steak." She was forced to watch as a mosquito landed on her thigh. Its body pulsed as it fed on her blood. She tightened the quadricep muscle, holding the parasite fast so it couldn't pull out. Its abdomen became huge in comparison to the rest of its body.

"And Don? Get some Bactine and insect repellent—they're having me for dinner." Unable to pull its proboscis out, the mosquito suddenly exploded in a splotch of red.

"Bactine and bug stuff, right?"

"How long do you need?" she asked. "Ian could leave any second."

"Give me five."

"You got it. I'll call you back."

"Bye."

She pressed the "end" button, slipped the phone into the hip pocket of her shorts and looked down at the dog.

Growling louder now, it set a paw on the baked asphalt of the road and looked up into her tree.

"Go on, dingo," she whispered, noticing for the first time that the cicada and crickets had suddenly quieted.

The front door of the house opened and Ian and the other dog emerged. Ian spotted the first dog at the road.

"What is it, Cain?"

His voice was only slightly muffled by the distance between them.

He followed the dog's line of sight, and when he did, Bridget swore she felt his gaze sweep over her for a split second.

"We'll walk when I get back, boy." Ian rubbed the base of the other shepherd's ear in rough strokes and that dog leaned in against his touch.

From her vantage point in the tree, Bridget stared in dismay.

How could a murderer be so nice to a dog?

In a few minutes Ian got into the big car. It roared to life and a geyser of blue-black exhaust spewed from the exhaust pipe. He backed the Olds into the high grass, turned around, and slowly drove out until the front bumper hovered above the road directly across from her. After a pregnant pause he turned out on the road and sped away. A cloud of dust rose from his dirt driveway like a ghost from a tomb.

The dogs silently watched him go.

Bridget waited a few minutes to see if he'd return. When he didn't, she dialed the number Don had given her, reading it from the back of her glistening hand.

Don picked up on the first ring. "Bridget?"

"Hey, thanks for being there."

"Told you, I would. Is he gone?"

"Just left."

"How do you want to handle this?" he asked.

"Pull into the driveway and push the steaks out through a gap in the window, then back out and wait for me fifty yards down the road. I'll watch the dogs as best I can from up here. I'll climb down and wave to you from the road when I think its safe, okay?"

"You got it."

He was at Ian's house three minutes later. The dogs growled and barked viciously as he pulled into the driveway. Bridget could see their white fangs from up in the tree. They even clawed at his window with their front paws. To his credit, Don didn't get swayed from his task, though it had to be frightening despite being protected inside the car. He slid the sizeable steaks through the crack in the window. The dogs took one sniff each and seized the offerings, running with them like hyenas onto the porch and immediately tearing them apart.

Don backed out and drove slowly the way he'd come. He leaned his head out the window, apparently searching for her in the trees but unable to spot her. She lost the car in the leaves a moment later.

Don Mayhew is a good guy. Bridget shifted her weight on the branches. *A rare find.*

Fifteen minutes later both dogs were lying on their sides on the porch. A crow landed on the porch railing, a black splotch within the shade. It cawed three times to the oak trees around the house and then turned toward the house itself, perhaps looking for a morsel on the porch. It angled its head toward the dogs and suddenly its wings were out and flapping in a panic. It took to the air and was gone. A single greasy feather drifted to the ground.

The dogs didn't move.

Bridget picked her way carefully down the tree, finding it harder to get down than to climb up. But she made it safely and stepped out onto the road. She started to wave to Don but he was already speeding toward her. Seconds later the car stopped alongside her. He rolled down the passenger side window.

"I'm pretty sure they're out," she said, peering inside the open window.

"God, they wanted to rip me apart! Let's not take any chances—get in."

Though he had the windows rolled down, the car seemed cooler than the soupy air outside. "It feels good in here," she said.

"I was parked in the shade."

"Something else—maybe I feel safe, I don't know." She flipped the visor and then the mirror down. "What a mess," she said, wiping her sweating bangs from her eyes.

"You're no mess," he said. "That shirt has seen better days, though. Oh man—your knee! Are you okay?"

"Yeah, it's nothing serious."

Suddenly Don was a flurry of activity. He reached in a plastic shopping bag, took out a white and red can and sprayed her knee. She gasped as he coated her knee with the antiseptic. Then he ripped the top off a cardboard box and produced a square bandage. Firmly grasping her ankle, he pulled her leg over his own. His touch was unexpected and, despite the circumstances, she found it oddly erotic. He applied the bandage, pressing gently with his fingertips on the adhesive borders.

"That should do until we can clean it out properly," he said.

"Thanks. I didn't even think to ask you to get the bandages," she said.

"Some men do think for themselves, you know," he said with a smile, letting go of her leg.

They pulled into Ian's driveway and parked in front of the house. The dogs didn't stir, even after Don repeatedly beeped the horn.

They got out and tried the front and rear doors. Both were locked. The shades were drawn over the few windows.

"There's no easy way in," Bridget said, stepping over the snoring dogs on the front porch and trying to peer in through the gap between the shade and the edge of the front window. She was about to look for a rock when Don produced a wiry-looking device from his wallet.

"Let me try this." He held it up for her to see.

"Is that a pick?"

"Uncle John's a locksmith. He was always showing me different locks and how easy it is to pick them if you knew what you were doing. I've got this nasty habit of locking myself out of my apartment. Now I keep a pick in my pocket and one under the mat instead of a key. Get locked out enough and you get good at it."

"Why not just call your girlfriend?" The question slipped out before her better judgment could squash it.

"I've been flying solo for a while now. Do you always call your boyfriend when you get locked out?"

"I don't have a boyfriend."

Don glanced over at her. "Good."

He eased the pick into the lock and worked it around delicately. Moments passed. Just when she thought it best to go find that rock she heard a click and he swung the door open.

She saw his Adam's apple rise and fall as he looked inside and then at her. "Well, here we go."

"Let's do it. We may not have a lot of time."

He went in and she was right behind him, looking around at the well kept but sparse home that held the lingering odor of disinfectant. There were two rooms, a bathroom, a kitchen and a small living room. There was also a door to what was either a closet or the basement. Don started in on this lock and in a few minutes it, too, clicked.

He opened the door. They looked at one another for a moment and then together they descended the creaking stairs.

Shouldn't be in here.

Have to be in here.

What if Ian comes back?

We've got to find out about him and this is the only way to do it, so shut up!

At the bottom they turned the corner and halted as if they'd run into some invisible wall. They stared at the labyrinth of tubes, connecting valves, bays, and beakers on one of the tables.

"Wow," Don said.

Bridget studied the configuration. "Wow is right."

She looked around, ignoring the counters along the walls and the cabinets, instead focusing on the large refrigerator and the electron microscope and the computer linked to it.

Bridget opened the industrial-sized refrigerator. The temperature inside was cool but not cold. She stared at the racks and racks of petri dishes and test tubes with organic material inside each. There were also slides. She carefully removed one of the slides and closed the refrigerator. Quickly she went to the table with the microscope and computer and turned the equipment on. They were similar to what she'd used in the Hematology Lab at Chambers. She placed the slide she'd taken from the refrigerator beneath the lens and studied the associated image on the computer monitor.

"Well?" Don asked, pacing about nervously, checking out the glass tubes and beakers and then going to the shelves near the sink.

"It's the same virus," she said, leaning forward to peer closer at the monitor. "He's been manufacturing it down here."

Don stood beside her and stared at the spiral-shaped organism suspended on the monitor screen. "How many people has this guy murdered with this virus?"

Bridget looked away. "Eleven. Jo is the only one to live longer than three days."

"Why is she different?"

"I don't think she was a target. I think Jo just happened to come into contact with what was left over for Margaret Morrison. She accompanied her father during his cleaning visit and probably took a drink of water from Margaret's coffee cup or something."

"The virus is strong enough to live like that?"

"Evidently. He must have mixed it with some kind of suspension compound to render it undetectable to the victim."

Bridget returned the slide to the refrigerator and then carefully removed a sealed test tube. "Here's our evidence."

"Should we call the police and wait for them?" Don asked.

"I don't think so. I'm not sure they'd look favorably on our breaking and entering. And I'm really not confident they'd listen to an intern who just got canned."

"Yeah, but anybody could see that your getting thrown out was political."

"Even if some crime lab agreed to study the virus, they wouldn't know how to trace it to the victims since the virus gets absorbed after unleashing the leukemia. No, I think they'd probably arrest us and tear this equipment down because they'd think it's a still for moonshine or a meth lab or something. They'd probably just question Ian and give him a fine or a couple of nights in the county jail. And who's to say he won't get tipped off that the police have raided his place? He might just turn and drive off in another direction—free to make the virus somewhere else." She eyed the intricate constructions on the lab tables and walked to the stairwell. "Come on, I want to find out who this guy really is."

With a final look around they went upstairs. Bridget felt every muscle in her body trying to tense up on her and she had to fight them so she could simply move. The air seemed to press down on her shoulders.

"Can you keep watch at the window?" she asked Don.

"I was just about to do that," he said. "Maybe we should have parked farther down the road instead of right in front of the house."

"I think we'd better hurry," she said. "I'm getting really nervous."

"Getting? I've had the shakes ever since I fed that meat to those killers out there."

Quickly, she looked around the kitchen and, finding nothing of informational value, entered the main bedroom. There she saw a stack of business envelopes on the dresser, bills and junk mail. Not one was addressed to an Ian McGuire or a Mike who-the-hell-water-guy. The name in the little window at the center of the envelopes was a "Mr. Anthony Burgess." She pulled out the top drawer of his dresser, felt below the neat rows of socks and underwear without disturbing them. Pressed flat at the base of the drawer was a simple manila folder.

Don asked something from the living room.

She opened the folder. Inside was a collection of newspaper clippings and legal documents. She got on her knees and pulled out the contents of the folder onto the bed. "What, Don?"

"The dogs—how long will they be out?"

"Thirty minutes, maybe twenty-five. I didn't want them out when he returns, in case he was just out on errands or something."

"We've been here a while already. The dogs might wake up any minute now."

"I know. Believe me, I know. Come here and look at this."

The newspaper articles taken from the Raleigh paper were about how health care organizations were snatching up physician's independent practices. There was an expose on how one doctor, a Dr. Andrew Raynorr, had vowed to keep his private practice in place regardless of the pressure the HMO's put on him to sell.

She read to the bottom of the piece. It is continued on A-13 of the Sunday edition, dated May, 1990. Bridget's hand trembled as she flipped the article over to see the remainder of it, cut out from page A-13. There was a picture of a man in a white lab coat, balding but distinguished, listening with a stethoscope to the skinny chest of a young boy.

Bridget's face went slack. *"That's Ian."*

Don leaned over. "That's also our water guy—younger, but it's him. Actually, it says in the caption that he's Doctor Andrew Raynorr, general practitioner."

They poured over the other articles.

"It says here he was forced out of business by the health organizations," Don said. "All legal, but man, they squeezed him out by opening two practices right next to his. They treated people with the HMO's health insurance plan. Within nine months Doctor Raynorr lost his practice and then his license! Then he was arrested and released for practicing medicine *without* a license!"

"God," Bridget said. "Look at this."

She turned over the article and found a stack of legal documents and more articles. She flipped one over and then the next. There were divorce papers between Elizabeth Raynorr and Andrew Raynorr. Next was a document specifying custody rights for their three daughters. Then there was a restraining order, followed by newspaper articles of Andrew Raynorr being arrested for violating the restraining order against his wife and kids.

Then there were no more documents. It all ended, as if the man's life itself had suddenly ended.

There was a loud rapping at the front door. They leaped to their feet.

"Shit!" Don exclaimed.

Bridget placed the folder with the articles and legal documents back into the top drawer of Raynorr's dresser, her heart racing away in a mad rush of seemingly continuous beats.

"Out the back?" Don asked, his voice higher pitched than normal. "Should we run for it?"

"It can't be him—why would he knock?" Bridget said. "We need to go out the front. My car's there."

Bridget peered through the blinds at the front window. "We might be okay."

She opened the door to see an attractive woman with a lot of blond hair and a curvaceous figure standing on the porch. She was perhaps in her late forties. Bridget and Don stepped through, closing the door after them.

"Hi," Bridget said, as friendly and nonchalantly as she could. She reached back and held Don's sweating hand boyfriend/girlfriend style.

"Hello," the woman said, backing away as they stepped forward. Her brows were knitted. "I was looking for Tony."

"Daddy?" Bridget blurted, trying to think and walk down the porch steps at the same time.

"Well, yes. I thought I would stop and see Tony, uh, your Daddy. Is he in?"

Bridget shook her head emphatically. "No, not right now."

"Oh, that's too bad," the woman said, following them as they slunk toward Bridget's car. "I'm Madeline Harper."

"I'm Denise...Denise uh, Burgess," Bridget said, remembering Raynorr's alias on the junk mail and bills. She held out her hand and gave a brief shake when Madeline took it. Madeline had a heavy southern accent. Country girl. Country girls respond to fellow country girls. Judging from the white pickup truck parked next to Bridget's car, this woman was working-class Southern, not snooty society elite Southern.

"Good to meet you, Madeline." Bridget dragged out the "oo" sound in "you," adding more to her own southern accent.

Madeline smiled. "He never told me his daughter's names. So you're one of 'em?"

"Yep, the youngest. I'm past twenty-one but Momma would hate like hell to know I been here. You know, with the divorce n all."

"He said it'd been a rough ride."

"Sure was. Look, Madeline, I'm not even goin' to pretend. You know how it is. This is my boyfriend, Donny. He and Daddy don't really get along. If Daddy finds out you caught me and Donny in his house while he was out, well, I'm scared he'll never get to likin' Donny. And Donny, well, he's…he's asked me to marry him! You know I'm achin' to tell Daddy but I want to tell him at the right time. I'd hate to have it all spoiled by this. If Daddy ever found out about this, I—I just don't know what he'd do. He'd probably never want to see me again!"

Bridget looked beseechingly at Madeline as Don got in the driver's seat of her car, started it and let it idle.

Madeline smiled. "My Daddy never liked my husband, either. Turns out I shoulda listened to him. But I won't tell your Daddy, honey. Girl's got to go with what she thinks is right. Just maybe you should find another place for you and your beau to go an' be alone, is all."

Bridget smiled and rolled her eyes in false relief. "Oh, I will, Madeline. I will. Thank you so much! Oh, you're wonderful! I hope Daddy brings you to the weddin'!"

"I hope so, too. " Madeline looked down at the dogs. "Say, are these dogs okay? They're usually alert. I live in that little subdivision down the road, and every time I drive by they're always watching from the porch or runnin' around in the yard. I hardly ever see them sleepin'."

"They're fine. We took 'em for a long walk. You know, the heat an' all wears 'em out. That's why I'm all sweaty."

"Oh, is that why?" Madeline said with a wink and a knowing smile.

Bridget tried to look embarrassed as she got in the car. She waved as Don backed out alongside the white full sized pick-up truck. "Bye, Madeline! Thank you!"

Madeline waved back. "Bye, Denise. It was nice to meet you. Y'all stay out o' trouble, now."

As they sped down SR 1202 Don turned to Bridget. "Talk about scary. That was quick thinking on your part. What now?"

Bridget thought for a long moment, biting her lower lip as she did so. "Do you have a video camera?"

"Yeah."

"We've got to get some hard evidence to link the former Doctor Andrew Raynorr with the virus itself." Bridget pulled the test tube she'd taken from Raynorr's refrigerator out of her pocket. "We'll send this sample down to the CDC in Atlanta. At the very least they can examine it, maybe they'll figure out we really do have a lethal virus, here. But that could take time and we don't have that much."

Bridget watched the trees blur past. "We've got to somehow neutralize him. If we video the virus, his house, his lab equipment, the newspaper articles—all of it, then maybe the police will at least investigate and shut him down. The thing is we've got to video tape it all soon, before Raynorr kills again."

Don looked at the road and then back at her, his eyes wide. "So the bottom line is that we need to come back and break in again."

Bridget squinted against the sunlight streaming in through the windshield. "I'm afraid so."

* * *

Pushing through scattered thunderstorms that left rising wisps of steam on the road, Raynorr drove eighty miles an hour down I-95 South. Halfway through South Carolina, he took I-21 West toward Columbia. Four and a half hours after leaving his house, he pulled into the parking lot of a half-hidden motel on the outskirts of Columbia.

At some point he'd stopped whispering to himself. But *the bastards have done it again* kept rolling on in his mind.

It kept rolling as he mumbled a false name to the desk clerk and paid for the room in cash and the clerk handed him a room key.

It kept rolling as he carried the briefcase into the room.

It faded somewhat, but still did not disappear, when, from the briefcase, he produced the laptop computer and a pad of paper with Internet home page addresses listed on it in heavy bold print.

Brown stains spotted the bedspread and the throw carpet over the tiles was worn and frayed on the edges. Cobwebs hung from the ceiling and entire regions of paint had peeled from the walls. He made his way to the end table beside the bed and the scratched and chipped phone.

Raynorr disconnected the phone from the wall jack and replaced it with a line from the laptop computer. Using a false account he'd set up for just this purpose, he went on-line with the Internet. He clicked into the home page of Foundation Health Net Corporation. He ignored the corporate propaganda and clicked the *contact us* link. Inside the electronic mail form, he imported a previously created file into the body of the message, marked it as *urgent* and clicked *send*.

He electronically faxed the same document to a series of fax numbers for the company, then repeated the process for the other five targeted companies.

Afterward, Raynorr unplugged the internet phone line and reconnected the motel phone. Then he withdrew the laptop's operating system disk from the briefcase, inserted it in the disk drive and initiated a hard disk reformat. That would ensure all files would be swept clean from the drive. During the process he sat diligently by, patiently waiting for the computer to finish.

The front office was closed by the time he was ready to leave. Raynorr dropped the key through the mail slot and began the drive back home.

This is it, he thought. *Ultimatum time.*

TWENTY-THREE

Don's apartment complex in north Raleigh was much like Bridget's own, except it had flawless siding and spotless gutters and gleaming white trim on the many gables. The bushes in the landscaped areas were small and freshly planted. Young maple trees had wooden stakes on either side, with support lines for stability. Borderlines were still visible in the sod.

They were about to drive past the petunias and pampas grass surrounding the fountain entrance when Bridget spied, in the neighboring shopping plaza, a mail-anything store.

"Let's go there first," she said, pointing.

"Going to send that test tube on a trip?" Don asked.

"You got it."

As he drove into the plaza parking lot he spoke in a more tentative voice, "I know this is kind of a dumb question considering everything that's going on, but are you all right?"

"What gave me away?"

"The way you're shaking, for one thing. Another thing—and please don't take this the wrong way—is that as beautiful as you are, you look, well, exhausted."

She lowered the passenger side visor and flipped up the covering on the little mirror there. The dark semicircles beneath her eyes were nothing short of frightening. She raised her eyebrows then lowered them. The fine lines on her forehead lingered. Her skin felt as if it had been stretched too tightly across her skull. She looked at her hands as they rested in her lap. The fingers of her right were practically tap dancing, while the hand holding the test tube did a mini version of the Stagger Lee.

"God, I'm a mess," she said, staring down at the show.

"I'm sorry," Don said. "I shouldn't have—"

"No, it's all right. Surprise! I'm scared. I'm scared about what this ex-Doctor Raynorr will do next, and I'm scared Josephine Woods is going to die like all of Raynorr's other victims. On top of that, the adrenalin has worn off and I'm dragging—worse than normal even, thanks to this cold that's lingering on." She looked at Don. "So, how are you holding up?"

He held up his hands. Like hers, they also trembled. "Not a care in the world."

She smiled. *Strange how this Don Mayhew can make me smile, even at a time like this. And did he say I was beautiful? He did, didn't he?*

"I think we'd better rest before heading out again with the camera," Don said. "I've got cold medicine at my place that might help with your bug. Or you could write a prescription and I'll get it for you, like we did with the tranquilizers for the dogs. Uh, one thing though: You don't think you've been infected with the virus, do you?"

She thought for a moment, renewed fear rising inside her like a sudden black cloud on the horizon. Had she somehow been infected from the blood samples she'd studied?

"No," she said. "I'd be a lot worse off than this if I had that virus inside me. It debilitates in hours." *Except for Jo,* she silently added, *who was exposed to a much weaker concentration. It took two days to manifest itself in her.*

Don nodded. "I'm glad."

"Thanks. Me, too."

They got out and went into the mail-anything store.

"I need to ship bio-hazardous material in dry ice," Bridget told the clerk. "You've got the proper containers and all the warning stickers, don't you?"

He did.

Bridget scrawled a note to the CDC. In it she described the virus, how it had killed her patients, and where it came from. She signed the note "Bridget Devereaux, M.D." and enclosed it in the orange cylindrical container along with the test tube.

"This needs to go out overnight to the Center for Disease Control in Atlanta," she told him, placing her credit card on the counter. "You can get the address from your computer there, can't you?"

"Sure can," the clerk said, reaching for the bio-hazard stickers. "Want to insure it? How much are the contents worth?"

"It's priceless."

At the car Bridget got in on the passenger side while Don went to the driver's side.

Funny, she thought. *I'm letting him drive my car again and this time there isn't a compelling reason—that's not like me. I didn't even like it when Travis drove my car. Why allow Don Mayhew, a guy I've known for all of eight hours now?*

And what's really funny is that I don't mind.

"How long have you lived here?" she asked, after they'd driven the short distance to his apartment.

"Just had my six week anniversary. They were running a special. First thirty tenants got two months free rent. I jumped on it."

"It's great."

"Sure beats where I used to live. They're still apartments

though, no matter how nice they make them look. After I finish my degree, I'm going to get a real job. Then I'll be able to afford my own house—a house with grass, or at least dirt, on all four sides. Maybe a place to raise a family someday."

She smiled. "Wouldn't that be nice?"

They plodded up one set of stairs and then another until they reached the third floor landing. As Don worked his key into the lock of his apartment door, she looked out the hallway to see the bold purple and orange hues painting the western sky. The purple rumbled and was advancing rapidly this way, snuffing out the late afternoon sunlight.

"Another thunderstorm," she said, turning to Don while leaning on the bright white railing.

"Man, it seems like we've had one storm a day since summer began," Don said, looking over her shoulder. He swung the door open. "Come on, let's get inside. I'd rather not get struck by lightning."

No sooner had he said it, a vein of silver flashed from the swollen underbelly of the purple behemoth. More ominous rumbling followed.

"Inside's a good idea," Bridget agreed.

He stood to the side and gestured inward.

She went inside and looked around. There was a couch, a single chair, a small television with rabbit ears, and a wooden table beneath the small light fixture in the kitchen. The walls were still eggshell white and completely barren.

"It's not much," he said, closing the door behind them. "But it'll do for now. Uh, let me get that stack of laundry off the couch. It's clean and folded—I just haven't put it away yet." He spread his arms out wide and scooped up the laundry.

"Don, don't worry about—"

But he was already heading for the bedroom.

She stood before the large glass sliding door and watched the storm clouds move into position overhead. A shadowy net fell over everything that she could see: the plaza where they had shipped the virus specimen, the young trees on the apartment grounds, the pool area and tennis courts, and the cars in the parking lot. The cars on nearby Strickland Road had their headlights burning like radioactive bugs.

And no more than a half mile away, to the southeast, just off Six Forks Road, Bridget could see the giant water tower that supplied north Raleigh's drinking water. It loomed above the trees, like the rising stem and bulbous end of an incredibly huge light bulb.

The storm hadn't passed over the water tower as yet, and the diminishing rays of sunlight chose its smooth surface to hold a last stand against the approaching storm. But even as Bridget watched, the copper glow was fading quickly, replaced by dull battleship gray.

Strange that they built office buildings around a water tower. Land in Raleigh isn't getting any easier to find, I guess.

She heard drawers sliding open and shut inside the bedroom. "You wouldn't have anything about my size, would you?" she asked, over her shoulder. "Maybe some shorts and a tee shirt and some socks?"

"Sure," he called out to her. "Let me dig a little. My aunt sent me some stuff from Sea World and it was all a size too small. It'll still be big on you, though."

"I don't care as long as it's clean. Mind if I take a shower?"

"Not at all. Come on in. The shower's off the master bedroom here."

He handed her a dark-blue tee shirt with dolphins on it and a matching pair of shorts, as well as a pair of white socks. "Uh, I'm afraid I don't have any underwear for you…" he trailed off, his face reddening.

She laughed. "A briefs guy, huh? Don't have any boxers at all?"

"Come to think of it, I do have a few. I even have a pair that I shrank by accident." He began fishing in a drawer. A moment later he had them. Orange-striped.

She took them from him and held them up. "These are perfect! Thanks."

He looked relieved. "Shower's all yours. I'm going to check my messages and see if Lisa at the office has any more info on that suicide while you're in there. Want some of that cold medicine?"

"That'd be great, Don," she said, then closed the bathroom door.

When she came out, he was sitting on the couch, staring out at the falling rain. A steaming cup of what smelled like orange medicine was on the coffee table, next to an empty beer bottle and a small video camera with a curled shoulder strap.

"What's wrong?" she asked, walking out in the clothes he'd given her and rubbing a towel over her damp hair.

He stared straight ahead. "According to Lisa at the office, someone has threatened to infect Raleigh's drinking water if he doesn't see some kind of statement in tomorrow's newspaper from the area's HMO's."

She stopped rubbing her head and looked toward the water tower in the distance. Dark now, only the flashing lightning revealed the massive structure. "Thousands could die in days."

"The problem is that no one is taking him seriously," Don said. "In his faxes and emails he says he has 'chosen' half a dozen other companies, as well. They all think he's a crackpot trying to take advantage of the deaths of the execs. I tried to tell Lisa it was real. Tried to tell her and that vice president you ran into earlier, but they both thought I was crazy."

"So will the police, then," she said, stonily. "We have to get his lab on video tape."

"Tonight?" he asked, looking up at her. His tie was off and the first couple of buttons of his wrinkled dress shirt were unbuttoned, revealing his chest hair. His slacks were dusty and wrinkled.

Poor guy looks completely wiped. And even with that shower, I'm a walking zombie.

"No, not tonight. He's got to be stopped, but we can't do it if we're going to pass out on our feet. Besides, we don't even know if he's back home yet or not. You said he demanded a statement in tomorrow's paper?"

Don nodded, mutely staring through the sliding glass door as the lightning flashed outside like saber-play of the Gods.

She sat on the couch and stared outside along with him. "We've got until tomorrow to rest, then. We have to hope maybe he's still going to deliver the water like normal. When he's gone we'll give the dogs each another drugged steak and try to film what we can of the basement lab. Even if we tell the cops it *is* a moonshine still, at least they'll come and investigate. But I want to get it on tape first. You don't have to come with me, Don. I—"

"Hell if I'm not coming with you! You think I'd let you do this alone? What kind of guy do you think I am?"

She searched his eyes and then once again turned to watch the storm outside. "Thanks. I was hoping you'd feel that way. Mind if I crash here? I don't really want to drive across town to my place."

"I'm not about to let you go out in that storm. You can sleep in my bed—I'll take the couch."

"Oh, I can't take your bed. I'll sleep out here."

"Sorry, management won't allow it."

"Management won't…yeah, right. And who's the management?"

"I am. And the management says you take the bed. I put clean sheets on it while you were in the shower. You wouldn't want me to have wasted my efforts, would you?"

"Okay, okay. Thanks. Look, you can sleep in the bed with me. We can't—you know—*do* anything. Not that you're not cute an' all but…" She cleared her throat as the blood rushed to her cheeks. "Uh, anyway, I'm not going to make you sleep out here on the couch. You can sleep in the bed with me as long as that's all we do."

He smiled. "Even as bone-sagging tired as I am, Bridget Devereaux, I wouldn't be able to sleep a wink next to you on that bed. No, you take the bed. I'll stay out here after I get a shower. Agreed?"

She smiled. "Agreed."

She sipped at the hot cold medicine in the cup, eying his beer bottle. "Have another in the fridge for a new friend?"

"Sure, but I thought you were sick. Besides you're drinking cold medicine."

"Not prescription. One beer won't hurt. And in fact, it'll help me sleep that much better."

"Is that your official doctor's remedy?"

"You could call it that."

He laughed and rose from the couch, returned a moment later with two cold beers. They sat and drank and watched the storm.

Bridget was glad to be warm and dry and in his company while the storm raged outside, but even this couldn't keep the worry from preying on her mind. She suspected that after tonight, the lid was going to get blown off her world.

✳ ✳ ✳

"Jesus!" Bridget said, bolting upright in the bed.

Don's clock radio glared at her with 5:00 on its face. The constant buzz spewing from it was loud and raw and tugged on every synapse of her brain. With her head under attack, she groped for the light. Bumbling into it in the dark, she found the switch and flicked it on, then cried out as the bright light cut into her eyes. She turned from it.

She wished it away but the alarm blared on. The demon kept right on prodding at her brain with that goddamned pitchfork. With her eyes squeezed shut she fumbled along the surface of the alarm clock with her fingers, pushing a variety of square buttons without succeeding in shutting off the unfamiliar apparatus.

Suddenly the dreadful noise was silenced, just as her fingers encountered warm flesh.

She squinted and barely made out the vague form of Don Mayhew standing there in shorts and a tank top. Bridget found her glasses on the bureau and put them on. She forced her gaze upward, noted his flat stomach, the lean muscles of his arms and chest, and the stubble on his tired but handsome face.

"You ought to take that alarm out and shoot it," she said.

"Believe me, I've thought about it," he said, his voice hoarse. He turned toward the closet and bent to grab a pair of sneakers.

Nice glutes, she thought, forcing herself to look away before he caught her looking.

"How are you feeling?" he asked, sitting on the edge of the bed to get his shoes on.

"Not too bad. The cold's holding back. I'm a little achy but I'm not feverish. I think that stuff you gave me helped."

"Good. I don't know if you're hungry, but we should get something to eat on our way back to this Doctor Raynorr's house. There's a bagel place right at the plaza. I took out two steaks from my freezer last night that ought to be thawed by now. When we get to the house I'll go up that tree while you wait in the car."

Her heart started pounding away at the thought of waiting outside Andrew Raynorr's lair once again. It pounded even harder at the thought of going back inside. "We need to take shifts watching his house. I don't think we should try and stay up that tree longer than an hour or so at a time. We'll use the beeper and cell phone. If and when he leaves, whoever's in the tree will beep the other back in the car. Video camera charged and ready?"

"Charged and ready. Which is more than I can say for me."

"Me, too. Maybe some coffee'll help."

She drove this time. They stopped long enough to order coffee and bagels, then ate them on the way. She sipped at the coffee and put it in the holder. "Yesterday I noticed a dirt road, hardly more than a path, just before that subdivision near Raynorr's house."

"Yeah, I noticed it, too," Don said. "Think we should park there?"

"It probably leads to a phone conduit or circuit box or something. I saw a Southern Bell sign on a metal pole next to the entrance. I think we'd stand less of a chance of getting noticed if we park there instead of in the subdivision itself. That woman we ran into yesterday—what was her name—Madeline? Didn't she say she lived in that subdivision?"

"I think she did, but I'm not sure. I was so nervous I could barely think straight."

"Well, we don't need her or anyone else telling Andrew Raynorr that we're hanging out in the neighborhood taking turns spying on him."

The first rays of dawn met them on SR 1202. Bridget slowly drove past the gap in the embankment and the simple, rusting mailbox and faded green newspaper box that marked Andrew Raynorr's house.

At the end of Raynorr's driveway she could just barely make out the dark trunk and chrome bumper of a large automobile.

"He's back," Don said, reaffirming her thoughts.

A quarter mile later she pulled into the dirt access area for Southern Bell. Don stepped out, armed with the cell phone and small bottle of insecticide. Glancing warily at the woods, he held his hand up to her in a kind of still-motion wave.

Bridget returned the gesture and he started toward the woods. She was about to lean out the window to tell him to be careful when the forest seemed to lunge forward and engulf him within its darkened maw.

TWENTY-FOUR

THE MORNING AFTER his return from Columbia, South Carolina, Raynorr drove the water truck through the industrial park, with its low roofed buildings and gaping truck bay doors, until he spotted the blue sign with the oversized diamond painted in silver upon it. He parked in front of the steps leading up to the small dispatch office and swung down from the cab.

Morgan, the supply manager with the watermelon belly and stubby, cigar-stained fingers, burst out of the office. "You can't park there, dip-shit! You gettin' senile or somethin'? You know the rules—get yer mother-fuckin' rig outta here!"

Yankee foreman.

Unhurried, he started up the metal stairs. The entire framework shook beneath the weight of the charging supply manager. At a nearby docking bay, other workers, stacker grunts and drivers, hovered in a loose-knit group.

"Uh, oh! Morgan's goin' t' kick some ass again!" one of them said, his eyes gleaming.

"Aw, he ought t'leave the old guy alone," another said. "Hey, Pops! Morgan don't like trucks in front o' the office. Better move it out before he gets his hands on you."

Morgan slammed onto the midway landing and leaned over the rail. The iron bars pressed deeply into his belly. A charred stub of a cigar was clenched between his yellowed teeth, and his bloodshot eyes were round with rage. "Are you hearin' me, old fart? Move that fuckin' truck!"

Raynorr glanced at him and continued to ascend the stairs.

"Better do it, Pops," the worker who had warned him to move the truck said. "Give me the keys, I'll move the damn thing."

"No thanks," Raynorr said.

"Yer gonna move that piece of shit, you piece of shit, or I'm gonna bust you up!" Morgan said, once more thundering down the stairs as Raynorr continued to climb. Only eight steps separated them, then six, then four.

Then two.

"I'll kick yer fuckin' senile ass!"

Raynorr's head tilted to the side. "Is your mother aware of

your vulgar speech habits?"

"My moth—*you fuck!*" Morgan's hands balled into fists. He raised a meaty right arm. Elbow up, his fist was cocked in position and aimed in a downward angle at Raynorr's head. He took one more step down.

Like a cobra strike, Raynorr's hand shot out, just as Morgan's size fourteen construction boot was about to land on the next stair. His fingers hooked beneath Morgan's huge metal belt-buckle, the one with "BOSS MAN" standing out in bold letters.

Raynorr gave the buckle one quick tug.

The mass that was Morgan's body flew by in a blur of dirty white. The man had time to utter a startled cry and then his two hundred seventy-five pounds of vulnerable flesh met unforgiving steel in a single jarring thud.

"Ouch!" the workers at the bay door said.

"Had t' hurt!"

"Morgan's cigar is covered in blood, man! Look at that!"

Raynorr didn't bother. He walked up to the office just as the route manager flew out.

"What happened?" she cried, looking down the stairs toward the moaning heap and then at Raynorr. "What did you do to Morgan?"

"I defended myself."

"You attacked him!"

The worker who had offered to move the truck spoke up. "Naw, he didn't. Morgan threatened him and my man had to defend himself. Maybe Morgan won't be so quick t' throw his weight around now."

Raynorr threw the truck keys to the route manager. She tried to catch them, missed, and they bounced off her sizable chest to the floor.

"What's this?" she said. "You forget who you're dealing with, Mister! I'll have your job!"

"Save it. I resign."

"You what? You can't just quit on me! I got to have coverage for the route, bastard! Who's goin' to cover your route?"

In one smooth motion Raynorr took off his uniform cap and placed it on her head. He gave the brim a quick flick. "How about you? Surely, as a woman, you can do the job better than a man for half the pay. Think of all the money you could save the company."

The men at the loading bay howled.

The route manager stared at Raynorr in shock, her jaw working up and down but no sound issuing forth.

Raynorr turned and walked down the stairs, stepped on Morgan's thigh and continued on. "I'm donating my back pay to this gorilla, here. He appears to be a good candidate for plastic surgery."

Raynorr walked to the parking lot and his small compact commuter car that he used to get back and forth to Crystal Water, left here overnight when he'd driven the water truck home. Without a backward glance he climbed in, started it up and drove away.

✳ ✳ ✳

Thirty-six hours had passed since he sent out his demands to the insurance companies.

Deadline time.

Raynorr rocked back and forth on his front porch as the sky gradually brightened from black to light purple. Cain and Abel were laying beside him, their heads on their paws but their eyes open. Now and then their heads went up, ears rotating toward sounds no human could detect.

He heard the beat-up station wagon approach on SR 1202. It slowed as it neared the vicinity of the house. At six-ten in the morning there was a scrunch of tires and ensuing cloud of dust. The deliveryman was older than Raynorr. Slowing but not stopping completely, he jammed the Raleigh News and Observer into the green plastic container beneath Raynorr's mailbox and then drove away, the car kicking up gravel.

An instant later Raynorr was at the mailbox. He yanked the paper out of the green plastic box before the dust from the station wagon had cleared. Quickly, he thumbed through the paper as the air around him brightened.

The A-section held the same crap as the day before. The same crap…and nothing more.

I don't understand. They received my demands. All my email had registered as "delivered" and the transaction reports from my faxes had been error-free.

Raynorr walked slowly back to the house.

He threw the newspaper on the foldout table that served as his kitchen table and leaned down on it, setting it to trembling. He gritted his teeth and forced himself not to smash the toast and orange juice he'd prepared. He went through the A-section one more time and then the rest of the paper. The printed words lacked any acknowledgement of his demands. He stared at the meaningless columns and editorials.

They ignored me.

Ignored me!

He slammed his fist on the table. Orange juice leaped from the glass to splatter the table and the plate ejected the toast.

Where's my control?

Fuck control!

He backhanded the orange juice, toast, and every last section of the paper from the table.

Breathing hard, he glared around. The dogs had disappeared. He leaned on the kitchen table and then sank into a chair.

Why am I upset? I knew this was a possible, if not probable, outcome. Fools that they are, I should have counted on their silence. I overestimated the impact my sniper hits would have on them.

Bastards!

The initial demand had been simplistic: a single advertisement, in bold print, taken out by at least one of the health insurance companies he'd targeted.

That's all he'd demanded—up front that is. He had also demanded sweeping policy changes over the next six months, but that was reasonable. He knew they would need time to implement the changes, and six months was more than enough time for those changes. He had made it clear, though, that if he didn't see direct evidence of the changes in printed policy documents made public through the newspapers and magazines, then he'd be forced to increase his victim base.

There was no ad—no acknowledgement whatsoever.

In his mind he could see it, a full page dedicated to just two words:

WE UNDERSTAND.

But there was no such ad.

Perhaps they didn't believe him. Didn't believe he'd actually caused the deaths of their executives. They probably thought he was some crackpot taking advantage of the random misfortune of others. It seems he'd been *too* proficient as an undercover operative. Now he'd have to follow through as a known entity, like the Unabomber, but on a far greater scale.

I'll use Raleigh as an example for all the others. I'll release the new, self-replicating strain of the Raynorr Virus into Raleigh's water supply. The people of Raleigh will drop like flies. These managed care companies will be forced to answer my demands!

A knock at the front door made him start. He craned his neck to see who it could be. Had he been discovered despite his careful plans? Was it the police?

The dogs ran for the door, barking and snarling.

He rose and warily approached the door, heart beating wildly, hammering against the walls of his chest. He parted the blinds near the door and could make out a single form on his porch step.

He noted the curves, the long, blond hair.

I should ignore Madeline Harper. I was weak to involve myself with her. But then, it had been so long since I shared my bed.

He called the dogs back and opened the front door, leaving the screen door between them, casting a gray shade over her form.

"Well, hello!" she said, smiling.

"Hello, Madeline," he returned, watching as a soft breeze stirred her hair. He breathed in the scent of wild flowers on a clear sunny day.

"I hope I'm not imposing," she said.

"No, not at all. I...I was just having breakfast. Care for some?"

"No, thanks. I ate earlier."

"Coffee, then?"

She smiled. "Always could use another cup of coffee."

He popped open the screen door, holding it open for her. "Please come in."

She followed him into the kitchen. The dogs sniffed at her, growling low until Raynorr cut them off with a sharp "*No.*" They immediately quieted and went to curl up in the living room.

She noticed the floor near the kitchen table. "Tony, what in the world happened here?"

"What do you mean?" He looked, suddenly remembering. "Oh, that—I was a clumsy fool! I slipped and shoved everything over while trying to catch myself on the table."

"Here, I'll clean it."

"No, that's all—"

But she was already kneeling, gathering the paper and the plate and glass together.

"Not working today?" Raynorr asked, pouring Madeline a cup from Mr. Coffee.

She put the dishes in the sink and the newspaper in the trash, then took a sponge to the stained wall. "Not today. I work Saturdays at the nursery and they give me Wednesdays and Sundays off."

"How are your boys?"

She returned the sponge to the sink. "They're fine. Went to their father's place again. He's got a pool in his backyard. You know, it's summer vacation an' all. How are your girls?"

He looked at her in surprise. "My girls? They're not girls anymore. They've...all grown up. I guess they're working or going to college or having babies or something. I haven't seen them for so long...not since the restraining order after the divorce. I'm really not sure how they're doing." He placed the coffee on the table before her. "Cream and sugar?"

Her eyebrows knitted together, as if the choice confused her.

"Uh, yes, thank you."

He poured the cream and moved the sugar bowl toward her so she could sweeten her coffee as she saw fit.

"You've at least talked to your youngest lately, haven't you?" she asked, stirring her cup and leaning against the counter.

Why was she asking him about his family? He'd told her the truth about them when they'd first gotten together. He had to clear his throat before answering. "I haven't seen—or spoken to—any of them in years."

She stopped stirring. "Now that's strange."

"Not exactly a Norman Rockwell print of classic American life, is it?" He poured a cup of coffee for himself. His hand decided to start shaking and he spilled coffee on the counter. He cursed and grabbed the sponge. When he was finished wiping the counter, he turned to find Madeline regarding him with a curious expression. He sipped his coffee. It was bitter, but far less so than his memories.

"Now, this is strange," she said. "I stopped by the other day and was going to invite you to dinner–"

"Why is that strange?"

"Well, because your daughter was here."

"My daughter?"

"I-I promised her I wouldn't say anything, but when you said you hadn't seen or even talked to them for so long…I feel I should say something."

"My daughter was *here?*"

"Now, don't be mad at her! She was just tryin' to get up with you."

"What was her name?"

"Denise."

"Denise what?"

"Why, the same last name as yours: Burgess. She said her name was Denise Burgess."

Raynorr moved suddenly to loom over Madeline. "Describe her."

Madeline chewed the inside of her lip. "Tony, I feel so bad. I promised her I wouldn't say anything, on account of you and her boyfriend not gettin' along, and all. Wait a minute—if you haven't seen her in years, how could you disapprove of her boyfriend?"

"Describe her."

She blinked at his tone. "Uh, quite a striking girl—pretty, even with her glasses on. Maybe twenty-five. Seemed smart. Nice figure. Dark hair to her shoulders. She has kind of a direct way of lookin' at you that makes you think she's lookin' right into your soul. Least, that's the impression I got."

"And did she look into your soul with blue eyes or brown?"

She eyed his hands warily. He realized he was clenching and unclenching them and forced them to stop.

"I'd—I'd say her eyes were...green. I didn't see her for very long but they were definitely green. The color of jade, I remember thinking. She and her beau were coming from inside the house. Your dogs were sleeping when I pulled up, so I got out of the truck and knocked on the door, and when they came out I asked if you were around. They said no, but looked at me kind of curious—I don't blame 'em, they don't know me." She flashed him a placating, almost inviting smile. "Hell, you didn't even know me until last week."

Bridget Devereaux! Raynorr's mind was spinning. *She was here in my house! How did she get past the dogs? Did she wreck the lab or compromise the Raynorr Virus? I checked the basement lock but I didn't check the lab itself...haven't checked the lab during the past day and a half!*

His hand dove for the keys on the kitchen counter. He rushed to the basement door, shoved the key into the lock and threw the door open, almost running down the stairs.

His equipment appeared as it had been before his trip to South Carolina. The conglomerations of glass tubes and beakers and hoses and burners appeared untouched. He checked the large refrigerator. The petri dishes and test tubes containing successive generations of the virus seemed okay, as did the electronic equipment in the corner.

Everything appeared unharmed.

Madeline suddenly spoke from directly behind him. "Wow! What is all of this stuff? You got a moonshine still cookin' away down here, or what?"

He turned and she blanched at the look on his face.

"Madeline—you startled me," he said. "A still? No, no. I'm a retired doctor, remember? I do the water job just for some quick cash. What I've got here is my real work. You see, I've created a strain of bacteria that will break down petroleum-based solutions in large quantities. They've got others on the market, but mine stay alive a lot longer...long enough to replicate. I've got a patent pending on them, as a matter of fact. I don't have to tell you of all the possible applications for oil clean up in the modern world."

Her eyebrows rose as she gazed about. Suddenly, she looked up into his eyes.

"You're lying."

He took her arm and tried very hard not to crush it in his grip as he led her away from his lab equipment. "Why don't we talk about it upstairs?"

In the kitchen he told her she was right; he had been lying. Then he told her who he really was, what he'd done, why he'd done it, and how he planned on introducing his self-replicating virus into the drinking water of north Raleigh.

"But you can't...all those innocent people!"

"Sacrifices."

"My boys are in Raleigh for the week with their father!" Her eyes brimmed with tears.

"Then they are in danger," Raynorr said, reaching into a drawer. His fingers closed around the handle of a long fillet knife.

"You can't!"

"I must." He grasped the knife from the drawer and held it at his side.

"No. Please, Tony—no!"

She backed away from him, eyeing the gleaming blade. He followed her, unhurried and undeniable. When they were outside, Raynorr didn't see her white pickup. Evidently she had walked the half-mile to his house. Good.

She fell once and he waited as she gained her feet. "Don't do this, please! *Please! How can you do this to me?*"

"It's war, Madeline. Unfortunately, you know too much now."

Her lower lip was bloody from the fall and now trembled. "But this—this won't help. Oh God, my kids! *Please don't!*"

Remaining within striking distance, Raynorr forced her down the driveway. As she backed away, she glanced over her shoulder and then at Raynorr's knife. They crossed the road, barren and without traffic at this time of day. He forced her continuously backward, back within the tree line.

"I'm sorry, Madeline," he told her, once they were deeper in the woods. "But I can't risk any interference with my plans. It will be easier for you if you close your eyes."

She closed her eyes. Tears seeped between her lids, soaking her long lashes before tracing separate paths down her cheeks.

Raynorr struck, quick and deadly.

Madeline gasped and tottered, unsteady on her feet, eyes wide with shock. Her severed carotid artery shot bright red spurts with each beat of her heart.

Raynorr moved behind her and caught her in his arms, turning her head so her life's blood jettisoned away from them both. Inevitably however, some flowed over his upper hand. It was thick and hot, something he'd felt almost daily while in Africa. He'd always thought that fresh blood felt like motor oil draining from a warm car engine.

He carried the bleeding woman deeper into the woods.

Inside the protective camouflage of trees and leafy vines

Raynorr walked until he spied a massive oak. He leaned against the ancient trunk. The cool shade provided by its huge canopy embraced them both. With Madeline Harper in his arms, Raynorr slid to the forest floor.

He caressed the sides of her face as her life drained away.

She stared up at him, her gaze already distant. She breathed in a series of rapid, shallow gasps that became weaker and weaker until, with a final, powerful exhalation, she breathed no more.

Raynorr eased her body to the forest floor.

"Cain—Abel! *Come!*"

TWENTY-FIVE

G OD, BRIDGET HATED this. What was worse than waiting and worrying?

She tugged on a strand of hair and tried not to glance at the dashboard clock but it was useless to resist. The hour and a half of waiting for Don's shift to end passed with all the speed of a charging glacier. She put her finger to her lip, only to realize she had chewed her fingernails to the quick yesterday.

Great. Now what was there to gnaw on?

She scoured the glove box for some gum or breath mints or even an appetizing pencil, only to slam the little door shut with a curse when it became evident that the napkins and wrinkled receipts and owner's guide and vehicle registration harbored no such luxuries in their midst.

So she sat in her car in the small dirt clearing just off State Road 1202, the engine silent and her windows rolled down, sighed and stared at her surroundings. For the millionth time.

Getting brighter out. It's got to be my turn.

A few yards from the car, in plain view, stood the large relay box with the faded Southern Bell Telephone sticker on it. Clumps of tall grass and weeds encircled it like disciples gathered around the base of a sacred monument. Early morning dewdrops sparkled like diamonds as the first shafts of sunlight penetrated the surrounding broad leaf and pine trees. The once-yellow paint covering the box had long since faded and was now yielding to large rust spots that Bridget swore were getting larger as she watched.

Beyond the rusting box loomed the forest where Don had once again disappeared. He had insisted on taking the first shift to spy on Andrew Raynorr. He had taken a flashlight, and in moments the darkness had claimed him.

Time's slipping away. Come on, Raynorr—leave! I don't want to spend the day out here in this heat taking turns watching you.

Bridget peered into the woods, but could penetrate only the first few feet before the mesh of green and brown shut her out. Sweat beaded on her brow. As she wiped it away, she realized the air was not moving at all. She caught herself taking deep breaths, as if normal breathing could no longer capture enough oxygen for her body's needs.

Why aren't you here, Don?

The brightening sun and consequential rising heat of the day, normally welcome occasions for her, now served as barometers for her growing apprehension.

In the trees, hidden birds whistled and chirped. Instead of finding their songs soothing, she found them disjointed and chaotic, territorial warnings that threatened violence to invaders like her.

A swarm of dragonflies suddenly appeared and buzzed about like tiny fighter planes. She counted eleven but it was hard to be exact with their intermingling flight patterns. They commanded the airways of the tiny clearing, attacking and devouring a rising stream of young termites as they flew with delicate, temporary wings from a nearby rotting stump.

One dragonfly chose Bridget's car antennae as a landing pole. Grasping the thin metal pole with its four rear legs, and holding its double-set wings in a wide X-pattern, it proceeded to feast on a termite, holding it helpless with its forelegs while munching down on it, headfirst. Bridget blanched as the tiny legs of the termite kept moving, even as its head was bitten off.

She looked away.

Not a single leaf stirred in the trees before her. With the exception of the air battle between dragonflies and termites, the morning air remained jungle-humid and completely still, as if it were in the process of hardening into another, thicker substance.

All right, Don. She pumped her leg up and down alongside the steering wheel. *It's your turn to watch the dew drip while I go up that tree again.*

She suddenly had to swallow.

Oh, boy! Nothing like a good dose of acrophobia to get the stomach fluttering. You'd think I'd be over it after yesterday...

She fingered the sides of the beeper and held her breath while waiting for it to go off. After a minute the air *whooshed* from her lungs. The beeper remained silent.

What if Don fell from the tree and broke his neck? What if he's lying on the ground, dead or injured, right now? What if Raynorr spotted him—would he kill him? Would Raynorr kill to protect his deadly scheme?

Damn right he would.

She tried to tell herself to be patient—*ha, ha! The blackballed intern who wanted to be Doctor Devereaux now had to be patient! Get it? What a hoot! Patient...Doctor...Doctor...patient. God, that's funny, Bridget, honey*—that it was a waiting game. It might take days for Raynorr to leave the house once again so they could videotape his lab and the documents she had discovered in his dresser drawer.

She got out of the car, left the door open for quick access should Don beep her with the cell phone. She checked her watch then checked the LCD readout of the beeper to make sure the watch wasn't lying to her.

He should have been here ten minutes ago. Another five and I'm going to go looking for him.

Just as she took her first step toward the woods, a twig broke in the underbrush. She backed up to the car.

A vague shadow emerged in the gap between two massive trees. Gradually Don appeared, his light brown hair damp and his face glistening with sweat as he ran out of the woods.

His face and arms were scratched in a few places but he was moving normally, with no evidence of broken limbs. Bridget's shoulders plummeted from the sides of her neck. "So you didn't fall from the tree."

"Hey, nice to see you, too."

"I was getting worried," she said, moving closer.

He took a deep breath. "Thanks, I'm okay." He leaned back against the passenger side fender and wiped the sweat from his face with the bottom of his shirt. "That woman's inside Raynorr's house, though. What was her name…Madeline? I was climbing down from your tree when I saw her walk up Raynorr's driveway and knock on his door. She didn't drive this time. She's only been inside a minute. Think she's in danger?"

"I don't know. From what she told us, it sounded like they had some kind of relationship going. But if Raynorr thinks Madeline is a threat to him or his operation, then yeah, she's in danger big-time." She saw the fear in Don's eyes and knew it was a reflection of her own. "You've still got the cell phone, right?"

"Yeah, here." He handed it to her and in return he took the beeper she offered.

"Oldsmobile still there?" she asked.

"Yeah, along with a little compact car, but he parked it around the back in the dark this morning. If he leaves in that little one while we're doing the changing of the guards thing here, we won't be able to tell he's gone—unless we circle the house."

"…and risk getting attacked by his dogs."

Don swallowed, nodded once. "And risk the dogs."

"I'd better hurry." Bridget passed the phone relay box in four strides.

"Be careful," he said.

"See you," she said over her shoulder, running into the forest.

Yet again she dodged mature trees and briar patches and young trees that were leafy but no taller than her. The goal was the giant beech tree across from Raynorr's house. The route she took was getting familiar—always parallel to the road. Apparently, Don took a similar route, since many of the spider lines were already broken.

There was the hollowed oak trunk and the burnt cedar she could only guess had been struck indiscriminately by lightning during a storm. And there was the rising, gnarled root that had tripped her. Sharp stabs of pain came from her knee as she ran. She risked a quick glance down. The fresh bandage she had applied while in the car was red around the edges, and now some blood seeped down her lower leg.

As if that wasn't enough, the cold virus made her very heavy on her feet, as if she had blocks of concrete for shoes. Her breathing came in gasps, but she didn't let it slow her…much.

She had to get there, and get there fast. Every minute spent in transition was a chance for Raynorr to slip away without them knowing about it.

She looked at her watch. Ten minute point. Thank God she could stop soon. She ran on for another minute and then slowed to a fast walk. State Road 1202 was just barely visible to her left through gaps in the fauna.

Where was the giant beech? It shouldn't be so hard to find a big boy like that…there! She glanced toward Raynorr's house though she couldn't see much of it from this low-level vantage point. She didn't see or hear Raynorr or the dogs, or Madeline. She hurried to the tree, reached on her tiptoes for the lowest branch. As her fingers closed around the branch she froze.

What was that? Had she heard something just as she crunched those dried leaves?

Then she heard a voice call out from the woods behind her.

…*behind her*.

Not across the road, but deeper inside the woods—on *her* side! It was a man's voice, though she couldn't recognize it as Raynorr's. It was harsher, more commanding than Ian's voice had ever been.

Two heavy bodies crashed through the woods.

The dogs.

Raynorr was coming this way and he was calling his dogs to him. He must have come out to the woods during the transition with Don.

Get up the tree!

Fear of discovery slammed her acrophobia to the back of her mind. She scrambled from one massive branch to another, reached and pulled and pushed, tried to get higher before—

The crashing was too loud, too soon. She was only twenty feet up. The large branches she had climbed stood between her and the ground, providing some cover but not nearly enough; the leaves at this level were many feet away, farther out toward the end of the branches. A sickening feeling knotted her stomach as she looked down and realized the gaps between the branches could still reveal her to searching eyes from below.

She climbed one branch higher, one that took her to the opposite side of the massive tree and away from Raynorr and his dogs. She leaned back against the tree trunk. Her legs shook so violently she thought she might have to sit on the branch.

The crashing crisscrossed behind her tree. She heard growling and more crunching on dried leaves. The dogs were running, possibly playing with one another. She could see the big German Shepherds, muscles stretching and flexing as they raced with one another and jumped fallen branches and roots.

"Cain! Abel!"

Bridget shuddered.

Raynorr was directly beneath her. His call brought the dogs charging back toward her tree.

She bit her lip to stifle the cry that threatened to escape. She squeezed her eyes shut but then had to look down as the sound of Raynorr's passage took him from behind the tree to the front of it.

There he was, dressed in blue jean shorts and a white t-shirt. She could only see his backside. Then he turned as the dogs raced by him.

Bridget slapped a hand over her mouth.

The front of his shirt was splashed with crimson.

Raynorr wasn't hurt, the way he was moving. The blood wasn't his; it had to be from something or someone else. Maybe the dogs had hunted down or happened across the carcass of a wild animal. Judging by the amount of blood, it was probably a deer. But Don said Madeline—

Oh, God.

Bridget bit her knuckles. *Madeline.*

The dogs milled around their master, tails wagging. Their muzzles were covered with the same red as Raynorr's shirt.

He killed her!

As if hearing her thoughts, Raynorr suddenly halted and looked around. He scanned the forest, turning slowly.

Bridget didn't breathe. Every muscle in her body trembled now. Drops of sweat ran down her back and arms. She stared, waiting for him to look up the tree and discover her.

After several unendurable moments he turned and strode quickly through the last few feet of woods before the road. He no longer petted the dogs. He didn't speak to them as they crossed the road with him, one on either side, like canine bodyguards.

Across the road now, Raynorr turned in her direction once more. Again he searched the woods.

But never elevated his gaze.

He spun and charged up the dirt driveway to the house, the dogs at his heels.

Bastard! she wanted to shout at him. *Murdering bastard!*

She dialed 911 and pressed the SEND button.

The phone slipped from her sweaty palm.

"No!"

She grabbed. Her fingertips brushed it, only to propel it farther away.

It hit a branch and fell end-over-end in what seemed like slow motion, until finally it slammed into a base root of the tree and ruptured. Electronic innards sprang in every direction to lay scattered on the forest floor. The main electronic panel trailed behind the rebounding, spinning, plastic frame. Blue wires dangled, free form, like severed umbilical cords.

"No!" Bridget cried. "No…"

And then a thought cut through her disbelief: What if Madeline was still alive in the woods? As a doctor, she might be able to save the woman's life.

Her muscles quivering like jelly, Bridget hurried down the tree, nearly falling with each move she made.

She jumped down the last six feet and ran headlong in the direction from which Raynorr had come. She looked for signs of Madeline's body up ahead, but could see only forest. A root clipped her and she flew for a split second and then struck the ground with the same knee as the day before. A rush of pain slammed into her and black formed at the edges of her vision.

She tried to stand, but her leg buckled on her. Bridget hit the ground once more, this time landing on her hip. It didn't feel good, but at least she spared her knee. She rolled, put her palms on the ground, intending to push off and up—

The ground was wet. From last night's thunderstorm? The storms had been isolated. It didn't appear to have even rained here at all.

She looked down. No, it wasn't water.

Her hands pressed into a trail of blood.

Visually she followed the blood trail. It led straight to a massive oak, the trunk half again the size of her big beech. Bridget pushed off the ground and half-ran, half-limped for the oak.

She pulled up, her fears realized. Madeline lay across a bed of enormous roots. No attempt had been made to hide her body.

"Oh, Jesus. Oh Jesus."

Bridget's stomach hitched and threatened but did not vomit.

She knelt. No need to check Madeline's pulse. The woman no longer had a throat. The skin, muscles, and ligaments—where still present—were hanging in shreds, severed in a jagged manner that spoke of fangs and canine teeth.

But wait—

Bridget's gaze zeroed in on a slice of skin that dangled below Madeline's left shoulder, almost out of sight. The edge of the skin was uniform. Madeline's throat had first been cut by a blade.

"Madeline, I'm sorry," Bridget said, her tears splattering the blood beneath her.

This was not a cadaver lying prone in an advanced biology room. Even the adrenalin junkies of the emergency room would choke at the sight of this murdered woman.

"Madeline, I am so sorry."

Madeline didn't say anything.

She couldn't, of course. Couldn't do anything now. Not now. Not ever again.

The muffled screech of tires on asphalt wormed its way through Bridget's shock.

Raynorr. He's leaving.

She rose unsteadily and looked away from Madeline's body.

Think, Devereaux, think!

The trees and undergrowth offered no help.

Can't call the police. Can't page Don. Could run back to Don at the car, but that's ten minutes wasted. There's a phone in Raynorr's house. Take only a minute to get there, even with this knee.

Bridget swallowed.

The only problem is…the dogs.

TWENTY-SIX

THE SCREECH OF Raynorr's tires echoed in Bridget's ears as she tore through the last of the lacerating undergrowth and skidded to a halt on the gravel shoulder opposite his driveway. Chest heaving, she gulped air like a fish trapped in a stagnant pond. Desperately she tried to peer through the blue-gray smoke rising from the molten strips of rubber that snaked westward on the sun-baked road.

Where are they?

Madeline lay dead in the woods behind her.

I'm losing time! Can't see anything!

Madeline's image appeared in the undulating wall of smoke, her ruined throat in obscene crimson contrast with the rest of her unscathed body. Suddenly nauseous, Bridget bent and retched but did not vomit. She forced her eyes up, where they remained fixed on the gradually clearing smoke that shielded Raynorr's house. Her body may react to the horror she had seen, but she'd be damned if she was going to let it paralyze her any more than it already had.*No way am I going to let Raynorr get away with murdering Madeline and the others. No way.*

The smoke hung over the road for another lingering moment and then, animated by a sudden puff of a breeze, bore down upon her like a massive shroud. She blanched as it passed around and over her. The rank odor of burnt rubber clung to her nasal passages and curdled in her stomach.

Where are those damned dogs?

Finally, the air above the road cleared. Bridget squinted, tried to locate Raynorr's Oldsmobile in the distance. But the long black car had disappeared, though the road was a straight shot for five miles. Was the car really that fast?

Look for the dogs, dummy!

She yelled for the beasts. Swore at them while poised to race back to the nearest tree should they come charging toward her.

When they didn't show themselves, Bridget scooped up a handful of gravel, cocked her arm back, and whipped the rocks at Raynorr's mailbox.

She had played varsity softball throughout high school and

two years in college, before it began to eat into her study time and she'd elected to quit. In her first collegiate practice, she'd fielded a grounder at third base and threw the ball to first so hard the poor girl had to drop her glove and massage her hand. From then on, Bridget had owned third base.

The jagged rocks struck the mailbox in a tinny barrage, scarred and dented the faded black surface. Still, no sign of the dogs. She grabbed another handful of rocks, and, cocking her arm back to throw, sprinted across the road. No sooner had she set foot on the dirt trails that constituted Raynorr's driveway when the blast of a car horn made her leap clear off the ground. Thoughts flashed like lightning as she spun in the direction of the blast.

Had Raynorr come back? Was this a trap?

Tires crunched on the rocks and dirt. The car was instantly familiar. Don Mayhew waved frantically from behind the wheel.

"Get in!"

Bridget bent and shouted, "Raynorr killed Madeline!"

The color drained from Don's face. "Jesus. Hey, don't stand out there. Where are the dogs? I heard a car peeling out—"

"That was Raynorr's car. We've got to call the police."

Stuffing the handful of rocks into her pocket, Bridget bolted for the house. Don drove the car up the driveway paths and cut the engine. A split second later his heavy footfalls sounded on the porch steps behind her.

The door stood ajar.

"He wouldn't have left it like this if he was coming back," Bridget said, pushing the door open.

The living room appeared the same as it had the day before when they'd broken in: same sparse furniture, same two lamps, same books on the table. The kitchen was likewise unchanged. They ran to Raynorr's bedroom. The bed was made but the spread was wrinkled, as if items had been thrown on it and then collected in haste. The dresser drawers were open and empty, sagging downward as if mourning the loss of their contents.

Don pushed a couple of the top ones in to see the lower drawers. "He's cleaned out all of his personal stuff. We're too late."

They looked at each other.

"The lab," they said, almost in unison.

They dashed out of the bedroom. Like the front, the basement door was also unlocked. Their feet thundered on the simple wooden steps as they went down. With Don on her heels, Bridget pushed off the cement wall at the bottom of the steps, turned the corner, and was once again inside the laboratory of a madman. Shivering and sweating at the same time, she gazed in the dim light at the labyrinth of tubing, containment bays, test tubes, and beakers. It seemed un-changed.

"Maybe he didn't leave, after all?" Don ventured.

Bridget went to the large, almost industrial-sized refrigerator from which she had stolen a sample of the virus. Slowly she opened it, not wanting to shatter any of the test tubes or petri dishes Raynorr may have left behind.

"Gone," she said, staring at the empty shelves. "All of it." She wrapped her fingers between the metal rows of one of the shelves, felt the dissipating coolness of it. "He could go anywhere and start all over again."

She jerked the metal shelves out and hurled them to the concrete floor.

From over her shoulder Don peered into the empty cavern. "He wouldn't really infect Raleigh's drinking water with the virus, would he?"

"If he thought murdering thousands of innocent people would force the managed care companies to meet his demands, then yeah, he'd do it." Bridget glanced around. "I know I saw a phone down here the other day…There!"

At the counter she snatched up the handset. "Maybe the police can set up road blocks or something. Come on, damn thing! Where's the dial tone?" She mashed the button again and again.

"Think he closed his account with the phone company?" Don asked.

"Why would he bother?"

"True. What about the cell phone I gave you?"

"Sorry, it took a dive out of the tree."

"Then let's drive to the nearest house in that subdivision and call from there."

"Good idea…you go. I'm going to video this stuff while you're gone. Is your camera still in the car?"

"We don't need evidence that he's the creator of the virus anymore, Bridget," Don said. "He'll get the death sentence for what he did to Madeline."

"That's what they said about O.J." She paused, sniffed the air. "Do you smell that?"

"Smell what?" Don inhaled. "Wait a minute. That's—"

"Gasoline," Bridget finished. In their haste they hadn't noticed the distinctive odor before. Now it enveloped them. The vapors were starting to make Bridget's eyes water. She peered down at the basement floor. Crisscrossing trails of clear liquid led to a shallow pool of the stuff at the base of the stairs at the far end of the laboratory. More trails led to the cement walls all around them. She looked down. Her sneakers were soaking in the gasoline, as were Don's.

Quick, heavy thuds sounded on the floorboard above them. Bridget jerked her head up, eyes wide and searching the naked joists above.

"Someone's upstairs!" she said. "We have to get out of here!"

She raced for the stairwell with Don on her heels. Just as she was about to turn the corner and reach for the railing, a sharp *crack!* jolted her to a stop. She cried out as a chunk of cement exploded from the center of the foundation wall at the foot of the stairs.

"I wouldn't come out any farther," a man's voice warned from the top of the stairwell. "Bullets do considerable damage to the human body, especially these hollow tips that flatten on impact."

She could see only his twisted shadow on the far wall of the stairwell, but she knew it was *him*.

He had them trapped.

His voice sounded a little like the Ian McGuire she had briefly known, or thought she had known, back in the hematology lab at Chambers Hospital, but it was no longer the warm and kindly voice of a lab technician gracefully easing into retirement age. Now his words were caustic, steeped in acid. To Bridget he sounded like a man who had been beaten down and resurrected into a new being, one who had been dealt far more than his share of life's insanities and was now ready for some payback.

That isn't Ian McGuire up there. It's Andrew Raynorr, ex-physician turned murderer, the brilliant, twisted creator of a lethal virus he uses to take innocent lives. Soon he'll add genocide to his list of dark credits unless we can stop him, and the prospect of that happening just evaporated like a drop of water on a hot frying pan.

"I'm really a blade man," he informed them, cutting through their shocked silence. "Guns are so impersonal. But seeing as how there are two of you, I'm not taking any chances. Of course you realize I won't hesitate to shoot both of you if you show yourselves."

"You murdered Madeline, didn't you?" Bridget said, trying to breathe through the gasoline vapors while searching for something—*anything*—in the lab that could help them. Then she saw it, the one thing that might save them when Raynorr made his next inevitable move.

"I beg your pardon?" Raynorr said.

"Her throat was ruined by animal teeth, but the dogs didn't kill her."

"Didn't they?"

"It was you!"

"Really? What makes you think so?"

"Your dogs weren't as thorough as you may have thought. I know a little about you, now. You're so caught up in your personal vendetta that you're willing to kill anyone who gets in your way. Did you know that while you were murdering those executives you also infected a young girl with your leukemia-conjuring virus? Did you know that, *Doctor* Raynorr?"

"So, not only do you know who I am, you also know about the true nature of the virus? I knew you were talented and astute, but I really had no idea, Doctor Devereaux. Ah, but it's not really *Doctor* Devereaux anymore, is it, Bridget?"

She bit her lip.

"Oh, yes, I know all about *you*," Raynorr said. "I called an old acquaintance at the hospital and he provided the sordid details. Gerard Handlaw makes Bill Clinton look like a boy scout, doesn't he? They did you just like they did me, Bridget. Don't you just want to tear them apart for ruining your life?"

"The girl, Doctor," she said, trying to fend off his attack."What about the girl?"

"...the girl? I've seen *thousands* like her perish from human cruelty. The one you mention is simply the first truly innocent victim in my war. Madeline was the second. Now I'm afraid you and your friend there will be the third and fourth.

"It's too bad, really. When I first saw you walk into the hematology lab at Chambers I knew you were different from the other interns. Oh, you were young and naive like the rest of them — but you had a drive, a determination to push through that went far beyond the norm. You didn't accept the dismissive opinions of your superiors concerning the strange leukemic episodes, even when they pressured you to do so. You kept running your tests, kept trying to save those who were beyond saving. Handlaw was a fool to throw you out. Had you not challenged your superiors quite so openly, you would have made an outstanding doctor."

Bridget backed away from the stairs and into Don. At first he stood like a stone statue, but when she pushed he moved back along with her. They exchanged a look. It was obvious he didn't understand her intent, but was willing to follow her lead.

"You know they'll catch you," Bridget called up to Raynorr, raising her voice as she and Don retreated. They contacted the far wall and could retreat no further. There were no windows, no doors other than the one Raynorr blocked with his gun. The gasoline stench was making her eyes water.

"They have no idea of what they're up against," Raynorr said. "My new virus can reproduce. It thrives in chlorinated water. I can now infect thousands, and hundreds of thousands, perhaps even millions. I can release the virus into the drinking water of any number of cities. I can destroy any population of my choosing."

"You can't want that."

"The war has escalated. The greedy fools have chosen to ignore me, so now I have to beat them across their snouts with a two-by-four to get their attention, as an over-priced, pompous ass of a lawyer I once knew was fond of saying."

"You can't commit mass murder," Bridget said. "The people of Raleigh had nothing to do with what happened to you."

"Innocent lives carry the most impact, my dear. Just ask McVeigh or the Irish Republican Army or any terrorist from the Middle East." He paused for a moment as if retrieving something from his pocket. "Well, goodbye then, Bridget Devereaux. It has been a pleasure. And to your silent friend, well, I'm afraid for you this is one of life's unfortunate circumstances."

"Murdering bastard!" Don cried. "To hell with you!"

"All in good time, my friend. All in good time."

"The police are on their way!" Bridget shouted.

"But I'm already gone. My essentials are in the car. By the time they connect me to Madeline I'll be in another part of the country. The virus will grow and soon everyone who drinks Raleigh's water will come down with a case of drastically accelerated leukemia. They'll perish by the thousands."

"You can't do that!" She kicked her gas-soaked shoes off and pointed for Don to do the same. He complied, his eyes wide and fearful.

"I *can* and *will* do it," Raynorr snarled. "This is war, *my war!*"

"But you're a *doctor*. You were meant to heal, not murder."

"Life changes when they take your soul."

"You swore to protect life when you took the Hippocratic Oath."

"That oath was shattered by managed care."

"I don't buy that. Companies don't take the oath."

"No, but they have turned it into a farce. Managed care—and now our government-run, socialized medicine—murders by denying timely treatment. Like presidents who lie under oath, they get away with fucking the American people. Doctors are now bound by financial considerations and the whim of a government stooge, not patient need. And it doesn't stop with the insured—now the uninsured are more fucked than ever. They get turned away at the hospital door to bleed out in the gutter. Hippocrates' ancient ghost has been spinning in his long-forgotten grave ever since managed care took over."

Bridget opened her mouth to respond but nothing came out. What could she say? Much of what Raynorr said was true.

Raynorr spoke softer this time, "Do you know what it's like to lose everything, Bridget?"

She didn't hesitate. "Yes, I do. And I don't hurt people because of it."

"Then you know the hell of it," he said. "Perhaps you'll rise from the fire like a Phoenix...but it would be better if you didn't. The world doesn't deserve you."

As if sensing the end, Don suddenly pressed forward. "I'm

going to rush him!" he hissed to her.

Bridget stepped in front of him, her hands up. "He'll shoot you."

"I can't just let him fry us."

"He won't. He'll try but he won't—"

They heard the *ch! ch! ch!* of Raynorr striking up a lighter.

"He's going to—*hey*!"

Bridget shoved Don inside the open refrigerator. He twisted, landed on his side, then, understanding her meaning, pulled his legs inside. He held his hand out for her.

She caught a glimpse of the flaming Molotov cocktail as it flew down the stairwell. The walls glowed eerily with its passage.

Bridget leaped.

She landed inside the refrigerator beside Don, but she was turned the wrong way to close the door. The flaming bottle shattered. As she struggled to twist around, Don grasped the edge of the door and hauled back on it, slamming it shut just before the basement burst into yellow and blue.

From inside the refrigerator they heard the *whoomp!* of flame igniting gasoline.

She and Don held fast to one another in the darkness. Bridget was too terrified to speak. Don was silent. After a moment she cocked her head, picked up the muffled crackling and snapping that surrounded them. A minute passed. It began to get hot in the airtight vessel that had saved them from becoming charred meat. Beads of sweat formed and rolled down her face. The hot air didn't seem to fill her lungs with enough oxygen.

The crackling and snapping grew louder, then louder still.

Bridget forced her tongue from the roof of her mouth. "Don?" Her grateful relief at escaping the initial flames was replaced with a new fear. "Don…?"

"Here," he said, as if answering roll call. His voice was weak and fearful, like her own, but at least he was responding.

"The gas must have burned off by now."

"I know."

"I hear wood burning. We…we have to get out."

"I know."

"Help me with the door."

Together they pushed on the door. It didn't budge.

"Oh, shit," Don said, frantically slamming his hands into the door. "Oh shit!Oh shit!Oh shit!"

Bridget was silent but in her head she was screaming. Her mind hearkened back to a public service warning she'd seen on television long ago: *Every year children die from asphyxiation inside improperly secured abandoned refrigerators.*

They pounded at the door and were soon gasping for air. Sweat sprung from every pore in Bridget's body.

"Wait!" she said. "Use your legs."

"Yes."

After a few precious seconds of squirming they managed to sit with their backs pressed against the rear panel of the refrigerator and their feet on the door, as if ready to do a leg press. There was just enough room to cock their legs back in preparation for the kick.

Bridget tensed. "One, two, three…!"

Their feet slammed into the door. The latch rattled but did not give.

Bridget opened her mouth to breathe but no air came in this time. It was as if she was being smothered with a pillow. She had just enough air left in the furthest recesses of her lungs to hiss, *"Again!"*

Amber light attacked Bridget's eyes as the door flew open. She gasped for air…precious air. It was there, but it was hot and smoke-filled and felt like it singed her throat and lungs as she breathed it in.

Popping and crackling, then a more subtle—but infinitely more ominous—whooshing noise crowded in around her.

Still gasping, she looked out into Hell's belly.

Tornadoes of barreling flame twisted and writhed and ran horizontally beneath the ceiling toward the upper stairwell. Thick black smoke began to fill the space between the floor and the ceiling. The counters and cabinets were gone, replaced by dancing fire demons. Everywhere Bridget looked there was fire.

Except the floor.

The gasoline had burned away in a manner of seconds, catching flame to all it could before consuming itself. The concrete showed white where the gas had burned. Dust and other particles had turned to ash. The fumes and smoke were almost overpowering. She couldn't get a decent breath. Her eyes watered and she began to cough.

Pulling Don with her, Bridget crawled from the refrigerator, keeping her head low and as far away from the roiling clouds of yellow and red as possible. The gasoline had quickly burned away leaving the concrete floor warm, but not scorching hot. On all fours, she pulled her shirt up over her nose and mouth and tried to breathe. Don did the same, his eyes huge and round. The fire's reflection played in his pupils as if the house around them was Rome and he, Nero.

The ceiling writhed.

She stared. The room was amazingly quiet considering the ferocity of the burning, just a kind of whooshing, punctuated here and there by crackles and explosions. The flames were hideously beautiful.

Sudden pain on her head woke her from the stupor. Something knocked her to the floor. Don was on top of her and his shirt was off. He struck the top of her head again and again with his shirt.

"Are you crazy?" she managed to yell while trying to fend him off.

He kept on pummeling her for a second and then backed off. A new stench invaded her already overwhelmed nostrils. "Your hair was on fire!" he shouted.

On all fours, gasping for breath, he pointed to the refrigerator that had both saved and nearly destroyed them. The coating of paint on the outside had caught fire. Melting, blazing paint ran down the front of it and pooled on the floor to form a lake of fire. Soon the entire refrigerator was an inferno. Her hair must have caught when she came out.

She tried to swallow but her mouth was too dry. The unmistakable odor of burnt hair mixed with smoke and other noxious fumes made her woozy. She nodded and grasped his arm in gratitude.

"The stairs!" she cried.

A wall of undulating orange and yellow and red claimed the stairwell, blocking their only escape route. The upper third of the fiery wall parted, giving way to the side-spinning, flaming tornadoes feeding on the ceiling. In the stairwell they righted themselves. As Bridget stared in horror the flames parted just enough for her to catch a glimpse of naked wood on the far side of the stairwell.

"It's our only way out!" she shouted, catching another glimpse through a gap in the flames. Raynorr had left the door open at the top of the stairs.

The fire greedily sought this fresh supply of oxygen, snaking around the corner to eat its way to the upper floor. The doorframe blazed like Hell's gate.

Then the wall of fire closed in and she could see the door at the top of the stairs no longer.

Don turned to her. "Oh, man."

Like rabbits ducking from a swooping eagle, they kept their heads low. They crawled near the blazing staircase but had to back off from the heat.

"We have to jump through and run for it!" Bridget cried, straining to be heard now over the increasing pops and crackling and the ever-present *whoosh!* as flames claimed more and more of the house.

"No!" Don shouted, shuffling back from the fiery stairwell.

She caught at his shoulder. "It's our only chance!"

His face was black with soot. "No—we'll use a table!" He

pointed. Raynorr had pushed together two tables, both six feet long, to accommodate his lab equipment. The tables, with much of the plastic and glass apparatus still intact on them, stood upright, even as their wooden legs were consumed by fire.

Bridget nodded. The tabletop was covered in thick Formica finish that hadn't caught fire...yet.

They scrambled on their hands and knees to the first table. Bridget grasped beneath the top overhang and pain shot up through her hands. Crying out, they yanked their hands away. Blisters were already forming on Bridget's palms. There was a metal support beneath the tabletop.

Don dove for his shirt, now complete with fire holes and charred edges. Wrapping it around his hands, he tried to shove the table toward the stairs. Unable to stand upright and gain necessary leverage due to the thick smoke, the table moved only a few inches and stopped. The smoke and noxious gases poured over everything. Bridget breathed as best she could between coughs. On one knee now, Don lowered his head, his shoulders and neck working up and down as he coughed violently. Bridget yanked her shirt off, squatted beside him and shoved at the table with all the desperate strength in her body. Don joined her and together they succeeded in pushing the table—its wooden legs torches now and burning at a frantic rate—to the bottom of the fiery stairwell.

"Over! We have to flip it over!" Don cried between coughs. "We have to run through the break when the table hits!"

They pitched the table over into the fiery wall. The flames parted, then began to lean together as if drawn to one another magnetically. For a waning moment they had an avenue of escape that was disappearing fast.

This time Don shoved *her* forward. "Cover your hair with your shirt! Go!"

Catapulted by Don's shove, Bridget sprang between the columns of fire that had been the table legs just a moment earlier. The flames that had parted for the table now grabbed for her as she raced by. Bridget scrambled up, up, up! She couldn't feel her legs and arms and for one horrific moment felt as if she was suspended in the air, not moving anywhere, limbs pumping impotently. But a stair passed beneath her, and then another, and now a new burst of adrenalin kicked in and she rocketed into motion, somehow avoiding the livid flames on the outer edges of the stairwell. No time to ponder—just go! The naked skin of her shoulder and side of her body shrank from the heat.

Bridget leaped over some, but many of the stairs were now burning all the way over to the foundation wall. She had no choice but to hit them.

*Don't break!*she thought.

She registered pain at some distant, lower level, but the terror at being burned alive and the adrenalin pumping through her body kept her sprinting upward. She couldn't turn to see Don but she thought she sensed him behind her. There was only up and out and keep moving. Keep moving! Keep moving!

The spinning fire tornadoes blazed out of the stairwell and into the ground floor of the house. Following the oxygen, they writhed like demonic snakes, twisting and flowing and burning—always burning—but at the same time leaving a foot or two of space near the cement foundation wall that was as yet untouched.

It was into this space Bridget sprinted. She swore she could feel her skin charring and her blood boiling. Terror beat in at her from all sides, but there was nothing she could do but keep pumping her arms and legs. Her bare shoulder scraped the foundation wall as she sprinted up the stairs, and the relative coolness of it made it feel like she had rubbed against an iceberg.

The door was alive with snaking, spinning columns of fire that greedily consumed the oxygen of the ground floor and belched black smoke everywhere. There was no time to pause. No time to think. Bridget pressed her shirt on the top of her head, closed her eyes, and leaped through the doorway.

She had no air to scream with, but she tried anyway.

The skin on her arms and legs and her breasts under her bra quivered beneath the sinister caress of the flames. She leapt into the wall of fire and felt it *pass over her*, as if a great dragon had cocked its head back and blasted her with the fire from the kilns within its scaly hide. There was a split second of pain, of blinding yellow and orange and then—

She crashed onto the landing and cried out as she hit on her elbows and knees.

Made it! She patted madly at her hair with the shirt. For some reason she hadn't caught on fire. She rolled to make room for Don.

The hardwood floor was oozing something she was sure was flammable. The living room, bedroom, and kitchen walls and ceilings were engulfed in flame. Black, oily smoke smelled of death and hung in a thick cloud below the ceiling. The couch and La-Z-Boy chair in the living room hurled flames high enough to hit the ceiling and run laterally.

The kitchen tiles were porcelain, and hadn't caught fire. The back door was straight ahead. It was their only escape route, *if* they took it in the next few seconds.

"Don!"

Coughing violently, Bridget could only wait on her hands and knees.

The doorway was a wall of flame from top to bottom.

Why wasn't he…?

"DONNNN!"

The wall of fire parted. Out came the head and shoulders and then the rest of Don Mayhew. The flames appeared to wash over him. He hit the landing hard, his arms crumpled and his head struck the floor with a heavy thud.

"God*damn!*" he cried. He clutched his forehead even as he kicked and slipped and went down again.

His shirt landed like a flaming meteor beside him. She kicked it away, grabbed beneath his arms and hauled backward, away from the flaming doorway.

"Kitchen!" Bridget gasped, and she could feel the smoke particles bounce eagerly down her throat and fill her lungs. Her head felt like a balloon. The world melted into a canvas of orange and yellow and black.

They staggered through the kitchen toward the back door. The doorknob seared Bridget's palm. She cried out but did not let go. Instead, she turned the knob and flung the door wide. She and Don half-tumbled, half-ran out the kitchen door. The smoke and flames followed them in a last-ditch effort to claim them.

Bridget collapsed onto the close-cropped grass and weeds outside Raynorr's small cement porch. Though it had to be a hot summer day, the drop in temperature was immediate, and the *air, sweet precious life-giving air!*

Chest heaving as she hacked and spat, eyes watering so badly it was like looking through shattered glass, Bridget crawled a few feet on her hands and knees. Blisters had formed on her hand, arms and legs. Miraculously, except for scrapes and bruises, their feet had not been burned.

I'm alive! She swiped at her watering eyes.

Don fell beside her, also hacking. He was bleeding a little from where he had hit his head on the landing. His hair was singed and smoking visibly in two patches, but he appeared okay.

Bridget slowly pulled her shirt back on, smoke holes, rips and all. "Do I look…as bad as you?" She tried to smile through her coughs.

Don's teeth glowed against his blackened face. "You're beautiful."

"No, I didn't mean—"

"Oh, but that coal miner look…" he suddenly bent and hacked, the veins in his neck bulging terribly. "It's you, babe!"

Bridget laughed, reached for his shoulder. "We made it."

Don squeezed her hand. "Talk about scared shitless! Barbecue's never going to be the same for me, now."

They watched and coughed as the entire house was consumed

by the fire. Thick black smoke belched into the hazy sky.

A faint wail drifted in the distance. Just as Bridget's smoke-dulled senses figured it was coming from a siren, she noticed, for the first time, a large metal tank next to the house.

The silver paint on the surface melted and dripped before her eyes.

Bridget's jaw worked but she couldn't get the words out at first until she dug her nails into Don's shoulder. "Propane!"

Don spun. *"Shit!"*

Another rush of adrenalin. She leapt to her feet an instant before Don. Ignoring sharp rocks and tufts of dry grass that cut the soles of their feet, they ran like hell to the front of the house where Don had parked her car. It waited placidly where he'd left it, only twenty feet away the house. They'd scarcely reached its doors when behind them the house went up like balsa wood soaked in kerosene.

"Should we wait for the fire trucks?" Don choked out. "Down the road, I mean."

"No time!" Bridget said. "We have to get out of here if we're going to stop Raynorr!"

They jumped in the car, Bridget taking the driver's side. Hands blistered and hurting, she grabbed the wheel, turned the key and pumped the gas pedal with her abused bare foot. The reluctant engine sputtered to life. She jammed the vehicle into reverse and they shot out of the driveway, tires spitting gravel and dirt. Bridget found first gear and now the tires squealed in protest as they fishtailed away from Raynorr's inferno.

There was an earsplitting *BOOM* as the propane tank was fully introduced to the fire. Flaming wood and shingles shot high into the air. Thrown to the side by the force of the blast, Bridget lost control and the car ran up the far shoulder. Somehow she recovered. She stepped on it, the tires spitting gravel as the back end fish-tailed. Only when the engine screamed did she remember to shift.

"Jesus, all those huge trees around the house are on fire!" Don said, staring out the back. "Looks like the entire area was hit by Napalm."

Bridget glanced in the side view mirror. "Oh my God."

After a moment Don sat back down, coughed a few times. "Where do you think Raynorr went?"

Never taking her eyes from the road, Bridget shook her head. "He said he'd infect the drinking water of Raleigh first and use its dying population as an example. He'd have to have access to Raleigh's water supply to do that."

"Not the reservoir itself—that'd take too long to get results."

"Right. Not Falls Lake."

"The water treatment plant?"

She coughed violently for a moment, fighting to keep the car inside the lane. "Maybe. It wouldn't take as long for the virus to infect the drinking water from there, but it still wouldn't be quick enough for him. He's looking for a much faster hit."

"Where, then?"

"Why not infect the water that's already been treated and just waiting to be summoned through the pipes and into the households of thousands of unsuspecting victims?"

Don thought for a moment. "You're talking about a water tower, aren't you?"

Bridget looked at him.

Don nodded. "The one near my apartment would make an easy target."

"I'm afraid so." She swallowed and tasted smoke and fear.

From Don's apartment, the water tower had looked like a massive metal turnip sitting atop a seven-story pole. Though Bridget had gazed on it with little more than detached interest before, now it stared back at her.

She didn't want to think about how high it was up there. Didn't want to think about the fact she had seen no protective fencing at the very top, only a simple handrail—one that was completely open, completely exposed.

We have to catch Raynorr while he's still on the ground. But what about his killer dogs? And his gun?

TWENTY-SEVEN

FROM A DISTANCE, the water tower on Six Forks Road was merely impressive. Its conical base rushed upward and narrowed at the top without so much as a hint of a right angle. Atop the base was a rounded vessel so vast it could pass for a small planet. A reporter for the Raleigh Times had dubbed the water tower, "a captivating blend of high engineering and grand-scale artwork." Bridget figured the reporter must have observed the tower from a distance, because now that she was up close, there was no way the tower was a captivating blend of anything. Up close, the Six Forks Road water tower was something else entirely:

Pure *monster*.

The clusters of pine trees and the two five-story buildings located at the tower's perimeter…these were children at the monster's feet.

Don leaned forward in the passenger seat and whistled. "Big boy."

"I noticed. Do you see him anywhere?"

"Not on the stairs around the stem—maybe he hasn't gotten up here, yet. Maybe he can't get past the fence at the base."

"We're not that lucky. A fence wouldn't slow Raynorr long. Let's just hope he hasn't already made it to the top." Bridget jerked the car into the right lane to get around another motorist who, pissed-off at her poor road manners, blared his horn and offered his middle finger. She ignored the motorist and closed in on the tower.

A low rumble filled the air.

"I didn't just hear that," Bridget said.

"Yeah, I'm afraid you did," Don said. "Looks like a bad one, too."

Bridget leaned forward and glanced out Don's window. Purple clouds were plowing over the horizon.

"Not now," she said, at the same time knowing how pointless it was to complain. One of her favorite Mark Twain expressions: Everyone complains about the weather, but no one ever does anything about it." She knew the heat and humidity almost mandated afternoon or evening thunderstorms. As hot and humid

271

as the past two days had been…

Bridget eased up on the accelerator. She could see the car's blurred reflection in the glass panels of one of the business buildings near the water tower. Coming rapidly toward them was a simple gravel entrance. Bridget braked firmly but not hard enough to cause the tires to screech, turned into the gravel entrance and let the car idle.

Where is he?

She leaned forward on the steering wheel.

The gravel driveway curved and then led straight toward the tower. Several tall shrubs blocked their view of the gate. She inched the car forward. The tires crunched on the gravel. The chain-link fence around the base of the tower was maybe twelve feet high. The coils of razor wire at the top of the fence gleamed with the promise of sliced flesh. The only way in was through the gate and so far she hadn't seen any signs of Raynorr.

Maybe he didn't pick this as a target after all. Maybe I was wrong.

"There's the Olds." Don pointed at a black fender just visible behind a clump of thick rhododendrons near the fence.

"And there're the dogs," Bridget said, staring at the wolfish forms watching them from *behind* the gate.

The big German Shepherds growled for several moments then barked outright, their ears low on their skulls as if ready to attack. With each bark came flashes of white fangs.

"He knows we're here now," Bridget said.

No sooner had she finished her sentence than the windshield exploded inward. She cried out as was showered by tiny glass pebbles. Something tore through the dashboard and then into the narrow space between her and Don. She smelled the heat from the passing bullet and heard the gun's report.

"He's shooting!" Don cried.

"Hang on!" Bridget pinned the gas pedal to the floor.

The engine screamed and the wheels spun, kicking gravel up into the air. The car was slow, unbelievably slow compared to the bullet. Bridget tensed, sure they'd get shot. But in another second they were racing toward the gate and the barking dogs.

A hole appeared in the hood, buckling the metal. Steam hissed from the wound in a white column just as the front bumper slammed into the center of the chain-link gate.

The enraged dogs didn't move until the car was almost on top of them. One of the beasts narrowly escaped by leaping out of the way at the last possible moment.

Metal poles tore. Chain mesh bent and snapped and burst apart, springing in all directions like dried spaghetti noodles.

A sharp yelp came from beneath the car. Apparently, one of the dogs hadn't moved fast enough.

A ruptured pole shattered Bridget's window. The cubed pieces sprayed her upper body and fell into her lap.

Then the engine died, and the car rolled to a stop beneath the massive water tower.

No sooner had Bridget started to breathe again when a dark snarling blur appeared at her shoulder. The dog's ears were pressed low to its head. Its white fangs streaked for her throat.

She couldn't move.

The seatbelt, meant to preserve her life in an accident, now trapped her in the seat as the raging brute's head came through the window opening.

Bridget strained against the strap, trying to lean away from the enraged dog. She held her forearm up in what she knew was woefully inadequate protection. The dog clamped down on her forearm and immediately she felt the crush as its fangs sank into her skin and drew blood.

She screamed, tried to pull away but the dog was too strong. Again and again she struck it in the snout but the animal took the blows as if they came from a child. The dog stared at her, its brown eyes full of the promise of death. It jerked on her arm and growled, working her throat closer to the window.

Don shouted at the raging animal. His fist careened into its snout twice, to no effect. Bridget felt her seatbelt give—he must have pushed the release button. He tried to pull her away from the dog and now she was caught in a tug-of-war between man and beast.

She was sure if she didn't do something her bone was going to snap.

Don disappeared from her side. "Bastard mutt!"

The growls and snarls from the dog were horrible. Bridget struck at the dog's snout but she had become so weak so fast the blows had no impact. White dots drifted around her like pixie fairies.

Don reappeared—this time *outside* the car.

Bridget could only watch as he ran around the front of the car toward the dog. "No! Don...no!"

But he ignored her. He kicked at the dog's exposed flank, cracking its ribs audibly. Still the dog didn't release her, despite the first signs of pain that entered its eyes. Then Don's arms encircled its muscular throat. His head appeared above the beast's, his lips pulled back to reveal human fangs.

Don heaved backward.

Still the dog would not release her arm. Bridget slammed into the door.

A gunshot cut through the growls and cries. Don spun off the dog's back, his arms pin-wheeling.

"Don!" Bridget screamed.

She watched helplessly as he went down, his shoulder a mass of brilliant red. "DON!"

He didn't answer.

The dog, as if feeling the weight of the man lifted from it, growled and jerked at Bridget's arm with renewed vigor.

This is it, Bridget thought, *fight or die!*

Frantically her free hand groped for something—*anything*—that might hurt the dog. On the floor in the back her fingers contacted her lab coat. She felt her pockets. Maybe there was a pen or pencil or—

Her fingers brushed something hard, a familiar shape. Her hand closed around the syringe. She pulled it from the pocket, prying away the protective cap over the needle.

The dog let out another fierce growl and, with another massive tug, yanked her completely upright. This time Bridget went with it.

And buried the needle in the dog's left eye.

"LET GO, GODDAMN IT!"

The dog did let go, but before it did she jammed the plunger down, injecting 20 cc's of air directly into the animal's brain.

The dog let out a terrible cry and sank from the door. She watched as it tried to walk away in trembling, hesitating steps. Suddenly it halted, as if confused. It didn't try to paw at the needle protruding from its eye. Its entire body shuddered in a way that, despite what it would have done to her, almost made her feel sorry for it.

Almost.

The dog dropped to the ground and convulsed wildly, paws and skin twitching and jerking. Its long tongue protruded through its fangs. The syringe quivered in its ruined eye.

Pain was everywhere at once inside Bridget. She stiffened and clenched her teeth.

Her left arm was in agony from the elbow down. She used her right hand to unlatch the door and then kicked it open. She crawled on her knees and good hand while cradling her injured arm until she reached Don, who was lying on the ground a few feet from the rear of the car.

"Don—oh, God!"

He was on his back, his eyes open and staring up at the tower that loomed over them. His shoulder was a raw, bloody mess and there was a livid cut on his neck. At any moment, Bridget expected another shot to bring her down. But either they were protected from Raynorr's gun by the car or Raynorr had moved on to bigger and better things.

Don turned and smiled as she crawled toward him. "Good

going, Dev."

"You're alive!" She moved to inspect his shoulder.

"Hell yeah, I am. This ain't bad." His voice was little more than a whisper.

Blood ran slick on his bare chest and side, and the crabgrass beneath him was stained as if someone had kicked over a can of red paint.

"Jesus, Don."

"Not really attractive, huh? We're still going to go out...after this, aren't we, Dev?"

Still? Bridget thought.

"Of course, we are," she said.

"I'll get myself all cleaned up first, naturally."

No sooner did he say it than his face screwed into a mask of pain.

He must have registered the horrified look in her eyes because with a show of incredible willpower he forced his face to relax, though the muscles around his eyes were still contracted. "Hey, I knew that dog didn't...have a chance against you, Dev."

She couldn't catch her breath. Whether it was from the danger they'd narrowly escaped or the shock her body threatened to succumb to, she couldn't tell. "That's why you tried to pull the mutt off me, huh? Because you were sure I could beat it? That was a stupid move, Don Mayhew, but thanks."

"Ha! I would have spanked that puppy if Raynorr hadn't gotten a lucky shot in!" He shook his fist at the monolith that was the water tower. "Lucky shot, bastard!"

She pushed his arm down. "I think you're a little lightheaded."

"Well that's a helluva thing to say to a man. I swear I don't have a little head. At least, nobody ever *said* I did. You don't think...you don't think my old girlfriends were just bein' polite, do you, Dev? I mean, it ain't like, *huge* or anything, but I always thought it was *respectable.*"

"Shhhh."

"Hardly reassuring, babe. So, what's my diagnosis, Doctor?"

"The bullet nicked the back of your neck and passed right through the thickest part of your rear deltoid. Luckily it missed both bone and artery, but you're losing a lot of blood."

Way too much, Bridget thought.

Her left arm useless, Bridget hooked her right hand in the armpit of Don's good arm and tried to pull him upright. She couldn't budge him.

She took her shirt off, gasping as she passed her injured arm through the sleeve.

"You have to sit up, Don."

"What's on your mind, Dev?" he said, looking up at her and grinning. "As much as I like the idea, I'm not sure this is the right time for us to be getting naked an' all—though I have to say, you do look stunning in that bra."

"Okay, big boy! You need to sit up now. Your heart has to be lower than your shoulder...it'll slow the blood loss."

"I'm already bleeding less. Since you took that shirt off, I got blood pumping to another part of my body."

"Well, you're a man, all right," Bridget said, playing along. She knew how bad it was for him, knew he was keeping his spirits up, and hers at the same time.

"Let me tell you somethin', Dev-o-mine. You are in the midst of one hun'red per*cent* pure *man*!" Don laughed, a high-pitched giggle.

"Let's go, Mister One Hundred Percent."

Don nodded emphatically. "Put my ass in a solution, and I'd be the one hun'red percent solution!"

And despite it all, a laugh escaped Bridget. It took some of the tension off. Not a lot, but enough to breathe and not go into shock with her own arm hurting the way it was. Bridget helped him sit up, then he pushed with his legs as she half-dragged him to the driver's side rear tire. She folded her shirt into a square, pressed it to his bleeding shoulder and had him lean against the tire to gain some amount of pressure.

"I have to go up the tower, Don," Bridget said, as they both fought to control their breathing. "I have to try and stop Raynorr."

"Wait—hear those sirens? Someone heard the gunshots. The police're comin'. Fire trucks, ambulances too, maybe. They'll be here in another minute or two." He squinted at her, and his face became serious. "Uh, I hate to break this to you, Dev, but I'm having a hard time seeing you as Raleigh's alternative to Rambo right now. For one thing, that arm of yours has got to be in a substantial amount of agony. Am I right?"

"It's okay."

"Can't move it, can you?"

"I have to try and stop Raynorr."

"Let the cops take care of that bastard!"

"They won't get here in time to stop him," she said. "You know I'm right. Thousands of lives are a sip away from death if he infects the water with his virus."

Don sighed. "Raynorr had a point, you know."

"What do you mean?"

"Health care today does suck. I can't get a doctor to wait on me even when the alternative is a lunatic on a water tower with a gun in one hand and a lethal virus in the other."

Bridget smiled despite the pain that leaped from her arm and slammed into her head like a spiked glove. At least she'd avoided going into shock—so far.

Don's words came weaker this time. "You get to have all the fun." He couldn't quite manage the grin this time.

Bridget's heart sank. Don was turning so pale.

"I'll be back," she said, rising unsteadily to her feet. She smoothed the creases in Don's forehead as best she could with her trembling hand. "They'll bandage you up in the ambulance and take you to Wake Med for the real stuff. It's an excellent hospital."

"Maybe so, but I ain't leaving without you." He seemed to have a sudden surge of strength.

"We'll share a room at the hospital."

"I'm not going without you."

"God, you're stubborn."

"Look who's talking."

She opened her mouth to retort but nothing came out.

"Watch yourself, Devereaux," he said. "I'll be here when you get back...leave the light on for ya."

Bridget didn't know what to say. She barely knew Don Mayhew and yet she'd almost died with him, twice. She bent and kissed his lips, turned and ran as best she could for the stairs leading up the massive water tower, expecting Raynorr's gun to end it for her any second.

But the shot never came.

That was good *and* bad.

Either he's out of bullets, Bridget thought, *or he's busy.*

She pictured him up there, dumping his virus—a virus that he had said was immune to the viral-killing properties of chlorine—into Raleigh's largest single reserve of drinking water.

Bridget ignored her pain and sprinted.

The world darkened as she reached the gate to the caged stairs. Deep rumbling churned overhead, now, punctuated by flashes of bright white light. The thunder was getting stronger, as if warning her to stay low to the ground. But that wasn't an option. The narrow gate, more like iron rods welded together in a rough frame and put on hinges, was open. It had been locked but one of Raynorr's bullets had persuaded it to release. The metal shards were jagged and hanging from the exit hole in the lock.

Ignoring the agony in her painfully throbbing forearm, raw knees and the jelly she had for muscles, Bridget forced herself to sprint up the caged stairs. As she got above the tree line her fear of heights grabbed her stomach and squeezed. She was grateful the stairs were caged in, but as she traveled around the stem of the water tower once more she found herself already some sixty feet up, and the thin metal rails to the sides and overhead did not appear anywhere near as trustworthy as they had when she'd been on the ground.

It wouldn't take much to slip through these rods, Bridget thought *Wouldn't take much to see the ground rushing up at my face.*

Look at the stairs then, she told herself.

But the stairs were mesh and had way too many air gaps in them. Drainage was one thing, proper support was another. What if the metal was rusted through? The stair might break and she'd tumble to her death!

Screw that! There's no time. Concentrate on what you're doing woman, and get your ass up the stairs!

Around and up the huge stem of the tower she went, working her legs and climbing and gasping for more and more air. She crashed through the pain in her knees and her torn and bleeding arm, crashed through the limits of her known endurance, crashed through because she had no other choice. Time and time again she bumped the inner rail with her injured arm and each time she cried out as new waves of pain slammed into her. The white dots circled her head almost continuously. But now the pain—

Kept her going.

Kept her *focused*.

Bridget poured her entire will into running *up*. All the time *up*.

Then she could climb no longer. The stairs were gone. She had reached the top.

The surface of the water tower extended into the sky around her. The upgrade at the middle allowed rain, ice, and snow to slide off the smooth sides instead of laying flat and adding tons of weight to the structure. From a distance the vessel had a pleasant rounded appearance. Now she found the entire structure decidedly unnerving.

The dark storm clouds raced through the surrounding skies She crouched against the winds that gusted and whipped at her Her hair flung against her cheeks like tiny pinpricks. Then the hair on her neck and arms stood at attention. Lightning suddenly flashed, the veins of brilliant silver so close overhead she felt she could almost reach out and touch them. The resulting thunder jarred her, reverberating in her chest as though she were hollow.

Surely she had climbed to the surface of some alien, storm torn world.

Where are you, Raynorr? she asked herself, peeling her hair from her face with her good hand.

There was a single metal rail, waist high, leading out and up to the center of the containment vessel. She squinted, following the rail with her eyes.

At the center of the water tower Raynorr stood like a gangl

scarecrow. His tee-shirt and shorts rippled in the wind as he grasped the rail with one hand and used the other, his arm fully extended, to aim his gun down at the tower surface. He fired once and Bridget barely heard it through the storm's fury. There was a brief shower of sparks, then Raynorr knelt, grabbed at something, and threw the object he'd fired at to the side. With a muffled clang it hit the tower and slid down the sloping surface toward Bridget.

Metal shards protruded from the ruined center of the lock.

Raynorr hurled open a trap door and reached for the large antifreeze container beside him. At that moment lightning streaked overhead and caught him in a flash of blinding white light.

There's no cover here. No place to hide from a bullet.

Without a plan of attack, without knowing what else to do, Bridget grabbed the metal handrail and used it to catapult herself forward. Her feet seemed to barely touch the steel of the tower. Right now, a cheetah couldn't have sprinted any faster.

"NO!"

But her voice was drowned in a barrage of thunder.

He knelt and raised the large container, his fingers closing around the white cap. Perhaps he sensed her presence despite the buffeting winds, or perhaps he felt vibrations in the steel surface. Whatever the reason, he turned in her direction as she ran headlong toward him.

His eyes widened and he raised the gun, a big revolver. As the hammer of the gun cocked back she launched herself into the air, diving at him with her head and her good shoulder lowered.

Bridget felt the top of her head crunch into his face and then their bodies collided. He groaned and was hurled backward. The container with the lethal virus fell from his grip.

Bridget twisted so her good arm hit, but the impact still sent a shock wave from her injured arm. She gasped as her brain seized up, pain receptors overloaded.

What's he doing, what's he doing...?

She blinked, forced herself to stay alert. There was the downward-sloping surface and the churning purple clouds of the storm that seemed to swirl and dive around her. Lightning streaked in every direction, illuminating the skies like a massive strobe light. Every move she made was captured in glaring frame-by-frame. Thunder exploded continuously now, jarring her very soul.

And there was Raynorr, crawling on his hands and knees like a zombie clawing from its grave, dragging the container holding the virus along with him as he moved toward the fallen gun. His gaze was fixed on her. His nose oozed thick, red blood. It flowed over his lips and chin and strands of it were pulled from the edge of his jaw by the winds and sent flying some distance away like string kites.

Bridget rose to her knees just as Raynorr grabbed the gun and gained his feet. He spread his legs wide to brace himself against the wind that howled down at them. He was no more than a dozen feet away.

"You are *tenacious*, Doctor Devereaux!" Raynorr shouted, wiping his blood-covered mouth with the back of the hand that held the revolver. "I thought the fire and then the dog would finish you, and yet here you are."

"The police are here, Raynorr. It's over."

Grasping the rail, she pulled herself up, preferring to die on her feet. A barrage of raindrops pelted her and she winced. The rain also hit the steel tower surface around them in large, exploding drops, then in sheets. It was cold and it stung, but at the same time it felt good, maybe because she knew it would be one of the last sensations she felt before dying.

Raynorr grinned with blood-covered teeth. "Over? No, Doctor Devereaux, this is far from over." He raised the gun and pointed it at her chest. "Pity you survived this long only to die up here. But as a reward for your perseverance, I'll allow you to witness the onset of a hundred thousand deaths."

"But you're a doctor, a *healer*."

"I am the catalyst for change! You've seen how they deny proper care for your own patients. We have robber barons dictating health care. How logical is that?"

"You can't murder people because the system is flawed."

Raynorr spat a mouthful of blood at the glistening surface of the tower. "*This* is the only way they'll listen! They understand two things: money and death. And since I'm not a billionaire, I offer the alternative."

Bridget let go of the rail with her good hand and dropped it to her hip. Her palm glided over her pocket, felt the lumps there—

Lumps?

The rocks!

The gravel rocks she had stuffed into her pocket at Raynorr's house in case the dogs attacked. Paltry defense against dogs, but against a man...

She turned her side from him and slipped her hand into her pocket.

A gust of wind moved her like a possessed statue a few feet down the slick metal surface of the water tower. A few feet closer to Raynorr.

He trained the gun at the middle of her chest.

"Think of your daughters!" she cried, trying to stall him. "Do you want them to spend the rest of their lives knowing their father was a mass murderer—a monster no better than Hitler?"

"My daughters care nothing for me. Their mother poisoned their minds long ago."

"You're still their father."

Raynorr scowled. "They're strangers to me. *Strangers!*"

Through the wild brilliance of the flashing lightning he stared at her. She didn't know which was more intense, the lightning or his eyes. Ice seemed to cling to every single vertebra of her back.

"But you...you are different," Raynorr said. The scowl vanished as if washed away by the driving rain that fell between them. His eyes became less focused. The gun barrel drifted downward. "You should have been my daughter, Bridget. Not only beautiful, you are intelligent and kind and brave enough to challenge a corrupt establishment."

"Andrew..." She inched toward him.

I have to get closer, she thought. *Have to make sure the rocks do more than glance harmlessly off him.*

Fighting the wind, she took a step down the slick surface and pulled her hand from her pocket. "Father."

He caught the movement. Fire leaped into his eyes.

"*Liar!*"

Buffeted by the storm winds, he again raised the gun and aimed the barrel at the center of her chest.

TWENTY-EIGHT

B RIDGET WAS CLOSE enough to see Raynorr's thumb pull back the hammer. Tears, or was it just rain, ran down his cheeks. The insanity in his eyes told her she was going to die if she didn't—

She whipped her arm up and over. As the rocks flew from her hand she threw herself down and to the side.

The sharp report from Raynorr's gun cut through the shrieking wind and driving rain. Bridget felt the heat of the bullet slice the air an inch from her cheek. She hit the tower surface on her mangled arm and cried out but watched as the rocks struck Raynorr full in the face.

He fell backward, the gun going off once more, this time into the purple storm clouds that swirled and dove around them.

Above the shrieking winds she heard him scream, "*NO!*"

The gun was gone when he reappeared.

Then the winds had her. She slid down...down toward the smooth edge of the tower. Splintering her already short nails, she clawed with both hands at the slick surface despite the agony it brought from her injured arm.

The slick steel ignored her efforts.

The edge grinned.

Better to have taken the bullet, Bridget decided, than fall from this thing.

Twenty feet before the final rounded lip of the tower she succeeded in driving three fragmented, blood-covered fingernails into a tiny gap where the metal sheets were joined together.

Over the toes of her bare feet she stared down at the edge, noting in horror how the metal just *disappeared*, and how the bruised clouds took up the space beyond that. She forced her eyes away from the view.

What's this sliding down, now? Raynorr's container with the virus inside. Where is he? Did he go over the—no! I'm not that lucky.

Some twenty feet above her, Raynorr had one claw of a hand gripping the water tower. He sat up, his face bloodied all over again. Jagged slices and gaps were there. He yelled incoherently, swiped the blood from his eyes with his free hand, and spotted the sliding container.

It isn't moving fast enough. The wind has changed direction. It had no problem whisking me down the slope but when it comes to that jug, it's pushing it in the other direction!

Raynorr stretched out on the tower and groped for the container. He missed by only inches. Evidently the blood coming from the cuts above his eyes was flowing fast enough to at least partially blind him. He swiped again at his eyes.

Bridget kicked, made it to her knees before crashing to the tower once more. Her adrenalin was gone. She had no more strength. She slid down a few inches before catching another crack and stopping.

"Oh, Jesus."

Chunks of hail stung like attacking hornets. The clamor the hail made as it struck the surface of the water tower told her this was just the beginning—hang on a minute and there'll be a real pounding on the way.

Can't stay here!

With little left inside but desperation, Bridget fought against the water tower. It wanted to see her plummet over the side, wanted to see her twist and turn like a rag doll as she fell.

"Not if I can help it," she muttered to it.

She gained a few inches and then, miraculously, a few feet. She used the hand of her injured arm to hold her in position as she extended for another reach. The incredible agony may have actually helped her. She crawled toward the container that was spilling its contents even as it slid to a halt mere inches from her groping hand.

"Go, go, go!" she screamed, clawing for it.

I might take the plunge off this tin turnip, but I'm not going without taking this pukey orange anti-freeze container!

Raynorr evidently heard her scream. His shout of rage filled her ears and then she heard another sound.

Ching, ching!

Metal on metal.

Ching, ching, ching!

She grabbed the container by the handle. "Got you!" she cried. She kicked and tried to force the fingers of her damaged arm into the unforgiving steel. Her nails found another minute crack and she held on, scarcely daring to breathe.

She looked up. "Oh God."

Raynorr was half-crawling, half-sliding through the rain and hail *toward her.* Blood ran in streaks down his face. He stabbed at the water tower with a long knife as he approached—Blackbeard charging down the timbers at some double-crossing knave.

"Give it to me!" he shouted.

She shook her head. "No!"

"Give it or I'll cut your goddamn throat!"

"Like Madeline? You come and get it!" She held the container up for the wind to jerk around.

He came at her faster than she expected, all caution abandoned. Just above her now, he gained his knees and held the knife high overhead. Lightning streaked behind him, illuminating his bloodied and crazed countenance in a wash of blinding white.

Hail careened into them like icy meteors.

In a last-ditch effort, Bridget rolled onto her back, spinning on the slick surface even as she started to slide once again. She used her momentum and kicked. Roundhouse.

Bridget's shin crashed into Raynorr's ribs. He toppled, but at the same time lunged with the knife. She jerked her head away felt the tug of the knife in her hair. Then the knife missed and bit into the tower, into a hairline crack between two steel plates Raynorr's eyes grew even wider as fear mixed with his rage. He shrieked and worked to get the knife free but now gravity had him in its clutches, twisting him at an odd angle. Raynorr cried out, flailing his arms and empty hands. He'd lost his grip on the knife. He was sliding down the tower now, fingertips scraping at the water and steel, unable to gain purchase.

"Nooooo!" he shrieked, sliding faster away.

Bridget rolled onto her stomach and slid face-first toward him.

A crack was coming.

Now!

She dug into the shallow seam with her splintered fingernails She stopped sliding and watched Raynorr claw at the water tower Suddenly he halted, just as the lower half of his body disappeared over the edge.

Sheets of water leaped from the edge everywhere around him It also ploughed into him, splattering his bleeding, twisted face An armada of white hail nuggets sailed over the edge.

The world's largest man-made waterfall, Bridget thought, inanely

Something nudged her. The bright orange anti-freeze jug had come to a precarious halt against her side.

Bridget groaned and tried to hold on, three hundred feet above the ground. Her head pointed down the slope, toward the rounded edge of the water tower. The rain and hail whipped the bare flesh of her back. Through the barrage of flashing lightning she stared down at Raynorr, who hung at the edge with a single hand.

"Help me!" Raynorr cried, the whites of his eyes glowing against the swirling grayness. "Help me, *daughter!*"

Images of the victims he'd murdered with the virus flashed in Bridget's mind, along with those of Josephine, who was probably dead by now, and Madeline, who was very dead and lying in the woods like some fallen wild animal.

"Yeah, I'll help you."

She bumped the jug away with her hip. The jug parted hail nuggets like a misshapen orange torpedo.

"No!" Raynorr cried.

The container struck him full in the face. His arms flew upward and for a moment he seemed to hover at the edge. Then suddenly he disappeared, his scream drowned by the wind and hail and rolling thunder.

"See ya, Pops," Bridget said.

No sooner had Raynorr vanished than Bridget's own slide started once again. The same forces that had worked against Raynorr held no favors for her.

The edge winked at her.

I'm not going to make it, she thought, oddly calm. *At least it will end all this pain and exhaustion. Sis'll be upset, but maybe I'll see Mom again.*

Her teeth chattered.

So cold. So very cold.

Her fingernails could slow the inevitable no longer. She felt the hard cold surface passing beneath her.

I'll just close my eyes. Close my eyes and it will be over soon enough.

But when she closed her eyes, a single image hovered before her: Raynorr's knife.

Her nails had found the crack again. Agony with the one hand because of fresh new pressure, but her slide slowed…

And halted.

Slowly, she looked over her shoulder. There was the knife, close enough to kick. The lightning flashed blue-white over everything, making the knife seem huge for a split second. She waited for it to fall and get swept down and over the side but it remained, straight and true while the water flowed around it.

Her fingers bled into the water that ran off the tower. They were barely snagged in the crack, at about Bridget's waist level. If she pulled, no, heaved herself backward and upward, she might just be able to hook her leg over the—

And then what?

NOW!

Bridget screamed in equal parts pain and terror. She heaved and twisted, fully expecting to follow Raynorr's lead over the side, but some inner chord deep within her snapped tight and refused to loosen, refused to let her surrender. She caught the knife behind her left knee and clamped tightly over it. The knife wriggled but did not come free. She had pictured herself pulling the knife out with her leg and bringing it to her hand via leg motion, but now her nails failed and she lost her base. With a cry she did a sideways sit-up, leveraging knife and knee. Simultaneously, she dug the nails of her bad hand into the same crack as the knife and clamped the fingers of her good hand around the knife's handle. She gasped, unable to believe she was still at this...but the trick wasn't over yet.

At least she was facing the right direction. If she didn't make it, she could at least stare up at the storm as she went over.

To use the knife she'd have to pull it out, move her leg, stab the blade back into the crack and twist it just enough to hold.

Before she fell.

The hand without the knife, the one attached to her damaged arm, with fingernails barely hooked into the crack, shook violently and shrieked for her to stop. The arm was badly mangled but the ligaments would have to pick up the slack. Her whole body shook, but it was this hand that worried her most.

Quit thinking and go, girl! Pull and go...now!

Expelling a primordial scream she forced her body to move.

Bridget kicked like she was doing *The Running Man* on the dance floor. It didn't move her upward on the tower, but the friction kept her weak hand from failing completely, and that was friction she had to have.

Bridget gasped again, sucked in water, and vowed not to scream again and waste her energy, though she couldn't get any more terrified than she was right now. Squinting against the rain and hail, she wouldn't let her gaze follow the cracks more than a foot or two at a time. The knife, what was left of her nails, her arm, and her kicking feet all went to work, pulling overtime—because it could very well be the last few moments they'd ever move... ever.

The blade found enough purchase for her to pull up and dig her nails in, half an arm's length higher, and then she held on just long enough to pull the knife and stab at the crack ahead of her other hand.

The slope eased a bit, and then a bit more.

The rail! There. It had a post! Bridget lunged for the post, located at the highest point of the tower. She wrapped both arms and legs around it and clung like a barnacle against a hurricane. Her limbs almost completely numb, she pulled herself around until she sat above the post, then pressed herself into it and let gravity help her for a change, pinning her there.

Crying, she shook uncontrollably. She'd made the rail! *ThankGod! ThankGod! Thank God!*

She was too tired to go on. After a little rest, she might try to move, but not right away. It was too nice here, hugging this cold metal post.

Bridget put her head down and closed her eyes.

Something shook her. Wind. Getting stronger. Teeth chattering, Bridget clung tighter to the post. The shaking again and now the wind sounded like a voice trying to cut through the wind. Bridget swiped at her eyes and blinked. A cop was in her face. She could tell from the plastic wrap thingy around his hat. A cop with a hat rubber!

Bridget giggled.

"Let's get out of here, Bridget."

The wind and hail all but drowned his voice.

He pulled her bodily up to him, as if she weighed nothing. The cop was short, shorter than herself, but he may as well have been a giant. His strong arm encircled her waist like an iron band.

"Put your arms around my neck," he shouted, as he reached around her, tightening something. "We won't fall, we're both tied to the rail now."

"Where did…you come from?"

"Hold on to my neck!"

"Can't. My left arm…"

He shifted her to his left side. She hooked her right arm over his neck and held on as best she could but couldn't feel her arm enough to know if she was much help.

"Can you walk?" the cop asked.

"I don't think I have anything left. I'm sorry."

"Don't be! I'm sorry we didn't get here sooner to help out. Hold on, now!"

He gripped her even tighter, so tight she almost had to tell him to back off a little so she could breathe.

"My friend down at the car…?" She spoke in the policeman's ear, watching as hail bounced off his hat.

Almost crushing Bridget to his chest, the cop gripped the rail with his free hand and went sideways, step-by-step, down Tower Planet. A brilliant yellow rope made a tight line to the rail, and he pushed the knot ahead of his sliding hand with each step.

"Don's okay! He told us and the CDC agents everything."

"He was hemorrhaging so much—did they take him away?"

"The paramedics are with him. He's in the ambulance but he refused to go to the hospital. Said he was gonna kick ass if they tried to take him away without you, and even with that shoulder he looked like he meant it."

Other cops appeared, braced against the wind and rain at the end of the caged stairs. They wrapped her in a blanket, covering her semi-nude condition. God, she'd never felt anything so warm.

"Cut the rope!" Bridget's cop told them, then he practically ran down the stairs with her.

"Are you a mountain climber?" she asked, weakly.

The cop shook his head. "No way—heights scare the shit out me!"

"But you would have come out to the edge get me."

"Yeah, but you made it back by yourself. If I had to go out, I was hoping all the rain and hail would make it hard to see down. You're one tough lady, taking the bad guy out and dealing with this tower."

"I'm not tough. Raynorr had to be stopped and I was closest."

"Lots of people wouldn't have done it, believe me."

"What's your name?"

"Terry Blevans."

At the base of the tower, blue and white and red lights flashed over trees and grass and a crowd of cars. There were television crews with bright white lights and men and women with microphones. The lights suddenly flooded over the two of them. The reporters yelled questions but other cops kept them at bay.

Officer Blevans handed Bridget to the paramedics beside an ambulance.

She laid a hand on the cop's shoulder. "Thanks."

"Hey, the thanks goes to you. You saved me and my family and a whole bunch of other folks. I'll need a statement from you after you've rested up." He smiled. "I'll be in touch."

Then he turned and walked to his squad car. As he did the reporters circled around and threw a barrage of questions at him.

"My superiors will issue a statement after all the facts are clear," was all he said to them. Two men in long coats appeared from the sidelines, walked up and took positions on either side of him.

Inside the ambulance, Don was lying on a gurney with his upper body propped up on several pillows. Blankets covered everything but his head and bandaged shoulder. Blood had soaked the bandage dark red.

"Hey you," Bridget said, as she was guided to a gurney next to him by the paramedics.

"Hey yourself," Don said, smiling.

"Nice shoulder."

"You were right—bullet went clean through. These nice paramedics gave me a shot to slow the bleeding and one for the pain. I haven't felt this good in a long time." He raised his head feebly. "Glad you're back."

"Me, too."

"Your arm?"

"Maybe broken, but I'll take that over a high-dive from that tower any day."

He smiled. "I knew you'd beat Raynorr."

She arched an eyebrow. "Liar."

"I'm not lying."

"You'd better come clean, Don Mayhew."

With a paramedic already putting an air cast on her arm, she gently pushed Don back so he could rest his head on the pillow. She looked fretfully at his shoulder. The bandage was soaked with blood, but the paramedics had done a good job; the flow had slowed and he was hooked to an IV with fresh blood coming in.

"I did," Don said. "I knew you'd beat him and I knew you'd come back."

"Well, that makes one of us." She wiped her eyes. "You damn hard-head, you should have gone to the hospital."

Don's smile grew into that lopsided grin. How a guy could look charming at a time like this she had no idea. He held out his hand.

She couldn't stop the tears now.

Didn't bother trying.

It was over. It was all over.

Raynorr was dead. He wouldn't hurt anyone again, ever.

"Told you I'd wait, Dev," Don said.

Bridget couldn't say anything. She could only hold Don's hand.

EPILOGUE

NURSE WATKINS LEANED against the wall, her posture perhaps a few degrees less rigid than the steel in *Jo's* bed frame. Bridget had never seen the woman so relaxed.

"I pushed and pestered and used every trick in the book to keep them from deviating from your treatment plan," Barbara said. "This little girl's remission is due to your care, Bridget—not theirs."

Jo, sitting cross-legged on her hospital bed, took first a blue marker and then a yellow one and continued with her artwork on Bridget's forearm cast.

She's so alert, Bridget thought, shifting her weight slightly on the bed next to Jo. *So alive*.

"Jo, here, did all the heavy lifting," Bridget said. She looked up. "But I'm glad you stuck with me, Barbara."

"Well, I almost walked out when that blankety-blank Handlaw bounced you from the program."

"Good thing you didn't. Who knows what would have happened to Jo if you'd left."

Jo tilted her head, pursed her lips, and worked the yellow marker back and forth on Bridget's cast.

Bridget smiled. This is why she had risked everything to stop Andrew Raynorr. "It's great to have you back, Jo."

"It's great to be back," Jo said, without looking up from her work. "I almost feel like I was before. Not totally, but almost."

Bridget glanced at the folks sitting in the chairs near the window. Mrs. Woods dabbed at the corners of her eyes with a handkerchief while Mr. Woods squeezed her shoulder. The only person to survive the Raynorr Virus tapped Bridget's cast with her marker. Bridget turned.

"Did it hurt really bad when that dog bit you?" Jo asked.

"Yeah, but I'll bet nowhere near as bad as the chemo you went through."

"I don't know. The chemo was bad, but I think havin' your arm chewed on by a dog is bad, too. Probably both of them were bad just in different ways."

Jo put the finishing touches on her artwork and then scribbled her name beside it in bold letters. The large flower with orange petals and a beaming lemon-yellow center was the finest Bridget had ever seen.

"There you go!" Jo said, then reached up and gave Bridget a hug, which Bridget returned with her good arm. "Can you visit me at home sometime? Maybe watch me swim? I was county champ last year, you know."

Bridget smiled. "I know! Sure, I'd love to visit, as long as it's okay with your folks."

"Of course, it is," Mr. Woods said immediately.

"And bring Don, too!" Jo said, pointing at Don who sat in a stiff-backed chair in the rear corner of her room. His arm was in a sling but not in a cast.

"Thanks, kid," Don said, pointing back at her.

Jo leaned forward. "He's hot, you know."

Don laughed.

Bridget took a sidelong glance at the man who had been a stranger to her only ten days ago but now was so much more. "He *is* good-looking, isn't he?"

"Good-looking?" Jo said at full volume, her eyes wide and incredulous. *"He's a hunk!"*

Bridget felt her face flush as laughter filled the room. "Are you really just ten years old?" she asked.

Jo giggled. "And do you know what else?"

"I'm afraid to ask."

"He's nice. I can tell."

"You're going to go places, kid," Don said.

Jo raised her chin in an exaggerated, superior manner and nodded regally. "Yes, yes. Thank you, thank you."

"Lady Josephine," Bridget said, shaking her head in a show of disbelief. "Do you tell fortunes, too?"

"No, but I bet you and Don are going to get—"

"Uh, that's enough, Jo," Mrs. Woods warned, cutting her off just in time.

There was a knock on the door.

"Come on in!" Jo called.

A middle-aged man in a charcoal blazer and white slacks walked smoothly into the hospital room. His shock of gray hair was offset by warm blue eyes that made Bridget think of the waters of the Caribbean she'd seen in magazine pictures.

"Excuse me for interrupting…" the man said.

"Who are you?" Jo asked bluntly, the way gregarious kids are wont to do.

Nurse Watkins gestured. "Everyone, this is Doctor Avery Sheldon."

"Thanks, Barbara. Hello, everybody." He shook hands with

everyone. When he shook with Jo, he said, "I'm very glad to see you're doing well, young lady. You've been through quite an ordeal."

"Thank you, sir."

He smiled broadly and turned to Bridget. "So, you're the Doctor Devereaux I've heard so much about."

"*Was* Doctor Devereaux," Bridget said. "I've been—"

"Handlaw's a boor with dollar signs dancing in his eyes."

"Well, I'm glad word is getting out."

"It's getting out, all right. They've already removed him as CEO thanks to the formal complaints and the article in the News and Observer."

"I haven't seen any article," Bridget said.

"That's because it's coming out in tomorrow's edition. Actually, there are two front-page articles—the one I just mentioned and another that chronicles the struggles you and Mr. Mayhew, here, undertook to stop Andrew."

"You sound as though you knew him," Bridget said.

"We went to medical school together at the University of North Carolina. We practiced medicine as friends and colleagues for many years in the Triangle. I tried to help him after he lost his practice but he wouldn't allow it—the shame was too great, I suppose. He didn't stay in touch after he went to Africa. I didn't know he'd returned—or that he was even alive—until he called my office at Duke Hospital a week ago. I didn't recognize his voice at first. It was him, but there was an underlying current of tension in his voice that hadn't been there before. I had a thousand questions for him but all he would say was that I needed to seek out a young intern at Chambers Hospital named Bridget Devereaux. Intrigued, I began making inquiries. Then the news hit with the incredible events surrounding you."

"Wait a minute—you're *the* Doctor Sheldon?" Bridget said. "Head of Oncology Research at Duke Hospital?"

"That's me. And though they're going to reinstate you into the program here at Chambers Hospital, I'd like to counter their offer."

"Counter?" Bridget asked.

"That's right. I'd like you to complete your residency at Duke Hospital, after which I'd like you to consider joining my staff. Any intern who can treat patients, perform research, *and* confront a deranged but brilliant man armed with a deadly virus would be a great asset at Duke. Duke will waive all future expenses, pay off your current loans, and provide a salary as you complete your residency. We can negotiate again after that. What do you think?"

Bridget swallowed. Duke was *the* premier hospital in the southeast, ranked on the same level as Johns Hopkins and any of the other big names. She looked around the room at the expectant expressions and eventually settled on Nurse Watkins' smiling face.

"Can I bring Barbara?"

Barbara Watkins smile broadened.

Doctor Sheldon said, "She's already on board. I thought it might help persuade you."

Bridget squinted at the nurse. "You didn't say anything about this."

"I wanted it to be a surprise," she said, trying to look innocent. "Gave my two-weeks notice yesterday."

Bridget looked down at the flower *Jo* had drawn so beautifully on her cast. "I—I don't know what to say."

"Say 'yes,'" Doctor Sheldon urged.

Bridget tried to think, tried to scrutinize exactly what was being offered here, but no thoughts came to the fore. For once she didn't feel inadequate. For once there were no contending voices, no contending thoughts—positive, negative, or otherwise. Instead, there came only the sudden image of Christine, the love of a proud mother shining in her eyes.

"I'll do it."

Cheers and clapping broke out in the room.

Doctor Sheldon handed Bridget his business card. "Take four weeks to rest and get healed up. It'll take half that alone to sort out the details with the CDC and the FBI and the press. Keep me posted and give me your start date. We'll mail you some forms today. Get those back to us and we'll get an advance out to you." Once again he held out his hand. "Welcome aboard, *Doctor Devereaux*."

Bridget gripped his hand, pumped it wildly. "This is so incredible. I don't know if this is real, but thank you, Doctor Sheldon."

"Thank *you*, Doctor Devereaux. See you at Duke." He said goodbye to the others and left the room with a wave and a smile.

"Did that really just happen?" Bridget asked, staring after him.

"Yeah, it did!" Jo said.

Don stood and laid a hand on Bridget's shoulder. "Good going, Dev—I mean, *Doctor* Dev! Hey, I hate to break this up, but we're late for your sister's pig-pickin'."

Bridget hugged Jo, Mr. and Mrs. Woods and Barbara Watkins, then turned to Don. "You sure you want to do this?"

"I've never been more sure of anything in my life."

As they walked out of the hospital, and into the sun and summer heat, Bridget held Don's hand a little tighter. "My nieces will be all over you, you know."

"Hey, I crave attention."

"And my nephew will want to throw the ball with you until you need a sling on your other arm."

Don smiled that easy smile of his. "Sounds great, Dev."

"You like kids, then?"

"Yeah, kids're cool."

Bridget considered him. "Ever thought about some of your own? Not now, of course. But later…?"

The End

JOHN KARR

According to John Karr, fiction writing each day helps keep the demons at bay. As an IT Analyst in Raleigh, NC he balances his day job with family life and writing. As best he can, anyway.

His horror novel DARK RESURRECTION was reprinted in 2007. His short stories have appeared in e-zines "Worlds of Wonder", "Allegory", and "The Absent Willow Review".

HIPPOCRATES SHATTERED is his first novel with Asylett Press. Currently he is working on a mystery with paranormal leanings.

Visit his website for more information:

www.johnakarr.com

New Releases by Tsylett Press...

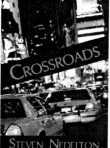

CROSSROADS
Suspense/Thriller
Steven Nedelton

Tallman's received a new assignment. He's not certain he believes in this new secret technology, but he's only the handler. It's the men under his command who have to perform. But he wonders about the Russian, Mikhail. They say he's the best in the field. They say he's defected...

She knows her supervisor Sokolov doesn't trust Mikhail. He believes Mikhail has defected and is revealing Soviet secrets to the Americans. She knows he will destroy Mikhail if he can find him. But Tatiana will keep him safe. Sokolov doesn't realize the power she possesses...

ISBN: 1-934337-55-2

AS THE WIND WALKS
Historical Fiction - Civil War
Harvey Tate

This is a story of two men, their wars and loves in two different eras. David Werner is a ninety-four year old veteran of the American Civl War. His great grandson, Edmund, faces maturity in 1940s Baltimore. While his great grandfather recounts his time in the Union Army, after enlisting at the age of fourteen, Edmund wonders about his own future, standing, as he does, on the brink of another crucial time in America's history... World War II. The candle burns low for David, but Edmund's flame and passion are just igniting—not only for war, but for a remarkable girl...

ISBN 1-934337-53-6

ALONG CAME A FIFER
Mystery/Suspense
R. Michael Phillips

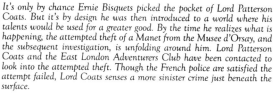

It's only by chance Ernie Bisquets picked the pocket of Lord Patterson Coats. But it's by design he was then introduced to a world where his talents would be used for a greater good. By the time he realizes what is happening, the attempted theft of a Manet from the Musee d'Orsay, and the subsequent investigation, is unfolding around him. Lord Patterson Coats and the East London Adventurers Club have been contacted to look into the attempted theft. Though the French police are satisfied the attempt failed, Lord Coats senses a more sinister crime just beneath the surface.

Murder and villainy are seldom far from the center of the inquiries of the East London Adventurers Club.

ISBN: 1-934337-61-7

DAYS OF SMOKE
Historical Fiction - WWII
Mark Ozeroff

DAYS OF SMOKE offers a compelling, mold-shattering view of World War II and the Holocaust from the unique perspective of German Luft-waffe pilot Hans Udet. Across aerial battlefields ranging over much of Europe, Hans progresses from a naïve young Messerschmidt pilot to an ace of increasing rank and responsibility. But unfolding events pit Hans' love of the Fatherland against his natural compassion for humanity.

ISBN 1-934337-44-7

GOTHIC SPRING
Gothic
Caroline Miller

Victorine Ellsworth knows something about the death of the vicar's wife... but what? Is she the killer? Or the next victim?

Victorine is a young woman poised at the edge of sexual awakening, and cursed with more talent and imagination than society will tolerate. The conflict between her desire, and the restrictions that rule her life, lead to tragic circumstances.

ISBN: 1-934337-67-6

AARYN OF THE HIGH ISLANDS
Fantasy
Glenn Swetman

There is treachery afoot in Randast. An evil plot to harm the Pantocrator, Alan the Just, is being hatched and Aaryn is summoned from the High Islands to thwart those involved. Using his various magical talents and powers, he must ferret out the conspirators and bring them to justice.

Before he reaches the City, however, he finds himself rescuing a mysterious young woman, Jordana, and a dubious thief named Zompre from a band of vengeful gypsies. Together the trio enter the imperial city on the eve of the Banquet of the Gathering and Aaryn enlists the help of Zompre to gather the information he requires. But he soon learns the evil he pursues is more dangerous than he imagined.

ISBN: 1-934337-53-6

LADY LUCK
Western/Historical Fiction
Julie Lence

Lucas Weston isn't too pleased when he's roped into escorting Missy Morgan back to her home in San Francisco. Fate has dealt Missy more losing hands than she cares to remember. Against her will, she's drawn to Lucas' blue eyes and honesty. Would it be so bad to put her trust in him? The odds say yes...

ISBN 1-934337-57-9

BRIDGED BY LOVE
Historical Fiction
Patricia Lieb

"Bridged by Love," by Patricia Lieb - Spring Hill resident Lieb has written a historical adventure set in the late 1880s in Texarkana, a city that straddles the Texas-Arkansas line. Lieb draws on a bounty of historical knowledge to craft a tale of two women - one native American, the other white - linked together in a fight against injustice. ~ Tampa Tribune

ISBN 1-934337-41-2 (Print)

Other Recent Releases...

Demon Lord
Dark Fantasy
Jason Jeffery

Talbot McCreary is dead...gone... reborn as a half-demon named Heretix. And the demon world now has complete access to our world. Alongside his friends and ex-wife, Heretix must find a way to close the gateway and prevent the Demon Lord from crossing over with his massive army to enslave the human race.

ISBN 1-934337-59-5

Fortune's Pride
Historical Romance - Americana
Michele Stegman

As long as no one knows who Irish really is, she will be safe. But Tyrus Fortune seems determined to uncover all her secrets. Can she fully love him without revealing her true self to him? And if she does, will it also put him and his family in danger?

ISBN 1-934337-24-2

Murders in the Swampland
True Crime

Patricia Lieb

A collection of true murder cases and crimes that took place in the swamplands of Central Florida from the late 1970's to early 1990's. Reported by Patricia Lieb for The Daily Sun-Journal, Ms. Lieb includes personal notes from her own journals as well as 2007 updates on many of the convicted felons.

ISBN 1-934337-46-3

Gee-Whiz Meets S.H.A.F.T.
Romantic Spy Thriller
Valerie J. Patterson

Milton Gee is investigating the death of his partner, Chaz Whiz. He never could have guessed the investigation would lead to his recruitment by the UU to fight the worldwide evil organization The S.H.A.F.T. Or that he would come to face to face with The S.H.A.F.T's powerful leader...SHE.

ISBN 1-934337-49-8

LaVergne, TN USA
21 April 2010
180114LV00001B/1/P

9 781934 337400